The Deceitful Kingship

Kelan Gerriety

Author's Note

Dear reader,

This story was never just about vampires or kingdoms or blood rituals. It's the parts of myself I didn't know how to say out loud. A love letter I wrote for myself when I wasn't sure I could love myself.

Lorcan was all of my anger — the rage that comes from being made to feel like too much and not enough at the same time. Cormac was the way I shut the world out, the armour I built so no one could see how much I needed something, anything. Orahn was everything I *wanted* to be: strong,

steady, selfless, the version of me I hoped might exist if I tried hard enough.

And Adelira? She was who I might've been... if I'd been loved the way I needed to be. She's not the kind of strong that shouts. She's soft and gentle and quietly defiant. She chooses to love even when it costs her, and she doesn't harden just because the world tries to make her.

The gentleness across this story is my rebellion, a refusal to become what they try to shape me into.

If you've ever felt like your softness made you weak, if you've ever felt like you had to become someone else to be safe or worthy or *enough*, then this story is for you.

With all my heart,
Kelan

Content Warning

Slow burn, book 1 is clean, in book 2 the relationship takes a physical turn by the end, and book 3 continues the series onwards with spice.

Emotional vulnerability / Intense emotional and physical intimacy

Ambiguous consent / Emotional manipulation / Power imbalance

Intense psychological distress / Supernatural blood drinking / Family Trauma

Intense internal conflict and self-worth struggles

Diminished control / loss of bodily / personal autonomy

Exploration of intimacy through violence, and violence through erasure

Depictions of coercive sexual dynamics

The Kingship Series

Dedication

For Gina

This book would not exist in this form without you.
You shaped this story for years — scene by scene, idea by idea — and I felt your fingerprints on every page.
The Wall, the Battleyard Blood Ritual, the rooftop, to name a few — those moments are here because you saw them before I did.
Thank you for believing in this story, and in me, every step of the way.

1

Chapter One

FIT FOR A KING

"Run," Talion murmured in her ear.

Adelira stiffened mid-yawn as her guards moved to cut off her view of the excited early morning crowd. Her sister, Princess Odette, handed out spring festival gifts as if nothing were amiss.

Her brother, Prince Kieran elbowed her. Adelira shot him a pointed look before he smiled politely, stepping forward to shake someone's hand.

"What?" she asked her head guard under her breath.

"Run," Talion repeated with that spark of mischief in his eyes.

Her siblings had a single guard, while Adelira had four. At least half of them were Talion's fault, for instigating antics like this.

Talion wasn't quite smiling, but the glint in his eyes was. She must have looked desperate if Talion was encouraging this. Subtly, he motioned for the other guards who moved even closer, shielding her from spectacle.

A cheeky smile played on her lips. This was their game, the one he had encouraged since she was a small and trembling child.

Adelira broke into a run, leaving behind the royal procession.

The cold morning air hit her face as she sprinted. Her feet moved nimbly over the ground.

Dawn woke lazily over the Elven Kingdom. Nonchalantly, her guards peeled away and followed after her.

She shot up a tree, kicking off her shoes at the base and letting the bark bite into her soles. Her fingers clawed into the grooves as she made her way up.

Adelira climbed higher through the trees until she breached the canopy. Her grey eyes, which had glazed over during the morning ceremony, now shone bright with wonder. From the treetops, Adelira could see all of Ebedene, her Kingdom, with its ivory spire towers enclosed by forest.

Even at this height, someone watched her.

And not her usual four watchers.

A flicker of movement. A hooded figure on the ground darted toward the festival, too fast; purposeful and gone before she could place him.

His cloak wasn't Elven. Though their gates were open to all the Kingdoms, he struck her as odd. Too hurried and jittery for the joy meant for today.

"Did you see him?" she asked.

Adelira looked down between the leaves. Her long, fiery hair caught the wind. The trees rustled loudly around her like they were all shouting at once, speaking to each other. Very few Elves could still understand them. Adelira sometimes managed to grasp a word here and there.

"Talion?" she said hesitantly.

"Princess?" he called up.

Talion and her three other guards waited below, chatting quietly among themselves.

"Are you ready to come down yet?" he asked after she didn't respond.

Her long pointed ears twitched. Trees spoke again. Brushing her fingers along the ingrained bark. She shut her eyes tight and listened. Finally, she caught one word: *Rip*.

Her gaze flicked to where a discordant portal cut the sky.

The Rip still haunted her sleep; a tear in the heavens that spilled monsters into the world. The danger had fallen into Tharth, but surrounding Kingdoms felt the effects as creatures came through the portal and filtered outward. Sometimes she dreamed of the wolf-like Shifters that emerged from it, but she'd never met one.

Talion had to read her books at night to calm her trembling when she was still small.

"The Rip is in Tharth. Let the Vampires deal with the Shifters. Now Vampires are too busy to concern themselves with Elves," he'd murmured. *"We have to be more careful these days, but we're safe here."*

"I'm scared," she had cried back then. "The Rip. Vampires."

"I'm the Vampire King, big and scary! I'm a Shifter! I am every nightmare. And I'm going to gobble you up, if you don't run," Talion had said, making big claw hands at her, throwing up the blanket, crawling under it.

She'd shrieked and laughed and scrambled out, running from him.

And they hadn't stopped running since.

She would probably still be hiding under blankets if it weren't for him.

He'd lent her his bravery until she had courage of her own. That pushed her up into the canopy, dared to leap between branches, or climbed the tallest trees; just to prove she could.

If she stopped chasing danger, she might slip back into familiar fear. And she refused to go back to that, she pushed herself toward bravery to fend off panic.

"Are you going to stay up there all day, Adelira?" Talion called up, his voice half-amusement and half-worry.

"I was thinking maybe I would," she said pensively, touching her finger to her chin. "Seems a shame to miss the festival though..."

Music swelled with strings and drums rising through the leaves. Laughter echoed as the spring harvest festival began.

There was a pause, before he yelled up the tree, "Don't make me climb after you."

"You wouldn't dare, Talion!" she half-shrieked with a laugh at the thought. "Your old-man knees would never survive it."

He puffed a laugh. "I can still manage that much, at least. But if I can't, then Rayno volunteers."

A groan from below confirmed Rayno had, in fact, *not* volunteered.

She grinned, confident that she could outclimb anyone in Ebedene. Tempted to stay there long enough to challenge him, she leaned back on the branch, dangling her legs. A lone firework shot off in the first-light sky over the city spires, hours too early. Adelira delighted in the flames that exploded across the sky in front of her.

The guards braced, then settled once they understood an overzealous youth had set it off, and they chatted amongst themselves once more.

Her family travelled along the path she had traded for trees. Being the third-born had its benefits, Adelira could vanish, and no one would mind, for a while.

But her thoughts snagged on the hooded man. He was headed towards the festival, too.

A twig snapped under her palm and she flinched and chuckled nervously at herself.

"Be brave," she told herself, determined to follow the mysterious man. She'd keep her distance, watch him, and confirm her instincts one way or the other, without panic.

During the royal procession, Talion had only meant to offer her a reprieve, but he'd ignited more than that. Yearning to experience the festival her way, to be with her people, and maybe chase the unknown. Her guards meant well, but crowded her. Sometimes she wanted the freedom to remember she could move without them.

Toes curled around the bark, Adelira inhaled deeply. The warm scent of blooming flowers filled her lungs.

Then, she exhaled, and dropped.

One hand caught the branch below, and the next, all the way down. She kicked forward, sliding silently through the leaves, feet finding the moss below. Back against the tree trunk, the four hushed voices of her guards told her they hadn't heard her. A beetle landed on her foot, tickled and flew away.

Smiling, she pushed away from the tree and moved quietly. Into the path the hooded figure had taken and towards whatever awaited her next.

2

Chapter Two

Piercing through festival goers, the stranger's gaze found hers.

His angular face was too severe to be Elven and he had a scar beneath one eye.

Adelira's shoulders rounded and she fell back a step. Almost forgetting how to breathe, that familiar childhood fear gripped again, willing her smaller, more timid.

His interest only landed on her briefly, before pushing deeper into the festivities. The jerky way he moved triggered a memory she could almost hold.

A voice cut through the streets and the memory vanished before crystalising.

"Something's coming," Mirhan, the town's old storyteller, called out to Adelira. "It's on the wind. Trees talking."

Adelira looked behind her to be sure the old woman hadn't drawn her guards' attention. No one was behind her, yet. She sighed in relief. Talion probably wouldn't approve of her chasing strange men through the town.

The hooded figure was gone. She looked around and couldn't find him.

Adelira tried to reassure the old woman, "The trees said something about the Rip. Shifters must be moving through the Blood King's Kingdom and causing him trouble. Maybe that's what you heard?"

Mirhan looked horrified that she'd dare speak *that* name.

Speaking his name sent a long *slow* shiver down Adelira's spine.

"Princess!" Mirhan chided.

She gave a half-attempt at a bashful smile. "They keep each other busy."

Once, the Vampires in Tharth had hunted the Elves. But then, without explanation, they simply stopped. Only a few short time into the reign of their new monarch; the *Blood King*.

She still considered him their greatest enemy, though his gaze had turned away from Ebedene for some years.

The Blood King may have stopped preying on Elves, but in her heart she knew they were still *his* prey.

The Shifters coming through the Rip were likely a big enough concern *even* for the King of Tharth that it held his attention steadfast in the darkness. Just as Talion had assured her in childhood.

"Always running off somewhere, can't sit still long enough to listen," Mirhan said sternly, shaking her head. "You must be careful. And if you can't be careful, then you should get closer to your enemies. *Much* closer."

"I... will remember that," Adelira said with a nervous laugh as she walked towards the city.

Adelira belonged in the wilds just as much as she did in the heart of the city, woven into the lives of her people. Not in the careful existence the Elves now called protection since the Rip. Everyone was still afraid, like Mirhan, like Adelira was as a girl. Not everyone had Talion to talk them back from the edge of fear.

Adelira looked around for the stranger. His movements disjointed in a way that made it seem like his body could barely contain his form. Had she read something about that?

But before answers could take hold, someone smaller and sweeter captured her heart.

"Come on, Princess Adi." Little Leina snagged her hand.

Her thin fingers held on tight, trying to pull Adelira along. Her parents, deep in conversation and unnoticing, tugged Leina away further down the path.

The distracted parents hadn't noticed that their child had added a princess to their daisy chain.

Freeing herself delicately, Adelira waved goodbye to the girl.

"Soon! I promise, Leina."

The scent of fresh bread and mead drifted on waves of music through the main square. Elves danced and sang. Children chased kites strung with ribbons. Adelira clasped hands and shared smiles with friends.

Steel-capped boots struck stone, making their way towards her, breaking the rhythm of the day.

Her smile strained as she glanced back. Her guards successfully caught up to her. Steady and proud at her back, they scanned the crowd, standing near enough to let her know she hadn't evaded them at all. Rayno looked smug, like he was making a show of how effortlessly they located her. Talion at least had the decency to appear unaffected by the entire thing.

I guess they were bound to notice I wasn't still up that tree eventually, she thought.

With a crown on her head, the person she became felt less like Adelira and more like the frightened little girl hiding under blankets waiting to be coaxed out. It was dressed in gold, but the crown was just another hiding place. Without it, she could slip between the crowds and breathe like herself again; like a dare for her to live, not hide.

Talion's seasoned eyes fixed on Adelira, only shifting to ensure the surroundings were still safe before locking back on her.

Doing a double-take, she spotted the hooded figure in the crowd. Had the man bared his teeth at someone? No, that was ridiculous, someone would have said something.

The man stepped around some people and moved out of view. She wanted to follow, but risked running into more guards than just the ones following her. And others might insist she return to her royal duties, instead of following mysteries. Not all guards were as generous as hers.

She didn't turn, she just said, "Talion?"

He didn't respond, but the metal of his armour clinked as he shifted his attention towards her.

"How many guards are there?" Adelira asked softly.

A moment passed before he answered, "By my count, nine."

"Where?"

He paused and she knew he understood why she asked and was debating handing over that information. "Four behind you. Two ahead. Three to your left."

Her grey eyes flitted around the busy festival, but she only felt the four behind her in the dense crowds. Could she avoid the rest?

She nodded slowly. "Okay."

"Okay," he said quietly and began moving as she stepped forward again.

Even if her guards chose to follow her, she was determined to enjoy today, surrounded by her people as a part of the celebration, not removed by royal protocols.

"One day, you'll run somewhere I won't be able to follow," Talion said softly behind her.

"But I'm not running," Adelira said over her shoulder.

"*Yet*," he corrected.

"Then stop scowling and look around. This place is wonderful," she teased and pointed at the leather stall with coin pouches and belts.

That got no reaction from him, but she knew where to go to get one. It just took following her nose.

Freshly baked bread, still warm from the oven, lured Adelira in.

She examined the table of spiced breads and delicious baked delicacies. When she spotted them, she waved excitedly to Talion to show him they had his favourite sourdough. They would circle back for a loaf or two at the end of the day when he was more inclined to let her shop the market for him.

His eyes lowered to the bread and then her face, before he scanned the crowds again. Talion's face was his usual no-nonsense mask of professional stoicism, which only made her *more* determined.

Adelira always made it her mission to get him to smile at least once before she escaped. She liked his smile, she liked seeing him happy, and knowing he wasn't going to be too upset with her for leaving when she inevitably would.

Looking back at Talion, she pointed dramatically at the table of breads while popping a small bun in her mouth.

She moaned and mouthed 'soooo good.'

Talion watched her before his glance dashed away to scan the crowd again, the hint of an eye roll and an almost-smirk crossed his face.

She winked at the stall holder and thanked them for the bun, exchanging a few coins before she set off again. With a satisfied smile on her face; she thought, *good*, he was starting to lighten up.

Earning Talion's almost-smile made her feel triumphant. He was finally relaxing and enjoying himself even if no one else but her saw it, and now she could enjoy her day, too.

She scanned the crowd, half-hoping and half-dreading a glimpse of the hooded man. Instead, she found something more enthralling.

The guards' focus waned for a second, a fracture in their attention that Adelira slipped through like sunlight through leaves.

She bolted into the crowds before they could see her.

"Princess!" Talion called out, but there was no fire to his tone. It wasn't a command, only a plea.

She glanced back and she met Talion's eyes. A silver streak of his hair caught in the sunlight and she saw how he'd aged in recent years. Despite that, he was sharp-eyed and quick on his feet, she'd never earnestly escape him.

Holding her stare, seeing the desperation in her grey eyes, Talion finally gave a small nod and... let her go, a gift he gave to her when he could.

Throwing him a grateful grin, she vanished into the festival.

Talion resisted the impulse to lurch forward.

Instead, he let her gain ground before he followed. The crowd closed around her, swallowing her up. Behind her, Talion kept his distance, letting her think she'd gotten away.

She knew he was honoured to be her personal guard, but beneath that pride was a layer of guilt from knowing Adelira wished they could leave her be.

Their protection felt like suffocation and that was painful knowledge to hold alongside a sense of duty and purpose.

He cared deeply. He wanted her happiness.

So, he let her go.

3

Chapter Three

Adelira slipped through the crowd, nimble as she cut between Elves and stalls until the festival closed around her.

She ducked under garlands of flowers, the heavy boots lost behind her.

Moving deeper into a busy street and winning smiles back from festival goers, her shoulder's relaxed. Some bowed, but most were accustomed to her, familiar enough to take her hand and share passing jokes and friendly greetings.

Adelira cast a quick glance over her shoulder; no sign of Talion yet. Had he really let her go this far?

Behind her was the castle of Eloryth with slender towers and balconies with twisting branches grown to hold them.

Adelira stopped to listen as Mirhan recounted old magic tales to a captivated group of children.

"The old magic gave Elves the Elder Celestite, a crystal only those with royal blood can use," Mirhan told the child.

Adelira fought not to roll her eyes. She tried talking to the crystal sometimes, with little luck.

Mirahn said. "There's still plenty of magic in Tharth, if only used to chain up the Vampires."

"They scare me," one child said.

"They scare everyone," Adelira added. A shiver ran down Adelira's spine as she thought of the Vampire King, the warlord of Tharth. The Blood King in the shadows.

"Old magic holds Vampires to this rule, children, listen close and mind it well," Mirhan said. "If a dark stranger comes a-knockin' on your door after the sun's gone down, never, never invite them in. For if you do, you'll end up drained of every drop of blood, leaving your poor parents without a child to hold."

"The old magic still protects us," one child said in awe.

Mirhan clapped her hands. "Even when it's far away, child."

Adelira smiled. Stories of magic captivated her even if she'd outgrown the children's fables. She hung onto Mirhan's every word until the crowd moved her along.

A stutter in her heart, spotting the hooded figure standing motionless as the festival swayed around him. He was utterly in defiance of it. That scar on his face...

"Hey—wait," she called, spinning around.

Looking back, the man was gone. Sweeping the crowd for him only revealed the guards scanning for her.

"Adelira!" called Riann, a boyish grin lit up his freckled face.

The young boy of about seven was already pulling her further into the maze of stalls and fluttering banners. She knew him from a farm she snuck onto just to hear the whispers in the wheat fields and soak up the sunlight.

"Don't worry, we'll keep the guards off your trail!" he said.

"I'm trusting you!" Adelira called out.

Riann saluted, he was taking this role seriously and they darted past some children with wind spinners. Leina waved as Adelira passed.

Nearby, Oisín, the foreign trinket merchant, called out, "Princess Adelira! Your guards are searching the mead stands!"

Her people spirited her through hidden paths and under tables whenever the guards came too close, helping her evade her escort. Their laughter became encouragement of her mischievous escapades. They were used to seeing her sneak away from the palace guards and always made space for her in their world.

Slowing, they moved towards Riann's mother who held out a cup of tea. Adelira took the cup with a grateful sigh, the spiced tea mixed with honey sweet along her tongue.

Waving goodbye, Adelira stumbled across a trio weaving blankets on delicate looms. Their finished wares were on display and she stepped near to look at the bright fabric.

Thumbing the colourful drapery of a blanket, Adelira asked, "Where do the patterns come from?"

"We weave what we see in the dreaming world," one of the women answered with a proud smile.

"You must see incredible things." Adelira thumbed a textile drape depicting a tree entwined with stars. "This one feels alive, like it's breathing."

The artisans nodded, pleased. "You see it then. You've a touch of the old magic in you."

Adelira straightened, a smile tickling her face.

"Stay closer to your guards, the tall one looks worried."

"Talion?" Adelira stood on her tiptoes and peered over the heads in the crowds, immediately concerned for him, but she didn't see him anywhere and after a moment she brushed the feeling aside. "He'll be fine, he just needs to eat some pastries and enjoy the festival."

"Pastries will hardly soothe him," the woman laughed.

"Madame Caroselli's pastries could soothe me on my deathbed. He won't know till he tries them! I'll pick some up when I collect his sourdough..."

The women laughed.

"Oh, wait... Is there...a beast in this one?" Adelira asked, leaning closer to examine the fabric.

"Is that what you see?"

"I don't know..." Thread gleamed, changing from claw to a trinket, like the ones Oisín fashioned. "Maybe... I see Oisín, too?"

One of the women shook her head. "It's simply the light."

Chanting loudly, a group of musicians called Adelira over until her feet followed their calls and the music. Dancers had gathered in the square.

"Come, Adi!" Leina called, taking her hand and pulling her into the circle.

Laughing, Adelira danced with the small group.

Someone pressed a violin into her hands.

Her fingers found the strings instinctively. "I'm not very good," she admitted, but found herself playing anyway.

"We just love how your face lights up," the violin crafter assured her.

So, she played, a beat behind the other musicians.

The final note played. The dance slowed. Adelira bent over, catching her breath again, cheeks flushed. She belonged here, in the sunshine, in the glow of her people, with laughter on her lips.

A strong wind rushed in through the archways surrounding the square.

The din of the festival wavered. Flutes paused, birds fled the treetops in a flurry. Laughter trailed into uneasy murmurs.

In the archway's gloom, a massive wolf Shifter emerged with black fur and yellow eyes burning with destruction. Blood dripped from its jaws in slow, sticky pools around its feet and a growl rumbled towards them like rolling thunder.

Then, the wolf barreled in, a blur of muscle and fur tearing through the square too fast for her to track. Its jaws snapped around Oisín in a sickening crunch. His body crumpled. More red. Limbs twisted in on themselves before being discarded like a forgotten doll.

Leina screamed into her parents' arms. They scooped her up and ran. Everyone was running. The streets were crowded with people pushing and shouting.

Adelira jostled along, swept up with the stampede. Her legs stumbled along, kept upright only by the push of people behind.

"Princess Adelira!"

She knew that voice. She tore free of the stream of people fleeing and searched for him.

Talion sprinted toward her, shouldering through the hysterical crowds, his movements frantic.

Glowing wolf eyes locked onto her. Talion moved. Spear glinted between the Princess and the wolf. The wolf's heavy paws clapped against the ground, limbs disjointed like someone dropping the strings of a puppet.

Driving his weapon into its shoulder, he hit bone and lodged it in the shoulder blade. The massive wolf staggered. It shook off the shock of the attack and lunged again, ripping into him before he could move. Talion screamed. Blood splattered the stones crimson.

"Run!" Talion said to Adelira, his lips dark with his blood.

He didn't give it like an order. He said it like their whole lives had been built around this one word and it was their promise to each other; the game they always played.

But for the first time in her life, she didn't know how to play this game. Her feet planted like the roots of her trees and she couldn't run.

The wolf dropped Talion on the stone and turned to face the soldiers running over.

Her Talion...

He had taught her to ride and be brave, stood watch outside her chambers, told her stories when sleep wouldn't come, stood beneath her trees ready to catch her if she fell.

She clutched the wall with trembling hands for support. The music had turned to screams, but she didn't know who was screaming. *Her, maybe?*

They were only this far into the festival because he'd followed her. A sharp sob tore from her lips. Pressing a hand to her mouth, tears welled in her eyes. All around her, people were running and screaming, but she still couldn't move.

"I'm so s–sorry," Adelira choked. "I—"

Another spear. The wolf roared. Adelira shivered even though the heat of the battle was all around her.

The soldiers circled and the wolf lashed out with snarls and razor-like claws. Adelira didn't see how they'd cornered the wolf. Her eyes still couldn't leave Talion. She refused to fall. The world spun, red and violent, but she only saw him and tried to will her limbs to listen to his last words.

A younger officer jumped back out of reach and lodged the tip of a spear into the wolf's side. It howled in pain and tore away. Another spear pierced the wolf and with a final cry, the creature collapsed into a bloody heap.

Talion still hadn't moved.

Finally, her legs caught up with her mind and she bolted. Stopping only to see the wolf slowly morphed back into the man he was. The transformation was brutal, bones snapping and flesh twisting. Fur receded, claws shrank back into human hands. Monstrous features became *familiar*.

Angular face, small eyes, a *scar* under his eye. He was tall, muscular, with skin that looked as though it had been marked by years of harsh winters and covered in deep battle scars. His return to humanity was graceless; brutal remnants of a life spent fighting.

She still didn't know him, but his *eyes*, she'd seen those eyes in the crowd, and now she could see they belonged to someone who had lived too long on the fringes of survival.

With a final shuddering breath, the Shifter closed his eyes forever.

And now she understood why his movements had been strange, why the festival seemed to slide off him like rain against rock. The hooded man she'd followed all afternoon.

None of her books had prepared her for the way the man and the beast could be the same creature.

It was easy to imagine him as nothing more than a rabid animal, but now she could see the man behind it. This was someone thinking and feeling, who had chosen this path or had been forced into it.

Suddenly, she was a child again, hiding under blankets and Talion was telling her Shifters never came this far.

Talion was gone. So was her blanket. And shifters *had* come this far. She wasn't a child anymore, but she still trembled.

"Scouts have seen more Shifters on the border!" a soldier shouted as the army descended the streets.

Adelira wanted to see Leina and Riann, just to see their faces and stop the panic in her heart, but she'd watched their parents run off with them and she knew they were safe, somewhere deeper in the city. She kept running.

Trampled garlands and splintered stalls were thrown across the blood-slick stones. One of the wind spinners trailed red behind it down the street. The metallic tang of blood filled her lungs. A dirtied sourdough loaf on the ground.

Adelira's hands shook uncontrollably as she reached for the nearest guard. He steadied her.

"Where's Rayno?" she barely squeaked, short of breath.

"Here. We're all here," Rayno said, taking over from the first guard.

Not all, she thought, but she couldn't say that.

Adelira had heard the rumors of a rising conflict between the Rip Shifters and the Twelve Kingdoms.

She longed to run through the forest, to laugh and celebrate with her people, but that was gone now. If more of this destruction reached Ebedene, there might be no forest left to run in and her people would be in danger.

The pull in her chest begged her to act. She knew they'd need the old magic. There weren't many Kingdoms left who still knew how to wield it.

The strongest magic belonged to her greatest enemy; the Vampire lurking in the shadow Kingdom. Yet, that magic *weakened* him.

Even weakened, he was a near-unstoppable force.

Adelira gripped Rayno's arm. "T–Take me to the council."

4

Chapter Four

When Adelira entered the grand council chamber, the twin moons were high in the sky. Polished floors gleamed under her blood-caked feet.

King Hara was saying, "...and the wolf Shifters grow bolder with each passing fortnight. My reports estimate a dozen or so villages have been burned along the border. Their attacks grow more cunning. We cannot wait any longer."

Adelira bit back a gasp.

"Double the guards patrolling the woods tonight," her father King Hara said. "The attack in the festival was probably not singular."

He shot her a pointed look.

She froze. She knew that look.

It was the look he gave when she returned mud-covered from the forest after slipping past her guards to dance with friends.

Her father *had* tried to tell her it was this dangerous every time he sent guards to drag her home.

Her parents, the Elven King Hara and Queen Juli, stood at the long table. Next to them were her older siblings. Though she was separated from the royal procession when the attack happened, word had spread quickly of her safety. Her mother's gaze darted down to her daughter's feet as Adelira slipped into the room and tucked them under the table, out of sight.

Queen Juli nodded. "How are alliance negotiations going with the Fellin Kingdom? Now more than ever, we need that alliance, we cannot do this alone."

Adelira hesitated to place her stained hands on the table.

A strong ally. She considered her mother's words. The strongest Kingdom.

"Could the Vampires defend themselves from the Shifters indefinitely?" Adelira asked directly as she looked up.

A few gasps sounded through the chamber. The Vampires hadn't fed off Elves in years and no one wanted to remind the Vampires their favourite blood flowed just two Kingdoms away.

General Cillian, their seasoned general, answered first, "I... suppose. It's hard to know what they do in the shadows. Their fortresses are formidable and their ruthlessness is unmatched. If anyone were to survive, it'd be..."

She nodded thoughtfully.

"But they won't fight for us unless it suits their interests," he cautioned. "If the wolves weaken us, then the Vampires might just wait until they're the last power standing in the twelve Kingdoms."

"We won't beg for their protection," Adelira said. "We give them the means to destroy the Shifters on our terms. The Elder Celestite could be used to bargain."

Odette, her older sister, leaned forward with a scowl. "And hand them that kind of power? We'd be trading one threat for another."

King Hara said, "We may have no choice. If the Vampires demand concessions for their aid, so be it."

"Concessions? Is that what we're calling the Elder Celestite now?" her brother Kieran asked, folding his arms.

"We know the crystal is powerful," King Hara said, ignoring his son's objections. "My scholars tell me it could open the doorway in the Rip, but even if it did, we would need allies to face the Shifters on their own ground. We're not equipped for war the way the Vampires are."

Ebedene was a peaceful nation. The Vampires weren't a warring nation, they were *the* war nation.

Without some form of old magic, no one had seemed to be able to cross through the Rip despite the many attempts various Kingdoms had made.

"If the Vampires went through the Rip," her father continued, "if they were able to pass without permission, then perhaps they would be able to attack the Shifters' strongholds from within."

"Yes," she said, trying to ignore how desperate her voice sounded even to herself.

"I see why you believe the Vampires would make a strong ally, but we can't rush an alliance with such a man, if *he* could be called a man, at all."

"The legends can't all possibly be true. Surely the power of the Blood King has been exaggerated, with no small benefit to himself," Adelira pointed out.

"The Vampires are so powerful that the old magic manifests to chain them. They are one of the last races that still have blood magic, a burden to them that suppresses the entire race," their father said. "Without it, I have no doubt Vampires would have conquered and destroyed the whole of Taipan by now."

"Vampires are bound by old magic," Queen Juli explained. "Sunlight burns them, and they cannot enter private spaces uninvited."

Cillian's voice was grim. "The Elder Celestite could erase the second restraint for them to enter the Rip."

King Hara said, "The only reason we haven't been destroyed for our crystal is because it only works for Elven Royalty."

Adelira heard the words immediately as the responsibility of her suggestion weighed heavily upon her shoulders.

"Someone in our family can invite the Vampires through? Royalty works the crystal, the crystal opens the Rip?" Adelira asked slowly, piecing it together.

"Can we really risk opening up the world, and other worlds, to a race that the cosmic powers themselves have bent natural laws to forbid?" Kieran asked.

Odette shook her head in disbelief, her own red hair shaking with the movement. "And hope the Vampires still protect us after they get it?"

Malon, a mage schooled in the theory of old magic, had been silent until now. "We establish terms through magic that they cannot break."

Queen Juli asked, "Is there even magic left that can do that?"

Malon spoke with a feverous gleam in his eye. "There may be a way... A Blood Ritual. The Vampires used it for this purpose; to force the fates of two bloodlines together. It enforces a truce where trust could not be reached naturally; a circumstance that they encounter frequently for, uh, obvious reasons."

"A Blood Ritual, yes," Adelira said hopefully, trusting the confidence in his voice.

"Blood Rituals are barbaric," Odette retorted. "Even the Vampires don't employ this method unless in extreme circumstances."

"But they work," Malon countered. "The bond would make betrayal impossible. We offer a marriage to seal the alliance."

"Fine," Odette snapped, sarcasm heavy in her words as she waved an exaggerated hand through the air. "Who do we sacrifice to this grotesque ritual? Who do we condemn to marriage with the Blood King himself?"

The room erupted in whispers. The debate circled the truth; fear was posing as reason.

Not one name was offered up. Not a single one.

No one dared condemn another to such a fate. Even the most ruthless of criminals in Elven culture, by-and-large, were seen as redeemable. This living hell could not be given even to a soul destined for the gallows. Somehow, a sudden end seemed kinder.

Finally, Adelira spoke above the debate.

"Me."

"Please, no," her mother begged.

Adelira held up her hands for the room to see, stained with dried blood and dirt.

"A wolf just killed Talion. And Oisín. And they weren't the first. I won't wait for another," Adelira said, her voice quiet but steady. "If this is what it takes to save our people, I will do it."

Her family protested loudly; Odette with anger and Kieran in disbelief.

But Adelira said, "I'm the third spare. You have a secure line of succession for the crown from my older siblings. If a Blood Ritual and our crystal grants the Vampires the chance to destroy the wolves... then, I–I must do this."

"This is not about your place in our family," her mother said. "You cannot marry a Vampire. Especially not *that* Vampire."

Her mother continued, "This decision... it will change you in ways you cannot begin to imagine."

Adelira's body shook at the memory of Talion's lifeless eyes. Her voice was soft, "I am already changed."

Kieran's eyes saddened, and then his jaw locked and his expression darkened. "You don't know what you're agreeing to, sister. He enjoys it. The fear. The hunt."

The Blood King was a warrior who commanded legions of undead with the destruction and the precision of a cunning strategist.

For the first time, she found it impressive. As a foe, he was terrifying, but that was what made him such an appealing ally.

Malon turned toward Adelira, his eyes aged with wisdom and his words heavy with responsibility, "Both Kingdoms, Ebedene and Tharth, would merge under one united goal, but the Blood Ritual is no simple vow."

She had longed for the return of old magic. She never imagined it would come at the cost of her own future. But that future meant nothing to her, if anyone else perished.

"I–I understand," she said.

"It will require a union of blood and magic, a bond etched into your very being," Malon went on and then glanced around the room.

Kieran sighed. "There is so little magic left in the world, and what there is we must fight to protect and pass down through the generations. But this which you offer us, this *violent* marriage proposal, is one we cannot accept."

"Violent? A marriage?" she asked, arching an eye at him.

"He is the *Blood King*," her father warned warily.

Adelira lifted her chin. "What better guardian than a nightmare; bound to our Kingdom by blood?"

"You don't understand—" Kieran said.

"—The Rip is something that we cannot solve alone," General Cillian cut in. "The violence is on our streets, at our doorstep. If we do not seek out the Vampire King's protection now, then we will be nothing when the Shifters come. And they are coming."

Queen Juli reasoned, "If this bond fails, we could be condemning Ebedene to the same fate other Kingdoms have fallen to when the Vampire King has finished toying with them."

Adelira's heart pounded. "Then the bond cannot ever fail," she said softly. "What's required for the Ritual?"

Kieran turned away, shaking his head in frustration. Malon murmured excitedly about glyph alignments.

"Blood, willingly given, and the binding of your soul to his. He'd have Elven blood in his veins and Vampire blood would flow in yours, a mix of two worlds. It will merge our lines and ensure the Vampires' loyalty through magic they cannot break."

"Magic neither of us can break," Adelira said, committing it to memory, binding her to the fate of a creature whose darkness might devour her.

"There's a cost," Malon admitted. "Beyond marriage, beyond trading sunlight for nightfall and staying with the Vampire King."

"What is it?" she whispered.

"You were right when you said magic neither of you could break. If you changed your mind later, if you ran away, abandoned him... everything would break."

"I–I don't run anymore," she said softly.

Kieran's eyes landed on her, his expression dark and imploring, begging her to reconsider. "You've heard the stories, haven't you?"

"Yes, but they are just stories."

"Just stories?" Odette looked incredulous.

"He's impressive. He's even formidable. But no one is capable of... *everything...* they say he is. If everyone believes the stories, he's won half the battle before his enemies even step onto the field. They've twisted the truth into a legend of gross proportions," Adelira said, her resolve solidifying even more as she heard the logic in her own words.

Her father sent a silent prayer of thanks to wherever Talion was now. Tragically, death had been the thunderclap loud enough to wake his sleeping princess.

"Stories, even exaggerated, have a layer of truth and he has far too many to be dismissed," Kieran said.

"We don't know anything about Vampire customs, really, except that they strive for fearsomeness," Adelira pointed out.

General Cillian added, "We might not know anything about Vampire culture, they only attend a few diplomatic events with the Southern Kingdoms. But I was there at the battle of Arvain. And Arvain's fall."

"You were?" she asked.

"Yes."

Arvain, the fortress of the Eastern Reaches, had been impenetrable for centuries, until the Blood King came, or so the stories go.

"He didn't breach the gates or storm the walls like any other invader," Kieran told, his voice barely above a whisper, almost as though speaking of it might call forth the very monster itself.

She glanced toward the windows, half-expecting the Vampire King to appear, as if summoned by the recounting of his victories. Adelira shook her head, feeling foolish.

Cillian continued, "He turned their people one by one, using his own blood to corrupt them until the fortress was his. By the time Arvain fell, there wasn't a soul left to defend it, just hollowed shells and loyal servants."

Kieran looked at her pointedly.

"He did it all himself, slowly. He made strategic appearances. Terrifying us. Breaking morale. He was, quite literally, playing with his food," Cillian said. "I narrowly made it out with my life. I still have nightmares about it. He made the stronghold feel like a cage."

This caused her to skip a beat. She had never met anyone who had experienced the Blood King's terror first hand. Cillian was a seasoned general in the Elven forces. He was not spooked easily. Suddenly, the stories had a face that had seen him with their own eyes.

"He rules through that same fear to this day."

Her resolve quivered, but she swallowed it.

"You're asking us to place the survival of our people in the hands of a predator," Odette said slowly, like the slower she spoke, the more the absurdity of it would sink in.

"Y–yes."

"What happens when the bond is no longer convenient for him?" Odette asked. "What will he do with the power of the Elder Celestite once the threat of the Shifters is neutralised? If he even decides to do that."

"I could..." Adelira's voice faltered because what could she do? Ask the Blood King nicely to please respect his wife's family and people?

"You'd be holding the leash of Cerberus," Odette said pointedly. "If he tears out of your grip, he will destroy everything."

"With respect, you don't understand," Malon said in earnest. "This Blood Ritual is not a promise, nor is it a leash that could snap."

Odette raised a perfectly arched eyebrow at him and dared him to prove her wrong.

Malon's eyes darted around uncomfortably before landing on Adelira. He spoke eagerly to her. "Should either Adelira or the Blood

King betray it, the consequences could ripple through both Kingdoms, breaking more than just the alliance."

Adelira nodded, encouraged again by this binding magic. "If the crystal is what the Vampire King needs to defeat the Shifters and the Blood Ritual is what we need to trust him, then I can secure both..."

"We will not make you pursue this madness, Adi," Odette said, lifting her chin in disgust. "We will find another way."

Adelira's heart pounded as she weighed their words. Fear, practicality, pride, all blending into a cacophony that demanded a decision.

Adelira closed her eyes and no sooner did her eyelids flutter shut did she see Shifters tearing through their lands, screams of her people as their homes burned... Her eyes snapped open and she knew there was no other way to protect everyone. Her father glanced up, a flicker of approval.

She stood and the room fell silent. All eyes turned towards her.

"There is no other way. My parting gift to my people will be the promise of safety," she said with finality. "Prepare the marriage proposal to the Vampire King."

Her hand instinctively touched her heart where she could feel the pull of this magic for the rest of her life...

Adelira felt it in her soul as she became the bridge between the Elves and the Vampires. Beneath that she worried she would also be the battleground. If she hoped to endure the court of the Blood King, she would have to learn to survive in darkness.

5

Chapter Five

Adelira sat in her chamber with the acceptance letter from the Vampire King. The paper was too thin for the way it felt like a rock in her hand.

The letter was written in *Tharic*. The Vampiric language was still taught to give their people the possibility of parlay. If you could not fight for your life, perhaps you could bargain.

She had found it frustrating to learn as a child, now she was grateful to be armed with something from Tharth. She doubted if anyone in Tharth could speak *Ehvayn*.

She'd give up her friends, her home, her language... Her safety? She shuddered.

But it'd be worth it if Taipan's greatest army became her strongest ally.

Her ladies-in-waiting moved about the room, packing away the remnants of her life. Flowing silky gowns disappeared into chests, one after another.

The sight made her chest tighten. Would she be the only person in Tharth dressed in flowery silks?

She shook her head. *No.* This was no time for vanity. She had bigger concerns. Like his eyes which were said to pierce the soul to see beyond pretence. Would he see through her, too? Would he know her weaknesses before she even spoke?

The invite was simple; an acceptance of her proposal and an offer to join him immediately.

They assured her that the King would protect her from the Vampires in Tharth.

But who would protect her from... the *Blood King*?

The King wielded his instinct like a weapon, sometimes holding it so tight that it almost ceased to exist entirely and then other times unleashing his wrath on his enemies.

He might not be able to kill her after the Blood Ritual, but he might make her wish for death.

Her stomach twisted.

Insatiable blood desire could turn the Vampire King from a calculating, political genius into a monster capable of slaughtering entire villages.

Th–that part had to be exaggerated... right? She bit her lip.

What would he demand? How much would she lose of herself in Tharth, when his control touched everything?

Adelira's fingers curled closed and the letter crumpled.

Nothing about this marriage felt like diplomacy. It felt like a trap she wasn't skilled enough to navigate.

What did she want beyond the survival of her Kingdom?

The answer came swiftly: liberation.

Her heart belonged to the untamed forests where the changing of the seasons was the only law and sunlight filtered through her every lens.

What right did she have to seek out the sunlight when her people needed her to walk into the shadows?

No safe carefree forests in Tharth for Elves, only hungry woods.

The Vampires' guards would watch her with unfamiliar eyes. Ironic, she thought she was stifled by her four escorts, but she longed to take them with her to Tharth now.

Even so, she would trade her whimsical dreams of freedom for something concrete. Her people's survival.

The hushed chatter from her ladies brought her back to the room.

She watched them pack her violin though she doubted there'd be much music to be played in Tharth.

Her ladies were talking amongst themselves, but it was the mention of Tharth and the King that snagged her attention.

"I heard... I mean, we've all heard he is as ruthless as he is calculated," Lerato said, she glowed in the sunlight that filtered in from the window but even in the warmth of day, she shivered when talking about the Vampire King. She shook the thought away, her hair bouncing around her face as she did so.

"H–He's lawless. He, uh, they say he's near-mythical powers on the battlefield," Marieke said, her voice holding a note of awe in it. "When he fights..."

Carys nodded, pushing back a stray strand of Marieke's long brunette hair from her face. "I know what you mean. He fought a mountain crag-beast—"

"—And won single handedly!" Lerato jumped excitedly. "Oh, sorry, continue."

Carys chuckled. "You heard that one, too? Apparently, he was fresh as daisies when he delivered its head as a trophy hours later to, uh, I think it was the Aclastic ambassador? But it looked like he'd just slept and bathed instead of, well, of being in a life and death struggle with a man-killer."

"Th–that's not possible?" Marieke asked with a nervous chuckle.

"Well, maybe not for anyone else, but for the Vampire King..." Carys shrugged and gave a cheeky smile.

"Knowing when to use force and when to use charm has worked well for him and I'm sure he'll be charming now, because it is best for everyone," Lerato said thoughtfully.

"My uncle said he held Ilver's Pass for fourteen days with something like just forty-three men. Convinced half of his enemies to switch sides and the rest fled before reinforcements ever even arrived," Marieke added.

Adelira bit her lip, which did not go unnoticed by her ladies who quickly pivoted towards lighter areas of the topic. His charm seemed to always carry the undercurrent of violence.

"My cousin was at court in the Fellin Kingdom for negotiations and she said the Vampire King was the most beautiful man she'd ever seen," Lerato said.

"He commands every room he steps in," Carys said dreamily winking at Adelira. "So handsome, how could he not?"

Adelira only smirked and shook her head, understanding exactly what Carys was doing. She wasn't entirely wrong though, there were plenty of rumours circulating about the Vampire King's beauty.

"You surely can't run a Kingdom on violence alone. He must also be a skilled diplomat. It's not like he never negotiates with other Kingdoms," Marieke said, trying to soften his image for her.

"I heard Tharth has peculiar customs," said Lerato, her voice barely audible as though it was almost too sordid to speak about out loud.

"Peculiar!?" Carys chimed in as she smirked across to Lerato. "That's not even the right word."

The girls giggled.

"They say the men outnumber the women," Carys said, her voice scandalously low. "A ridiculous number. Like three to one, or something."

"So then, it's not just the Elder Celestite they want... It's her, too," Lerato said.

Adelira could hear their cheeky amusement and the curiosity beneath it for this strange new land she'd be joining.

"What happens when there aren't enough women?" Lerato's cheeky smile almost answered what Carys dared to say out loud.

"Two husbands, maybe?" Carys teased.

They erupted into more laughter, the lightness soothing Adelira. Where she saw uncertainty and duty, they could afford to see adventure and novelty and it allowed her a moment to absorb that side of it as well.

Turning, she cast a mock scolding glance over her shoulder at her ladies, her voice coloured with warmth even as apprehension pooled in her stomach.

"You three are meant to prepare me for diplomacy," Adelira chided them playfully, "Not domestic mayhem."

More laughter rang out around the room, the warmth of their giggles filled her, pushing uncertainty away for the time being.

The ladies moved through the room in a flurry of light touches, unconscious gestures woven into their work. A gentle hand on a waist to reach around for an item, laughter spilling easily as fingertips brushed a shoulder.

Adelira picked up a wooden box.

Opening it, the crystal ball nestled on a velvet lining. Her finger traced over the smooth surface.

Carys stepped closer and took Adelira's hand in hers. "Your chests are ready. The carriages are waiting. May I help you with your coat?"

"Yes, of course."

Adelira allowed Carys to drape the warm Elven coat over her shoulders, the colour of the autumn sky.

Carys's hands brushed Adelira's long fiery hair into place. Her hair was often falling out of its pins. It was fashionable to have it styled in intricate Elven hairdos, though Adelira preferred it down and natural, but she let Carys fuss. Her hands were tentative as always with warmth that was every ounce of comfort.

"Fit for a King," Carys said with a small encouraging smile.

6

Chapter Six

Descending the bone-white winding staircase of the palace Elorth, Adelira saw the carriages lined in the courtyard below.

Eight mahogany carriages gleamed in the morning light. Horses with nostrils flaring and breath misting, stomped against the stone with the occasional thud of a hoof.

The carriages bore the crest of the Vampire King; three crimson swords carved expertly into the wood along the sides.

Adelira turned sharply to face the driver. She half expected a Vampire, but it was only Nodrick. The Royal chauffeur smiled, ready to open the carriage doors for her.

"*He* sent them for the Royal company," Nodrick explained to her.

"A gesture of hospitality, I reckon," Nodrick continued, he was only slightly shaking. "Breath steaming in the midnight air and without a soul to greet me. That's the work of... well, you know yourself, Princess..."

Reaching out, Adelira stroked the mane of one of the midnight-black mares, coat soft as velvet.

"Finest mares I've ever stabled," Nodrick said.

Her mother appeared, granting a sweeping glance over the carriages before turning her to her daughter. "Adelira, it's time."

Adelira nodded and as it always did when she was nervous, a stream of words flooded from her before she was able to think better of them. "I–I know. The Blood Ritual must happen quickly. Without it—"

"—Without it, we are at their mercy," her mother interrupted, her inflection hardening. "And mercy is not a currency Vampires trade in."

Adelira hesitated. "But they've given us their word."

Queen Juli looked to the distant mountains. "The word of a Vampire is smoke; impossible to hold."

Adelira felt the letter in her pocket, but she was holding his promise, she wanted to say.

"They live in murkiness and lies," her mother explained, "hiding from the light that might keep them honest."

Adelira felt doubt creeping into her heart despite how much she longed to believe every terrible rumour about the Vampire King was grossly exaggerated.

Juli frowned, seeing the doubt in her daughter's eyes, but it would do her no kindness to shelter her from this.

The wind shifted, colder now, as though warning them both of what lay ahead. Juli's hands rested lightly on Adelira's shoulders, her expression softening for the first time.

"I will do what I have to," Adelira said,

Her mother walked alongside her father to their own carriage. A half dozen nobles climbed into the carriages to journey with them over the next couple of weeks to reach Tharth. She said goodbye to her siblings, though Odette still seemed angry about the idea, there was now also a flicker of dread in her eyes. Kieran hugged her tighter and longer than anyone else.

Stealing herself, Adelira climbed into her own carriage. A faint scent of cool forest mist clung to the cushions. Despite the warmth of Ebedene, an unexpected chill awaited inside the carriage.

Her ladies reached in to clasp her hands, bidding her farewell. They placed a parting gift of sable-hair paint brushes and a basket of cinnamon buns gently into her lap. Adelira touched them lightly, the gesture as sacred as the connections she was leaving behind.

Carys climbed in to sit on the opposite cushion and stayed holding Adelira's hand. The touch, gentle and earnest, made Adelira grateful to have a friend with her.

The carriages lurched as the horses moved. As the palace receded, Adelira glanced back at the white soaring towers.

After the Blood Ritual, would she become like him?

She opened the box and the crystal hummed. "What would you have me do?" she whispered. It was silent. She set it aside on the cushion beside her brushes.

Carys was already eating one of the buns.

She looked at her friend and smiled. Carys had come a long way from the scruffy, orphan child Aderlira had demanded to be friends with all those years ago. Though no amount of plush palace accoutrements would ever make Carys forget that she had experienced both sides of Elven society.

Now, the two of them were often inseparable, often plotting escapes into the forest or ways to slip past her guards undetected. Adelira blocked out the thought of leaving Carys to keep it from breaking her.

Instead, Adelira leaned out of the window, waving her hand along the gentle breeze riding alongside the carriage, trying to catch the rays of sunshine on her skin.

She listened for the rivers or the trees. But it was as if the world was waiting in silence.

Along the roadside, a group of Elven children stepped out from the trees. They stood barefoot on the soft bright moss as the carriages rolled past.

"Princess Adelira, the Forest's Blessing for you," the girl said, her voice trembling.

The girl tossed a garland of flowers in the carriage window.

Adelira caught it, her tears catching in her throat. The blossoms were woven with care but hadn't yet bloomed. The timing of it was thoughtful, the petals would uncurl just before she arrived at the Vampire King's castle.

The children's bright eyes were solemn, mischief replaced by something heavier and older than their years. They knew where she was going. The stories of the Vampire King frightened them. They were frightened for her.

Adelira pressed it to her chest, her laughter replaced by their quiet ache. The children raised their hands in a gesture of farewell and mourning; kisses extended outward. They offered them to her on the wind.

Carys spoke, "They picked your favourite, Your Highness."

Adelira held the garland in her hands, a small smile on her lips. "I'll miss these, I doubt Forest Blessings grow in the cold climate of Tharth."

"Perhaps not..." Carys suggested, "That's why you'll make a grander entrance with it in your hair."

Adelira chuckled and, for a moment, she was herself, before duty secured its hold.

Carys went on, "I'm serious. Keep the garland on. Hit them back with some of those scare tactics they're so famous for. You'll be terrifying."

Adelira arched an eyebrow. "Terrifying? That's not exactly my aim."

Carys grinned slowly as though thinking up something new. "No, but maybe it should be. Let's work with that instead. Fear is a weapon to Vampires, right? You might as well play their game."

"How will flowers scare them?" Adelira said, twirling the garland in her hand.

Carys studied her with a thoughtful expression. "Not flowers. You. Dare to be yourself in a world where you don't fit, Adi."

Adelira raised a sceptical eyebrow.

"No one but you could have convinced me to sleep without a knife under my pillow. No one but you would have looked at a dirty, street rat, and seen a friend instead of a thief."

"But that's you, Carys."

"No, that was you. You notice people, Adi," Carys said. "I mean, you *really* see them. It is beautiful and it can feel terrifying; to be seen like that. It's exposing and vulnerable and somehow you're gentle enough for it to feel safe."

Adelira was unconvinced even as Carys' attempt warmed her. "You think I have the power to... What? *Acknowledge...* the Vampires into submission?" She half-smiled. "Yes. Terrifying."

"It is terrifying, Adi. Especially so when they live in the shadows. Their power is murkiness, but you will cut through to the truth of them."

"That's not a weapon," she said softly.

"No, not all power is a weapon," Carys said.

Adelira paused. "And what if I don't do any of that? What if I'm... nothing at all to them?"

Carys's eyes softened. "Then they'd be the first. But I don't think you'll have that problem. You're worth following."

"Me?" she repeated with disbelief. "I've spent most of my life wishing I could run away and live in a tree."

Carys leaned forward, her expression softening. "I don't see anyone running now."

"What do you see?" she asked tentatively.

"I see... a woman who gave up everything for those she loves. And that kind of sacrifice? Of loyalty? That's not something just anyone can do..."

Blinking hard, Adelira willed herself not to cry. "Oh, Cari..."

"And if you exhibit even *half* as much value to the Vampires as you've shown to the Elves," Carys said, her voice steady and sure, "they'll see you for who you are."

"I might need you to remind me of who I am a few more times before we get there..."

"I'll remind you every day and every night if you need for as long as they let me stay in Tharth."

Adelira watched the children running alongside the carriage for as long as their small legs would carry them.

Do the children of Tharth laugh?

∞

The sunlight grew softer and late afternoon was nearing. The road ahead wound into a meadow where deer grazed and bright birds dove in and out of the long grass.

Carys nudged Adelira and pointed to a fox darting through the fields, its coat jade green to camouflage with the grass.

In his letter, he promised her safe passage. No Shifters would attack as he had patrols set up along the route.

The carriages began to climb a gentle hill, and at its crest, the travellers stopped to rest on the last farm along the border of Ebedene.

Adelira joined the ladies beneath the tree, biting into a peach so ripe its juice ran down her fingers. She laughed as Carys tried to catch a falling petal on her tongue.

Drinking honey wine, Adelira listened to the farmers speak of the good harvest they had this season and smiled. Every so often, her eyes caught on the darkened stain in the sky and the closer they got to Tharth, the larger that scar became.

Carys' knowing eyes connected with Adelira. No effort to mask her distress would ever be successful with her friend. Carys offered only an easy smile.

"Don't be too sad," Adelira coloured her words with sarcasm, "I'm only going to live with monsters."

Carys laughed casually. "We'll see if they're still monsters when you're armed with flowers."

Adelira did not laugh back. She sensed no cruelty in Carys' words, but it still stung like the friendship was slipping away and only she ached for it.

Carys continued, "No matter which way I look at this, Adi, it doesn't feel like the end. Anyone that thinks the Vampires will defeat you has simply never met you."

Adelira thought that over. "You think I can defeat the entire court of the Blood King... alone?" Until now, Adelira thought of simple survival as a lofty goal. "What gives you so much faith in me? Or maybe you underestimate the Blood King?"

Carys smiled broadly. "Underestimate his Majesty, the Slayer of Gods, Tamer of Mountains? Never." Carys' eyes slipped away for a minute and her smile receded to easy confidence. "I just know you, Adi. I know what you did for me, and I know you'll do it again."

Adelira cocked her head, not seeing Carys' logic.

Carys asked, "Have you ever thought about what it means for the Vampires? That the Elves don't trust them?"

Adelira glanced over, frowning slightly. "That they won't trust us either?"

Carys nodded. "More than that. They don't trust *anyone*."

"That's... terrible."

"After spending centuries convinced the world is against you, then you stop believing in honesty... In *love...*" Carys said. "You start to think harsher and the world becomes that, too. Does that make sense? I don't know if I'm explaining it well... Like survival depends on expecting betrayal, before it comes, because eventually... it always does."

Carys' hands tightened around the stem of her glass. Glancing out over the golden fields, she breathed deeply. Adelira watched her fingers loosen again, but the sentiment was still lodged in her chest, tightening around her ribs.

"You think he's expecting me to betray him?" Adelira asked softly, bewildered by the very idea.

"I'm sure part of the reason he agreed to marry you is as much a security measure for them as it is for us. He probably expects the Elder Celestite to be laced with treachery; sees it as a gift that can't be trusted, not without the leverage of your life bound to it."

"I–I'm not going to hurt him," Adelira stammered.

She didn't know if that was true, if he was a monster who moved against her Kingdom, then she'd do everything she could to stop him. If she secured the Blood Ritual, then he couldn't move against her or her people, he could be a prince of darkness all he wanted then, but she wouldn't hurt him.

Carys turned her eyes to Adelira, meeting her gaze with quiet certainty. "No. But that's the world you're stepping into."

"That's normal for them?" Adelira shuddered at the thought.

"You're asking a man who has lived his whole life that way to believe in something... kinder... just because you do."

"Then what do I do?" She didn't know how to win over a Vampire. If such a thing were even possible, she was entirely out of her depth.

Carys was quiet for a moment before answering. "Don't convince him with words," she said softly. "You show him every day. He'll see it for himself."

"Maybe he can learn to trust me in time," Adelira said slowly.

Carys exhaled, her voice filled with something almost wistful. "It's a hard thing to do. And an even harder thing to accept, when someone finally proves they are exactly who they said they were the entire time and there was never any treachery to begin with."

Adelira nodded slowly, understanding this.

It had taken Carys a long time to trust her. But this was something they both had experience in, Adelira had put years into lowering Carys's walls and she could do that for the King as well.

It all felt so sudden. Her oldest sibling Odette had the same partner for the last decade and they weren't ready to marry, yet. Adelira envied the years of trust and dedication they built.

∞

The feast ran into evenfall. Finally when everyone went to sleep, it was the farmers who woke before the sun rose. Dawn peeked, stirring Adelira from her slumber.

She made her way outside and sat quietly on the grass in the fields, running her fingers through. She lifted her face to the sunlight and wished that the warmth on her skin could keep her in this world she loved so much.

A boy dashed past with a stick in his hand that he swung like a sword.

Riann! Adelira's face lit up.

He waved excitedly to her. He looked happy, like maybe he'd been far enough away from the heart of the festival not to have seen any of the things she had witnessed. Adelira's heart lifted.

"Seeing you before I leave is the best parting gift," Adelira called to them and walked over. "Maybe we have time for a quick sword fight?"

The boy blinked, looking around. "I don't have another stick..."

"That's okay," Adelira said with a shrug.

Talion had tried to teach her to use a sword, but she'd been half-way up a tree before the lesson ended. But now, she wondered if she might have needed that training after all. Even with Talion's training, she'd never be able to take on the Vampire King.

Flowers, the only weapons she could take. *Oh, and kindness. Flora and trust, was that enough?*

Quickly, Riaan stuffed his hand in his pocket and pulled out a small unremarkable pebble.

He held it out towards her in his open palm. "For you, Adelira."

Adelira accepted it and in that moment it was the finest gift in the world.

"I'll treasure it always," she promised. *Flora, trust, and a pebble.*

Riann grinned.

Adelira waved goodbye and walked back to the travelling party.

The shadows grew, and she knew her time in the sunlight was borrowed.

Her mother called, "The carriages are waiting. I hope you are rea dy..."

Adelira stiffened. She wasn't ready to trade sunlight for a life in the darkness of night. But what she wanted didn't matter anymore.

"It's not too late, Adi," her mother said. "We can turn back."

"No," Adelira said softly. "We're going forward."

Adelira cast one last look back to the farm as it disappeared from view. In her soul, she held a quiet life in the sun that would never be hers. Adelira squeezed her pebble.

The Elven Kingdom broke into rougher terrain, golden fields slipped away, their brightness replaced by the grey peaks ahead.

Each step grew darker as though the Vampire King was reaching to meet her.

7

Chapter Seven

Twisted trees with gnarled blackened trunks scarred by war, surrounded the carriage as it rode through Tharth.

Adelira peered out at the knotted branches weaving a canopy so dense that no sunlight was able to pierce through. Decaying leaves and tangled roots made for slow travel. Ravens with eyes like glowing red coals tracked them, guttural caws cutting through the eerie stillness.

A dilapidated tavern sat off the road, nestled in mist beneath the twisted boughs of trees, under the watchful eyes of the ravens. Blackened timber slick with dew and stone structures almost crumbling in places made it seem abandoned, but for the faint glow coming from within.

“We can’t ask for much more from the horses tonight,” Nodrick said as he jumped down, his gentle hands rubbing down the tired mares’ necks.

Adelira stepped down from the carriage, sinking into the damp soil. The dark forest around them was a different world to her. They were another day's ride from the castle.

The forest swayed and creaked, leaning in any time she dared to look away. This wasn't her Elven woods filled with songbirds and sunlight. She imagined if she even tried to climb one of these trees, it might just grow teeth and swallow her whole.

"We cannot possibly stop here," Carys said, trembling behind Adelira.

"We don't have much choice," Adelira replied.

She threw a wary glance at the road still to travel and then to the exhausted mares and knew they needed to rest. Her hand stilled on the flank of one of the mares as goosebumps crawled along her arm.

Her mother emerged from her own carriage and gasped audibly.

Adelira looked up and came face to face with a striking vampire.

He appeared beside them, watching. A smirk played on his lips, flashing fangs at them. He had piercing blue eyes and brown curls that fell messily in his face.

Then he hid his fangs and took a step closer to them.

The Vampire man moved with predator's poise, circling them like a shark. Each step was measured. Each look scanned them up and down, sizing them up hungrily. He paused before the princess, his unblinking eyes locking onto Adelira like a hunter studying its target.

"Well, isn't this an honour," he said in a voice so flat Adelira was convinced it was sarcasm until he cocked a smile at her.

His Tharathi accent was thick, but they understood his language when he spoke.

"I was expecting you. Please, come inside."

His clothes were worn, an old Vampire military uniform In a style that had been decommissioned several wars ago. Adelira guessed that he had long unwoven himself from the fabric of Tharth's civilization. It was as though he had severed all ties to society by retreating to the shadowed fringes of the world.

His clothes, the look in his eyes, everything was just a little too unhinged, except his smile was charming and his manners were impeccable, like he could just remember how to behave in front of guests.

With a casual flick, he shook his hair out of his face. He might be irresistibly beautiful if she weren't so afraid. His jawline was sharp and his lips kept pulling into a smirk that revealed his fangs.

This was the first Vampire she'd ever seen.

Elves were tall and she was used to feeling a physical advantage over most people from other Kingdoms. But this Vampire easily matched the Elves for height.

Where Elves were lithe and precise, but this man was muscled in a way that made Adelira think of a panther. If all Vampires were like this, no wonder they thought of all other races as inferior.

His eyes kept flickering over her. She couldn't move under his intense attention. She would have run all the way out of that forest and back to her golden fields, if her feet would just let her go.

All the horror stories of the Vampire King suddenly didn't seem so exaggerated after all.

"Don't worry," the Vampire said as though he sensed their fear. He grinned, fangs flashed. "The Blood King made it... painfully clear that If I hurt you, he would ensure not even my memory remains."

There was a long pause as the travelling party considered this. The King had anticipated they would need to stop here; the innkeeper was instructed, or rather threatened, into ensuring their safe passage.

Finally, as though the spell had lifted; they shook free, able to move again. King Hara thanked him, making his way towards the inn, followed by the all the rest of the Elves.

"Please, by all means, do come in," he said sarcastically, watching how Elves needed no permission from him to cross a threshold.

The Elven party strode inside.

Adelira passed him and he added, "Day creatures active at night, you must be tired."

She couldn't help but feel as though he was teasing her, but then he knew who she was and why she was here. Nighttime activity was something she would have to quickly adapt to if she was to live in Tharth.

Staff hurried inside to prepare the strange inn as best as they could. There were no lanterns they could spy, no candles, as though the red glow they had seen earlier folded in on itself and disappeared without source. They could only just make out the layout of the rooms without proper light.

She imagined with some love and attention, it could have been cosy. Judging by the cracked pictures on the walls and the faded upholstery; it once had been pleasant.

A creaky but stable staircase led upstairs to the rooms for let. An unlit fireplace made a nice centrepiece of the common room and the kitchen seemed spacious from what she briefly spied in her fleeting transition through the building. The structure held firm. But even good bones were creepy when lifeless.

"I would fix you something to eat..." he said nonchalantly. He watched them scurry around his space, quickly retreating into the sleeping quarters provided. "...But somehow, I don't think you'd like it," he called up the stairs with a grin that only grew louder with each door closing one by one.

8

Chapter Eight

Carys helped Adelira bathe, scrubbing the travel from her skin. They'd arrive at the Vampire King's castle tomorrow evening. Carys's fingers nimbly worked through Adelira's hair and they sat in a silence that was unusual for them, but comfortable, before they dragged themselves into bed for the night.

They climbed in, quiet and tired and hungry from their journey. But Adelira struggled to sleep. The mattress was stiff and clinical, almost as though no guest had ever slept there, and then she thought that perhaps Vampires don't sleep.

What would she do if the King never slept? If his bloodlust never took rest?

She bit her lip and rolled over, looking out the window at the trees surrounding the inn. She passed a glance to Carys who was snoring softly in the twin bed. She smiled, at least her friend was able to sleep. Adelira lay there for what felt like hours, unable to follow Carys into the world of dreams.

She had wanted to escape into the forest when she first saw this Vampire who lived here.

She understood her world, escaping into it often enough to map it with her eyes closed. But Tharth was a curious mystery to her.

She couldn't sleep now, not with her thoughts racing the way they were and not with tomorrow rapidly approaching.

The Vampire's last words haunted her sleeplessness with hunger. Surely Vampires had to consume something, right? Other than Blood? And then a detail clicked into place for her like a puzzle piece; she had seen a kitchen through the archway in the common room. It was dimly lit and dusty, but its existence implied food.

To face the Vampire King, she needed something — anything — to hold onto. Some kind of understanding of the world she was stepping into, even if it was as basic as what food might be prepared in their kitchens. There were answers right downstairs.

She hesitated, fear held her motionless.

Then, anger sparked.

She was tired of being afraid, tired and hungry. This was her last night before the castle, her last chance to gain some control.

She slipped out of the bed. The blanket was cotton and warm, maybe the only warm thing in the inn. She listened for a moment. Carys was breathing evenly and all around her, the inn was silent. Outside, a bird cawed and a branch of some scrawny tree scratched idly at the window. Everyone else was asleep.

Perfect.

Her Elven steps were light, making no creaking sounds along the old worn wooden floorboards. She knew how to move silently. Would that help her in Tharth? She stopped at the door, looking back at Carys resting soundly.

She wondered what Talion would say...

Run.

But surely if she was going to understand the Vampires, the answer was to investigate? She closed her eyes, wishing Talion was standing right behind her. But she had to do this alone. Brave, and alone.

Placing her hand on the handle, she slowly twisted the iron knob. Opening the door, she crept downstairs, maybe she could find something to eat, not quite believing the Vampire when he said she wouldn't like his food. Perhaps she might understand him and the Vampires she'd live with better if she looked around.

The stairs were gloomy and she held onto the wall to feel her way down to the common room where it was not much brighter. Feeling the weight of one step sink beneath her foot, she eased off it slowly, trying not to make a sound. This time, she skipped the step and landed on the next one below.

Along the wall there was a painting of a young girl, maybe six or seven years of age, with soft curls and a sweet smile. It felt oddly tender for a place like this, mysteriously clean compared to the dusty paintings and damaged bit of the tavern. Someone had hung that picture on purpose. Someone had cared about that girl. Not everything here was monstrous. It meant someone, somewhere in this place, had once loved.

She couldn't quite shake her nerves though, as she moved along, what food would a Vampire prepare? She half-expected a decaying corpse on the table.

Stepping into the living room, thoughts of food quickly left.

There in the centre of the lounge, under the shimmering moons straining to shine in through the window, sat the owner of the inn. The room was dark, hiding his form in the shadows of the armchair. Only his shining eyes gave him away. If not for that, she might have missed him sitting there, quietly.

His eyes locked on her.

"Oh," it was the only word she could muster, frozen in place between the steps behind her and the Vampire before her.

He was awake. *Of course* he was awake. Night time. It was just so quiet she assumed he was in his room or out or... suddenly, she didn't know what she thought, every thought felt ridiculous.

"Oh, to you too," he said and this time she knew he was teasing her.

She wanted to climb under the blankets and hide until morning. The room was too gloomy and she was too alone. It was too much; seeing him there, his grin, all of it.

But something inside her begged her to stand her ground, because if she couldn't face just one Vampire, how would she face the King's *entire* court?

There was a strange clink of metal that she couldn't place, coming from somewhere in the darkness.

She forced a deep breath and recovered her movement with a small shrug, trying to shake the terror from her shoulders.

He seemed amused as he said, "Your kind looks so... sunny. How long do you think that'll last?"

His words paused her. She swallowed hard, pushed that fear down, and walked again.

"A–as long as it needs to," she said, hating that her voice shook. Then she took another deep breath, set her shoulders back and grounded herself in determination as she looked for the Tharic words. "Some of us aren't afraid of shadows."

She lowered herself into the seat opposite him, crossing her legs with performative ease before meeting him with a challenging stare.

Though they were blanketed in darkness, she could make out his shadowy figure and the pointed grin. That odd chime of metal again.

His eyes flicked down to her hands clenched in her lap. His grin grew.

He responded to this challenge with one of his own, "Are Princesses allowed to sit with common folk?"

"We make exceptions for innkeepers," she said as nonchalantly as she possibly could, though she knew he could tell most of her bravado was paper thin at best.

"Ah, lucky for you I chose to be an innkeeper today. It's much better to sleep safe and warm in here than... out there." His eyes flashed to the window.

She dared not ask what he was when he was *not* an innkeeper.

Adelira followed his look to the forest that lay beyond the glass, suppressing a shudder, but she would not let him win; "We could simply have ordered that you give up the inn for us."

"Oh, no." He smiled in a way that was both hungry and sinister, she could just make it out in the darkness. "No, you couldn't. You're not in Ebedene anymore, little rabbit. You don't command this Kingdom, or its people."

Whatever warmth she thought was in the room suddenly extinguished and she wished she had stayed upstairs instead, but she refused to back down. If this was her only opportunity to speak with a Vampire before her whole world turned to shadows and blood, then she needed to learn what she could from him.

She wondered what her parents would say about this; a Princess out of her room at night was improper enough, but alone with a Vampire unarmed and unguarded was reckless. On top of that, she was meeting his every challenge with a threat of her own. But she could not help herself. She was made for climbing forest trees and jumping in rushing rivers, so sometimes Elven etiquette slipped by her, and she could not hold her tongue.

"I don't command you... for now. But *soon* this will be my land, too."

She hoped it sounded confident, but she really did not know how much political power the Vampire King would let her have.

The innkeeper had pulled her into a game of chicken and now she dared not back down. But the smirk forming in the corners of his mouth told her he had ripped through her bluff; reading her uncertainties. It was difficult to see him, backlit only by moonlight through the window, he sat in a sea of darkness. The wind picked up and the scratching sound was at the windows downstairs too. Something howled in the distance.

"Have you met him?" he asked. His grin was sly. "The Blood King?"

She didn't need to answer. He knew she hadn't.

"No?" he probed. "Ah, well then, best of luck to you."

"You say that like..." She searched for the right words.

"Like... I'll never see you again?" he offered with a raised eyebrow.

She couldn't quite figure out if he simply meant because she will never go back to her Elven Kingdom and so she would not pass by his inn again... or if he meant to imply that she'll die at the hands of the Blood King.

Suddenly, the thought of never even getting a chance to ask for the Blood Ritual gripped her.

What if she got there and the King took one look at her and deemed her too weak and insignificant to bind himself to? And kept her, silent and bound, locked away in some forgotten wing of his castle?

No sun-filled skies. No trees. *No trees*! Her pulse was hammering in her head and she couldn't breathe, like she'd forgotten how to draw air in the dark.

Her world would be endless stone and blood and shadows.

Fear gripped her with an icy chill that shuddered through her body and the innkeeper smiled, like he was tasting something growing more delicious by the second.

With a snarl, he lunged at her.

Restraints jerked him back, his own momentum working against him and landing him back in his seat with a violent thud that held him in place for only a second before he lunged again. A feral growl rolling up from within him and his teeth snapping a fraction away from her face.

Adelira scrambled back in her seat, colliding with the furniture, almost scaling over the backrest of her chair. A shriek threatened to tear from her lips, but instead remained trapped and silent in fear.

The sharp clash of chains sounded through the room as they went taut, arresting his leap mid-air and leaving him straining against the restraints.

Adelira's eyes swept downward, finally catching sight of the thick iron chain locked around his neck and two more around his wrists.

It rattled again as he tugged at the one around his neck with one trembling hand as though to show the links bolted securely into the stone walls. His body shook.

All the while, his grin stretched unnaturally between pain and amusement. His breaths were quick shallow pulls in. The strain to control himself wore on him heavier than the chain about his neck.

With a low growl and the chink of metal, he shook his head sharply once, lowering himself into the armchair. His body was jerky, a complete opposite to the fluid and confident, cocky man he had been even seconds ago. The struggle against his own instincts had him on the verge of shattering.

He sat there, head tilted slightly, fixing her with a predatory stare that pinned her on her perch. Still curled up against the backrest, half perched on top, like prey too frightened to move; her eyes darted around.

She might bolt at any movement only that she dared not move an inch and test the strength of those chains.

"A beast in a cage," he murmured. His voice was shallow like it cost him to speak, but there was a cruel draw to it like he'd pay the price if it meant scaring her just a little bit more. "That is what you will make him."

His lips twisted into something that tried to smile, instead it was a sneer. "Tell me, little rabbit, are you meant to be the collar or the pet?"

"You're—" she started, but her voice failed her. She tightened her fists, swallowed hard and forced herself to try again, "You're just trying to scare me."

The Vampire leaned in. His grin widened, but there was only pain in his eyes. She could clearly see his fangs. But just in case she couldn't, he leaned even closer until the chains began to groan in protest.

"*Trying*?" he said mockingly. The tremor in his voice betrayed how close he was to losing control. "Little rabbit... I could smell *your* fear before you even entered my forest."

Adelira flinched, but made herself meet his striking blue eyes. The flicker of her defiance only served to amuse him further. His laugh was broken and full of spite. His eyes flashed red, before he blinked and they were blue again, unsteadily so, but blue.

"He's testing us both," the innkeeper said, more to himself than to her as he looked out the window. "I wish it were with anyone else, trust me. I'm not sure he anticipated you making me feral... I can only follow his orders when the man in me is stronger than the beast. Unfortunately, with me, that isn't very often at the best of times."

The chain rattled again as he shifted in his seat. His head cocking to the side like he was studying her. His voice dropped, but no less dangerous.

"I fed for three weeks straight in preparation for your passing through my forest... And it wasn't enough."

An almost nervous chuckle sunk him back against his chair. His hands fidgeted with the chain. The links clicked against each other in an uneven rhythm, betraying the tension in his grip.

"Your blood, it's richer than any other Elf I've smelled before. Lucky you I took these measures, when I was feeling more... *responsible.*"

Adelira wanted to run, to hope he couldn't escape his chains before she escaped his forest. But still her legs refused to obey.

He broke the silence, his voice carrying a thread of resignation. "You should go back to bed. Staying any longer would endanger us both..."

She gaped at him silently.

"Please." His eyes stayed locked on her too long. "I will break free. Sooner or later. I'd rather hunt for my supper in the woods... than in my cabin."

Her voice came out in a small whisper, but she knew she wouldn't sleep until she got an answer, "Wh—what will you hunt?"

For the first time, his grin faltered. He wasn't hunting for pleasure tonight, he was hunting because he *had* to.

Leaning forward just enough for the chain to groan under the strain again, he whispered back an answer chilling in its simplicity. "Anything."

Adelira wished to make a confident and unintimidated exit, but she scurried over the back of her chair and up those stairs.

She lay awake in her bed, listening to the innkeeper breaking his chains and almost immediately taking down something large and angry in the woods surrounding the terrifying dwelling.

Just before dawn, her parents rose, anxious to leave the inn and make their way to the castle. Perhaps they heard the innkeeper's hunt in the forest as well. How Carys slept through it, she'd never know.

Adelira had not slept at all. She was ready to go when the knock came to call her downstairs. She walked into the common area as her parents stepped into their carriage. She glanced out and saw the pre-dawn brightening the forest only a subtle shade lighter, sunlight refusing to touch the Vampire King's homeland.

The innkeeper stood back on the pathway, allowing his guests to leave, forcing them to walk past him. His hands were clasped pointedly behind his back, she wondered if he had chained them again. She saw the dark circles under his eyes and knew he needed sleep quite desperately, too.

As Adelira walked by him, he leaned in just a fraction too close into her space and winked.

"Tell the King I say hello," he teased as she left.

Once safely in the carriage, the wheels began to turn, pulling her away from the hunter in the woods. She released a sigh of relief that she saw mirrored on everyone's faces as they left.

"Things will be... better in the Vampire King's castle," Carys said by way of comforting her and hoped that it was not a lie.

Adelira wished she could believe that, but the night's conversation kept replaying in her head.

By nightfall, she would find out if Carys was right or not.

9

Chapter Nine

Tharth was not built to be conquered.

Cradled by the ruthless embrace of the Feronia Mountains, the castle was hewn into the cliffs and the city was built from the bones of the earth in the belly of the valley. The Kingdom itself was a fortress and at its heart the Blood King had claimed his castle. The untamed mountains curved around the land to guard the city. Few who entered unescorted ever survived.

The passes into the valley were few and treacherous, winding narrow paths where a simple misstep could send an army tumbling into the abyss.

Their peaks would be cloaked in snow in a short few months and suddenly she didn't know if she could survive the cold winters here. Mist rolled down the mountain forests and pooled in the belly of the Kingdom.

The Obsidian Keep, where the Vampire King ruled with his blood court, was an unyielding monolith. It was a blend of fortress and rock that was indistinguishable from the cliffside from afar. They were close enough that she could see the towers of the castle and the gargoyles crouching along parapets.

Where Eloryth was a seamless blend of nature and architecture with the trees growing through the dwellings of Ebedene, here the Obsidian Keep dominated the land. The Vampires had made the mountain bend to their will. They quelled rock until it suited their needs strategically. And aesthetically, it did just as much work to showcase their strength and power.

The carriages rolled through the winding mountain path.

Adelira peered out the window and Carys squeezed her hand before reaching for the garland and placing it gently atop Adelira's head. After all this time, the blossoms had finally opened in earnest and there was a sweet floral scent in the carriage.

The sun had set when the carriages rode through black fortified gates. Before them, stretched the towering architecture of the castle of Tharth. The Obsidian Keep towered to overlook the city. Both a palace and prison.

Lines of vampire servants waited to greet them, stiff and formally dressed entirely in black. A row of nightjars sat on banner poles next to men dressed like soldiers. Banners in gold red and black; the colours of Vampire Royalty, were blowing in the wind, the face of which had the Vampire King's emblem of three swords, one in the middle and two crossed over it. One of the birds let out a high-pitched trill. The twin moons were bright in the sky and several clouds threatened to gather over the cliffs.

Fortified gates closed after they rolled in. The metal locked shut was a deep and final clash that made Adelira jump. The servants stood in line, it felt less like a wedding greeting and more like a funeral.

The air here was colder, thicker. The castle, ever-growing larger, clawed its spires disappearing into the overcast sky that hid the evenfall stars.

A Vampire doorman opened her carriage.

Adelira passed a quick glance at Carys before she looked down at him, though he kept his eyes on the cobblestone. She lifted her dress and made her way down.

Her attention was on the row of statue-still staff in front of them and the waving banners. She'd thought one Vampire in the forest was intimidating, the fleet of Vampire staff that waited in the courtyard were worse.

She misstepped and stumbled climbing down from the carriage.

His gloved hand caught her arm hard enough to bruise. Once she was steady, he dropped her hand as though she was a hot coal he'd grabbed by mistake.

"Thank you," she said to him.

He didn't so much snarl as grimace, like the encounter pained him.

Without a word, he shot off away from her, his eyes flashing in a way she could not interpret. The way the hairs on the back of her neck stood on end made her grateful for his departure.

She rubbed her arm where the bruise had already blossomed beneath her skin. Unease was growing into anxiety by the minute.

All the vampires approaching her, seemed to hold their breath. They refused to look at her, but they moved towards her all the same. Adelira turned to look for Carys, the panic of Vampires stalking towards her was too much.

But Carys wasn't there. And neither were her parents.

Her eyes darted around, scanning for them until she finally spotted the Elven royal procession far ahead being led quickly into the castle, leaving her behind. She tried to call out to them, but a wall of Vampires were in front of her now.

Tharathi staff whisked her away. One moment she had the familiarity of the nearby carriage and the next moment she was in the castle before she could process anything.

Glancing behind her, she still couldn't catch sight of her family. She faced forward again, trying to keep up with the escorts. Obsidian floors were polished to a shine. Adelira looked around and caught her reflection in a mirror along the wall, the only person in the frame, pale and wide-eyed.

The corridors were a labyrinth of twisting halls and endless stone passageways. Hallways wind between chambers and walls inlaid with deep-set alcoves, some empty, some containing statues of past kings or beast-like creatures she'd never seen before. Occasionally there was a guard standing motionless inside an alcove, kept company only by candlelight and his sword.

Servants strode with exact precision, each step mirrored to the person beside them. Every action was stiff. More soldiers than castle staff.

Doors opened before she reached them and closed behind her, the sound of wood shutting against frames followed her through the Keep. The messages and luggage passed between hands were so fluid that any time she turned her attention to it, it had passed.

No words were spoken. Not to her. Not to each other. The silence was terrifying. Even if their eyes were lowered, their instincts latched onto her. Noses turned up as she passed, eyes flashed onto her, fangs concealed behind tight lips.

She kept turning her head around, trying to make sense of what she was seeing in her peripheral vision, trying to lock eye contact with someone who might speak to her, trying to see any of her travelling party.

"Wait—!" She couldn't finish before she was ushered toward the double doors of the throne room.

Looking around, the escorts had already retreated into the shadows.

She turned her gaze up to the doors towering in front of her, stretching to the ceiling. The doors groaned, a guttural sound, like it had been hungry for centuries and was finally allowed to eat. *Her? Was she about to be eaten?* She shook her head, that was a ridiculous thought.

Adelira braced herself against the sheer magnitude of the chamber that awaited.

The herald announced, "Behold the bride of The Vampire King Orahn Viremont, Lord of Tharth, Sovereign of Shadows — Princess *Adelira Delvane* of Ebedene."

She flinched at the herald's announcement as her name was amplified like it didn't quite belong here. The Tharathi accent was unfamiliar with Ehvayn names and it was punctuated over every syllable, none of it coming out smoothly enough to create her name accurately. Not even her name belonged here.

She steeled herself for a moment.

...And then walked into the hall.

A sudden gust of air rushed past as the doors slammed shut tightly behind her, sealing her inside. The abrupt silence was immediate. Every pair of Vampire eyes honed onto her.

I can do this, she thought, willing her feet forward.

Her first step forward shook. Her shoe caught on the stone floor and she bit back a gasp.

Straightening, she forced herself forward, letting her heel land with a poignant click. Then another.

The soft clack of her heels struck the tiles like cannon fire.

Each step was defiance, an assertion: *I am not prey.*

Vampires dripping in jewels tracked her every step with sharp eyes and even sharper teeth. They were unblinking and unmoving and absolutely unnerving.

By the time she reached the dais at the end of the aisle, she'd forced her breath to be steady. Trembling hands smoothed the folds of her gown. The silk was cool against her clammy hands, she brushed them over her thighs.

She had been so focused on the Vampires surrounding her, still and unnervingly watchful, that she hadn't noticed him. Not until he was standing right before her. She gasped, her eyes snapping up.

The Blood King.

King Orahn was striking, dangerously so. His black hair slipped out from beneath the heavy crown and framed his face as sharp as a blade. She could hardly look at him as the air around him tightened.

From his place on the raised platform, Orahn's figure dominated the room, his authority seeping into every corner.

And then, he *stood.*

Adelira dropped into a curtsy as though him towering above her was a weight she could no longer bear and her knees gave in beneath her, then she caught herself and began her ascent, chin tilted up.

Rising from her curtsy, she locked eyes with his.

His eyes — oh, gods help her, those eyes — intensely shifting between hunger and something far more disarming, and utterly unexpected, *warmth.*

His eyes were an arena in which Adelira watched gentle kindness battle animal instinct. As she watched, he settled into himself. The kindness had won.

She was prepared for a predator in every sense, but he was far more complex. The flickering torchlight played over his features, casting sharp shadows. The faintest smile curved his lips, yet did little to soften the intensity in his gaze.

The innkeeper was handsome, a little unstable, a little menacing, but handsome all the same. The court Vampires were colder. Beautiful, yes, but in a clinical, polished way.

Orahn was nothing like them.

His beauty sent a warm flutter through her. Just on the edge of desire, there was something more forbidden; *hope.*

Smoke and snakes. A familiar fear returned. He was a Vampire.

Adelira's eyes hardened as she steeled herself. It would take more than a dashing figure to win her over. Time alone would reveal his true self.

His gaze held her in place, reading everything he needed to know about her in an instant. And he smiled. Did she have no secrets? Her eyes widened as she tried to decide what she'd do if Vampires could read minds.

It took him no more than a heartbeat to see her for exactly who she was, but he liked what he saw.

His smile caught her breath.

The rest of the room disappeared from her mind until she only saw him.

The faint glint of his fangs caught the candlelight, a deadly reminder of his true nature. Though he was no raging beast and not the nightmare from the tales told. She could almost believe he wanted this alliance as much as she needed it.

Beneath the surface, there was a promise he held out for only her to see.

It was more complicated than safety, but she was yet to fully understand it.

Could she trust it? She wavered in her resolve.

He sensed her unease, her shaken will. He waited, motionless, content to let her take the first step. The instinct to flee thrummed in her veins, but his patience held her in place.

Then, he extended his hand to her.

The softness in his expression couldn't erase the hunger she'd seen glinting in his eyes, nor could it quiet the warnings her mother had drilled into her. Centuries of warnings pressed against her instincts that urged her to flee.

She looked at his hand, his palm open to her, a gold band of a ring around one of his fingers. His smile deepened, without demand, as though he could remain motionless in that moment forever, waiting for her choice.

In the depth of his dark eyes, he held a quiet reassurance throughout her hesitation. Like if she looked through the darkness, there was a light inside, guiding her through. Her fear slipped through her fingers as she placed her hand in his.

His grip locked around hers, keeping her steady even when her body threatened to shake again.

He lifted his hand towards him and she followed a step forward. He lowered his face to hers.

"Welcome home, Adelira," he whispered in her ear in Ehvayn.

10

Chapter Ten

For a heartbeat, it was her mother's lullaby, the whisper of her homeland's trees.

When he spoke her language, her fingers tightened around his. The cold metal of his ring bit into her fingers.

Vampires watched her from the peripheral of her vision.

She would stay here in this cold, unbending place. Her choices had led her to this and now she would endure.

But then there was *him*.

She wished this could be real. Even a little real; the warmth in his eyes and in his hand. The stories she thought were exaggerated, sounded real in his presence. If even only a fraction of it was true, she was placing her life in his hands completely.

The Forest Blessings garland still poised in place and she lifted her head, allowing the flowers' scent to waft down and ground her. Exhaling quietly, she squeezed his hand.

His eyes flickered with approval as he watched her swallow her fear.

The floors turned to sand when Orahn moved, destabilising her. It was only his aura, she told herself. He stepped down from the platform, his presence enveloping her. Tucking her hand into the crook of his arm, he steadied her against him.

Orahn led her through the throne room. He was graceful, surprising as she could feel the strength in his muscles. He had the attention of every Vampire. Even those who claimed disinterest shifted subtly, bending the room around him.

As they moved around the room, nobles gave nods or made quick hand movements. She sensed a subtle divide between the nobility in attendance. The younger houses goaded each other, daring one another to meet her gaze. The elders surveyed, gauging whether she was naïve prey or a threat.

The King acknowledged everyone even if it was just with a sweeping glance, whether they bowed or not, but the looks he regarded them with was pointed and performative.

Adelira followed his example, though all of her greetings were careful and small. Hoping she could disappear even while they kept walking deeper into the room and up closer to his Vampires.

She was familiar with this public display of royal graces, only now she didn't know the players. She tried to commit as many faces to memory as she could, pre-empting the time when the memory of which faces smiled and which faked smiles would be useful.

She watched in disbelief as her parents were escorted from the room, along with the few other noble Elves until the room was entirely Tharathi.

Orahn exuded a calm that set her nerves on edge.

He seemed genuine to her, yet her mother's warning made her doubt herself. Smoke and snakes.

Some Vampire gazes carried the raw hunger she had seen before, eyes gleaming with a feral intensity that terrified her. They passed swiftly, Orahn's hand tightening ever so slightly on her arm.

Many Vampires barely acknowledged her presence. Their expressions dismissive; she was beneath their notice. They spoke in hushed voices and she never quite made out what they said. A hand resting on the pommel of a sword or the side of a goblet, the shuffling of feet and arranging of jewels.

Their disinterest was forced, they tried too hard. The act of ignoring her was undoing all the work of ignoring her. They'd have to know *exactly* where in the room she was to constantly have their backs turned to her.

Was it because she smelled too delicious or too much like weakness? One was instinctual, the other was political, and she suspected it was probably both in varying degrees.

"I understand it might be customary for people of the Elven Court to come up to meet us," Orahn said to her, but his attention was on the room, nodding to the people they passed.

She startled when he spoke, though his voice was so light it floated between them without drawing attention. His tone belied the thick and gravely weight of his accent which she was quickly associating with Tharth.

He spoke in Tharic, slowly, like he was making sure she had time to translate his words. "But here, we walk among the Court."

She listened carefully, eyes ahead.

"They are dangerous," Orahn continued. "Every single one of them in their own right. Do not let the gowns and jewels deceive you."

They looked pretty, but more than that, each of them looked intentionally deadly. And hungry. His words settled like frost, a smell she was beginning to associate with him, and she shivered.

A jewelled bracelet clinked in the crowd, sounding like steel being drawn.

She jumped, expecting a fight, yet everyone appeared composed. They all seemed just a little too aware of her every movement and it left her jumpy.

"As I walk through the crowd, we are equal for a moment," Orahn explained the Tharathi custom. "We will see what they will do with that."

Beneath it, this was a battlefield of power and politics clashing for dominance. And Orahn wasn't simply moving through it, he claimed the danger as an extension of himself by making it another weapon in his command. The room and its predators became his; falling into line beneath him.

A group of younger nobles, in house colours and emblems she didn't understand, were the only ones who openly looked at her. Their eyes and teeth gleaming with a youthful excitement that cut smiles into their faces.

A prompt stern look from one of their elders immediately locked their gaze to the floor. Though they tried not to smile, she could still spot their smirks straining with the effort to remain composed.

Orahn shifted slightly, angling his stance so his back was to them as if he found something far more interesting in another noble.

The young men's smirks faded. Their eyes dropped, shoulders tightening as if bracing for something.

She wasn't sure what had just happened.

They were no fragile novices; each carried a sculpted, solid frame that spoke of regular training, and the arrogance of youth that met most challenges certain of victory. But not this one. This challenge shook their confidence; it made them look away instead of standing tall.

Orahn glanced at her. She sensed it immediately, like his gaze held a heaviness, previously distributed across the room, yet was entirely upon her now.

The heat of his body was a steady reminder of his presence at her side. She could get lost in how handsome he was, how deep his eyes were, but there was the thundering of her heartbeat and the Vampires close enough to reach out and snatch her up that kept pulling her gaze away from him to make sure the room drew no closer.

Even standing by the King's side, Adelira felt like nothing more than a guest in a room full of ghosts. Neither of them were really a part of the others' world.

She wanted to replicate his confidence, but she still hadn't seen anyone from her court yet and she longed for one familiar face to hold her together.

"Have... all the Elves been removed?" she asked so quietly she wasn't sure he'd hear her.

"They are safe," Orahn said.

"Where?"

"Your people were escorted to the guest wing," he answered. "This is not a place I'd have them wait, because there is still a chance someone might feel brave enough to harm them as a method of challenging me."

"Would they really?" she asked in dismay.

"No one here is a threat to my crown."

If the Blood King was concerned for her people, just what was his court really like? She looked around to make sure no one had been forgotten or left behind.

“Were the carriages to your liking?” Orahn’s voice low through the muted hum of conversation around the room. Like he knew she was still scanning the crowds and he wanted to draw her into other subjects.

She hesitated, aware of his eyes on her. They still walked slowly through his court, but his attention had turned from the room to her.

It was harder to look away now and her attention slowly drifted from the room to the beautiful cut of his jaw line and the way his lips moved while he spoke quietly to her.

“Yes...” She didn’t know if the carriages were a display in reach and power designed to intimidate her or an act of generosity, perhaps simple diplomacy. She leaned on diplomacy, “...Your horses are lovely.”

He tilted his head slightly as he glanced her over, his dark eyes catching the light.

She looked up at him. Her cheeks flush and a slow heat that pressed up her spine and threatened to push her closer against him.

“You’re exhausted from your travels, I’m sure,” he said gently. “I will get through the formalities quickly so you can retire for the evening.”

“No, please,” she said quickly, her words rushing together. “I need to get used to the nights.”

“I have no doubt that you will adjust in time, perhaps I can even help with that. But I will end the night early. If you are to see the Kingdom, you’ll need your strength.”

“Thank you,” she murmured, unsure whether to feel relieved or uneasy.

Climbing into bed now sounded wonderful.

But then she wasn’t so sure... Would she go to bed alone?

“Where—” Adelira began, but the words caught in her throat as a strange feeling fell over her.

She glanced over her shoulder, an odd prickling sensation creeping up her spine. The wall behind them was bare. But the feeling remained; a set of unseen eyes *watching* her.

There was no one back there. Only a wall.

Taking a deep breath, she turned back to Orahn and finished her question. "Where will I sleep tonight?"

"You'll have your own chambers," he said simply.

She had braced herself for her sleeping arrangements to be something far colder, perhaps even cruel, before she met him.

He nodded to a lady with a crimson necklace and her partner who greeted him back.

Orahn continued smoothly, not skipping a beat, "You may keep your room even after the wedding ceremony, if that is your wish."

"Oh," she murmured, startled by his kindness, but also a little disappointed.

His lips turned up, her surprise entertained him. The smile was a reminder of the warnings of the Vampire King. He was a calculating creature. This might be a part of that calculation.

She came for politics but still found herself hoping for affection.

The Vampires seemed to be moving closer, like the room was closing in on her, trapping her in suffocating tension, breathing shallow.

She stopped moving.

Her eyes snapped up to Orahn. Searching in panic for that reassurance she had seen when she first took his hand, when this all seemed safer and the Vampires and the room weren't closing in around her and she wasn't looking for the hidden treachery in everything.

He met her gaze and tilted his head subtly towards her, an elegant motion that somehow felt intimate; as though *she* had his full attention, not the room around them.

He stopped walking and shifted into a stance that looked very intentional, like he had intended to stop here all along and it wasn't her shaking legs holding them hostage there.

"You're holding your breath," Orahn said.

She released a shaky breath.

"You'll make them think they frighten you."

"They *do* frighten me."

"Good." His reply was smooth, as though her fear was perfectly natural, expected even. "I won't downplay the court, that would be a disservice to you. But I also won't have you terrified."

"I don't know how."

"I'll show you." He motioned subtly, his fingertips only just brushing along her arm. "That bruise is fresh. Did you get it here? Did someone...?"

She looked down at the purple mark and his fingers hovering above it. She could feel the heat in his hand, but covered the bruise hurriedly with her sleeve. He dropped his hand away.

"No, no. I... tripped," she said. She didn't want to get his staff in trouble; the Vampire had gripped her too hard, but he'd only done it because she had tripped.

He considered her words but pressed no further. "It is difficult for my Vampires to be here now, with a fresh injury like that, even if the skin didn't break."

"Oh, um..." she started, but she wasn't sure if she should apologise or accept it.

"Look at them, Adelira. I mean, really look at them."

She tried to do what he asked, dragging her eyes away from him to look around the room again. Noting how each Vampire's attention was keenly on them. For every step she took forward, they took a step away. Barely a whisper of a step, but a step nonetheless.

Now she realised they were restraining themselves. It was her own adrenaline that made them seem too close.

"Elven blood sings, but yours is... a little louder than most."

She looked up at him in surprise.

"They are hungry, even tempted by you. I'll confess, in some small part, I am as well. Though my control is above that of the courts."

"Y–you want me?" she asked and the glint of amusement in his eyes made her curse herself for phrasing it like that, her cheeks colouring red.

Orahn forced down a surprised chuckle, fighting to keep the smile from his lips. He didn't answer her question.

"The Vampires want to come closer, but they are scared of me," Orahn said instead. "By extension, they are scared of *you*, too. You're everything they want. And yet... they are terrified to come near you."

Terrified of her? She didn't know which way was up when the world's axis tilted like this. Carys hadn't been so wrong after all.

"I hope that might comfort you during your time here," he offered her, "in some strange small way. Remember it when you need something to cling to."

Adelira looked around the room again.

Respectful gestures passed quickly through the court, a ticking of fingers as though the room was speaking in code to their King.

He tracked their hands signals and gave respectful nods in response.

Some people smiled, some bowed, but all of them were drawn to him and the way his presence completed the room.

"You have them trained," she said softly as they walked. And then immediately regretted saying it aloud, thinking how rude that must sound. She only meant that no one here was chained, like the innkeeper was, and no one was coming closer to her, because of him. *He* was their chain.

Orahn chuckled low in his throat, the sound rich and velvet smooth. "Oh, they are far from tame. I simply remind them that I bite harder."

Her cheeks flushed despite herself. His confidence was magnetic, an anchor to soothe her nerves.

She hadn't even noticed they were moving again until they were half way across the floor. Somehow, he'd gotten her legs to stop shaking.

"You're smiling," Orahn remarked, his words mixed with mischief.

"I—" She faltered, her voice trailing off as she realised a faint smile was tugging at her lips despite herself. "You're... unnervingly good at this."

"At what?" Said low and steady with just enough curiosity to keep her talking.

"Disarming me," she admitted, meeting his eyes briefly before looking away.

His smile shifted, soft but with a flicker of something darker beneath it. "That's hardly a challenge."

Her eyes snapped back to his, surprised by the boldness of his claim, but there was no arrogance in his expression.

"And why is that?" she asked.

"Because your armour," he said quietly, "was never meant to keep someone like me out."

The words fell between them, not as a boast but a simple truth. She could feel her pulse quicken from the intimacy of his observation.

Slowly, around the room, Vampires began to tap two fingers into their left hand and then hold their closed fists in the air. They uncurled their fingers and revealed age-old scarred palms up towards the King.

Only a few had no scar at all. Some hesitated before making the sign, but the gesture spread through the hall, one by one, like a slow wave of submission.

With that silent declaration hanging in the air, the King simply nodded once and moved towards the doors without looking back.

"Everyone seems to respect you," she said, her voice soft. "Or fear you."

Orahn's inflection shifted, taking on a reflective quality. "It's both. They respect strength. But without grace it becomes brutality. Fear alone is effective, but respect makes it sustainable."

"Grace and respect," Adelira repeated, testing the words against the image of him in her mind. The image everyone had painted of him. The image of the Blood King. "And yet you still use fear, even when you say respect is more sustainable?"

"It has its uses."

"But then you tell me to be unafraid..."

"You misunderstand. You should be afraid. And so should they. You should fear them. They should fear me. And because I am here... you don't need to be afraid *now*," he murmured back though his eyes were fixed ahead as they walked out the doors.

She straightened her spine, chin tilting up instinctively. *Never again prey.*

She'd work hard her whole life to not let her terror create a trap she might not be able to escape. His gaze flickered to her and there was the ghosting of admiration in his smile.

Her heart fluttered again, not from the watching eyes around the room, but the quiet intensity of his attention.

For the first time since arriving in Tharth, she was steady. The room hadn't grown less intimidating, but Orahn had made it seem as though it didn't matter.

11

Chapter Eleven

Adelira's eyes opened slowly, her chamber dim with the setting sun.

The din of distant staff performing evening duties travelled through the thick walls. *Right*. She'd need to get used to waking up at sunset. Glancing around, on one side of the room, beyond the bathtub, was the private enclosed garden.

A knock at her door, a guard stood there. He had sky blue eyes that darted quickly over her, and then, over her shoulder into her room, before landing back to her again.

"I'm doing a security search of your chambers. May I come in?"

"Yes, come in," she said and stepped aside.

The air hummed with magic receding as he passed the threshold. His gaze lingered on the tall windows with a reading seat beneath it, before he made his way towards the indoor garden.

Over the garden, a glass ceiling enclosed starlit skies. He turned abruptly, moving around her and returned to the main door.

He looked down the corridor. She peered out, seeing no one else there.

Facing her, he gave a quick bow. "All seems clear. Your ladies are arriving presently. I'll take my leave."

"Thank you," she said.

A minute later a second knock came and she opened her door to her ladies in waiting. Behind them was a hanger of dark Vampire style dresses.

"May I come in?" the one lady asked.

"Yes," Adelira said, stepping aside.

"May I come in?" the other lady asked.

Adelira frowned, and then less confidently this time, "Y–yes."

They pulled in rails of clothing, explaining that the King had a dozen Vamperic styled dresses sent for her. Stiff bodices appeared to have a steel structure or boned corset.

"That was thoughtful of him," she said.

The women exchanged a glance.

"Was it... *not...* thoughtful?" Adelira asked uncertainly now.

"I'm sure it was," one responded without the assurance in her tone to match the words and placed them in the wardrobes.

One of them lit a fire in the hearth and lit candles she placed on tables around the room. Vanilla incense filled the space and the room seemed to breathe easier. They informed her of the plans for the evening before disappearing from her chambers quickly.

She pushed the outfits aside and pulled out her own clothing.

The evening was hosting a formal banquet. She dressed in a long Elven gown, peach-coloured. The straps were thin and her shoulders bare and while the chill of Tharth made the long sleeves sensible; her heart raced at the thought of venturing among the Vampires again.

She dressed and did her hair alone, missing Carys's chatting and effortlessly weaving her hair into something that passed for formal dinner dos. Adelira finally gave up after the third attempt and settled for leaving her hair down.

Once she tamed her hair enough, she made her way out onto the balcony, hot and frustrated.

The cool air was soothing along her flushed skin. The noises from below drew her gaze downward.

The battleyard crackled like fire, the energy of the soldiers barely contained to that space. Steel of weapons rang through the yard. Bat hawks did daring aerial displays at the whim of their handlers. One glided passed her, bright yellow eyes watching her briefly before it nose-dived. Rocketing downwards to catch the lure the handler yanked away at the last second, the bird shot up again without its prize.

She spotted her parents down below. Her father had likely requested a private demonstration of the army he had secured with the Elder Celestite and his daughter's hand.

Of course her parents were okay, what else had she expected?

Orahn strode up and down through the rows of soldiers in his army. He was dressed in the same military uniform with his squared back, every step struck the ground like a warning. His deep voice shot through the battleyard and even from up in her tower, she could hear him clearly. His army responded with precision.

He moved to the front of his regiment and began complex demonstrations with his longsword. Immediately mirrored by his entire army, move for move. Every soldier was in sync with him. They were deadly and singular while the King moved like a flame.

Around the outskirts of the battleyard, a number of guards stood at attention, it was clear they were not a part of the army. Their uniform was different. Her attention was caught by one of them who kept moving nervously, only subtly, along the wall and then back to his position again. He glanced up at the sky and she saw the paleness of his blue eyes. He was the guard who had checked her room earlier. She held his gaze for a long moment until he pointedly broke it and looked away.

Orahn's voice called out a command and his soldiers moved into a new stance.

Shouting instructions, the Vampire King moved in front of the ranks. He was the haunting vision of eternal night.

He snapped his face upward. His eyes locking onto hers. Adelira felt pinned under his attention.

He inclined his head and a smug smirk tugged at his lips. Before she even fully realised he had winked at her; his attention snapped back to his soldiers, and he didn't look her way again.

Adelira walked back into her chambers with pink cheeks, her thoughts tangled with the memory of his gaze.

The Vampire women she had seen in court all looked like beautiful nightmares; dark red lips, agonising corsets with lace and plunging necklines.

She had long tanned limbs from her hours in the sun, red hair that caught the light like a flame and grey eyes that held more wonder than shadow. She dressed in ethereal silks, stitched with the quiet beauty of the forest she'd come from.

Surrounded by creatures carved from nocturnal essence and desire, she suddenly felt... delicate.

Orahn had looked at her like maybe he'd seen something deeper in *her*.

The pull of the temptation to transform, to trade silk for shadow. Could she ever replace softness with steel? It lasted only a breath. Even as the thought crossed her mind, it felt like a betrayal of herself.

She was carved from sunlight. And she would not smother that light to match their darkness.

Crossing the room, she opened a chest she had brought with her and retrieved her jewel box from within. Sitting neatly on top was the small pebble, its surface smooth and worn. She held it tightly. The gift from Riann was a steadfast reminder of why she had come here.

Don't let me change, just let me survive, let us all survive.

Placing it near her bedside, she knew why she was here and why she'd stay even if this honeymoon period was too good to be true.

A casual knock at the door broke her thoughts.

She hesitated, glancing toward the door. She hadn't expected an escort to fetch her for dinner.

Opening the door, there *he* stood.

Orahn poised as ever, dressed for dinner already, like he could shed his military uniform effortlessly and step into diplomacy as though he was born to wear both armour and silk interchangeably.

Surely not even he could cover that distance or change his outfit so quickly.

He wore a deep crimson tunic framed in a black jacket. The fine cut emphasised his broad shoulders and built frame. He towered over her, without being intimidating. He held back, just a fraction out of her space.

A small smile played at the corners of his mouth, her surprise amusing him.

"You're impossibly fast," she said, slightly disoriented by what she had just seen in the battleyard and seeing him now.

"Am I?" he asked. His voice was light, trying to conceal a smile there.

Adelira bit her lip. For a man so dangerous that legends were written about him, he seemed almost kind. She wasn't sure Vampires could move that fast.

He smelled fresh. *Fresh as a daisy? Was that what Carys had said?* But he didn't smell like a daisy, he smelled like forest frost and maybe the hint of something alcoholic.

"Shall we go, Adelira?" Orahn extended his arm. His voice was smooth. Only the subtle traces of his lethal command in the battleyard.

A whisper from his lips could be a promise or a threat and the line between the two was dangerously thin.

She laced her arm through his, it was almost too easy, like they'd done this a thousand times already, and they walked through the corridors.

Everything in Tharth was quiet. Was that just what the evening was? A hush that was respectful to the sleeping world beyond their borders.

"How did you sleep?" he asked.

She hesitated, caught between whether to be polite or honest. It was exhaustion that allowed her to sleep. Now she wasn't sure she could close her eyes in sunlight and find slumber instead of finding herself outside.

"I will have some tea sent to you in the mornings. It'll help you sleep easier during the day," Orahn said. "How do you take your tea?"

"I don't think I need a calming herb to sleep. I just need time to adjust to the new routine."

"Yes, that is true, but tea can help you adjust... quicker. Besides, I'd like to know how my new queen likes her tea."

Blushing, she caught herself smiling. "Honey if the tea is spiced, otherwise plain with floral tea."

"I'll remember that," he promised.

"And yourself?"

He looked down at her in surprise.

"How do you enjoy your tea?"

"I, well... How about this? I'll join you some time. I can try both and see what I prefer."

She fought back her smile, knowing the King didn't drink tea was oddly amusing, but knowing he would for her was sweet. It occurred to her then, that he didn't drink tea because he drank *blood*. He was willing to expand his world for her.

Unnaturally thin pillars held the vaulted ceilings impossibly high above her. Some of the windows had stained glass which caught the twin moonlight and shone colour across the shiny floors. Chandeliers of wrought iron hang from thick chains.

"There are several layers of protection within the Obsidian Keep."

"For the people here?" she asked tentatively.

"For you," he clarified.

"Oh..."

"My court has free range in public spaces. Any bedroom is off limits without explicit consent. Like your room," Orahn said. His voice was smooth, like he wasn't actually subtly telling her about the dangers lurking in his castle.

She nodded. She had felt the permission give way to the guard and her ladies.

"Be intentional with that. Your ladies will ask to enter, always," he went on.

"Yes, they arrived earlier with, um, your gifts. Thank you."

"I'm glad you received them. Those who can't handle the task required of them will forfeit the privilege. The ladies will need permission from you every time, just to be sure," he paused. "That requires nothing of you, save to allow them access. I will handle all other affairs in the background."

"W–Why wouldn't they be able to do the task?"

"They might feel... weak," he said carefully choosing the word, "in your presence."

This made her frown. "There's a lot to get used to," she said softly.

"There is," he agreed.

"Can you speak Ehvayn?" she asked after deliberating the question for a while.

He smiled, almost embarrassed. "No. I learnt the greeting I spoke for when you arrived. I could learn to speak it though, if you would prefer that?"

She looked up at the quiet way he waited for her response. "I... I speak Tharic fine, don't I?"

"You do," he agreed.

"Then, we can keep speaking this," she said.

His gaze flashed towards her again, though he simply nodded.

The Keep was a fortress of stone broken only by moonlit windows. Fires lit in endless halls gave her an idea of how large the palace was. The castle housed more than just its ruler. It held past betrayals. And the promise of future bloodshed.

Descending the grand staircase, voices from the banquet hall threaded through the corridors towards them. As they entered, the air was laced with wine and fresh bread. A few chairs scraped on the floor and goblets were placed down. Adelira noticed that the floral scent was masking another smell. *Blood*.

The room, full of chatter seconds ago, fell silent. All eyes turned to them. Orahn didn't call for the room's attention. He drew them in like the tide, deep enough to drown.

She looked into his dark eyes and could almost see herself drowning too, but the warmth was so welcoming the drowning almost felt *kind*.

Adelira caught her mother's glance from across the hall as they escorted her family to the far end of the dining table. She was again relieved to see them, even across the room.

Carys shot her hand out and waved. Adelira grinned widely, bowing her head to hide it, fingers twitching the smallest wave back that she dared. The King didn't look at them, but his eyes lowered to her hands before returning to the room again.

Orahn led her to the head of the table, his hand light against her back. Once everyone was seated, he stood, his regard sweeping the room.

Orahn began, his voice commanding yet inviting, "Tonight, we celebrate the strength of alliances forged through stone, blood and sacrifice."

He glanced at Adelira, his expression softening before his voice turned resolute.

The room raised glasses in agreement.

"To Princess Adelira, to unity and to assured victory." He lifted his goblet.

"To victory."

12

Chapter Twelve

The Vampires played their roles; court seated for a grand feast. Plates were filled and passed up and down the tables. Movement furrowed through the hall and cutlery clanging was *almost* convincing. Yet, not a single bite was taken.

The Vampires only drank from their goblets.

She fought to keep her hands steady in her lap as she tracked the illusion.

"How is your food, Adelira?" Orahn asked.

She looked around the feast. The Elves were eating and enjoying themselves. Was this care genuine, or calculated?

His hand brushed lightly against her fingers, her skin tingled, pulling her attention back to him. The motion was so elegant it was almost cruel for how much it left her wanting.

His eyes roamed over her face in amusement, pleased with the way he'd made her heart flutter.

"It's wonderful," she replied, steadying herself. "It tastes as though it came straight from the royal kitchens of Eloryth. Is that why no one else seems to enjoy it?"

She hadn't intended to draw attention to the fact that she saw through the performance they put on.

But Orahn only smiled. "They are usually much more convincing. I suspect you are distracting them."

Her eyes snapped up. He was definitely teasing her, but the truth of his words was there as well. When her eyes connected with any particular Vampire, it was as though the attention made them falter, cutlery slipped. But she looked around the room and found they *were* convincing enough, none of her Elven party seemed to notice the act.

"Food matters more to you than it does to us," he continued. "Most don't care much for the taste, though some take pleasure in eating occasionally. If it makes you more at ease, we can eat what you're accustomed to. If you want it, my kitchens will cook it."

There was a subtle ravening edge to his assurance. She wasn't sure if she offended their culture or if she should be relieved he'd make adjustments for her.

Adelira glanced down at the spread before her. The watermelon caught her attention most, simple and sweet, something she'd eat under the trees in Ebedene on a warm sunny day.

Her silk gown was bright and, in this stifling darkness, it felt as alien as the food arrangements. Two worlds colliding, oil and water trying to mix, destined to remain forever separate.

A server behind her poured wine into her glass. Afterwards, he didn't move away. He breathed in deeply. Adelira froze with the predator's hot breath on her neck. Each inhale was a slow panic that crawled up her spine and still he would not move, drinking in her scent.

Orahn was calm, but she couldn't replicate that. She couldn't even breathe.

Casually, Orahn picked up his glass and leaned back in his chair, taking a long sip and passed a lazy glance over to the server whose muscles tightened as soon as the King's gaze landed on him.

The server immediately peeled away and Adelira drew breath again.

Adelira didn't know if she should truly fear Vampires or not, but her body responded instinctively.

She picked up her drink, then glanced over at Orahn's glass. His wine was a different shade of red.

"You prefer blood," she said, the statement escaping her lips when she understood what was in his hands.

"Yes." His response was unapologetic.

In Ebedene, no one would have dared to speak about Vampires drinking blood. Yet here, under Orahn's intense attention, there was a thrill to it, an intoxicating sense of freedom.

"Ask it," Orahn said. He said it gently, but insisting, like he could see the questions race through her mind, he just needed her to say it aloud.

He waited in silence for so long that she became braver than the thumping beat of her heart that was too scared to hear the answer.

"W–will you drink my blood?"

The smirk that curled his lips made her skin flush.

He leaned in, his words murmured along her neck, "Do you want me to?"

Stiffening, her fingers tightened around the fabric of her dress in her lap.

He pulled back and chuckled. A low rich sound that warmed her.

"I won't do it unless you ask me to," he said, the playful lilt of his voice undercut by a predatory undertone.

His eyes flashed and she saw both his hunger and desire.

She didn't look at him again, staring instead at her lap as silence stretched between them. Did she want him to?

The King was handsome and charming. Longing for his bite was dangerous to entertain, her thoughts brought her there regardless. She imagined his lips on her neck. A warm tingle ran down her spine. Orahn slowly savouring every drop, tasting every secret she'd ever tried to bury.

He shifted further away in his chair, like her body had reacted a little *too* loudly to that idea, and he needed the distance.

Finally, she spoke, "That's the Blood Ritual though... isn't it?" Her voice barely a whisper, "That's why I'm here."

Orahn's laugh was indulgent, yet his eyes gleamed darkly.

"No, that's not the Ritual," he said, leaning back. "Drinking your blood? That's something I'd do... for fun." He shrugged, as though that wasn't quite the right word, but would suffice.

"So, the Blood Ritual... requires no blood drinking?"

His smile was kinder now. "You thought you would need to offer yourself up like that, and you still agreed to this?"

She hesitated in answering, but he got what he needed from that.

"Drinking your blood can be sensual," he said. "It can create an intimate bond between us."

Sensual. Her lips parted.

His fist curled closed as he watched her face and his words came out a little strained. "Some blood is spilled for the Ritual, but there's no feeding involved."

Adelira's shoulders drooped a little.

Then, her eyes widened. *Wait,* was she disappointed?

She shook her head to brush the thoughts aside. Her cheeks were pink. Him drinking from her was terrifying, but also tender, like a surrender. Like she could let go of the duty and fear and simply relinquish herself to her fate. To him.

His eyes lowered to her fallen shoulders, but his expression remained unchanged. "It's performed by blood priests."

"Is it like... marriage vows?"

He tilted his head, a thoughtful expression in his eyes, like he was weighing what he thought her idea of what that looked like against what he understood it to be.

She was struck by the idea that even in simple Tharic, in the most basic form, they were worlds apart from each other. They could potentially talk past each other, because their definitions didn't always align.

"No," he said. "It's not a marriage vow like you would call it."

She nodded, but said nothing.

"Blood Rituals fade slowly over time."

She looked up at him in shock. She could not risk the Blood Ritual deteriorating. She *needed* it.

"If we wed as well, then the Ritual will endure forever," he finished.

"But..." She started in confusion. "You accepted my marriage proposal. Isn't the Blood Ritual a magically enforced Vampire Marriage?"

Regarding her, his face revealed none of his thoughts. "In theory, the Blood Ritual will make your blood smell more like mine—"

"—In theory?" she asked in horror. "You don't know?"

"This hasn't been done before with an Elf."

"Right..."

He paused, glancing as she clutched her glass. "Afterwards, my Vampires should smell Vampire Royalty in your veins. Right now, your blood brings out their killer instincts."

She felt that. All around the room, everyone's attention was honed to her while they pretended to eat instead.

"I will be bound to protect you and your people. But it will not last forever. A marriage is what seals it 'until death do us part.' They work best *together*, but, you understand, they are not the same thing."

Adelira bit her lip. "Then, it doesn't necessarily need to be done simultaneously? We could do the Blood Ritual first? Before we get married? We can do the Ritual *now*?"

He leaned back slightly, eyes locked steadily as he took her in. He spent a long time studying her. She began to shift uncomfortably.

His voice was quiet. "The Ritual... is an agreement written in our blood."

In blood, she repeated to herself. The idea stuttered her heart, even though she'd known all along that they would be tangled together in blood and in fate. Could she do it? What exactly *was* the rest of this Ritual?

Adelira's chest was taught. Frustrated with herself, she'd crossed mountains for this and *knew* it required blood, in some form.

She lowered her eyes to her lap. Trying to steady the sudden rush of fear coursing through her veins, she twisted her fingers around the folds of her dress. Movement snagged at the corner of her vision, vanished before she could make it out clearly. Exhaling slowly, she thought of her pebble, of the flowers wilting in her room, and tried to be fearless.

"It's *harrowing* and raw." He slowed, like it was too personal to easily voice.

Adelira's pupils widened. He'd *done* this before.

"It's not a wedding. It will rip and break us apart, before merging us together, again. Trust me, the marriage will feel...easy... in comparison."

Orahn watched her closely, his sharp eyes catching every flicker of uncertainty in her. Then, slowly, he leaned closer, his presence consuming all of the space between them. His voice was a whisper of velvet that brushed over her ear.

"You're not ready for that, yet."

She knew she wasn't ready for the Blood Ritual, she felt it in his careful pause as he gauged her reaction.

She lifted her eyes to his. Her throat was tight around the words, but she forced herself to ask, "What if I'm never ready?"

His smile was barely there, like he was trying to be comforting, but somehow just couldn't quite manage it. "We will find another way."

She thought she saw something in his eyes; secrets carved into his very soul.

He sounded kind. She could feel beneath her skin her choices slipping away, covered up as a surrender he was gently coaxing out of her. And she almost let herself believe they might find another way.

No, she had to secure the Blood Ritual, *ready or not*.

Her words came out brittle, without the bravery to complete it, "W–when will we...?"

Orahn's expression softened entirely.

"When the time comes," he said, leaning out of her personal space. "I will teach you everything you need to know about the Blood Ritual, but that time is not now. In the meantime, we can perform the Vow of Intent."

Adelira swallowed hard. "What is that?"

"The Vow is spoken beneath the twin moons," Orahn said, "Once our intention is declared before the court, it cannot be taken back... Not without dishonouring us both."

In her future was not just the Blood Ritual, but a separate wedding event and, to give them some time, a public declaration of alliance.

She couldn't tell if delaying the Blood Ritual would help or make it worse. All she knew was that the alliance, for now, felt safer waiting for clarity than rushing into something she didn't fully understand.

"You'll adjust in time and I'll ensure you feel at home here, Adelira."

She looked down at her plate, not so hungry, after all. She noticed he hadn't eaten, either.

"How... how do you get your blood now?"

Questions had circled endlessly in her mind while she listened to the innkeeper hunt in the forests. Now, with the weariness of her journey easing, she couldn't rest without at least one solid answer.

Orahn shrugged as he casually adjusted his sleeve, rolling it past his elbow. "We have blood donors."

The subtle tracking of his eyes suggested he'd noticed her shiver.

Who were these donors? Did they come willingly? How often did the Vampires feed? She couldn't voice them, each new horror crawling up inside her reminding her how out of her depth she was.

The questions piled upon each other, threatening to overwhelm her. Until Orahn's voice broke through her racing mind.

"It must all be strange for you and difficult for you to feel like you can talk to me," he said. "But I would urge you to, if only for your own ability to adapt quickly to your life here."

His intensity made her lower her eyes. "Yes, Your Majesty."

He let a playful lilt coat his words, "That's too formal. Just Orahn."

"But..."

"Please. I insist," he said. His voice was lighter now and he leaned back into his chair. "You call me Orahn and I'll call you..." His eyes swept over her, thinking. "Lira? How does that sound?"

She stifled a smile. Lira was different. She was used to Adi, but Adi climbed trees and ran through golden fields. Lira stayed awake all night and dined with Vampires.

13

Chapter Thirteen

Torchlight along the gothic stone walls followed Orahn's movements as he walked alongside Adelira, a ripple of light through the halls. She'd never been out on the sea, but she imagined this soft bobbing was what the ocean felt like, calm and endless.

There was the constant smell of copper in the Keep. Blood.

Orahn turned to her. "What would you like to do now?"

The patience in his eyes gave her courage. "Am I… allowed to see Carys?"

Orahn's brows lifted in confusion, processing the request before he responded, "*Allowed?* That's a peculiar way to phrase it."

Her cheeks burned with embarrassment. "I only mean… Do I need your permission?"

His brown eyes narrowed, like finally understanding what she was saying. And he didn't like it.

"You don't need my permission for anything."

"Oh."

"You are not my prisoner here. You're free to see whomever you wish. Do you understand?"

"I–I know. I meant no offence. Only... I..."

Softer now, and with the kindness returning to his eyes, he said, "If you'd like to see her, I can help arrange that."

"I'd like to see Carys."

Orahn inclined his head at the request. "Wait in this seating room. I'll send someone to bring her to you."

"Thank you."

She waited in a plush chair by the hearth and wondered if he meant what he said before. Her fingers brushed over the velvet seat, her fingerprints leaving patterns in the soft material.

Hairs pricked along the back of her neck as though someone was watching her. She was alone though. Out the window, beyond where she was able to see, a nightjar squawked.

Moments later, her friend bounded into the room, disturbing the stillness.

A smile broke across Adelira's face. "Carys."

They embraced tightly.

"You're well?" Adelira asked, stepping back but keeping her hands on Carys's shoulders, inspecting her.

Carys wriggled out of her grasp. "The food is divine. None of my gowns will fit by the time we return."

They moved to the seats.

"The Vampires are dangerously appealing," Carys sighed, "particularly that King of yours."

"Isn't he?"

"How has the King been treating you?" Carys asked seriously. "Has he tried...?"

"Tried what? To drink my blood? No. He's been kind, truly," Adelira said, but held back gushing about how he'd charmed her in other ways. She was too unsettled by how few Elves she'd interacted with since arriving. "Please, tell me about the others. How is everyone?"

"We're fine. If I'm honest, we're more than fine. We're pampered. There's no work to be done. We're treated like guests, all of us... It's so dark here. It's beautiful, but the night is intense even though everything is... fine..."

It feels like everything is designed to keep us comfortable and our guard low."

"The Vampires are polite," Carys started slowly, "though sometimes their stares linger longer than I'd like."

Adelira hesitated, then added, "The way they look at us, it's like we're being measured for something."

"I see that in the way they move almost too fast."

"I never quite know where they are in the halls, one moment there and gone the next. When I arrive, they vanish."

"Do you think they might hurt you?"

Adelira shook her head. "No. It's not like that, I don't think. Or, at least, maybe not like that for *most* of them anyway... But there's something they're not telling us."

Carys leaned in. "The Blood Ritual."

Adelira tensed. "I don't know, Carys. I'm not as confident as I was before. When I spoke with Orahn... There's something about him and the Ritual."

Carys frowned, holding Adelira's hand. "I worry about you in that room in the tower, so high above the earth. I hope you get to go to the forests, feel the rhythm of the land beneath your feet. That you'll get out of this stone castle often enough that it won't rob you of your fire."

Adelira smiled. "Thank you for thinking of me, Carys. But I will be okay, even if I never step in another forest again."

They both frowned.

"If everyone at home is safe, I'll learn to love the stone for granting me that," Adelira added.

Carys smiled then, hearing the truth of it.

"Do you think anyone is listening to us?" Carys asked.

Adelira bit the inside of her cheek at the thought. "Gods, I hope not. The King admitted he can't speak Ehvayn."

"Let me tell you about all the wonderful things we've seen and done since arriving," Carys offered.

"Yes, that sounds wonderful."

She curled up against Carys' side in the armchair and they spoke until the sun was shining and the day drifted between them.

Carys' eyes fluttered closed and Adelira heard her breaths become shallower as sleep pulled her under. Tucked up against her friend, Adelira let her eyes close as well.

The sound of footsteps broke the quiet.

The door opened to reveal Orahn paused in the threshold, his sharp regard swept over the room and settled on Adelira.

She startled awake. Then, she relaxed when she looked up at Orahn.

"Hello, Orahn," she said quietly, sleep falling away slowly. "Have I kept you waiting?"

"I am not here to keep time for you. And I don't mean to interrupt." He paused as though he wasn't sure if he should have said anything at all.

"What is it, Orahn?" she asked softly.

"It's just... I only thought a bed might be more comfortable."

Adelira nodded with a small, reluctant stretch before turning to kiss Carys' cheek. "Wake up. We must figure out this day and night routine."

Carys groaned, half-shooing her away, lazily sitting up. "Fine. Fi-iine. I'm awake. It's going to be hard to visit you, if you keep these nocturnal hours."

"Yes, but you'll do it for me," Adelira said with affection and Carys rolled her eyes.

Then Carys' eyes swept the room and landed on the King. She sat up straighter. "Your Majesty," she said and then jabbed Adelira's ribs with her elbow.

Adelira smiled and shifted out of reach of her friend. Orahn didn't smile, but his eyes did, and Adelira's smile grew.

Orahn offered politely, "I'll walk you to your chambers, if you're ready, Lira."

Adelira rose, turning back to Carys for one final comforting embrace.

"I'll see you soon," she said.

Carys smiled faintly, her eyes flicked warily to Orahn before returning to Adelira. "Tread lightly, Adi..."

"I always do, Cari."

Then, Adelira moved with the King and the hallway opened up.

Guards became motionless when Adelira passed, muscles tensing.

She frowned, her gaze drifting from one set of rigid shoulders to the next, tracking the weight of her presence. Their faces revealed quiet strain and the air thickened around her. It was an unspoken truth, lingering in the silence of the halls she walked.

And Orahn besides her was keeping them in even sharper check. Anyone moving through the halls immediately parted when he walked in that slow and unhurried fashion. Together they seemed to chase everyone away, like the breath that disappears on cool glass.

Orahn's control and her desire, an aura made to tease everyone within the Obsidian Keep.

He spoke quietly as they strode down the dimly lit corridor.

"I've arranged for a set of guards to be stationed at your door and to escort you through the castle when I'm not around," he said, matter-of-fact. "Soldiers stationed at one of my outer territories. They won't be tempted by Elven blood. They'll arrive in a week or so."

Adelira glanced up at him, brow furrowing. "Was there a problem?"

"I did not anticipate the strength of your... allure. I won't blame a weaker Vampire for caving into it, but I can't allow it, either."

She nodded, though her mind lingered on Carys' words and the part where Orahn said she was no prisoner, except for the guards he had stationed throughout the castle. And the new ones he'd assign to her.

She sighed and brushed the thought aside, in truth this was no different to her life in Ebedene with private guards and escorts everywhere, except that Ebedene had *Talion...*

Orahn's dark eyes washed over her and he almost frowned, but he said nothing.

Orahn walked unhurriedly through the Keep, like a man who had all the time in the world. Adelira was half-convinced that time would rather wait on him than risk him appearing late.

They walked towards her chambers in silence where there were ornate silver doors with intricate carvings etched into the wood; attempts at Elven artistry.

The sweeping patterns almost captured the grace of her people. The execution was foreign, like it had been crafted by hands that only half-understood Elven carpentry.

He said evenly, "Rest well, Adelira."

He pushed the doors open, but didn't step inside. Instead, he turned to her, taking her hand in his. He lifted her knuckles to his lips; the contact brief but searing.

The kiss's warmth spread slowly through her until her cheeks began to burn. She told herself she didn't want his kisses, that he was too dangerous this close, and she only needed his Blood Ritual and protection of her people.

He didn't let go of her hand.

"You can come in," she offered nervously, "if you would like to."

His smile was instant. So was the flash of his fangs.

She blushed deeper. He let go of her hand. His eyes shone with a thirst he tried to quench before she saw it, but she caught the look, the near glow of red.

"You give up your protection too easily," he murmured, teasingly amused.

Beneath his amusement was something older, hungrier, like a shadow that had turned its head to look at her.

He lingered at the threshold like a ghost. She took a deep breath, trying to sip her fear instead, and looked up at him. There was a subtle glint of approval in his eyes.

Then, he *stepped* in.

She fumbled backwards, gasping. *What have I done?* She had only meant to be polite, maybe keep him a little longer, not... *forever.*

He took only one step over the threshold. Now he stood in her room.

The wards didn't spark to stop him. There was no resistance in the air, it hummed like he was welcomed.

The space around them *tightened* and held her in a warmth she couldn't escape. Vast only moments ago, the room felt smaller and charged with him in it.

"Don't invite a Vampire in, Adelira," he murmured. "It's not something you can take back."

Her breath went cold in her chest. The old magic hadn't stirred. She'd undone it with a whisper and now the Blood King was inside. She had given him everything, and she didn't even know what it cost, yet.

"Oh..." Her face paled at the realisation that somehow it was *she* who had made the Blood King even *stronger*.

His face close to hers, his body almost touching hers, the heat of him pressed against her.

"The exception being to your personal servants, who need your permission each and every time they wish to enter your chamber."

The room held her tighter.

He added, "But for the rest of us, *once* is enough."

She swallowed and nodded, not trusting her voice when he pressed into her space like this. Frost, pine forests, mountains, he smelled like Tharth.

Half a step closer and she caught the scent of something strong as well, whisky perhaps. He looked down at her, towering over her. She almost took a step back, but it was as though he wouldn't let her. Or she wouldn't let herself.

"Your heart races when I am near," he murmured.

"C–can you hear that?" she whispered.

"Yes." His gaze flickered to her lips and back up. "Is it an invitation, as well?"

"I..." she started, but didn't know what to say.

"Good night, Lira," he said, her name a low hush, rich and intimate like he'd keep this secret between them, like he'd never tell anyone he had access to her room.

Her hand tingled where his lips had touched her skin. Her heartbeat quickened. She couldn't tear her eyes away from his.

"Good night, Orahn," she barely whispered.

He fell away from her, through the door and disappeared.

The bed was impossibly large in the centre of the room.

Her mind betrayed her then, conjuring an image of Orahn at the end of the bed, his piercing eyes locked on her, his smile inviting.

Pressing her fingers into the back of her palm, she tried to quiet the place where he planted his kiss, but it had already taken seed beneath her skin.

Climbing into bed, she tried to think of anything else. There were stars painted on her ceiling, she hadn't noticed before.

She'd invited him in, he hadn't come far, but now she knew he always could.

Somewhere, beyond the silver doors, Orahn waited, patient as the night.

14

Chapter Fourteen

The next evenfall, the Elves were invited to the Onyx Hall.

Adelira caught her reflection in the floor, skidding across the polish before catching herself. Steadying herself along the wall, she watched couples twirled in slow, graceful dances. Others stood along the sides, talking and laughing softly.

There were fewer Vampires tonight. They moved with elegance, though none of them could fully relax, whispering to each other as they passed and checking windows. Their clothes were dark making them look like the shadows of the Elves in pale silks.

Rayno caught her eye from across the room.

"Your Highness," he greeted.

"Rayno..."

"Are you alright?" he asked quietly in passing.

"Yes," she assured him. "Please, enjoy yourself tonight."

His eyes lingered on a Vampire nearby who seemed to sense they were being watched and walked away casually.

"If you start, I can follow," Rayno said.

She grinned and shook her head.

"Alright," agreeing, she made her way towards the table with drinks. "You've made me smile, now you have to go enjoy your night."

"As you command," he said with a quick bow and his own grin, grabbing a glass from the table and moving away to find his companions.

Seeing everyone the night after Adelira had expressed concern for them, made her believe the King created this event entirely to calm her.

Things were arranged around the Elves' arrival, like reducing the number of Vampires tonight, designed to keep her comfortable. The King had to have requested it all, the music, the warmth of the room. Ebedene and Tharth were allies now, after all.

Part of her wanted to join Carys, the other part of her wanted to watch the room carefully until she discovered which parts were genuine or honey-traps.

Her father spoke, "The army's precision is unlike anything I've seen," he'd said with admiration in his voice. "...A truly marvellous war nation..."

Her mother spoke of the beauty of the portraits lining the castle walls. Even Carys was enjoying herself, laughing as she recounted some story that won laughs from the ladies she stood with.

Sighing, Adelira idly picked up the nearest glass from the table filled with wine and walked slowly around the room.

She would rather be up a tree. But everyone was smiling. She'd often escaped parties like this in favour of the wilder dances her friends hosted in the woods. Under the moonlight, drinking moonshine and playing whatever assortment of instruments her friends dragged out there.

"Not that one, Your Highness," a woman with long blonde hair said as Adelira picked up a glass.

"Oh," Adelira said but the glass was removed from her hand before she could think about it. "Was it blood?"

The woman laughed as she walked away without answering.

Adelira watched her walk, hips swaying, confidence in every step. A dagger glinted in the bodice of her corset.

Glancing around the room, the few Vampires that were in attendance *all* carried weapons as concealed as beautiful as the one the blonde woman carried. Jewels she dismissed as ornamental until she looked closer and saw them for what they were. The King's guests were guards dressed up for the evening.

Disappearing deeper into the party, Adelira watched the blonde woman until she was gone and then looked over the table of drinks again. They all *smelled* like wine to her.

Carys bounded up to her, planting a kiss on her cheek and then reaching across the table to pop a treat into her mouth. She nudged Adelira, mouth full, and said, "You look too serious."

"I am very seriously thinking and you're interrupting," Adelira said, forcing down a smile.

"Oh, my, that does sound serious," Carys said with a wink. "When you're done brooding, you should dance with me."

"I most certainly should not," she said in mock horror. "Can you imagine? That wildness just wouldn't stand in a place like this."

"Outside, under a tree, afterwards?"

"Still no. But I love you for asking."

Carys stole another tart and popped it in her mouth before dashing off to find Rayno. Adelira rolled her eyes affectionately and sought out the figure making her stoic tonight.

The Vampire King took a drink handed to him and flashed a smile at the Elven lady who brought it over, giving her just enough attention to win a rousing of cheeks, before he returned to the story he was telling the small group circled around him.

Adelira stood along the wall, watching the King.

Here, he wasn't the warlord her father spoke highly of. Perhaps not even the art collector her mother praised. Orahn smiled and worked the room *effortlessly*.

He laughed easily, his hand resting lightly on the waist of a noble Elven woman when they danced. People *leaned in*, rapt by his stories. When he moved away, they glanced after him.

This was a ruler who knew how to charm a room, becoming someone for everyone. And as she watched him move through the crowd, his expressions shifting so seamlessly, she realised; *he's playing them all.*

Smoke and snakes. Looking around, her mother was smiling and Carys was laughing at something new. No one else was concerned about deception tonight. A frown deepened on her face.

Where were her trees when she needed them...

Her gaze fell to the King who was mid-laugh through a story, winning the approval of his guests when her attention was pulled closer to herself.

Glasses clinked noisily beside her.

Adelira startled. A server collected the empty glasses from the table she stood near, stacking them on a tray. His hand began to shake, the glasses clinking on the tray, like she was making him unsteady. He stilled the glasses quickly with his free hand and hurried away.

"Hello," a smooth voice spoke behind her.

She turned. Orahn's dark eyes fixed on her with an intensity that made her heart stutter. He was deep waters with secrets hidden below.

She couldn't fight his current, dragged under and lost to him completely.

"Is everything to your liking?" he asked.

He glanced around the room, an action that almost confessed he had brought them all here for her.

She hesitated; it was like he could read her thoughts.

"They're happy. My parents. My people. Everything seems..." She looked for the right word. "...Perfect."

"Seems?" he asked, catching her gap.

Adelira's lips parted in a silent gasp, caught off guard by the word she had used and how much she'd revealed with it.

Orahn almost smiled, the ghost of a curve of his lips reassuring even its incompleteness. "Tomorrow night we'll perform the Vow of Intent."

She looked up at him wearily.

He fought back a smirk. "It's only a promise... I think you're ready to make at least that much?"

She blushed. "Yes, I can do that."

"Good, then we will declare our intentions to each other before our courts. That begins the path towards the Blood Ritual, and marriage."

He said it simply enough, but he didn't look at her as he clarified the meaning of the ceremony they'd perform tomorrow.

Then, she remembered Carys saying he'd have trouble trusting her, too.

She studied him, the effortless way he commanded the room, the ease in his posture. Did that seem like a man who struggled with trust? Carys had to be wrong. What could he possibly have to fear from her? She was no threat. Not to the Vampire King.

And yet... she wasn't like anything he had ever faced before.

She didn't come to his gates bearing steel and bloodlust during a time of war. Arriving without wrath or destruction, she came with open hands and flowers in her hair.

Maybe, faced with something unknown, he was being more cautious than ever.

His dark eyes gave away nothing, but the room behind him did. Wherever he had passed, Elves and Vampires alike turned subtly toward him, like he was a celestial polestar. Their laughter grew freer when he touched a shoulder or bent his head to listen. They smiled, circling his orbit, never realising they couldn't pull away.

"Will you come with me?" he asked, extending a hand.

"If I come with you," she said slowly, tilting her head, "will you tell me this was all for show? Like the first dinner?"

Her voice wasn't accusatory, simply curious, like she already knew the answer, but wanted to see if he'd admit it.

He smiled, quick and dangerous. "No. But I might dance with you."

Her breath caught. But her fingers longed for connection, reaching out, drawn as if pulled by invisible threads. His touch was warm.

His ring cool against her skin. Her hand wrapped in his was almost familiar to her now.

When he moved, she followed. To do anything else felt impossible, like the pulse in her heart willed her forward more than her legs.

The Elves were chatting, some dancing. Adelira wasn't paying attention anymore. The hand in hers was sure and strong.

Tall glass doors had curtains drawn aside. He pushed on the frame and opened it outwards. They stepped onto the balcony wrapping around the hall. The breeze was chilly. The wind carried the first promise of snow in the months to come. Behind them the party faded and gave way to the deep dark of night. Before them, the mountains stretched high beneath the starlit sky.

He didn't need to cage her, if he made her forget the walls existed.

Since arriving, she had never truly *looked* at the mountain range. Now, up close, it was monolithic, standing eternal against the night. It was a jagged bone that wrapped around Tharth. The peaks were the same shade of grey as her eyes.

Not noticing, he released her hand. Her fingers wrapped around the railing and she leaned over the edge slightly. His fingers flexed, the barest reach toward her.

"*Careful*," he murmured so softly she wasn't sure he'd spoken.

When she first arrived, the Keep surrounded by rock looked like a wall. Now, the mountains opened up under her careful breath and his control, appearing more like a gate.

"It's beautiful," she whispered.

She felt him watching her gently. Almost like he could feel the weight of this moment shaping something in her.

Melting against the railing, she wanted to reach out and touch the sky or the mountains. A breathy sigh fell from her lips. Not her trees, but so nearly the same feeling, outside and up high in the cool air.

Somewhere in a valley cutting through Tharth, a large cat roared.

"Was that...?" Adelira asked, her face lighting up.

A crooked smile pulled at the corner of his mouth and he nodded.

The tension between them lingered. Yet, for the first time the castle didn't feel like a fortress of Vampires. It felt steady. Like the mountains themselves.

The Obsidian Keep had stood here for an age, almost as old as the mountains themselves.

"I imagine the thought of your family leaving weighs on you," he said, his voice measured. "It's a lot to ask, for you to say goodbye to everyone you care about to stay here, with me." He glanced out at the mountains, then back at her. "I don't want you to feel like I'm keeping you apart from tonight. But I would like to show you the beautiful side of Tharth. You just need to choose to see it."

She turned slowly toward him, searching his face. Trying to see what lay beneath the words. An invitation. A choice. A step forward.

Her eyes held his gaze and for a moment he didn't blink. "I already see it," she said.

His eyes widened for just a second before he broke eye contact first and turned his attention to the peaks surrounding Tharth. A smile broke across his face.

Looking up at him, he was so close she could reach out and touch him. His face was striking in the firelight coming from the hall. Dark eyes impossible to escape, a black sea she was already lost in.

When he smiled at her like that, gently hiding his fangs, she chose to release the warnings she had carried with her.

... And smiled back.

15

Chapter Fifteen

In one of the highest towers was the Observatory. Domed-glass stretched from floor to ceiling, giving them an unclouded view of the sky all around them.

This spire nestled in the sky just like her ancient trees, except now the world around Adelira was glittering stars instead of sparkling sunlight. Polished black stone floors reflected the stars above like a mirror and she'd stepped into infinity.

Spoken under the watchful gaze of the twin moons, the Vow of Intent was declared.

Adelira stood on a raised platform. Vampires stood before her, elegant and eerie in their stillness, hungry eyes catching the candlelight like cinders.

She wore an Elven gown of midnight-blue, nearly black but shimmering to indigo under the moonlight. Her thick red hair unbound, save for a few silver clasps woven through the soft curls.

Across from her stood the Vampire King.

Orahn was dressed in ceremonial black. His broad shoulders draped in the heavy cloak, the collar wrapped around his neck.

Adelira could feel his attention on her even without him looking her way, like the pull of the twin moons above them. He was the gravity, his steadiness beside her was constant. She was a celestial star, eternal and full of hope. She couldn't tell if she was caught in his orbit, or falling...

When he crossed the threshold, the crowd exhaled. Orahn moved through the room like the tide and everyone turned to him like they were caught in the undertow. A calm sea at rest with silence reminding the same tide that cradled could crush.

"The Vow of Intent is not spoken lightly," the elder said loudly.

The room shifted attention.

"It is a step forward on a path that cannot easily be undone," he continued. "A declaration before this court, before the Kingdom, before the old magic that binds us."

Before them, the elder stepped forward, holding a strip of dark wax and a silver needle.

"The vow must be sealed," he said. "A drop of blood, offered to awaken the appetite of the Gods so that they might rise in the future to secure the Blood Ritual."

Orahn extended his hand first.

The needle was swift, piercing the tip of his finger, and a single drop of blood welled up before he pressed it into the wax.

Then it was her turn.

She held out her upturned finger towards the elder. Her hand trembled once, waiting for what felt like an eternity as the silver point drew closer to her skin.

She swallowed, bracing herself as the needle pricked her skin. A single bead of red bloomed at the tip of her finger and she pressed it to the warm wax beside his.

Their marks, side by side, sealed in crimson.

The moment her blood beaded, the room sharpened.

It grew colder, stinging her lungs with each breath she drew. The breathing was heavier in her ears. All of the Vampires were too focused, their intent honed towards her.

The gathered crowd began to crack under the strain of their control. Someone exhaled loudly. Someone lifted their nose and inhaled deeply. Adelira felt the restraint and hunger closing in around her, making it harder for her to draw a full breath.

The elder's hand twitched, just a fraction, as he lowered the wax seal. He refused to look at her, but his nostrils flared. Some eyes shone *red*.

One Elf's hand ghosted over the hilt of a ceremonial dagger, a gesture so subtle it could have been mistaken for adjusting their cloak.

The Vampires and Elves held themselves too tight, ready to release at the faintest tremor. Her blood was the spark between them.

None of them said anything, but their gazes danced between the Vampires and the crimson bead pooled on Adelira's finger tip.

Orahn's dark eyes swept through the crowd, his gaze holding them steady and the tension in the room simmered down.

Orahn's fingers brushed against hers, ever so lightly, as if by accident. But he didn't seem like the sort of man who did anything by accident.

Adelira drew breath again.

She looked up at him. His gaze lifted to her briefly and a subtle nod from him helped her steal her courage. Her breathing steadied.

"Your fates have been sealed and the Vow is clear, the path is set for you both," the elder said. "When the Blood Ritual comes for you both, may it find your Vow unbroken."

The doors burst open.

A Vampire messenger burst into the chamber, dropping to a knee before King Orahn. Orahn was already motioning him to the side of the room before the man's knee even hit the ground. The messenger rose and followed.

A Nightjar, a mottled bird with wings like moths, perched on the messenger's forearm. The feathers on its head like horns and a beak so wide it was almost grinning, the bird lifted its feet, pulling against the leather straps that held it there.

It let out a haunting trill as it flew smooth as smoke, landing on Orahn's arm and he pulled the small scroll message from its leg.

The messenger answered some questions as they spoke privately before Orahn exhaled deeply and then returned to the centre of the room.

"My soldiers posted on the border of Biryn Fields have reported smoke on the horizon to the west. Possibly a raid on the outer Elven villages," Orahn said to King Hara. "They believe it to be the war bands that have been lingering in the mountains."

The Elven King straightened immediately. "It will take us three days to get there. We have to leave now." Then the internal conflict betrayed him and he turned to his daughter, an apologetic look in his eyes.

Adelira's heart lurched, but she didn't want his concern for her to stall him. "Go now, father."

He hesitated, sparing a wary glance at Orahn.

Orahn spoke, "I have a troop stationed close to that village. They will get there before you do. I will send out a Nightjar with the message for my men to march to their aid. You and your warriors can meet them on the road and reinforce them if necessary, though I'm sure my army can put out the threat quickly."

The Elven King looked at the Vampire King, a lingering hint of scepticism beneath the surface despite the warm welcoming they had received. Then he turned back to his daughter.

"I'm sorry," her father said quietly.

It was a cruelty she'd always known was coming.

"You should go, truly," Adelira said gently, though the words were shaky. "I will stay and send word once we perform the Blood Ritual, but you are wasted here. Our people *need* their King."

Orahn frowned. Her voice trembled over the word 'need' and her shoulders had squared up. His fist curled slightly.

"We have made our intentions clear," Orahn finally said. "But an alliance is more than words. We must finalise our war strategy. My army will hold your border while we ensure this alliance is strong enough to win a war."

"What are you saying?" King Hara asked.

"I'd rather it not be said that we demanded a father abandon his daughter before the bond is even sealed. It would be a shame if you had to cut these last nights shorter than they already are," Orahn clarified. "Stay one more night. Let my army protect you. Leave tomorrow."

She saw her father hesitate. He, just like she was, weighed the Vampire King's words. Was compassion strategic kindness or true allegiance? He didn't trust Vampires, but he'd been prepared to meet monsters, not statesmen. And now, even before Adelira was fully handed over, he'd secured the Crimson army at his back.

That's what frightened him most, she realised, not the ruthlessness, but the cleverness.

"I'll be okay," she said quietly, when her mother's gaze swept over her like a tether stretched too thin.

Her father let out a breath, releasing something heavy from his chest. "We'll stay another night."

"Excellent," Orahn said.

"Thank you," she said softly, even if the intention wasn't for her benefit, she appreciated that it helped settle her.

Unseen eyes pierced the back of her head. It prickled along her skin. Glancing around, she found no source for this feeling.

This watching wasn't like the other Vampires' whose gaze was always hungry or distrusting. This gaze was possessive. *Cold.*

Soon, her family and friends would leave and she would navigate the blood court of Vampires alone. Her gaze slid to Orahn. Even as he spoke with a general and her father, he shifted his posture angled towards her.

She wouldn't be alone, Orahn would be here. And even if he did slip away later, even outnumbered in his blood court, she'd stand tall.

Skin crawling with unseen eyes that followed her as she moved towards Carys, she rubbed the back of her neck. Carys was comforting in her arms. Warm. Almost enough to distract her. Adelira froze. The faintest movement in the shadows behind her was a whisper crawling along her spine, ready to sink in its teeth. Or brush lips across her nape.

When she turned, there was nothing there.

16

Chapter Sixteen

Adelira said goodnight to her parents and Carys, watching them leave with the rest of the Elven party, before she turned and looked at the Vampire King.

Orahn and Adelira were alone.

He hadn't moved since the last of their people had gone from the hall. Standing with his hands braced on a stone table, his knuckles strained, and head bowed.

"Are you concerned that the raid is more than it seems?" she asked.

He didn't look up at her, but the confusion flashed across his face.

"*What?* Oh. No," he said, shaking his head. "No. My troops will be able to deal with it easily."

She considered that, "But something is bothering you. If it's not that, then what?"

Orahn's head lifted slightly at the question, his eyes meeting hers. It was subtle, the way he studied her, like he was searching for something in her face.

"My court just came from a blood feast. Everyone in this room was well sated. And yet, your one little droplet spiralled them to the brink of control," he said slowly.

"I asked if *you* were alright, not the court."

"I should be asking you that." His voice was quiet.

She almost smiled at his concern. "I asked first."

His lips parted, but no answer came. Then, "You asked first," he repeated with a smile that didn't quite reach his eyes. "I'm still deciding what the truth is."

Her brows knitted. That wasn't how truths worked, but then that was how emotions worked, sometimes they took time to digest. The prick on her finger throbbed.

Orahn exhaled, glancing at the table beneath his hands. She understood it, whatever she felt, he was feeling it too, and it left them both with uncertainty about their shared future.

She was everything he'd been taught not to trust. Here she was, in his home, and he had to promise to keep her safe... and hope against hope, *hope against his instincts,* that she'd keep him safe, too.

She looked up at him with big grey eyes, watching him collect himself. She wanted to reach out and hold his hand to tell him it would be alright. Before any words came to her, his mask was already back in place.

The magnetic warmth he usually exuded ignited the air around him. The chill in the room vanished. The Vampire King was back before her eyes.

His smile was soft, the deadly edge was subdued below the surface, but there all the same.

By the time Orahn straightened away from the window and offered his hand, she had almost convinced his moment of vulnerability was all in her head.

Her hand tucked lightly into his arm, they left the hall together. They passed a few Vampires in the corridors.

"I'm sorry this is difficult for you," she said softly.

"This is not difficult for me," he denied reflexively.

She saw the lie flash before his eyes, not entirely for her benefit either. If his lies comforted him, she didn't know. But she tried again to reach him.

"It feels like I've roped you into an uncomfortable situation."

"It's best for everyone."

Best? Maybe. But was it kind? She frowned. His feelings mattered, even if they were sacrificed for everyone else, they mattered to *her*.

The way he held himself at a distance, she knew he'd not admit his honest feelings about their arrangement to her any time soon.

She bit her lip and looked around the corridor. The dark paintings, the shadows, the way no one turned their backs to them.

She shivered before she could stop herself.

Orahn noticed. "Lira, I won't allow anyone to harm you here."

She nodded, unsure of how much of his statement was true and how much of that was him wanting to simply believe it so they could stay in this peaceful lull they'd fallen into.

When he called her Lira, she wanted to believe anything he said.

The portraits were watching. The faces of Vampire royalty stared back at her, their expressions lordly and imperious. She could convince herself their presence was nothing more than history captured in oil and canvas, except she felt it; the weight of them pressing down on her spine.

"You feel them watching, don't you?" Orahn's voice broke her thoughts.

She hesitated. He was good at reading her. Her heart rate spiked. "A little."

"They can't hurt you, either," he said with a small almost-knowing smile as he nodded to the paintings. "I promise."

There was something infuriatingly charming about the way he spoke, as though he were inviting her to uncover a secret she wasn't entirely sure she wanted to know.

Her eyes moved from the paintings to the slight, unreadable curve of his lips as he studied her.

Orahn's eyes swept over her with mild curiosity. "You haven't worn any of the dresses I had sent to your rooms. Were they not to your liking?"

Her fingers brushed lightly over her Elven gown self-consciously, the act grounding her.

"It's not that," she admitted, her cheeks warming.

"No?"

She looked out the windows as they walked, some stained with coloured glass, others allowed clear views of the courtyards outside. The night was still even though this was when his castle was awake, she heard nothing except the occasional pop of a sconce on the wall lighting their way and an owl outside hooting. Even the guards shifting away from her were silent.

"Part of it is that... I'm not sure how to wear them. I know that sounds ridiculous, it's a dress. Only... the fastenings, all the buckles, straps... There's lace and ties at the back that are so different from what I'm used to. And my ladies..." She hesitated. "They never stay long enough to assist."

"They're probably struggling with your scent."

"I thought it might be something like that." Then she looked him over, calm as he was, and said, "It doesn't seem to affect you though."

"Oh, trust me, it *does...*"

The tremor in his voice made her shiver.

"But I am King, because I am stronger than compulsions like this," he said firmly. After a pause, he added in a quieter voice, "But, gods, the fates sure do like to test that strength."

She blushed and looked up at him.

He neatly avoided her glance like he couldn't bear both his own confession and the weight of her gaze at once.

"I'll make arrangements for your ladies," he said instead. "I'll find someone stronger."

Adelira's expression softened, but she shook her head gently. "There is more, though."

He peered down at her, carefully, his strides were measured beside her. His focus on her entirely, like he knew the castle inside and out. He made it too easy to open up to him. She wasn't sure she should voice it though.

Her hands tightened on the fabric of her gown. She glanced down, her words a tumble. "I am Elven. Even if we marry... I will always be... My dresses are pieces of home. I want to hold onto that for as long as I can. It's not that I don't like your gifts. They're beautiful... It's... hard for me to let go of these small, familiar things."

The moment stretched so long she was about to apologise for offending him or not seeming grateful enough or whatever it was that kept him silent, but then he spoke.

He finally said, "You've left behind so much to secure a future for your people. If holding onto a piece of home brings you peace, then I want that for you."

She looked into his eyes and saw that reassurance reflecting outwards to her. His sincerity surprised her. "Thank you, Orahn."

"Don't thank me, yet. Because I *also* want you to be safe." A hardness tinged his tone that contradicted his earlier gentleness, "You're right, the dresses are complicated. It's not just buckles and corsets. It's reinforced steel with built-in armour."

"Armour? In my dresses?"

"Yes," he said. "Not everyone in my court is happy with this arrangement."

"No," she agreed, she could feel that much. Her own court had been against it as well, for very opposite reasons.

"If you can prove yourself, we will have more Nightjars supporting Ebedene. There will be fewer sent in silent rebellion against me."

She didn't know what to say. He said he wanted her to be comfortable, to hold onto home. Then he offered to replace it with armour. Maybe this was what comfort looked like in Tharth. Cold, beautiful and built for war.

"If you're not ready, I won't ask it of you now. But when you stand before the Blood Houses, they will judge you. They will look for weakness to exploit."

"Because Elves are weak?" she asked, more bitterness in her tone than she'd intended.

He politely ignored her jab and said, "If I could shield you from that, I would. All I can do is offer you shields; in words and in clothing," he said with a note of caution.

"You want me to act like a Vampire?"

"I want you to show them that they are wrong about Elves," he said.

Her eyes lifted up to his. *Did he believe there was more to Elves than his court did?*

"But it's also for my own peace of mind," he added. "There's real armour sewn into it; safety you wouldn't notice unless you knew. If I can't always be by your side, then I need to know you are protected."

She didn't want to change her clothes when she felt that she'd lost so much of her history already.

His eyes falling to her frown, he said, "I'll bring in more soldiers to compensate in the meantime. But when the time comes to meet the Blood Houses again, I cannot let you stand before them unguarded."

She wanted to say she wouldn't break that easily, but they'd both hear the lie in that. Maybe armoured clothing was what she needed to survive Tharth, but it wasn't what she wanted.

She wanted the Blood Ritual.

She didn't miss the careful way he weighed his words. He tried to give her space to adjust without letting go of what he thought was necessary.

Tucked into his warmth, he smelled like forest frost and the faint scent of scotch or whisky.

There was a lull as he considered something, wrestling with it, before he said, "Our customs must seem very strange to you."

"Yes, Tharth is very different from Ebedene."

"Maybe we can soften the transition."

She looked up at him with curiosity. "How so?"

"When Vampires arrange marriages, they typically waste no time. There might be a lot of formality and many steps involved, but it all moves quickly. One event after another until marriage," he started slowly, pausing beside her, "Plans are finalised so that vows are exchanged in rapid succession."

"That's... efficient," she said even while it all sounded rushed to her as she again thought of Odette and Grace and the years they had spent together, neither one ready for the next step.

"But Elves," he said carefully, "are much more patient. Time is something I can give you, Adelira. If you wish it, we can take this the Elven way."

She flicked her eyes up to his face, searching for any trace of insincerity. He started to walk down the corridor again, falling into step beside her. Orahn's willingness to bend to Elven customs demonstrated a degree of flexibility that his reputation in Ebedene did not maintain.

He said it with such conviction, as though patience were as easy as breathing for him.

He was a Vampire, no matter how carefully he concealed it. The slower pace might conflict with his nature, testing his patience and control in ways he wasn't accustomed to with a slow Elven tradition. Could he truly wait?

She now had teas and shadows and armour in clothing all in less than a week. She had known she'd have to give up her trees and her sunshine. She knew what she was stepping into. If she could slow this down, hold onto her Elven customs just a little longer...

Her heart ached for the comfort she could draw from this.

Adelira was confident that she could win his trust, if not his affection, with more time to nurture something between them. It might be what she longed for, for both of their sakes. The King and herself were the least important parts of this union, if she were honest. A knot of unease twisted in her chest, because accepting this offer felt like kindness to herself, but she owed her people a Ritual. The waiting endlessly and undefined felt like a betrayal of her mission.

Her mother flashed in her mind, urging her to make peace with this union quickly, to protect her people now. *Smoke and snakes...*

"I would appreciate it if we took our time with the marriage, but what about the Blood Ritual?" she asked finally.

Orahn paused mid-step, turning slightly toward her. His dark eyes flicked to her face, his jaw ticked once. "We just did the Vow of Intent to bide our time for the Blood Ritual."

Her stomach churned.

"I need this..." she said, her voice struggling to firm up and she avoided his gaze. Maybe her standing before him, expressing her own need might help him see why this mattered. "I feel fragile here..."

Orahn studied her. "I don't need a Ritual to protect you."

His assertion left her unsure whether she'd gained ground... or lost it.

She opened her mouth to argue, but stopped herself, unsure of what to say. The sconces burned, the smell of smoke followed everywhere they walked.

He folded his arms over his chest carefully like he was removing himself without going anywhere.

"I thought you might prefer to do this the Elven way, slowly and over time. So that we can get to know each other. Would you not?"

"I would," she said and forced herself to look at him then, so he would see the resolve in her eyes. She *would* put her people above her own comfort. "But I'd like to do the Ritual. As soon as possible. The wedding can come later, once we know each other better, as you suggest."

A moment of distress crossed his eyes and was gone before she could be sure she'd seen it correctly. Now, he simply looked tired. His shoulders drooped in resignation.

"The Blood Ritual is... *intense*," he said, inclining his head slightly as though he were saying something difficult for him to admit.

Her breath caught, ribs closing around her in dread.

"It's not some pretty, magical wedding," he said, every word careful and heavy. "It's intimate. Invasive, even."

Invasive. She bit her lip, her hand instinctively moving to her neck.

His eyes tracked the movement. "I won't need to drink your blood for the Ritual, but the fact that you asked about that before tells me you don't know anything about the rite. You're clearly not ready."

Cheeks reddened with embarrassment and rising anger. It wasn't her fault she didn't know what to expect. No one was forthcoming about what would happen. Her anger continued to simmer beneath the surface. Her hand fell away from her neck, because she understood how ridiculous it must seem to the King. And she was tired of his judgement, and his court's, for that matter.

She tapped her foot in annoyance against the stone as they walked. The sound reverberated down the halls.

"The truth is," he admitted with a fragility enveloping his words in a way that immediately dissolved Adelira's defensiveness, "*I'm* not ready."

He couldn't even look at her, his eyes fixed to the floor. She thought his reluctance was about *her*; her failings to meet his expectations of what he deemed as ready. Vampire kings didn't bare their throats this way. *He* was as much a part of this as she was.

If she delayed, was she protecting his heart or abandoning her people?

Her earlier anger dissipated when she looked at him. He finally looked up, his eyes connecting with hers, and she saw the shame there. He hated admitting this to her. She ached for him and the pain in his eyes.

He clarified in a low voice, "I'm asking you for some grace. A little bit of time."

He paused, jaw tightening, like he was swallowing something bitter. When he spoke again, his voice was even softer, raw around the edges.

"Please, Lira." His eyes softened entirely as he looked at her, unguarded like he'd set aside his crown and she was looking at the vulnerability of a man beneath it.

Her heart clenched. She almost crumbled under his stare; completely and utterly moved by his painful request.

Adelira was quick to tears, steadfast in her resolve, but she could not ever deny a call for help made in earnest.

When he asked like that, she couldn't dream of denying his request. She searched his face and searched her heart, and she chose to be gracious. A small voice inside her made her promise herself to make sure he kept his word.

17

Chapter Seventeen

Orahn suggested the stroll, a chance to 'see the court's workings.'

Showing her sculptures and paintings of Tharth's victorious history, Orahn spoke highly of their war efforts.

"Perhaps we move past the Fall of Arvain," he said, guiding her away from the Elven stronghold painting.

Her eyes looked over the painting quickly, the Blood King stood at the gates but the fort itself was empty of life.

"I like this one," he pointed to a statue of a crag beast.

Cut into marble was the image of a creature standing on crouched hind legs with claws reaching down for her. When she stood in its shadow, its paws were several feet above her head. Tilting back, she looked up into its open mouth. Even Orahn, large as he was, appeared small beneath the beast.

"Are they truly this big?"

"Oh, yes."

Walking through the castle, passing guards stationed periodically along the corridor and Vampires walked briskly by with scrolls or wooden chests.

"Tomorrow will be the final evening before your parents depart for Eloryth," he said. "After that, perhaps we could have dinner together, just the two of us?"

"That sounds wonderful."

"From then on, I'll be occupied for a few nights. I apologise in advance for my absence. Then the Fealty Ceremony, where the Vampires pledge their devotion to the crown," his eyes on her momentarily, "to me and my bride."

Adelira nodded, the enormity of the role she was stepping into wasn't lost on her.

"And the following evening?"

"Are you looking for an entire week's schedule?"

She bit back her own smile. "I'd feel more prepared if I knew what to expect."

"In that case, there's a council meeting with the Court of Shadows. They make up the representatives of the Blood Houses."

She nodded, listening closely to what she could expect after the Elves left.

"Would you like to hear more?"

"Yes."

He chuckled. "Well, I'm afraid there isn't anything exciting coming up for a while. After those events, the Kingdom should begin to settle and you'll likely find a less demanding schedule is expected of you."

"All the more time to explore then," she said.

Concern flashed across his face and disappeared in an instant.

"Orahn?"

He paused while he considered telling her what was on his mind.

"I only wanted to stress that, after the formalities are resolved, staying inside your chamber at *night* is safest."

She suppressed a sigh.

"And please," his voice dropped lower, a hint of urgency creeping in, "don't... don't get too close to any Vampires... Not everyone in my castle has mastered their own bloodlust."

He couldn't hide the sharp edges of his Kingdom entirely. She thumbed her fingertip where the needle had drawn blood.

When the corridor narrowed, he let her walk ahead, but not without his hand at the small of her back; light enough to be polite, firm enough to remind her of his presence.

"Your Majesty, I'd speak with you about the Hidden Jad—" a man started to say as he walked towards them.

Orahn's grip barely tensed at her back but she felt it. He stepped around her, his eyes flashed to her as they brushed past each other in the narrow corridor, before he strode forwards and pulled the man aside to speak quickly.

The warmth of his body remained as heat in her cheeks. Her heart stuttered, several heads turned to look at her, but they quickly moved away before any of them caught the attention of the King.

The messenger left and Orahn emerged into the corridor again. He stood there, watching her.

He studied her as though she were a blade he wasn't sure was sharp enough to cut him or dull enough to ignore. He had slipped the mask of the King back on.

Holding eye contact, she moved towards him.

"I know you have a way of running things which I don't understand, yet," she said slowly as she approached him. "But you don't have to protect yourself from me at the same time."

Blinking at that, he looked down at her in surprise. "Protect me? From you?"

"Well," she flushed. "You're keeping me at a distance, because you don't trust outsiders... I'm a liability."

His fingers flexed at his side and her eyes flared to the movement and then back to his face. He exhaled, his gaze still locked on her.

"The danger isn't you," he said calmly. "It's all around you."

She looked up at him.

"I keep my distance to make you safer..." he said. "Not me."

She waited for some hint that this was another deflection. But there was none. He meant it. She couldn't earn his trust by pushing him, but maybe he was looking out for her in his own way.

He said quietly, "Some things in the Keep are... unsettled. Arguing between my Blood Houses. Not all agree with my decision to..."

"Do the Blood Ritual?" she offered.

"I think they could care less about the Ritual. They'd prefer I didn't marry you, though."

She looked up at him, surprised that he'd shared that. "It's caused trouble for you and I'm sorry for that."

"Nothing I can't handle."

"I don't want to be another thing you have to handle." She paused, "That came out wrong. I only mean..."

"That's alright."

"Where are we going now?" She changed the subject quickly.

"I was taking you to the heart of the court where the Houses gather to conduct their work."

They continued towards a hall that opened up to them.

Before they stepped in fully, she was drawn to a section of the castle, the wall felt colder there. Like a piece of the castle was missing behind it.

She moved closer to the wall. What was it about this section? She couldn't quite place it. Nondescript and stationed between two large pillars with no statues or artwork surrounding it. As she stared, the wall seemed to stare back at her.

Brushing his hand over hers, he guided her subtly back to his side.

"The court gathers through here, Lira," he murmured in her ear. His breath travelled down her neck, making her shiver.

She hesitated, looking up at him before smiling, the charming King had returned to her. His mask lowered for her. In return, she gave him her attention, moving away from the wall and following him.

18

Chapter Eighteen

The corridors widened, the grandeur swelling to encompass the heart of the court.

Desks lined the hall, each crowded with scribes and mountains of scrolls and books. Stationed behind them were representatives of various Blood Houses. Each house had their own banner raised above their section of the hall. Her eyes lowered to the scribes hurriedly penning the whispers of the representatives behind them.

It didn't matter how much they spoke or moved about the room. *Orahn's* presence was the loudest in the hall, though he hadn't spoken a word.

They passed by imposing double doors sealed shut and Orahn gestured to them.

"Through that wing houses the council members' chambers. That's where most of the castle remains during the daylight hours."

"They have bedrooms through there?"

"Yes... Far from your chambers," he added.

"For now," he continued and they walked past without going in, "the council is mostly quiet. We'll resume weekly meetings once the formalities have settled down."

"I was told Tharth was a singular dictatorship."

"It was for an age. Vampiric leadership is chosen entirely by strength," Orahn said.

"I thought you were the crown prince of the last monarch? Born, not chosen?"

"Yes, our bloodline is that strength. Should it ever change, my family might not rule Tharth."

"Challenge the crown? Like when we walked through your court when I arrived?"

"Someone could have tried something then, yes."

"Are they scared to try or are the council meetings more than show?"

He chuckled. "They might put on a show, but the meetings discuss many important things. Modelled after the Fellin Kingdom council method."

"What will be discussed? Can I prepare for it?"

"There's no need. It's a formality really."

"The formality being my invitation?"

"The Blood Houses will want to see you attend a few events, but really they will spend the night arguing with each other. Even I rarely have anything to contribute to these meetings."

"They don't take the lead from you?"

"I'm there... to remind them I can take the lead. But I prefer to hear what they have to say. The Houses have matters to discuss amongst themselves. Decisions will be made. Alliances strengthened, or tested," Orahn replied, the tone betraying none of his thoughts on the matter. "It's always an interesting spectacle."

She was drawn in by him, wanting to discover all the ways he was different from how the legends and myths painted him.

"Tell me about what I am seeing?" she asked quietly.

He looked at her carefully and then glanced around the room, as though seeing it again for the first time, through new eyes.

"The banners belong to the different Blood Houses. There are six that you will see most commonly," he started slowly. "Though there are other smaller houses, too."

Banners of the Blood Houses draped from the ceilings to the floor behind the various work stations.

"House Marques manages the vaults," he said simply as he pointed to their banner behind where a dozen members sat poring over ledgers.

"What are the vaults?"

"Mostly blood vaults, but other goods and coins, too. They keep the city's books balanced, ensuring the market flows. If you need something moved or counted; they've already done it."

The tone made her stomach tighten. She imagined rows of ledgers filled with red ink and incurring debts.

She glanced up at the banner of a serpent coiled around balanced scales.

Then she looked at the men with their ledgers.

She'd seen very few women in Tharth, so she supposed her ladies in Ebedene were right about that at least. It made her wonder if maybe they were also right about women taking on multiple husbands.

Her cheeks reddened at the thought and she tried to turn her mind back to what Orahn was saying.

His eyes darted to her pink cheeks, but if he thought anything of the colour, he didn't say it to her. He simply continued moving them through the hall, each banner telling its own story.

"My generals mostly come from House Cazimer," he replied. "Like my General Victoria. They secure the borders, train the soldiers and execute the city's law."

That word, *execute*, landed with weight. She thought of soldiers who answered orders without question. His phrasing didn't leave room for mercy.

The scratching of pens and quills rang through the hall. Pages shuffling and seals stamped into wax. Suddenly, she felt unprepared for politics.

"Should I be wary of them?" she asked carefully, looking over the dragon's silhouette on their banner.

Orahn's gaze slid to her. He looked around the room and considered his court, weighing them quickly before he answered her.

"Them least of all. I'd perhaps give Delarosa a wider berth. They are courtiers skilled at making others feel seen... or wanted..."

She looked up at him.

He almost smiled. "Sometimes, that's the same thing."

Being seen sounded nice, but even *that* Tharth managed to paint like bait.

"Seen *how*?" she asked, though she suspected she wasn't going to like the answer.

He bit back the smile that was growing now. "Delarosa controls... appetites. Not just carnal ones. They know what people crave. Drugs, blood, gold. They'll have it boxed and ready before you realise you're starving."

Heat coloured her cheeks. "Right," she said.

"Smile, it unsettles them." His grin was wide now.

"Play the court?"

He looked her over again and the grin dimmed a little. "No, you best not play those games. Smile because you're not playing. Smile because you're sipping your fear, not feeding it to them to box for someone else."

"Is that their banner?" she asked, pointing to a silver rose against a purple velvet backdrop.

His approval flashed briefly across his features, that she could point them out just from his few words.

"There's so much to remember," she whispered, mostly to herself.

He caught it regardless. "In time, it'll seem less overwhelming."

"Who else should I know about?"

He glanced around again and then pointed to the next banner and scribes they passed.

"House Crowe sees things most would miss," he explained. "They prefer to work in silence. I'll leave it at that."

She got the sense *prefer* was a generous word. The way he avoided naming Crowe's exact role that made her skin prickle. Spies? Were they the ones who figured out the Elder Celestite's true power to the Vampires almost before her own scholars could?

Their banner was easier to identify; a golden eye circled with black feathers. She thought of the man who spoke with the King in the alcove. He'd met with his spy.

"Are my people alright?" she asked suddenly.

He startled. "Yes. Why do you ask?"

"Did you help them?

His steps slowed to a stop and he turned to look at her. "Yes, I helped them. Your borders are secure."

"T–thank you, Orahn."

He turned away quickly and scanned the room, drawing her attention back.

Goblets touching lips and placed down again before she could follow the action.

"The banner with the chalice. House Vontressa governs our laws, though those remain... flexible," he reasoned with a tilt of his head and a small glint in his eyes.

She wondered how much leeway they gave their laws. Was the line constantly shifting?

"My House, Viremont, you'll recognise them from the triple swords on the banners. I'd perhaps stay away from them, as well," he said, almost too casually.

She nodded, trying to take it all in.

Orahn paused, "And Le Rouge. They keep the old customs alive and protect ancient bloodlines."

When he spoke of them, the room cooled a few degrees and Adelira felt a faint chill wrap around her. Le Rouge's banner had two white circles on a black backdrop, one slightly larger than the other, just like the twin moons in the sky.

"And they all answer to you?"

"They do," he said evenly. "Though not always immediately."

He didn't look at her, but she knew he could feel the question in her next breath before she voiced it.

"And what will they expect from me?"

Orahn stopped walking and finally turned to face her. "Proof that you belong here. That you are not a mistake." He paused and said softer now, "But you already know this, don't you?"

It was not unkind, but neither was it comforting to have it confirmed that she was weighed at every turn. Not belonging felt like rejection even if the truth of that was a little ridiculous on her part. She was an Elf, different and 'other' in every way.

Adelira's jaw tensed. "And if I'm not what they expect?"

He shrugged, entirely too casual now. "Let them fear what they cannot understand."

She looked up at him. Did he understand her? The pounding in her chest betrayed how deeply she wanted to be understood by him.

She almost stepped closer. He saw the coiling of her muscles about to reach for him and offered her his arm instead; holding her out at a careful distance.

She looked down at his arm and then up at his face. There was that distrust again.

Still, she took his arm. She could work her way closer to his trust from this distance.

19

Chapter Nineteen

Out of the corner of her eye, Adelira saw three young boys, barely men, huddled along the side of the wall. She recognised them from her walk through the blood rooms.

They snickered and elbowed each other, one of them clutching something in his hands.

Orahn was speaking and she turned her attention towards him again.

Into the air, the youths threw the thing they'd been holding. An erratic flutter of wings shot past her. It spiralled in uneven strokes through the hall. She ducked, a shriek buried within her as she covered her mouth. Her heartbeat was as erratic as the creature's flight.

The court quieted in predation. The scent of her fear. Somewhere in the crowd, craving began to take hold.

In a smooth motion, Orahn's hand shot out, fast and precise, closing around the creature mid-flight.

He turned back and she caught the fire in his eyes, the boys stopped as his gaze fell to them.

"Was this a joke?" Orahn asked, his voice like steam rising. "Your idea of wit? A lesson in fear? I have better lessons."

Orahn held out his gloved hand, a tiny bat hanging upside down from his finger, before motioning someone forward who took the bat from him.

It was only a tiny thing, unexpected that was all. Though shock clung to her and the court had smelled it. So had Orahn.

She tried to turn that panic into anger directed towards the boys, but the sight of their father on his knees only made her worry more.

"Your Majesty," an elderly man grovelled before Orahn, "I take full responsibility for their actions. I beg for forgiveness."

"Take your sons and leave," Orahn instructed. "I will pass my judgment in due course."

The boys didn't have to be told twice, they left the hall with their father whose face was grim and anxious. The boys still looked smug, concealing their grins. She turned away embarrassed.

Orahn's focus was still on the youths when she felt a gaze, not mocking this time, but ravenous.

It was then that Adelira sensed it.

She didn't know how she knew, did prey always know when it was being hunted? She couldn't say. But she *was* being hunted now.

Nearby, a man's knuckles gripped the crook of his cane while he tried to keep himself seated.

The innkeeper flashed in her mind's eye; his teeth snapping at her face, straining on his chains. She'd seen this look before.

And this time, there were *no* chains.

The Vampire leaned closer. His face twisted into something that wasn't quite a grin, but revealed his fangs anyway. His gaze roved over her, slowly turning red. His pupils were big and round and pinning her in place. Any twitch of her muscle would give away her next move.

Her mind was screaming for her to hide, even if she just ducked behind Orahn. What she wanted was to run out of the hall and never come back.

The Vampire's hunger was so raw it felt like it was already taking chunks out of her. Her heart beat deafening; the louder it raced, the bigger his grin grew.

He'd been *waiting* for her distress.

Someone dropped a goblet, a trill ringing sound that went on until someone caught it. She didn't know if the blood inside it had spilled, she couldn't tear her eyes away from the man in front of her, sure that if she looked away for even a moment, he'd pounce.

His fingers twitched against the armrest, and for one dreadful second, she thought he would rise.

... And then he did.

Orahn moved so subtly it barely drew attention. He positioned himself squarely between her and the feral Vampire. Orahn's towering frame eclipsed her view.

Whether that made him her protector or her captor, she couldn't yet say.

He spoke once. "Be still."

The growl died in the Vampire's throat. Orahn's words hung in the air. The entire hall stopped moving. There could be no doubt who controlled the room. There was no hesitation in his presence.

They were fighting instinct with instinct in a now silent battle.

Violence had a root in the Vampire's heart, but Orahn's presence overrode it. The desire was no longer to fight, his life demanded flight now. There was something far more dangerous standing in front of him. Suddenly, his survival tasted better than her blood.

Adelira looked up at the King. Orahn held everything in a tight order, but it could easily be toppled. That was all of the fragility of his control. It's why the Vampires needed to fear him.

Guards moved swiftly, as though called into action by Orahn himself.

A woman emerged from the crowd. Adelira noticed the general's corset, embossed with the dragon crest of House Cazimer. When looking for it, she could make out the built-in armour that before she'd mistook for a deadly fashion sense.

The general moved like a panther, self-assured and lethal, clasping the Vampire's arm. The horror of tonight's incident flashed across his face leaving him panic-stricken as he was guided from the chamber with quiet efficiency. They were gone from the room before a full minute had even passed from beginning to end of the entire incident.

Adelira exhaled raggedly as she fought to suppress the memory of hungry red eyes, this Vampire's and the innkeeper's.

The fires popped in the long hearth set in the wall. The only sound in the hall. No one wrote. The blood in goblets was less interesting than her.

If anything, it grew sharper, the nobles' eyes flicking between Orahn and Adelira with renewed interest.

The way Orahn shut down the attack made the court reassess her. In truth, she was weighing her value too. She didn't have an answer for that.

"It's time to go." Orahn led her back through the room towards the exit.

She followed, uncertain in her steps, her thoughts still tripping over the encounter. And on the quiet, deadly authority that had brought it to an end.

She glanced over her shoulder, but Orahn pulled her focus.

"Eyes ahead," he murmured.

The instruction was steady enough to keep her moving forward, even as the shards of her fear lingered in the space between them and her legs trembled. It gave her direction.

One foot in front of the other. I am not prey. She willed herself to move.

"Everyone could smell me," she whispered, their footsteps echoing as they moved towards the exit, the sound piercing enough to shield her words so only he heard her. "Is the scent of my blood really that... tempting?"

She wasn't sure he'd answer; the silence stretched.

But then, he said, softly, like it was painful, "*Yes.*"

She unclenched her fist, a motion his eyes quickly tracked before flickering forward again.

They crossed the threshold, the corridor before them was completely empty. The hall doors shut behind them and swallowed the last echoes of court.

In a blink, Orahn slammed her back to the wall.

Hard enough to steal her breath, but not enough to bruise. His body caged hers, iron-strong and all heat, and his face buried into the curve of her neck.

Adelira gasped, instinctively jerking backwards, but there was nowhere to go, her hands catching at his chest. But he didn't bite her neck. He didn't speak. He *trembled* against her. His chest rising and falling with need; a desire that grew stronger by the second.

He inhaled. A long, deep pull of her scent. She felt a shudder ripple through him, down to his fingers now sliding into her hair; firm and possessive, holding her.

Against all reason, against all logic that screamed at her to move away, she *wanted* him at that moment. Instantly, she felt guilty for wanting when she should be running. She could try to push him off, but some deeper longing within her body betrayed her.

Her hips pressed back against him, her breath hitching. Her body responding, shamelessly begging for more.

He smelled like frost in the pine forest mountains and the whisper of whisky beside a fire. The strength of his body felt through every part of her. The evening's fear still hid behind her ribs, but gods help her, that wasn't what sparked the heat between her legs.

Her body pushed back against his. Her lips brushed along his cheek, longing for a taste of him.

Orahn stopped breathing. His fingers tightened just a little, but otherwise he froze, while her desire blossomed.

Finally, he exhaled slowly, control returning like a slow wave receding from the shore. When he pulled his face back from her neck, his eyes glowed with restrained hunger. He was shaking with need.

"*Fuck,*" he whispered. His jaw clenched. "I'm so sorry."

She heard his voice break. He couldn't pull away, but he couldn't stand being this close, either. The conflict in his gaze was unsure of his overstep or misjudging her reaction.

His hand lingered, thumb brushing behind her ear with gentleness that contradicted everything about the way he'd just claimed her space.

"The thought of anyone touching you..." His voice was low and frayed. "They have to *know*. You're mine."

"Yes," the word escaped her in a whisper before she could regret it.

His gaze fell to her parted lips, then returned to her eyes. "But you're not mine, are you? Not truly."

She looked up into his eyes. They weren't the same gentle ones she'd come to recognise, there was a hunger in them barely held back, and it spoke to the desire heightening in her.

Her gaze lowered to his lips and she moved in.

"I won't lie to myself and pretend fear is the same as want," he said roughly, stopping her. "And I won't let you lie about it, either."

He then stepped back, barely. Enough for her to breathe, but not enough to stop feeling him.

"I rule with instincts," he said. "But with you... it's hard not to let the instincts rule *me*."

She looked up at him and those damning deep dark eyes searched her soul for an answer to a question she couldn't hear over the thundering of her heartbeat.

"This won't happen again." he said with a pause before adding softly, "I won't lose control like that again."

Orahn fell away entirely, and started to walk down the corridor, his hand flexing at his side.

Adelira tipped her head back against the stone, breathless. She couldn't conjure up the embarrassment she knew she should feel, only the lingering smile that still played along her lips.

She heard the innkeeper's voice in her head, *a beast in a cage*, he'd warned. But gods, she wanted to open that cage now.

She pulled herself together and followed after him, falling in step beside him, her stomach fluttered. He walked slowly, confidently, looking like he hadn't slipped at all, except for the tension still flexing in the hand that had been in her hair.

Orahn had acted when she needed him, shielded her and kept her from harm from his people, but that very act reminded her swiftly that he too was a creature of harm.

A predator, a killer, more dangerous than the one he had removed from court.

Adelira cast her eyes up to him, though he didn't look at her this time, she felt his attention shift towards her. His boots sounded gentle along the tiles, like he was softening every step. This tenderness kept surprising her, so unlike the stories she had prepared herself for.

Yet, even with the effort, his nature was below the surface and she could no more deny its existence than she could deny her own.

He was a predator, of that there would never be any doubt.

But tonight, he was *her* predator.

20

Chapter Twenty

Adelira woke in the late afternoon to an unnatural stillness, the daylight rhythm of Tharth.

The castle was eerily quiet, a silence that belonged to the dead. If she'd drunk her laced tea, she might have stayed asleep with them. The tea was cold beside her bed.

The rest of Tharth only woke slowly under cover of darkness. Soldiers rose first, always braced for conflict. Servants followed, preparing halls and streets.

The general populace stirred late, but by midnight, the Night Market thrummed to its peak. Sometimes, she'd listen to the sounds and wish she were in the market.

Now, she was in a cage. Pretty as it was.

Adelira washed and pulled on an Elven dress before crossing to the balcony. She could see the battleyard below, the midnight gardens a bit further out. Then to the Keep's walls and on the other side was the market that faded into the winding streets of the city that stretched beyond the fortress. The city was cut in half by a river and surrounded by mountains.

Climbing up onto the thick banister, she held onto the column to steady herself. Gently, she lowered herself to sit on the railing and swung her legs over the side.

"Hello, Tharth," she called out into the day.

It didn't reply.

Sliding off the railings, her feet touched her balcony and she slipped back inside.

Adelira's room was a sanctuary in defiance against the oppression of the Keep. The room was large with a vaulted ceiling etched with painted constellations in silver and deep blue.

Her bath was sunken into the stone floor of a private courtyard, where her chamber transformed from bedroom to indoor garden. She had hoped for a tree she could climb, a star in the sky she could touch, but the plants were tamed and the sky was locked behind a glass ceiling.

Walking across the room, she slowly moved towards the garden, looking up. The clouds had moved off and her room brightened. Even if she couldn't touch the sun, she could step into her garden and the light could touch her skin.

She turned her face up to soak up the warmth. She hadn't felt this since arriving in Tharth, but this moment under the sun was everything to her.

"Hello sunlight," she murmured. Maybe it didn't answer either, but she felt its reply along her exposed shoulders.

The small twisted trees held their own strange beauty, nestled between thorny roses. Vines climbed over dark stone sculptures. It was no forest, a patio garden at best, with no depth in the soil for roots to support larger trees.

She ran a tentative finger along the curve of a thorn, careful not to prick herself, but determined not to shy away from sharp things.

The King floated into her thoughts. He was the sharpest thing in Tharth, but he moved around her with awareness of his strength and size. His steps were carefully thought through.

Still, he kept his distance, holding back his words and thoughts. He stepped back when she was overwhelmed, but remained close enough that she wasn't alone.

The King carefully held himself in check. Perhaps even more now that his control had slipped in the corridors outside of court.

The bat was something she'd have laughed about in Ebedene, maybe even used to frighten Talion, though he'd only have indulged her with mock-horror.

She brushed her fingertip over the petals. How long before the trees in Tharth decided to let her hear their voices?

"Will you speak to me?" she asked tentatively, not expecting a response.

There was a faint sound, low and pained. It wasn't the garden. That was definitely someone crying out. Her heart thudded.

Adelira followed the noise to a figure staggering through the sunlight still lingering in the garden. A Vampire guard. His skin sizzled and blistered under the sunlight, the navy uniform he wore couldn't protect him.

Running to him and pulling her cape from her shoulders, Adelira threw it over him to shield him from the sun.

The guard froze, his body trembling beneath the smouldering fabric. When he looked at her, his expression of shock and disbelief replaced whatever relief he first felt in the shadow of her cape.

"Princess! I—" He swallowed hard, his voice hoarse in protest. "You shouldn't—"

"What happened?" she asked and she adjusted the fabric to protect more of him from the light, lightly patting out the smouldering material of his clothing.

His hand closed around her wrist before she'd even fully moved to help him. His grip wasn't tight, but it stopped her. Weakened, burnt, it didn't matter. The man's true strength was obvious even in the flex of his fingers around her wrist.

She recognised him as the guard doing her security checks. He had beautiful blue eyes, the colour of the sky. And a strange look of fear she'd never seen before. It wasn't just pain, it was something more. That it might make him appear weak?

"I want to help you," she said gently, her voice soft but urging, but she didn't pull away. "What happened?"

His fingers trembled with indecision before he finally released her wrist. "Only a mistake. I didn't make it back before..."

Adelira hesitated. His burns were severe, his skin blistering where the light had reached him.

"You're hurt," she said gently.

He raised a hand, trembling in pain to try to wave off her concern, but dropped it just as quickly with a wince. His eyes lowered reluctantly to the ground. He allowed her to guide him toward the shadowed shelter of the chamber walls.

Holding the cape above him, she shielded him as they walked. Blood streaked his burned face, mixing with sweat.

His eyes darted to her face. His hunger flashed through the pain. "You shouldn't trust me," he said through gritted teeth.

"I don't need to trust you to see you're in need of kindness. If I can help you, then I will," Adelira said, her voice calm.

Fading sunlight caught the red waves of her hair. She smiled faintly up at him. She was so close to him that she could see his fangs, but he didn't bare them at her. He turned his head away from her face.

The guard's voice dropped to a growl. "You could get hurt."

"You mistake my kindness for weakness," she said. "But right now, it is you who is weak."

He stared at her in disbelief. Then a pained smile wavered on his face. "Do you always involve yourself in the troubles of servants, or is it just your lucky day?"

"Would you prefer that I leave and take my cape with me?" she asked while arching a questioning eyebrow at him.

Those pale blue eyes remained guarded. "You're too kind, Highness." But it wasn't said like the pleasantry Elven nobles used. "Far too kind. In Tharth, kindness will get you killed."

"It seems to me that you fear any form of strength that doesn't look like violence." Adelira saw the fear in his eyes even now. She thought about how everyone had kept their distance from her. "Tharth is too scared to try kindness."

"Fear is a resource. The wealth and currency of Vampires," he said after a pause, "But no one here fears you, Princess."

"No?" she asked, and then shrugged, it didn't matter to her.

"Tharth is not Ebedene, and your kindness may not be returned."

"What's your name?" she asked softly, looking up at him.

"Guards don't get names," he huffed.

"You still have one though."

"No. I don't." He stepped out of her arms and motioned to the doors, pulling the cloak tighter around him.

They reached her chamber doors and paused before opening them.

"I'll find the healers," he said gruffly.

"When you are healed, please come back," she said.

"Why?" he asked suspiciously.

"So I can see for myself, then I can stop worrying about you."

He paused, taken aback by that, then he scowled. Slowly, he said, "The King will be with the Elves. They'll be leaving soon. You might want to meet them... The war room."

He disappeared into the shadows beyond her chamber doors.

She was alone once more. But for the first time all week she felt like herself, Adelira, and not an Elven Princess trying to navigate something unknown. She'd helped someone and in doing so remembered who she was meant to be.

Turning to walk back through her garden, letting the shadows swallow her as the sun dipped below the horizon. This time she didn't flinch in the darkness.

21

Chapter Twenty-one

Every step outside this room before, she'd taken with Orahn at her side.

"Look at me," Adelira murmured, a breath of defiance. "Vampire saviour. Where's that earlier courage gone now?"

Taking a deep breath, she opened the door, stepping into the hall.

A lady approached; her expression wary. Adelira offered a polite smile, but the woman side-stepped sharply, muttering an apology.

"Could you show me the way to the war council? I haven't seen that part of the castle yet and my par—" Adelira started, but the woman simply pointed in the direction and walked down the opposite corridor in a hurry.

No Vampires would speak with her, most turned and walked back the way they came when they saw her.

She pushed on through the castle, everyone scattering away into hidden alcoves and down opposite corridors. She pressed on and neared the hall where murmured voices awaited.

In the war council room, a massive obsidian desk dominated the room. Her parents, other members of his war council and the Vampire King stood around it. Towards the back of the office there was another door which led somewhere unseen.

The scent of her blood hit each of the Vampires, the conversation dwindled and they looked up at her. Her parents exchanged glances, their expressions strained when they clocked the Vampires' struggle.

Orahn didn't glance up at Adelira as she entered the council chamber.

She stole a look at the King, standing in front of a floor-to-ceiling window where the city lights shone in and framed him. He wore a military cloak with a high collar around his neck that sharpened his already devastatingly handsome jaw.

The air around him bristled. He was the weight the world felt before it rained.

His voice carried over the room. "Using the Elder Celestite, we can open the Rip. The Vampire army will ambush the enemy on their territory. Until now, we've been at a disadvantage, unable to cross into their world all the while they can come and go through ours. We finally have a means to take the fight to them."

King Hara warned, "In their lands, their forces will be impenetrable. They will have numbers on their side."

"That's not a problem."

"By no means do we doubt your army," Queen Juli interrupted. "But they will hold the homeground advantage."

King Hara agreed, "You can't hope to defeat their whole force with such a small invading party. What are you planning? A scouting mission or an assassination attempt on their war general?"

The Vampire King's jaw tightened. His patience thinned in a way he'd never let show before. "We're not aiming to overpower them. Fewer soldiers will go unnoticed."

"Well..." Queen Juli started, her hand brushing over the chipped edge of her chair.

Adelira examined the map, the sections he'd positioned his forces and thought over his words.

"The target isn't their army or their general, but their crystal," she understood. "If we destroy that, we trap them in the Rip, the door slams shut. It won't matter if their army outnumbers us a hundred to one if they can't reach us. By destroying their crystal, we turn their perfect defence into a single stroke victory."

A look from her mother silenced her. Flushing, Adelira lowered her eyes.

But Orahn turned to her, a flicker of interest in his eyes as though he were assessing her place in the war room for the first time. He didn't seem impressed she could piece the plan together, instead he looked like he wasn't entirely certain he liked her astuteness.

At last, he spoke, "Correct."

She hesitated, then elaborated, "With our Elder Celestite, it's no longer a suicide mission. You will have the element of surprise and a safe way to return."

Murmurs rustled through the chamber. Several Vampires exchanged intrigued glances, their curiosity piqued.

She said softly, looking up at him, "This offers the least amount of bloodshed. It's almost... compassionate."

Snorts of laughter were blown across the room as the war generals shook their heads at the idea that the Blood King could be compassionate.

Orahn raised an arched eyebrow at her. "If the most efficient way to end this war was to rip their hearts out one by one, then we'd do that."

His words hung in the room for a time.

Then there was something lighter in his voice, "But somehow, I think this solution is faster."

She saw the almost-smirk on his lips and grinned back. "Faster and less messy."

The Vampire King's eyes locked with hers until a general's boot scuffed the floor as he crossed the room to examine the pieces on the table and the King's attention followed the movement.

"The rumours of your strategic prowess are well-founded." King Hara was full of praise.

The general reached across the table, knocking over a pot of ink which the Vampire King caught quickly, before any spilled on his map. The look he fixed his general with was enough to make the man back away from the table. Setting the ink pot aside, the King resumed focus on strategy.

"General Victoria," the Vampire King beckoned.

The woman snapped to attention, her dark eyes keenly on him. Adelira recognised her as the woman who removed the feral Vampire from court.

The Vampire King moved a number of pieces across the map with the precision of a surgeon, cutting through the land and reshaping their territories. He simply adjusted the pieces and looked at her pointedly.

Victoria's eyes darted across the map, following his movements quickly, then she nodded and left the room without a word.

He barely looked at the next person he called forward.

Gone was the patience of the Vows. This man was sharp-edged and ruthless as the evening went on.

When one of the generals hesitated, he didn't raise his voice. There was no need. The achingly slow and deliberate way he set his gaze on the man was enough to make the seasoned warrior falter.

She had an unnerving thought. What if this was the *real* him?

Sometimes kind and sometimes cold.

... Which man would she be left with after the war?

When the Elven leaders were satisfied, King Hara ordered his generals to prepare for their return.

Outside the Obsidian Keep, at the bottom of the stairs, Queen Juli turned to the Vampire King. "We've had a pleasant stay, thank you."

He nodded once.

The nighttime spring air was slowly giving way to summer.

Juli continued, "It's a lovely evening tonight."

He stiffened. "Yes." He glanced past the Elves, strangely eager to conclude the farewells.

"King Orahn," King Hara said, "I was impressed with your army. Thank you for sending them to our aid at the border, I will meet them upon my return."

He inclined his head. "I'm glad the tour was useful."

Hara nodded. "For the first time in months, I believe we might win this war."

"We've planned for nothing less," he replied. His words were firm but distracted, his posture angled as though already returning to the castle.

Carys gave Adelira a final warm embrace, holding back tears.

Her mother uttered in Adelira's ear, "Remember, smoke and snakes."

"I–I won't forget," Adelira promised, though she couldn't bear to admit to her mother that she had failed whatever test told Orahn she wasn't ready yet. "I *will* perform the Blood Ritual."

22

Chapter Twenty-Two

The carriages departed, wheels and hooves clattering softly against the cobblestones.

The Vampire King stood stiffly, angled slightly away, avoiding her gaze. When their eyes eventually met, he stepped back abruptly.

"Thank you for inviting me this evening."

"I didn't," he said.

Her smile fell a little. "W–What?" She blinked in confusion. "The guard in my garden, he said that—"

"—My guards aren't allowed alone with Elven princesses. The war meeting wasn't common knowledge. No one should be in your garden. Did you grant him access?"

"No, but..." she murmured, unsure how to respond, then she realised she *had* granted the man access when she very first arrived. "Oh, um... yes."

"*Yes*?" he demanded.

"He was your guard. In your army. He asked to do a security check," she answered, frowning.

"Guards are not soldiers. Soldiers do not conduct security checks on the Princess's private chambers."

Again, he only stated facts, expecting her to see how it didn't line up. She saw it clearly now. She also saw red.

"You cannot give up your only protection keeping you safe when I am not close at hand. You can't trust everyone at their word, Adelira," he said in exasperation.

"I..." she started, the gravity of what he'd said sinking in. She wondered if he included *himself* in that list. "I will remember that."

"Your blood is too powerful for the men I have at my disposal."

"I–If my blood is such a problem... What will we do?"

"I'm bringing in experienced men to station by your doors," he said. "When they arrive, you may grant them access. They should be the *only* people besides your ladies-in-waiting. No one else."

He regarded her with a sharp look, cold as a storm. His hands clasped behind his back. His gaze cooled.

She thought of Talion. And Rayno, on his way home now.

"I will look into this later." His words were clipped, as though the issue was an inconvenience to him.

His bluntness caused her to look him over again. The change was so sharp she almost believed he was someone else entirely. His eyes seemed so different, so far away.

She forced a smile. "Thank you."

"I will walk you back to your chambers."

The small smile on her lips was replaced by a slight frown. "Forgive me, Orahn, but I was hoping to see the Kingdom... or at least just the castle now that everyone's gone home."

After a pause so deliberate it was almost dismissive, he said, "Princess Adelira..."

"King Orahn," she dropped into a small playful curtsy, determined to draw back the teasing sides of him she'd seen this week.

He gestured to the castle doors. "Not tonight."

"I know you gave your word, and that holds a lot of value, but let us secure a date for the Blood Ritual now," she said coldly, her tone matching his.

He paused, turning slowly to meet her. The look in his eyes was calculating, but lacked the gentleness she had come to associate with Orahn's considerations.

His gaze missed nothing, revealed nothing either.

"We should return." He led the way through the castle's grand entrance hall.

"If it was all an act, you could just say that," she said, trying to keep the hurt from her voice with a smile that didn't reach her eyes.

"Would believing that make this easier for you?" he asked. Then he pushed her further, "Would it change anything?"

Her eyes widened. What would it change? Nothing except dash the hope she'd foolishly clung to.

"Sometimes I imagine you must feel like I forced your hand, linking our Kingdoms together with the promise of our Elder Celestite."

"You could not force me into anything if you tried."

"Don't underestimate me," she said lightly.

"A bold statement to make to the Blood King."

She swallowed a gasp. Blood King. Vampire. *Killer.* He'd swiftly reminded her not to get comfortable. "Sorry... It's... I–I don't mean to insult you."

"Before considering an alliance with Tharth, the Elves requested an alliance with Fellin Kingdom."

She flinched.

"You never received a response from them," he continued.

The negotiations had been abandoned in favour of her marriage proposal.

"...How do you know this?" She asked, a little disturbed.

For a while the only sound was their boots tapping along the polished floors.

"Why did your trees stop talking to you?"

Adelira took a full step back. He stopped and looked at her. She felt dissected. The sudden accusation in his eyes scared her.

"The old magic is leaving... I–I don't control that."

He didn't press. He watched her, waiting. And when she didn't offer anything more, he turned forward again.

If the war was the Vampires' only focus, then what was she to him?

Adelira grated her teeth and clenched her fists, Blood King or not, he was stoking her anger. "If you distrust us so much then why did you bother accepting the alliance at all?"

She reached for his wrist. Before her fingers closed fully, she felt him twist out of her grasp. He caught her wrist instead. The heat of his touch seared, but he let go immediately.

"I get that you don't trust us," Adelira snapped, rubbing her wrist though there was no mark, "but you do really need us, don't you?"

"Vampires cannot drink from the Shifters."

"Okay?"

"When their claws get into someone," he said, "that person changes. The Shifters are slowly poisoning our food supply."

She hadn't considered that the Vampire's motivation to fight was anything beyond war for war's sake until recently. And even then, she hadn't considered the Shifters were doing real damage to the war nation. At best, she assumed they were a problem either too distant or too small for their full involvement.

If the other Kingdoms around Tharth fell, the Vampires would fall into famine without the Shifters ever breaching The Obsidian Keep.

He walked several paces ahead, her face flushed with the effort of keeping up.

"That's enough!" she snapped in Ehvayn.

He froze. He went deathly still, before he turned. His eyes landed on her and pinned her there.

"Goodnight, Your Majesty," she said softer in Tharic. "I can find my own way from here."

"I have a duty to protect you," he said darkly. "Regardless of your preference right now, I cannot allow it."

His shoulders squared, jaw tight and the air closing in around them. She bit the inside of her cheek to keep from bolting. Once they were outside her chambers, he opened the door and she stepped inside.

Before she could turn around to him, he'd closed the door.

Adelira stood in the centre of her room, her chest tight with confusion. The breeze from her open balcony pushed back her hair. She crossed the room and closed the doors with a snapping sound.

It didn't matter if he could never love her.

She would never run away again.

She would get her Blood Ritual. One way or another.

23

Chapter Twenty-Three

They still had dinner plans later that evening. She changed her dress for formal dinner.

She made her way to the hall where a gentleman pulled out her chair for her and promptly retreated to the other side of the room.

The long dining table was surrounded by empty chairs. Her eyes drifted to the double doors each time she heard footsteps. She grew tired, as the night wore on.

Finally, a servant approached. He read from a small scroll, "The King regrets to inform you that pressing matters demand his attention this evening."

The first course was set before her, but she hardly noticed as she made her way through the menu with the same orchestrated pretend-interest in the meal as the Vampires had shown at the banquet. With an odd sense of irony, she wondered if she seemed more Vampire now.

When she finished, she stood to leave, but a crash turned her about.

A young servant kneeled beside a shattered glass, wine spilled across the polished floor.

A steward stepped forward and barked at him to leave it. "You've done enough damage."

Adelira quickly knelt beside him, steadying the young boy's trembling hands.

"It's all right," she told him gently and then moved to pick up the pieces.

"Your Highness, please." The steward stepped forward carefully, hands raised in caution, as though he himself was now *afraid* as well.

Adelira rose to face him calmly. "I'm not above cleaning up a little mess."

The steward stiffened, his bow shallow. "Your Highness, only that handling broken glass in a room full of Vampires is... unwise."

Adelira understood the warning then. The boy hurriedly gathered the remaining shards and fled the room.

Kindness was disruptive to the ruthless order and discipline of Tharth. Everything that she was seemed like it would be crushed beneath this formidable Kingdom.

Adelira returned to her chamber, velvet drapes, polished marble. It bore no trace of her, no warmth, no history.

Her eyes fell on the pebble beside her bed. Snatching it up, she turned the smooth stone in her hands, letting it remind her. A woman who danced in sunlight and sang to the trees.

The moons turned in the sky, sinking beneath the mountains and the sky began to lighten, threatening sunrise which would chase all the Vampires even further from her reach. Her tea was already brewing. She should drink it, let slumber pull her away from this night.

"Not yet," she whispered to no one.

A knock sounded at her chamber door, a heavy loud sound that startled her. Before she could reach it, the door swung open.

The Vampire King stood framed in the doorway. He was a shadow that came to life.

Neither of them spoke. A subtle tension in his shoulders coiled as though he might push forward into her room... Or walk away entirely.

The permission that she'd granted him nights before, when he had seemed a gentler man, left her exposed. She had no power to stop him.

Their eyes connected and she almost stumbled backwards. He didn't just look angry. He looked like a complete stranger to her; like she'd never peered into his eyes before.

"I didn't expect you to be awake," he said. There was fire in his voice.

Her hands began to tremble. His dark eyes fixed on them; losing the edge of resentment.

She closed her palm tightly around the pebble, hiding it from him. *Be brave*, Talion's words kept her upright.

"I couldn't sleep," she admitted softly.

His mouth twisted; not quite a sneer, but close enough.

"That makes two of us," he said, leaning against the doorframe, his arms folding across his chest. "Though I don't imagine we lose sleep over the same things."

He stepped no closer. And yet his presence filled the space around her, overwhelming her senses. Coldness radiated from him even at this distance. The tension in his muscles pulled tight.

An owl hooted. It sounded close enough to be perched on her balcony. She didn't dare take her eyes off the King to look. He didn't peer past her at it either. His eyes fixed on her.

He glanced over the dress she'd worn for the dinner he missed. Her hands brushed over the soft silk. Now she wished she was wearing one of his armoured dresses, maybe then he wouldn't see straight through her.

"We have a long path ahead of us, Princess," he said. "You should rest."

She nodded. Even though neither of them believed sleep would come easily. Her eyes betrayed her fear, but she refused to lower her gaze. The only act of defiance she could muster.

"Adelira..." he hesitated, about to say something more, but then, he withdrew.

She watched as he turned away from her room, his movements almost too abrupt. The door closed with a thud behind him. Alone once again, she released her breath and turned back to the view outside, her heart heavy, even as dawn broke.

Adelira felt it then, the truth in her bones. He didn't even trust her enough to let her know what game they were playing. A game where kings could deceive even those closest to them.

This marriage was a façade.

A deceit.

And she was caught in its deadly web.

24

Chapter Twenty-Four

Adelira's chamber doors opened. One of her ladies with dark hair in a plait down her back, carried hot water for her evening bath. The other lady was new, she had dark amber eyes.

"May I come in?" they asked for permission.

"Yes," Adelira gave it, wondering what happened to the previous lady.

"Your Highness." A flash of hunger in their eyes, before they locked their eyes safely back onto the stone floor.

The first lady with dark hair was semi-regular. Though no one stayed long and staff were rotated often.

They filled a tub with water silently.

The porcelain bathtub was sunk into the stone floor and nestled next to a roaring fire that warmed her water quickly. The bath overlooked the private garden, just outside enough that she could see the night sky from that angle. Above the gardens, the ceiling was glass. The far wall was partially hidden by roses and vines; and she could almost believe that she was not trapped here when she sat with nature, except for the slamming of that door each night.

The ladies dropped petals to the water.

"Which flowers are these from?" Adelira asked.

They had been talking to each other in hushed voices, but it died down as Adelira approached them. They backed away ever so slightly.

"It's Pantherlilly, Your Highness," replied her usual lady and felt the water.

The other lady lit candles and arranged them with care.

Adelira walked over, dropping her gown to the floor. The lady knocked over the candle spilling wax over the table, trying to back away quickly enough. She apologised, but kept moving towards the door, as though the nearness of Adelira's exposed skin was more than the servant could bear.

"I can do it. You can both go," Adelira said gently, turning the candle upright. She quickly climbed into the water, like it might mask her scent.

The ladies already slipped out of the door, closing the door behind them.

Adelira whispered, "Am I really too much? ... Nice to meet you, too... Please stay..."

Adelira sank into her bath, letting herself be blanketed by the water. Opening her eyes, she looked up and watched the stars shimmering and blurred by the water. When she could hold her breath no longer, she surfaced with a gasp and slowly began to wash.

She climbed out, ignoring the towel. Instead, she chose drying in front of the fire, the heat reddening her sensitive skin. She dried quickly like that and dressed.

This was it, her start of three days and nights alone before the Fealty Ceremony. Three days shouldn't have sounded long in theory, but Elves were never alone.

Adelira sat on the side of her bed. Row of Vampire dresses hung in her wardrobe. The gowns were in equal parts daunting and beautiful. The longer she stared at them, the more she thought they might bite back. Designed to intimidate as much as they impressed. She was used to light silks that slid against her skin, flowing like the warm breeze in her forests.

She left the dresses behind. Vines crawled up along the wall outside on her balcony and reached up to the roof of the castle. She could climb it.

Her heart ached to sit above the canopy again, not quite a creature of the earth, not quite a creature of the sky.

The innkeeper's forest came to mind, with its gnarled roots and twisted trees... she shivered. Perhaps not that *one*.

Her fingers stroked the vines on the balcony. She even gave it a gentle tug to feel the strength of it, it'd hold her weight. She could leave behind the dresses and the silences and bloodlust...

Talion.

His face came sharply into her mind. She had promised never to run away again.

She watched the sun chase the moons out of the sky and the daylight filtered into her room. If the castle was quiet before, it'd be dead now that the Vampires were banished to bed.

Closing the curtains, bathing in sunlight only made her return to darkness harder, and retrieved the violin case. She lifted the instrument tenderly and played in defiance of the silence. She played songs of home, of her forests and the rushing streams.

She played her violin until she didn't know whether she was soothing herself or trying to call someone.

No one came.

When the last note faded, Adelira placed the violin back in its case and waited for nightfall.

She stared at the closed door, beyond it were halls with dangers lurking in seductive gowns and teeth like razors.

25

Chapter Twenty-Five

Adelira tried, but Elves were not meant to be alone for days at a time. Even if the corridors had teeth, she couldn't stay in her room a moment longer.

She passed by a crowded hall on her way to dinner. Everyone inside was finely dressed.

"Ah! You must be the Elven Princess," said a man wearing the Ashbourne Kingdom's emblem. "I thought they were but rumours! Come in, come in, join us."

Her gaze fell on Orahn as he forced out a smile.

"Of course, join us," the King said. "The Ashbourne dignitaries are well known for their stalling tactic, but you are lovely enough that I'll allow the interruption."

She hesitated before walking into the room. The King returned his attention to the man before him, though his body remained angled slightly towards her.

The man who'd called her in, walked over. "I'm Bren."

"Adelira."

Bren made her laugh and fetched a drink for her.

"How have you found the hospitality of Vampires?" he asked.

She paused. "They... There are differences to what Elves are used to, yes. The war efforts require a lot of his attention."

Bren didn't miss the melancholy in her voice. "The Shifters have every Kingdom's attention, only few have all the pieces to deal with it effectively."

"Let's hope this alliance will benefit everyone then."

"That benefit can come from many different Kingdoms, given the chance. But what about your benefit? You do not have to sacrifice your future for it."

Bren leaned in close, his voice barely audible beneath the noise of the hall. He slipped a small vial into her palm.

"You shouldn't be alone here," he murmured. "Promises are easy to make when witnesses are watching. What will you become left alone in the dark?"

His eyes flicked briefly toward the Vampire King before returning to her. She followed his gaze.

Bren's hand brushed her arm, pulling her focus back.

"Ashbourne has long protected its allies without asking them to bleed for it. If you ever find yourself needing... leverage, this will keep you safe. He won't refuse a drink from you."

She gasped and covered the sound quickly.

"Think of yourself, here in *this* place..."

Then he fell away and Adelira glanced down at the black vial he left in her palm, her fingers closing instinctively before anyone saw.

Bren spoke loudly, some tale of the arduous journey here. She excused herself and made her way towards the King, picking up a glass of wine on her way.

The Vampire King hadn't done the Blood Ritual, she could take her crystal and go. He'd all but admitted this marriage was for show. But the way his fingers threaded into her hair, the way he looked at her, the show was starting to convince even him. Whenever he offered her his hand, he felt safe enough to hope, even with the silence.

More than that, Orahn had never asked her to poison herself morally.

The small crowd around the Vampire King leaned in to hear his story.

Orahn chuckled, saying, "And you know how they can—"

Adelira reached out and placed her hand delicately in his, the vial between their palms. He did a double take, glancing down at her, at their closed hands, at her again.

Slowly, he turned to the men. "If you'll excuse me, gentlemen. It seems my future bride would like some attention tonight as well."

The men made teasing remarks as they walked away. No sooner had they left, did the smile fall from his face and he dropped her hand. He lifted the vial, inspecting it.

"Ashbourne?" he asked.

She nodded.

"What did they offer you?"

"What I already have ten times over from you," she said softly.

His eyes connected with her. "Given a way into the Rip, they could win the war." His eyes sharpened. "And keep you untouched while they did it."

"I didn't make a Vow of Intent with Ashbourne. I made a promise to you... T–that means something... *to me.*"

His hard expression fell away. "Lira..." Then, it pulled back into place and he dropped the vial, crushing the broken glass beneath his shoe. "General Victoria, have the Blackguard escort the Ashbourne dignitaries to the Black Wards."

From the shadows, a number of soldiers appeared next to the Ashbourne people, grip locking on their arms.

"You will regret this," Bren sneered as he was ushered out. "When you see the monster you intend to marry, you'll wish you had listened to me!"

Adelira flinched.

Orahn slipped a finger under her chin, lifting until their eyes connected. "Don't turn away. Look at him."

She squared up her shoulders, stepping closer to Orahn. She turned around and watched Bren and his men be escorted from the hall and hoped the man beside her was the one she feared less.

26

Chapter Twenty-Six

When it was the evening of the Fealty Ceremony, Adelira bathed and did her hair alone.

A new set of ladies arrived, insisting that she wear a Tharathi gown. Their fingers like ice against her skin, conversation non-existent.

They secured the crimson dress around her. The gown clung to her like blood. The cut of it was sharp and commanding. Black stitching over the steel-reinforced corset cinched her.

She gasped as they pulled the lace tight. She braced against her bedpost. When they were done, she moved to the mirror.

The mirror didn't show a queen; it showed a girl playing dress-up in something crueller than her spirit could carry.

∞

Tall, unadorned columns lined the walls. The air stank of iron and burning incense. At the centre of the hall stood a raised platform of blackened marble, where those who sought allegiance to the throne would kneel.

She shifted uncomfortably, feeling like the dress was clutching at her throat too tightly. The collar on the dress came up her neck, stiff and immovable. She almost let herself believe he was protecting her neck from being bitten, but it felt too much like a literal collar he could show the court.

She panicked at her freedoms slipping away, but the armour around her ribs made it hard for her to pull a full breath. Maybe that wasn't just the dress, maybe that was the heaviness in the room and the way the Blood Houses looked at her.

And yet, despite it all; despite the discomfort, despite how much she longed for everything Elven, she still found herself wanting to belong *here.* And not by becoming someone else, either, she didn't want to surrender the parts of herself that mattered. But by carving out a space where she didn't have to choose between the two.

Why did that feel so impossible?

She tried to ignore the armour gripping her ribs. Instead, she focused on the room; the ceremony, the eyes, the blood.

The Vampires stepped forward one by one. Knives flashed as they cut their palms over the chalice. Blood spilled into the cup. An act of loyalty.

The youths who'd released the bat approached next, kneeling before the King and her.

They weren't laughing now. They looked scared.

One of them limped, dragging his foot across the marble. The last held his left arm strangely, fingers curled stiffly.

She looked down at them.

There were bite marks on them. Small, crescent-shaped punctures across the exposed skin of their hands and necks. One boy had them crawling up the side of his face, his ear nearly chewed through.

She glanced over to Orahn, but he wasn't even looking at the youngsters. They, in turn, weren't looking at her either, not anymore, maybe not ever again. They were looking at their King as they made their slices in their flesh.

The boy with one eye sliced his palm open and held it over the chalice. The blood dripped. The knife shook in his hand.

The second did the same, biting his lip hard enough to draw more blood from his mouth.

The third knelt for longer than he needed to, like he hoped the marble would swallow him or that his kneeling might win his King's forgiveness.

Finally, they rose in silence and moved aside for the next noble.

Adelira kept her expression neutral, but her pulse surged. She fought to keep it steady, she didn't want to be the reason anyone else suffered.

The King didn't request loyalty.

He *taught* it.

The court swore their allegiance to him. Tonight, Orahn gave her, and the room, nothing.

He spoke to no one, not even her.

The shadows lengthened when he had arrived, though the torches didn't dim. His cloak dragged behind him like something pulled up from a crypt. He didn't look at anyone. He didn't *need* to do anything other than arrive. His silence spread. It soaked into the cracks of the stone and filled the lungs of the nobles, until even the fire in the hearth seemed to shrink.

A woman stood before her and the King, glancing over Adelira, briefly, like she was barely a thing worth considering in all of this.

Except Adelira understood that she was the most important thing to consider. Following the Vampire King made sense.

It was *her* who was unlike the King in every way; a weakness they had to weigh carefully before deciding if they still stood by his choices and his rule.

Orahn could have done a trial, some set of challenges, or obstacles she would be forced to overcome in order to prove her place among the Vampires and *earn* their Fealty.

But there was nothing she could prove in a test that would mean more than the Vampire King himself standing beside her.

The last Vampire stepped forward. His knife slicing the air with a whisper before it bit his skin. The chalice filled, dark and shimmering.

She felt eyes at the back of her head. When she turned, there was only a wall behind her.

After their fealty was sworn, the ceremony gave way to a gladiatorial fight staged in the very hall where blood oaths were made.

It was tradition to celebrate with blood spilled purely for spectacle. The Blood Families competed with each other for the favour of their King, even though he wasn't offering that tonight.

Looking at the King, she saw only steel; a distant thunder she could hear coming but couldn't understand. He belonged here, as part of the rites, the harsh edges, the fortified walls.

His crown had hardened him. Or... had he always been like this, and she was only just realising how false their first few nights really were?

Searching his face for a fragment of the warmth he had once shown her. Was it beneath layers of duty and power? Or had Tharth claimed him completely, as it threatened to claim her?

He was part of this dark world.

And she... she was still searching for her place.

He turned and looked at her then. Like her longing had drawn him in. But when his eyes connected with hers, she didn't recognise them. Just as sharp as they'd been in the war room.

He looked at her like he'd seen her a hundred times before, studied her endlessly, watched her constantly.

But she hadn't seen him like this; very nearly a stranger to her tonight.

And then he turned away and the moment was gone.

They moved to the table while the fighters provided entertainment. The King did not offer her his arm. She refused to reach for it even as they passed the hungry eyes of the court, even as she trembled beside him.

"Wine, your Highness?" a server asked behind her.

"Bloodwine, please," she said in defiance.

He passed a nervous look at the King.

The King barely turned to her, but with a dismissive flick of the wrist he motioned to the server to carry out her wishes. Reluctantly, the server returned with a glass of bloodwine and set it down before her. He moved away quickly.

Adelira peered over the rim into the dark red glass. The smell filled her nose and burned. She pushed back in her chair and sat away from the table. She folded her arms and glanced at the King. He wasn't looking at her, but she felt his smugness all the same.

She wanted to ask about the donors. Did they donate willingly? But she hadn't reached for his arm to steady herself and if the King only gave her silence tonight, she'd be damned if she bridged that gap now.

The crowd roared as fighters tore into each other, their cheers louder with every spray of red.

After the victor stepped over his opponent's limp form, the rowdy crowd erupted into cheers.

A chalice of bloodwine was thrust into the victor's hand. Crimson rivulets spilled over the rim as he raised it high. He tipped the chalice back, the red staining the corners of his mouth as the crowd roared louder.

Somewhere beneath the noise, the defeated man groaned faintly. The victor didn't spare him a glance. Instead, he threw the chalice to the ground, the metal clattering against stone like a final punctuation to his triumph.

She flinched at the sharp metallic sound hitting the floor and instinctively moved closer to Orahn. Her fingers twitched, she wanted to slip her hand in his. Adelira's eyes desperately sought the King's gaze, some comfort in this brutal space.

He glanced down at her with a look that said, '*you can't crack here, not even for me.*'

She bit her lip, all the warmth she'd hoped for turned into more pressure. Grateful for the steel in her corset, without it she might have crumpled under the weight of what tonight demanded of her.

He was a storm held on the horizon. Not the lightning or thunder, only the silence that warns of what's to come.

The ceremony ended, she could still smell the tang of iron and rain.

27

Chapter Twenty-Seven

Adelira arrived at the Court of Shadows before anyone else from court had arrived. He'd asked her not to break for him and she hadn't.

The King was pacing rapidly along the front of the hall until he smelled her. He stopped, head snapped up.

Then, with practiced ease, he took a seat.

The effortless confidence and the casual sprawl was a quieter performance, but a performance nonetheless.

He wanted her to believe she didn't unsettle him, that he was above it.

But it was *too* easy. Just a fraction too much effort to be real.

"Hello, Orahn," she said softly.

His eyes narrowed as he watched her walk across the room, there was an almost snarl on his face which threatened to stop her. Last night his coldness had been for the fealty ceremony. Tonight, his coldness felt like an act of defiance... against *her*... Like she was his enemy.

Slowly, the court began to arrive in silent waves, gemstones and teeth glinting in the candlelight. Adelira tried to identify faces in the crowd she might have recognised over the last week and a bit in Tharth, but it was only a few generals and the feral Vampire from court that stood out to her.

There it was again, that tugging feeling she was being watched from places she couldn't see. When she looked back, she could see only the blank wall behind her. She fought the impulse to wave at her invisible watcher.

As his court arrived, the King moved less, like he was slowly turning to stone beside her. The heat off him suggested he was burning inside with the effort of it.

A nightjar flew into the room and the King's arm shot up, the bird landing expertly on his forearm. It gave a sharp thrill as he unfolded the scroll.

He read the message from the scroll it carried, the bird flying away across the hall to its handler. Abruptly, the King left the room.

A sea of eyes locked onto her. She couldn't move. They grew sharper.

Before the panic could fully set in, he returned.

The Vampire King walked in like a match dragged across stone, ready to ignite.

She didn't know what his message had revealed, but it had done nothing to improve his mood. One wrong move would set the entire court ablaze. He sat down heavily next to her.

"Are you okay?" she whispered.

He fixed her with an incredulous look before he turned away and reviewed the state of the room.

"Begin," the King instructed the council.

The room was a flutter of motion and sounds. Documents were pulled out and pens began scratching over parchment. Jewels clinked and boots struck polished floors as members positioned themselves.

In a semicircle, the Blood Houses sat around the room, stretched in rows that fanned the room in either direction. The chairs were high-backed and severe, marked with the crests of various powerful families, though some sat empty, their occupants having long fallen or forsaken their King.

"House Delarosa should speak first," a pouty woman purred.

"No, Ravena, we need to discuss real matters, like border disputes and district fighting between blood rivals," general Victoria said firmly.

"House Cazimer will take the lead," general Gareth said, blade glinting at his side.

"Who said you get to make that call?" Ravena demanded.

"The border disputes are a pressing matter. They're escalating again," general Victoria said. "It seems our northern neighbours have forgotten their place."

"Forgotten," the feral Vampire from the other night mused, his voice mocking. He was back in court and clearly back in control of himself, he didn't look at Adelira, but his eyes flashed in their direction as he said, "or testing? They've always been bold when they think the King's attention is... *elsewhere*."

Though Adelira didn't look up, she felt the room's attention fall to her, before darting back towards the members speaking at the podiums.

Besides her, the Vampire King shifted in his seat, like his body was fighting against the rigidity expected of him. The King ignored the jab, picking up his own pen and began hurriedly writing notes. She glanced at his pages but he flipped through them faster than she could catch.

Ravena gave a short humourless laugh. "Let them test, Lord Necos."

"Why?" Necos narrowed his eyes, twirling his cane in his hands.

He didn't appear injured, but the golden crow's eye surrounded by black feathers was a symbol on his tunic that her eyes kept coming back to. Adelira wondered why the boys had been punished, but the hungry Vampire was spared, and if his role in House Crowe had anything to do with his amnesty.

"To help them remember. A reminder can be delivered in many ways," Ravena said with a shrug.

"Burn a village."

"Drain a diplomat."

"They'll understand soon enough."

"Draining is messy," general Victoria retorted as simply as discussing the weather. "A famine in the outlying farms would send a clearer message. No need to raise a sword when hunger can do the work for us."

"Subtlety is overrated," Necos argued. "Let them see their mistakes written in fire. It's what the King would expect."

She had travelled here for this menacing world, but it was only unsettling in contrast to how her first week was. A war nation who was her salvation in her own war. She tried to reframe every cruel sentence they spoke as necessary for their war efforts, but her insides still twisted.

Somewhere, deeper in the Keep doors opened and closed, Vampires were moving through the castle. No one came through the doors, but this was the noisiest she'd ever heard the Keep. The council continued their discussions.

"We need to set a date for the Blood Ritual between the King and the Princess," Necos began.

Adelira looked up and sat a little straighter.

She could use their pragmatism to her advantage. And this particular Vampire likely had the added motivation of helping her secure her Ritual if it would keep him out of trouble and away from her blood.

"We wait," the King said sharply, he broke his stillness with the thrumming of his fingers along the table.

Her heart raced as the eyes of the room rested on her. They waited for her reaction to his words. She was about to speak up, when he offered more.

"We will continue to protect the Elven borders against the Shifter attacks." He sighed, shaking his head. "I need no blood promise to hold me to that duty."

Adelira looked at the King. While he honoured their deal with force instead of magic; her people had his protection. At least it gave her time to get ready for the Ritual, whatever that meant.

"Still, we will need to honour our part in the alliance agreement," Necos reasoned. "The Elven King will not like that we put this off."

"And we will do it. But not now," the Vampire King shut down the conversation.

She frowned, his face betrayed him briefly and she wasn't sure *who* she saw beneath it.

"Of course, your Majesty. There is another matter."

"What is it?" he asked tightly.

Moonlight filtered in from windows too high up for her to see. Raising her hand into a beam of moonlight, Adelira watched it dance over her skin. The King glanced down at her hand in the light and she tucked it back into the folds of her dress.

"We need to find a way to harness the crystal's powers," Necos said. "It wouldn't be safe to involve the Princess too close to the Rip. We will need to learn to wield its power without relying on her presence. So far, it has eluded all who have tried to awaken it."

Again, all eyes fell on her. This time she did not let the King take her voice.

She said flatly, as if the sentence itself resolved the matter, "The Elder Celestite works for Elven royalty."

Her words were met with blank looks from around the room.

Finally, Lord Necos pointed out, "That's what we're saying we need to work around. We're hardly sending a Princess to battle."

"What exactly did you believe marriages are?" she asked. "What about your Blood Ritual that mixes blood? Not just mine. His as well."

She looked at the court again, realising that none of them actually understood until now. Perhaps it was just too unfathomable for them to consider their terrifying Blood King as Elven Royalty.

"Once we do the Blood Ritual, my blood will flow through yours." She looked pointedly at the King. "Yes?"

A strange shocked expression crossed his face as he pieced together what she was saying. In the war room, the King had seemed a calculating strategist, but the man in front of her now hadn't realised that the Ritual would connect him as Elven Royalty.

Adelira continued, despite how his expression contorted, "You'd be Elven Royalty to the Elder Celestite after the Blood Ritual and you can harness its powers without me."

A loud crash sounded from the room next door, like something was smashed.

When she turned back to him, the look was gone and masked by fragile composure.

Necos turned a hopeful gaze to the King. "Then we can do the Ritual and solve that immediately."

"I said we wait! If we know there is a solution, we can hold it until it is necessary," he said, falling flat against the backrest of the throne.

"We're still months away from battle with the Shifters, so there's time to set a date for the Ritual," Necos said, skating dangerously close to a subject he had already shut down.

"It seems like they are building a force gradually, but these months will pass quickly. There's much to organise before they move against us," general Victoria said.

"We need to ready a small army of a dozen or so elite soldiers for the mission, but that's only to close the Rip, we'll still need armies to defeat the ones who made it through before we close it," General Gareth went on. "It'd be best to prepare everything we can quickly."

"I said," the King growled, but didn't lift his eyes from the floor, and there was hardly enough heat to his words, but they all knew how quickly that could change, "I'm handling it."

No one spoke after that.

Adelira just had to wait for him to come to her when he needed the Elder Celestite.

The rooms' chatter flowed again and soon everyone was engaged in some small side conversation, split across the various roles of the Kingdom.

Necos slammed his fists into the hardwood table. "What did you say?" he snarled with his fangs bared.

Ravena, with her long black hair curling down her back, rose slowly.

She repeated, "You should be cast out of the Blood Families for such weak ideas. Where is your honour?"

Necos reached across the table, his fist locked around her collar, a snarl in his throat that never finished. Ravena curled her fingers, her nails glinted; suddenly looking more like claws than hands, and she raised her arm to swipe his face.

Instantly, the King was there. Striking Lord Necos across the jaw and sending him sprawling to the floor.

"Discipline," the King growled.

He turned around. Ravena flinched as though she'd been the one struck to the ground.

"Do you know what that looks like in my court?"

The court held its collective breath. The quiet was punctuated only by the harsh breathing of Necos fallen on the floor. Ravena nodded, her head bowed. Necos didn't attempt to rise.

Adelira felt the strain it took the Vampire King to keep the court in line.

"Good," he said simply, brushing off his sleeves as though the matter had required no effort on his part.

Tonight, he'd used an entirely different method to hold the room in check and Adelira couldn't explain why.

The King scanned the room. His look sweeping over the court like a warning.

The fire crackled and roared as someone placed another log on it. When the King walked toward her, her hands trembled. She clasped them together quickly.

She couldn't reconcile this version of him with the man who had danced with her Elves and showed her mountains.

A sudden chill seeped into her as the King's voice slid down her spine, "You're quiet, Princess."

His dark eyes catching hers in the dim light. There was something unsettling about him, like he could see through her, see her fear, her doubts. And still, she could see no kindness.

"I have nothing to say," she replied, her voice tight.

"You should learn to speak," he said as he picked up his goblet. "Or someone else will speak for you, and they may not have your best interests at heart."

Did *he* have her best interests at heart?

"My silence is not weakness. I'm observing," she said.

He blinked, looking at her, and then slowly a smirk played on his lips. "You are learning."

Then in Ehvayn, beneath her breath, she muttered to herself, "I'd rather be silent than cruel."

The warmth she thought she saw in him had been a fleeting illusion. And she was all the hollower for having tasted it.

Adelira missed the sunlight kissing her face. Tharth gave her only its darkness.

28

Chapter Twenty-Eight

Doors kept closing in Adelira's face.

They didn't slam. They drifted shut, one by one, slow and final, until she found herself alone again, still searching for a way in.

She wasn't a prisoner officially, but captivity had more shapes than a cage.

Adelira tracked a lantern light glowing between the hedges in the castle gardens below her balcony. Somewhere down there the King walked alone. Just as isolated as she was.

Perhaps Vampires preferred to live that way; solitary, distant.

But *she* wasn't a Vampire. And *she* didn't want to be alone.

An owl hooted and flew away. Sunrise chased the castle into slumber, but she couldn't sleep. Even when tea to sleep was delivered to her room, she couldn't bring herself to drink it.

She sat on her balcony in the cool dawn. Tharth's effect on everything; slowly leeching all warmth.

The battleyard stretched unnaturally wide to hold a ten thousand strong army. Training dummies and wooden posts bent under the abuse they took from practising fighters. Racks of weapons with brutal points and cuts of steel glinted in the sunlight. The King's banners billowed lazily. They were immaculate, like everything in Tharth, despite the rain and wind that often tore through the valley.

In between the stone arches, daylight caught like streaks of flames illuminating the grounds. She hadn't even believed the light could spill in his courtyards. It did, though, and the effect was breath-taking.

The castle itself twisted and curved showing the rooftops and spires of towers in the other wings. Stone gargoyles stood guard on parapets stretched out in defiance of gravity. Stained-glass windows set in the cathedral-like castle seemed to shatter when the sunlight rose in a brilliant burst of light, colours scattered for a full minute before the angle changed and softened.

She stretched her fingertips up above her head and closed her eyes for a moment.

From up here, she spotted the Innkeeper's forest, densely packed and dark green, almost black, in the distance. She didn't know why she thought of it as the innkeeper's forest, except that was what he had called it.

It was probably Orahn's forest. Wasn't everything the darkness touched his?

The sun began setting, red spilling across the horizon in long slow streaks until there was only shadow left in the world.

And from the shadows emerged the Vampire King.

She slunk back on her balcony, sitting out of view on her knees, watching him between the stone slats in the railing.

He began a warm up regime so intense she wondered if he did this every evening before the castle even started to stir. He awoke before everyone; doing sets of sit-ups, push-ups, wall stands, and then he donned heavy armour and began again, weighed down by chainmail and solid steel weaponry.

He never slowed to catch his breath. He just struck his target with the same clean precision and force that rang through the battleyard.

She couldn't feel sorry for herself for how he changed after her family left. She didn't even feel scared anymore. He was every bit the war machine she needed.

His dark hair fell in his face and he pushed it back. His features were sharp, eyes focused. He was intense, and stunning to watch.

She shook her head and reminded herself; *war hero, not lover.*

The stars shone brightly and the yard began to fill with more soldiers, awake now and ready for the evenfall's training. The air thick with the sounds of sparring; steel clashing, boots scuffing, the occasional bark of instruction from an overseeing general.

Her gaze kept flitting over all the soldiers, her relief growing. Precise and lethal, the Crimson Army filled her with a renewed sense of resolve.

These were warriors who would win wars. The Vampire army was everything she'd hoped for and watching how deadly and efficient they were made her believe in her people's future. The King scared her, but he'd scare her enemies, too. There was something thrilling about knowing that, and knowing in all her time here he'd never actually turned that fear on her. He kept holding back just enough that she believed they were on the same side.

A small unsteady figure caught her eye. Entirely out of place in the army, but training alongside the recruits was a child. Dressed in heavy armour that weighed him down and struggling with the forms the soldiers were working through.

The boy, no older than ten, stood rigid in front of the Vampire King, his tiny frame tight with frustration.

The youths from court came to mind. Suddenly, her worry for this boy threatened to spring her into action.

She was about to turn for the stairs when a motion out the corner of her eye caught her mid-climb.

The King *knelt* in front of the youngster.

Tears streaked the boy's dirty cheeks and he clutched a training sword, before dropping it in defeat. Adelira expected the King to spout some curt command for him to toughen up. Instead, the King lifted a hand and brushed the tears from the boy's face.

Adelira straightened, startled, fingers tightening around the stone as she rested her head against the cool surface.

She couldn't hear what was said from this height, but whatever it was, the boy sniffled, nodded, then *smiled.* A moment later, he even *laughed*. The King flashed a grin, tapping his fist lightly to the child's jaw before reaching down and retrieving the fallen sword from the dirt. He placed it back into the boy's hands and rose to his full height, nodding for the boy to continue.

The boy squared his shoulders and returned to the beginning stance.

Adelira stayed watching them move through several more forms. The King corrected the boy's stance, his hand firm but patient on small shoulder, then they moved through the forms together.

If she had ever believed tears were met with understanding in the Obsidian Keep, she certainly hadn't expected that understanding to come from the King of all people.

The sight of it stirred *hope.* The King was capable of this kindness. Then she felt frustrated that nothing she'd done warranted this tenderness from him.

Where was the man who had turned cold the moment her family left? Where was the untouchable warrior? Why did she only get those parts of him now?

He had pinned her to a wall and... *trembled*. He was being careful now.

She didn't just want the Blood King who would bring her enemies to their knees.

She wanted *this* side of him, too.

Finally, she moved back inside her chamber, avoiding detection, and letting the heavy curtains fall shut behind her.

Who was Orahn? Which version of him was real?

Carys' warning flared in her mind again, sharper this time.

The King expects me to be laced with treachery.

And worse, maybe since learning the Elder Celestite wouldn't be easy to use without the Blood Ritual, he trusted her even less. Like she and her family *had* set a trap for him.

When she had turned down Ashbourne she knew it had surprised Orahn but that wasn't enough to let go of suspicion.

If she wanted this to work, if she wanted any kind of understanding between them, she had to change that. She *wanted* to change that.

29

Chapter Twenty-Nine

Adelira was summoned to see the Vampire King.

Her escort deposited her at the arena where he was the last man still training. A few nights ago she'd have been scared walking here, but she'd seen him show kindness to the child, and he had shown kindness to her in the past, too.

The King didn't stop when she entered. Sweat gleamed across his bare chest, his fists driving into the post, each strike fuelled by rage.

Adelira stepped as close as she dared. He was captivating from her balcony. Up close like this, his duality was startling. He looked like wrath and mercy all at once. His long black hair fell free of his warrior's braids, but he didn't move to sweep it back.

"The Blood Ritual," he said between strikes. *Thud. Crack.* "Know what you're walking into."

Thud.

"It's not a pact."

Thud.

"Not a trade."

Thud.

"It's a chain."

Thud.

"You'd belong to me."

Crack.

The wood splintered down the middle, but the thick pole stayed upright. A drop of his sweat hit the dirt.

"If I hurt, so will you. If you suffer, I'll feel it. Not a metaphor. Not poetry. Magic."

He finally turned to face her. His chest rose and fell like he'd come from battle. Skin flushed, eyes honed and turbulent. His knuckles raw, there were day-old bruises fanning along his ribs from an earlier training session. He looked like he was shaped by pain and it was the only thing he trusted not to pretend to be something it wasn't.

She tried to drag her eyes up, imagined kissing that bruise, trailing kisses up his chest, up his neck...

Her eyes lifted to his and the dark look he fixed her with, reminded her to pay attention to what he was saying and not how gorgeous his body was.

Once he stopped hitting the post, The silence hung in the yard and in that quiet, she felt shameful anger at how he left her wanting.

"It weakens you if my people are harmed," Adelira paused. "Magically?"

He didn't flinch when he answered, "Yes. Painfully. It turns against me. My mind, my body. And by extension, you'd feel that, too."

The horror of that answer flashed across her eyes. He almost grinned when he saw it in her face.

"You wanted a binding oath," he said, walking toward her. He didn't stop until they were close enough to share breath. "This is as binding as it gets."

She hadn't expected the heat between them to feel like temptation. For all the coldness he had shown her lately, she shouldn't have wanted this. But she'd had his body against her before. She wanted that again now, *without* the shirt this time.

He smelled like frost and smoke. She felt a little off balance and bit her lip.

His eyes fell to her lips. "Do you still want it?"

She wasn't so sure they were talking about only the Ritual anymore.

"Yes. This is, well, great, actually," she said, a little breathless. "It's everything I wanted."

His expression barely shifted, but she saw the flicker of surprise in his eyes, the hint of a fallen smile on his lips. Her relief looked like failure reflected back in his eyes, but she couldn't understand how her reaction had landed like a blow he didn't know how to block.

"... Great?" he asked, his voice thinner, not quite a whisper.

"This ensures my people are protected," she said.

Her voice was steady. Her pulse wasn't. He could hear it. *Feel it*, close as he was. He brushed back his long hair with a rough hand.

Adelira tucked a loose strand of hair behind her ear. He tracked the motion like he couldn't decide if it was nervous or calculated.

He said, his voice low. "It's painful."

She thought of the angry bruise on his ribs.

"I can take it," she said and he inhaled sharply before he huffed something like a laugh, but it didn't reach his eyes.

"You'd feel everything," he pointed out, his dark damp hair falling free across his face again.

She wanted to touch his bruises, his ribs, his chest. She wasn't afraid of the pain, being a part of it — of *him* — thrilled her.

When he spoke this close to her, his deep voice vibrated in her chest and there was a flutter inside her. She reminded herself who he was the last few nights, but she also remembered who he was when he smiled at her, held her hand, pressed her against the wall, his hand softly in her hair.

"I'd feel you," she said, her hand raising slightly between them.

The tips of her fingers brushed along his ribs. His breath hitched; sharp and involuntary. She froze, every nerve in her body alive with the sound. His skin was hot beneath her trembling hand and for one reckless moment, she wanted her lips pressed there instead.

He suppressed a shiver and she withdrew her hand, but not before she felt his body tense, like maybe he wasn't expecting it, or bracing because he wanted more. He looked at her like her touch could cut him deeper than any blade here.

"You'd feel this," he corrected as he lifted his own hand between them. His knuckles were cracked and bleeding, skin split raw.

She stared, eyes lingering over his large hand and the new bruise forming under the split knuckle in the middle. Gently, brushing her fingers near the blood, but not quite touching, she didn't want to hurt him.

"Every strike," he added pointedly. "Every break."

"I am asking you to bleed for my people. If I could take all the pain alone I would, but that's not how it works." Her gaze flicked to his eyes. "We feel it together. At least you don't have to carry it alone."

He stared at her as if she'd said something impossible. He blinked, just once. A muscle in his jaw ticked.

"Don't," he said quietly, pulling back his hand, curling his fist and causing fresh blood to drip from the wound. "Don't make this noble. It's not."

He watched her carefully, his breathing drawing slower, like he was trying to hold his breath and then she remembered her scent was difficult for him. She was too close, her blood too tempting. And she couldn't bring herself to move away.

Adelira said, "Pain is a fair price for the safety of my people. If you're still willing, I'd like to go ahead with it... When you feel more ready. I understand why you don't want to rush it though. It's not just magic, it's terrifying."

He almost smirked. It was almost enough to hide the fear. "I'm not scared."

He chuckled, a low amused sound and he unclenched his fists like the idea of fear was beneath him. Though his eyes flashed with anger like she had *insulted* him. "I don't even fear death."

He had met with death ten thousand times or more, and walked away each time.

"That's not even the scary part," he said, "but if that's where you've chosen to place your focus, what about you then? Aren't you scared of your own death?"

Her brows knitted in confusion. She wasn't sure which part was supposed to scare her then. Though death didn't sound fun, she wasn't sure how *she* could trigger that from the blood bond.

"That would happen, if you betrayed me," he pointed out.

He'd always be looking for that hidden blade from her. She looked up into his dark eyes, her exhale a whisper along his jaw and his fists slowly curled closed again. But he didn't step back.

She thought for a moment. She didn't know when certainty shifted into her bones. Her voice dropped to a whisper meant only for him.

"I'd never move against you," Adelira said softly and his expression faltered. "If you're keeping my people safe, my heart would always be grateful to you... no magic needed."

He looked at her like he was about to kiss her. Or cast her from his Kingdom. He didn't do either. Just breathed her in... and stepped away like it cost him.

He pulled all the way back. She felt the empty space between them like a wound, and let him go anyway.

His eyes flashed with obvious surprise at her words and then hardened into something she couldn't read, that he *wouldn't* let her read.

He shook his head, he nearly said something.

"Orahn?" she called out to him softly.

"What?"

"Thank you."

He blinked in surprise. "For what?"

"For explaining it to me."

He opened his mouth, then closed it again. His jaw ticked. Something passed through his eyes. Grief, maybe? Disbelief? Then, he smiled bitterly.

He turned sharply, pivoted on his heel, and drove his foot into the wooden post. It shattered with a sharp crack, collapsing like bone.

"Sure thing, Princess," he said.

30

Chapter Thirty

Drinking her tea, spiced black tea with just enough honey to stomach the knowledge that he was putting her to sleep with these concoctions, Adelira willed it to work. If she didn't see the sunlight, she couldn't be tempted to follow it home.

She woke, as the sun was setting, before the castle itself had even woken up for evenfall.

If she wanted to belong here, she had to stop waiting for permission. If she wanted trust, it required action, not hiding in her room.

The nights were hers now. She would claim them or she would never belong.

Opening her door, she walked down the corridors, mostly empty, save for a guard stationed along the wall every few meters or so. They stiffened as she walked by, hands curled tight at their sides, but they did not move.

Somehow, she felt watched again, in the back of her head and out of view.

Adelira turned the corner, nearly colliding with Orahn.

Taking a single step back, he neatly avoided their collision. He stood just inside the shadowed corridor, arms folded loosely across his chest and his eyes lifted to her face, his expression almost relieved.

"Ah, you're here," Orahn said smoothly as he stepped closer again, extending a letter towards her. The green wax seal was unmistakable Elven. "I was on my way to find you."

"You were coming to see me..." Her gaze turned down to his hands. "... With news from the Elves?"

"The borders have been secured. I assume your father wanted you to know."

"That's good news. Your army did well. Thank you."

Pulling a second letter from inside his cloak, smaller and sealed with a familiar emblem, he handed it over. "And I believe this to be from Carys."

"Oh, thank goodness." Adelira eagerly reached out for the letters.

Their fingers brushed, the touch was electric. It wasn't the hunger that burned between them last night, this was quieter. She didn't mistake quiet for less dangerous. Looking down at her, he didn't smile, but it shone in his eyes. The chill of the Fealty Ceremony and Court of Shadow nights frayed like a nightmare slipping away and this was the real him.

Adelira had prepared herself for whichever version of him she might find tonight, the smirking charmer, the cold statue, the restless force of war.

When she saw him, standing tall with quiet certainty, there was no arrogance or impatience in his stance; only warmth.

Maybe there was a subtle hunger beneath the surface, but for the way his restraint obeyed his authority, she almost reached for his hunger as eagerly as his kindness.

There was no game being played behind them now, no flicker of amusement at her confusion. No walls of detachment. Almost like, for this moment, he wasn't the King, at all. He was simply Orahn.

With a faint, almost imperceptible smirk, Orahn said, "Would've had more flare delivered with a Nightjar, I admit."

Adelira allowed herself a smile.

Before she could say more, he added quietly, not meeting her eyes, "I wasn't sure if you'd want to see me. I–After everything..." His fists curled at his side and he slowly forced his hands open again. "But I thought you'd want to hear from them."

Breath slipped from her lips. This Orahn was like standing in sunlight after a long storm.

"I want..." she started and then stopped herself.

Orahn studied her for a moment, his gaze trailing over her face as if seeing something he hadn't noticed when he first bumped into her.

He reached out as he asked, "Why are you here?"

His hand found her arm and she was cold to the touch. She shivered. Smoothly, he slipped off his cape and wrapped it around her shoulders, clasping it at the collar so it held. The scent of his coat carried forest frost and whisky. She pulled his cloak up to her face, her eyes closing briefly, her body remembering him pressed close.

Why was he so gentle, when these last few nights were all cold control, lessons and silences?

Her throat tightened. "Orahn..."

He inclined his head slightly, waiting. "Are you alright, Lira?"

She paused, no one had asked her that since she arrived. Tharth was strange and he was unpredictable. She wasn't okay, but that felt too heavy to hand to him. She looked for what else she could give him instead.

There were so many things she wanted to say. That she *hated* when he was cold and distant. That she *lived* for the nights when he looked at her like this, when he *remembered* her and it kindled something warm between them. That she was afraid of being alone in this castle, but the idea of being among Vampires frightened her just as much.

All she managed was, "I don't know."

His eyes softened further and he reached for her.

This was the man she remembered, but memories could be liars. Could warmth mean anything from a man made of so many masks?

She took his hand.

It had been so long since someone had touched her without consequence. Without pain or locking their eyes to the ground.

"I'm new to politics, but not life. Somehow, even my experience hasn't prepared me. My years mean nothing here. And—" Suddenly, she felt angry.

"Do you feel accused," he asked quietly, "for not being what this place expects?"

"Sometimes. No. I—" she stopped in frustration. "I feel out of my depth."

"We are immortals from two incompatible civilisations."

"Maybe a Blood Ritual will force compatibility," she said, quietly, hopefully, the thought slipping out before she could catch it.

He frowned. "Do you ever regret not taking Ashbourne up on their offer?"

She gasped and snapped her gaze up at him. "*No!* No, of course not."

"Fortunate for me, then," he said, looking away.

"I just... I don't know, Orahn."

He said softly, soothingly, "You have done well. You've stayed standing in a place designed to unsettle. That says more than certainty ever could."

Her hand tightened around his arm, she didn't think he'd understand what this week had cost her, but listening to him, she could almost let herself believe he did.

"I'm..." she tried, swallowed and then tried again, "I'll be alright, it was the Fealty Ceremony and Court of Shadows, it takes getting used to."

"It does," he agreed.

She felt watched again. The weight of invisible eyes pressed against her back, but she didn't bother to turn around. She knew she wouldn't see anything there.

"When I was younger, I found the Blood Court intimidating," he admitted.

She glanced up at him. Had the Vampire King really admitted to feeling anything other than composed and in complete control always?

"I imagine the experience was similar for you," he said. "There's much to get used to, for everyone, myself included. I'm sure you can see how difficult this transition is for my court."

"I know I'm making things difficult," she could hear the apology dripping off her words even though it wasn't logical, it wasn't truly her fault.

"It shouldn't fall on you to keep them in control," he added even quieter now, but his muscles tensed, she felt it through his arm and strain in his voice. "That's my responsibility. I don't like to admit when I've underprepared, but I suppose I'd rather admit it now so you can understand the impact than keep it secret, and you discover it in an unkind way."

"Unkind?" she asked, her stomach churning as she imagined the worst.

He didn't ease her fears by denying her worst assumption, instead he continued, "I'd prefer to take you to your room. My Vampires can only be tested so much in one night. Your blood is constantly tempting them."

"And does it... Does my blood still test you?" she asked tentatively. "Or have you grown used to me?"

His gaze darkened and he didn't answer for a heartbeat.

"Even now, you test me," he said in a rough whisper.

His pupils dilated with instinct he blinked away. He was fighting the instinct to kill her and the instinct not to trust her, and somewhere in the middle existed a space where he was trying. She understood then that his gentleness was a choice, not a promise.

"Will the effect fade?"

"I don't think I'll ever not hear your blood's song."

Adelira felt the hopelessness of her situation, unsure of how to help him. How could she win on both those fronts? The closer she was for him to learn to trust her, the harder she made it for him to control his bloodlust.

For all the effort she made to be harmless, her blood was undoing that diplomacy.

"Your personal guards have arrived at the Obsidian Keep. I'll send them up shortly," he explained. "They'll be stationed by your door, ready to go with you anywhere you would like to go."

Go? She thought wistfully. She'd be allowed to go places. She listened, even though the thought of having guards shadow her made her heart ache for Talion; a shadow she had openly cared for and still fought to escape.

"Thank you," she murmured.

When she stepped into her room, Orahn followed.

He stepped in like the dusk escorted him.

Turning, startled he was in her space, her hand flew over her chest like she might quieten the way her heart jumped.

He crossed the polished floors, crouching before her hearth and placing another log inside, stoking the fire back to roaring life. The muscles in his arms worked and the image of him breaking the wooden pole sprung into her mind.

"There, that should keep the chill out," he murmured as he rose slowly and walked back across her room towards her.

"Thank you," she said, looking up at him as he came to a stop before her.

He had never done that before tonight; come inside this far.

But then *he could have,* weeks ago when she had given him permission. Until now, he had never acted on it.

The room had been too big before. Now it shrunk down to a size that was comforting.

"Oh, your cape," she said, reaching for the clasp.

"Keep it. I like the thought of you wearing my clothes," he said.

Her lips parted in surprise and suddenly the cape around her shoulders felt more intimate than it had a minute ago. Colour rose in her cheeks. His smile softened as he watched her settle into his cape.

He glanced around her room briefly, taking it all in. The lingering scent of parchment from the worn book left open on the small table, the candle she had let burn too low, her pebble and violin.

Then, his eyes found hers again, unreadable even in the glowing light.

His fingers brushed against hers in a fleeting touch.

"You're not alone here, Lira, even if it feels that way, sometimes."

And then, just as easily as he had entered, he turned and walked out.

31

Chapter Thirty-One

Adelira slipped out onto her balcony, breathing in the cool night air.

Hearty laughter rose up to meet her.

She leaned as far as she dared over the railing and saw the King in the courtyard. He'd already replaced the cape with a new one. He was with a few guards, they sat along a wall, legs dangling and a drink in their hands and they were... laughing. His head rolled back in amusement at some ridiculous story one of the guards animatedly shared.

His laugh rolled in like the warmth that follows the winter months, a sound she'd now look for in every corner of Tharth.

The King was only a man here, exhausted, stealing a moment of joy among his own people. All the smiles he offered her were never this unguarded. She was tired of sitting outside and looking in.

The guards and the King dropped off the wall, heading inside.

She stayed there longer than she should have, letting the sound of his laughter echo in her chest like a call she wanted to follow through the castle.

The guards arrived at her door without him and without a sound. The camaraderie she had witnessed moments ago didn't extend to her.

She turned to them anyway. "Hello."

They nodded curtly. The spell of the evening broke, just like that.

They asked for permission to enter her room which she granted, but they never stepped inside. *A formality only*, they clarified. In case she ever needed them.

Their clothing was heavily armoured, though she could only tell this because Orahn had pointed it out.

"What are your names?" Adelira asked.

They didn't answer immediately.

"I won't have nameless shadows following me everywhere. If you insist on staying by my side, I insist on knowing who you are," she said firmly.

"I'm Benedict," said the elder of the two men.

"Finn," the other Vampire replied.

"Thank you, Benedict, Finn."

Benedict stood closest to her. His voice carried an undercurrent of old-world authority. His silver-threaded hair was pulled back into a soldier's knot.

Finn was the quiet tension of a soldier younger by decades, but no less deadly. He stationed himself at the wall, he'd checked everything twice before settling.

She looked at them and missed all of the warmth of Talion.

They weren't here for her, they were extensions of Orahn's shadow and will. The memory of the King's laughter still clung to their silence, teasing her with everything she could not have.

"Can we go for a walk?" she asked.

Finn's eyes glinted before he caught Benedict's stern gaze and cast his gaze down.

Her grey eyes still gleamed with hope, even as Benedict's eyes narrowed on her. She almost added a 'please' but that felt too much like begging.

Benedict shifted uncomfortably before saying, "It's best if you remain in your chambers until the King is free to escort you."

He didn't say more. Her guards didn't agree and the only reason she could imagine was that the King had told them something very different to what he had assured her.

Her gut twisted, her smile falling from her face. This cage was well guarded now.

She didn't want a tower. She didn't only want a war hero. She wanted laughter.

Her shoulders dropped as she returned into her chambers alone. She picked up her pebble next to her bed, willing herself to remember who she was outside of these walls.

From inside these walls, she had no way of proving herself to close the distance between them.

If she wanted him to *believe* her, she would have to leave her room again. If the guards were an extension of Orahn, could she get close to them and earn his trust that way?

She doubted they liked sourdough or climbing trees, but that glint in Finn's eye was promising. She knew mischief when she saw it.

32

Chapter Thirty-Two

Adelira took a sip of her tea and blinked.

Strange, Orahn never got her tea wrong.

She set the cup down, hoping for sleep that would not come, and paced her chambers until sundown.

She opened her door and her guards squared their shoulders, standing at attention. Benedict didn't turn to her, but she saw Finn tilt his head towards her ever so subtly, like he was waiting for her next move.

"Hello, Finn, Benedict," she greeted them.

Benedict nodded, Finn only watched her.

"I'm going to the dining hall tonight," she told them.

Stepping out of the room, she walked towards the hall. They followed soundlessly.

The Keep was dim in the evenings, lit only by the sconces evenly spaced apart down the hall and moonlight. The other guards stationed along the wall still reacted when she passed, but Benedict and Finn gave each a pointed look, and they seemed to relax in the knowledge that someone else was keeping her boundary safe.

"It took me almost two weeks to travel here from Ebedene," she said as she walked. "Though I think we moved slower with a bigger travelling party."

They moved no closer, but she knew she had their attention.

"It took you a bit longer than that," Adelira went on. "Tharth is very big, but you must have been on the opposite end. I hope the journey wasn't too taxing for you."

They didn't respond.

Eventually they'd thaw, her guards always did. She had done the same for Rayno when he first arrived and she'd done it for Carys, too. She would do it again now.

"I know the language," she continued, "But I'm afraid we aren't taught much else about your Kingdom."

Boots clicked behind her, a familiar sound.

"Perhaps we can find a map and see what Tharth looks like."

They didn't respond.

"That way, we can stay inside where it's safe, but I'll still understand the world around me a little better."

While she spoke, she listened to their footsteps soften out of duty and into attentiveness, honed towards the cadence of her words.

Another voice boomed through the halls. They stiffened at the sound, duty locking back into place.

Somewhere deeper in the castle, muffled voices rose and fell; sharp and commanding, like metal meeting stone. Her pace slowed. That voice was familiar and too charged to ignore.

The castle was quiet enough to carry the voices when she passed by the open doors of the war room. *His* voice drew her in and unsettled her all at once.

The King paced restlessly around the room. Brimming with energy that crackled around him, just like how he had looked when he crossed the Court of Shadows to stop the Vampires fighting. He wore his cloak like a statement, throwing it back with a flick of his wrist.

"The border skirmishes have doubled in the past month," he said sharply with irritation. "We should attack, not waste time reinforcing our defences just waiting for an ambitious Blood House to act first."

"I can take the Blackguard," Victoria said.

"I need you here. The Keep is just as unsettled. We know what they are upset about. And now they are testing us, because they think we are too busy with Shifters."

The space shrank around him. It was not a small room, holding the Elven party and war generals previously.

Now, he stood in the room with only general Victoria. It was just them, and the room could barely contain the King.

He spun suddenly, catching her watching. His eyes flashed with frustration. But then, as quickly as it appeared, it was gone.

Adelira stepped back, but she backed up into Finn and made a small jump forward again. The general and the King were watching her. Her cheeks warmed.

He looked at her longer before asking, "What is it?"

She didn't know how to answer.

He moved to close the door on her.

The guards started for the dining hall again. She lowered her head and followed them.

She couldn't understand how the man who stepped through her door last night was the same man who'd closed his door tonight.

The hall was filled with more food than one person could eat, the table stretched with various platters. She sat in the room and ate, kept there by reason somewhere between not wanting to let all this food go to waste and not wanting to return to her solitude too soon.

Finally, the food was cold and her statue-still servers were growing restless. A twist of a finger here, shifting of weight from one foot to the other. It was nothing overt, nothing that should have drawn attention to it, but Adelira noticed. And as soon as she noticed, she could trap them in their stations no longer.

She thanked them for the meal and rose to leave.

As she walked back down the hall, her guards followed. She still felt watched by something else, but the sensation was softened by the figures trailing behind her and she could almost trick her mind into believing they were the ones responsible for it.

Last time she left her room, she got Orahn to come back with her. She had managed to get him to come inside. There was no chance of that happening tonight. Maybe leaving had been the way to get him to notice her last night. But tonight, he had noticed her and for all the wrong reasons.

If she didn't need the Blood Ritual so much, then she'd almost ignore him entirely and simply explore her new home. But going too far kept triggering the pleading look on Talion's face to flare in her mind. She had to keep herself safe too, because that kept her people safe. She couldn't be reckless with herself anymore.

She rounded the corner in the corridor and came face to face with *him*.

The King was leaning against a stone pillar. One ankle hooked over the other and his arms folded over his chest. His eyes roved over her. A slow and assessing gaze that lingered too long on her curves.

The kind of heat in his gaze that made her want to jump into rivers with him and chase that wildness to the ends of the earth. The thrill behind his eyes teased at the restless parts of her soul. Wanting to know what secret hid behind those gorgeous dark lashes, he was a call to action and she had to will herself not to answer.

"You looked lovely tonight," he said smoothly, his voice a deep, rich sound. "I was surprised to see you."

Adelira hesitated as her mind screamed at her to remember that Vampires couldn't be trusted.

When he stood close like this, she could smell the forests and the frost and the fires that burned them down.

"You're... in a good mood," she said carefully.

His smirk widened. "Am I not always?"

No... No, he wasn't.

"You're always someone different," she said quietly, not looking at him.

There was tightness in his voice as he said, "Don't mistake who I am in the dark for who I must be in the light."

But before she was able to respond, he stepped past her.

He was again changing, so different from the Fealty Ceremony, or from last night in her room. Maybe not different from the Shadows of Court night, he seemed just as explosive tonight as he had been *that* night. But she couldn't quite keep up. Even her tea was changing now, too.

She should let him go, this wasn't a night for easy conversation. Before she could stop herself, she spoke.

"The tea you had brought me this morning," she called after him.

It highlighted a flaw that kept tripping up her evening. So much had been designed to be flawless, but the effort kept rupturing under its own strain.

He didn't stop, but he slowed his departure.

She continued, "The tea wasn't the same as usual."

He didn't turn back, calling over his shoulder, "You always take honey in your tea. That was what was given to you."

She tilted her head, expression thoughtful. "Well, no, not always. I don't take it in lavender tea. Only the spiced black tea."

That made him skip a step. Just for a moment, before he caught his footing. Just long enough for her to notice. Then he continued walking down the corridor without another word.

He'd never gotten it wrong before. She always sweetened spice, but never florals. He was often so careful. So calculated.

And yet, the act wasn't always perfect. There was something... just not quite aligning.

∞

The next night, she did the same thing; going out of her room, insisting on going to dinner, but asked them to make a suitable amount of food for one person.

Adelira stepped beyond her chamber, past the threshold where she had been expected to remain. Her guards stationed at her door watched her, more a warning than a leash.

"There's a chill in the air tonight, the seasons are changing," she murmured. "But we're going into summer, shouldn't it be warmer?"

After a long time, Finn said, "Rainy season."

Benedict fixed him with a sharp look and Finn swiftly glanced away.

She smiled, at least he answered, even if the seasons made no sense to her here. People made sense to her and slowly, slowly, she was thawing Finn, and in time, Benedict would follow.

They walked slowly down the corridor, Benedict and Finn remaining a respectful distance somewhere far behind her.

She paused outside a black and gold door that caught her attention.

She stopped to look at the design when a familiar voice from the other side of the door took her by surprise. Orahn was inside talking with... someone... No, not someone else... talking to... *himself*?

As her guards neared, only silence remained behind the door.

She shook her head and walked on, finally stopping by the war room. It seemed as though it had snapped back to its original size, no longer stretched out by the King.

It was so quiet inside, she thought it was empty.

But then a shadow moving made her look again.

Didn't she just hear the King inside the gold and black doors? She *had* heard Orahn.

Could he really move that impossibly fast?

Just like when she'd seen him in the battleyard with her parents and then at her door just moments later. Could she ask her guards how fast a Vampire moved? She didn't think they would answer that.

The sconces cast light over the Vampire King's form as he stood by the shelves, flipping absently through a book.

That's definitely him, she thought as she watched. So, he really wasn't in that other room after all...

The King didn't acknowledge her right away. He didn't turn when she stood in his doorway as she had last night, though she knew he sensed her there. Maybe she could have snuck by undetected, but both her and the guards together could not pass unnoticed.

She expected the air to shift, for his presence to flood the room as it had the night before. Instead... nothing.

The way he carried himself tonight was different from last night. Pensive, like light rainfall in the evening. Gone was the smooth arrogance, the knowing smirk. The room smelled like the frost forests mixed with ink and parchment, like a library filled with old books and living trees.

"You're quiet tonight," she said tentatively.

He exhaled slowly, not looking up, but he didn't sound surprised to hear her voice. "There's much to think about."

His voice was low, subdued.

"Orahn... Are my people okay?" she asked.

He half looked at her as he murmured, "I've heard nothing to the contrary."

"Oh... Thank you."

She wanted to say something else, something to pull at whatever he was keeping locked away, but he shut the book in his hands and turned toward the window, his back to her.

She saw an entirely different side of him then. A quiet sadness in the way he kept her, and everyone, at a distance.

"Would you join me for dinner?" she asked.

His shoulders tensed, his hand moving to the glass of the window as he peered out, avoiding her gaze. "Not tonight, Adelira."

She had the overwhelming urge to reach out, to pull him back from the canyon he kept between himself and the world. He didn't know how to trust her and she had heard the silent plea for her to leave. She would always do that when asked.

Her fingers hovered at the door frame, then fell away. "Goodnight."

Dinner was quiet as usual, but when she retraced her steps, the war room was empty. The King was gone.

Adelira made her way back to her chamber. Something caught her eye, like the section of the wall near the court that had drawn her towards it. A subtle break in the stone wall, a faint outline where no door should be.

She reached out to touch it.

"Don't—" Finn started but she'd already done it.

She pulled her hand back in surprise as the stones shifted at her touch. A hidden passage opened with a whisper of air.

She moved to step inside the long dark tunnel.

"Wait," Finn said sharply. His hand above her shoulder, but he never touched her.

She looked back at him, his gaze fixed on the darkness beyond.

Immediately, he retracted his hand and circled around her to go into the unknown first. He was stopped mid-stride by no force visible to any of them. He frowned, brow furrowing as he pressed forward, but it held him in place.

"That's strange," Finn muttered, turning to Benedict. "It's like I need permission..."

"To walk into a passage?" Benedict asked as he tried to put his arm through and found himself blocked as well.

"A passage isn't a room. Only private rooms need permission from the owner to enter, right?" Adelira glanced between them as she repeated what Orahn had told her. "Who could place a restriction like that?"

Her guards exchanged wary looks, but said nothing.

She gave them a thoughtful look. "I'll go alone."

"We cannot allow that," Benedict said abruptly.

"I'll be quick. There and back before you know it," she offered.

Benedict looked over the door again. "It could be dangerous."

"We don't know what's inside," Finn explained.

"Exactly," she said with a grin, but neither of them returned it.

There was that almost-glint in Finn's eyes, like he wanted to understand the mystery too, but he buried and said, "Not without us."

The draft coming from the tunnels was cold, suggesting a labyrinth behind the walls.

She thought about running past them. She only had to make it in and then they wouldn't be able to get her.

Then, she could explore the secrets that Tharth didn't want her to find.

But as she always did before she ran now, she thought of Talion standing out there on the other side pleading for her to stay where Benedict and Finn could do their jobs and not to make their lives harder for something as childish as adventuring.

Reluctantly, she let her fingers slip from the doorway. The stone shifted back into place, sealing the passage as if it had never existed.

"Alright, Finn, Benedict," she said softly. "No running away."

33

Chapter Thirty-Three

Crates of silks, wines and spices were passed along the courtyard as dozens of merchants unloaded their wares into the castle's reserves.

The guards were reluctant to let Adelira go since the courtyard was teeming with Vampires. But she spotted the King down there and they had to agree then that no one would lose control around him.

Orahn stood near a wagon speaking with a foreign trader and the diplomats who had travelled alongside them. His smile charming, posture relaxed, winning over diplomats was as easy for him as he made his training in the battleyard look, chatting freely and mixing in well-timed laughter.

Every diplomat felt as though they had won, even as the King walked away the true victor.

The crowd drew in and people gathered around him. He persuaded them to stay longer than they intended to, every 'I should get going' was met with 'Stay a little longer' and a reluctantly smiling 'Oh alright.'

Somehow he managed to get everyone to go down in price lower than they wanted to. All the while, everyone felt like they'd gained something.

Then again, they had won something.

Most people got a version of the Blood King who was ruthless and dismissive of everyone in his path. He was that person at least two thirds of the time, like the rarity of his good moods were wielded strategically for moments like this. Sometimes people got a King who was utterly charming and that felt like they were chosen *personally* by him.

She wanted his laughter too. She just didn't want to be manipulated to receive it. Watching him, she could see it clearly, but when he turned his light on her, she found herself forgetting how easily he tricked the people around him and she fell for the spell, too.

As if sensing her watching him, Orahn turned.

A broad smile on his face as his eyes locked with hers. He motioned her over. Her own guards fell away.

Adelira hesitated before she joined him. She didn't want the spell, she wanted *him*, she just didn't know how to reach the *true* him.

His hand moved to the small of her back as he drew her forward to introduce her to a man who had a family business in potions made from plants they grew in the northern mountain ranges.

The man greeted her and excused himself to finish unloading his stock. He moved too quickly, he almost didn't breathe. She guessed what no one was saying, that the Vampires outside of the Obsidian Keep seemed to have less control around her than the people of the court.

Striding towards them was another man who didn't slow his approach. Suddenly, his arms wrapped around the King's large frame and Orahn let out a low chuckle, returning the firm embrace.

Adelira blinked in surprise as she watched the King hug the man.

No one had touched the King since she had arrived.

But this familiarity and trust twisted in her before she could understand it.

Warmth between them or the unspoken exchange that flashed in their eyes. The murmurs that passed from lips to ears were too intimate, like they shared something from a time before her arrival.

The King released him, stepping back and introducing the two of them.

The man's gaze slid to her, the smallest flicker of sadness there, before he smiled and greeted her.

"I'd like you to meet Princess Adelira. And Lira, this is Tadgh. He's the diplomat for the Northern Ragnye."

"Hello Tadgh, nice to meet you," she greeted somewhat distractedly.

This time her mind wasn't tripping over Tadgh and their close familiarity with each other. She was tripped up by the fact that Orahn had used his nickname for her. He didn't always use it, but there seemed to be a pattern just on the tip of her tongue that she couldn't quite place.

Lira... Only sometimes... What did it mean?

Tadgh smiled at her and gave a bow before grabbing Orahn's shoulder and giving it a light squeeze. "It's good to see you again."

"You too. Next time, don't wait three years before visiting," Orahn said. And then Tadgh was gone, vanished into the crowd of merchants and staff moving goods in organised chaos across the courtyard.

"You two seem close," Adelira said softly.

"We were," Orahn said, turning to review a list handed to him by a tradesman, nodded once and the man moved away again.

Orahn didn't say anything more about Tadgh, instead his attention drifted back to Adelira and he began to point out other people of note and various goods as they passed.

"They've travelled all over Tharth, some even further than that, to bring what's left to the Obsidian Keep," Orahn said.

Wheels turned over stone as more carts as trinkets and valuables arrived.

"Does some of it make it to the city?" she murmured as she took in the busy activity around them.

He chuckled. "This is what is left after they've given supplies throughout the Kingdom first."

"Everyone else gets it *first*? That's... Unexpected," she said softly, like choosing to close the Rip permanently instead of slaughtering all the enemies within.

So many things about the Vampire King defied what she had been led to believe. He was unpredictable and harsh, but beneath that was a level of fairness no one in Ebedene could have imagined.

"What were you expecting?"

She bit her lip, unsure how to answer.

"A monster?" he guessed.

Her eyes shot up to his face, his smile was teasing. "N–No."

"Taking what I want first isn't a mark of my true strength. My Kingdom will feel my discipline when they see that I can wait."

"Can you wait?"

"Longer than you could imagine," he whispered, his breath along her neck.

Suddenly, she wanted her Blood Ritual *now*. She almost asked for it again, but he was talking again.

"I won't be ruled by my desires. How could anyone trust me to rule them if I follow something so fickle as wanting? No, that would make a weak King."

"Weak?"

"Indulgence makes for an easy weakness to exploit," he said.

"I think the people appreciate the consideration," she said.

"They probably do."

"It's more than consideration though."

"If someone could dangle a treasure in front of me knowing I'd bend to their will, I'd hardly be a King worth keeping," he admitted. "Then, the next time I walked through the Blood Rooms, I might be covered in jewels, but there'd also be daggers in my back."

She'd almost forgotten how vicious they were.

A large cat on a jeweled collar walked by, its leash held by a woman who looked more lethal than the panther. She didn't look at them, but the cat's big green eyes turned to Adelira and she stepped closer to Orahn. Big feet padded along the ground and it yawned, long canines gleaming in the moonlight.

"Talk me through what I'm seeing," she said.

"Of course," he said with an obliging smile.

Orahn spent a few more hours talking to her about the trade Tharth has going for it and the various families involved and when they expect shipments. How the fae pirates were occasionally a menace. How they navigated getting their wares home safely.

Most was managed by House Marquis, but they outsourced to a lot of smaller Houses, too, and they had networks and tradesmen set up through Tharth and into the surrounding Kingdoms. House Cazimer ensured the routes were kept safe and House Crowe kept sharp intel on all the dealings.

He spoke passionately. His light touches drew her gaze towards different collections while he showed her around.

As she listened, it occurred to her that this was the *third* night... That's why Orahn was talking to her.

No, that still didn't explain *why* he was talking to her, only that she noticed a pattern that tried to explain it.

Oh, gods, what did it mean? Her eyes widened as she looked at him.

The King only ever sought out her company every third night.

On those nights, he was at her side. He listened when she spoke, challenged her when she hesitated, and studied her with the quiet intensity of a man who enjoyed her company.

But then, the cycle would rotate, dependable as clockwork.

If she caught him in the corridors in-between-nights, his words were sharp. Or teasing, almost flirting. Or he'd simply *pass her by* as if she were no more than another fixture of the castle, almost as though they were nothing to each other, until that third night again.

34

Chapter Thirty-Four

The next night she saw the King only in passing, he walked with his generals, talking in quick commands. He didn't look at her, but as he passed, his fists clenched.

Her guards escorted her to her chambers and she drank the tea. Brushing out her hair and changing into a nightdress, she ran her finger over the pebble on her nightstand.

Just before dawn, she climbed into bed, the doziness seeping in and she stared up at the painted stars on her ceiling until her eyes fluttered closed.

A terrifying sound ripped her back into the land of the awake.

So loud that not even the laced tea could hold her in its midday slumber. Adelira bolted upright, breath catching in her throat, her heart hammering against her ribs.

A roar ripped through the sky like a dragon breaking free of iron chains.

The force shook the foundations of the Keep. The glass of windows quivered in their frames.

And then another boom sounded, closer this time, and a flicker of light shot through the gap in the drapes, lighting up her room in one brilliant sharp flash before vanishing again.

She leapt out of bed.

Barefoot, still tangled in the long folds of her nightgown, she shoved open the heavy doors. She tumbled out into the corridor, shutting the door as though she could lock the destruction outside.

She braced against the wall.

Her guards stood at attention just outside her chamber, their stillness broken only when they turned toward her in surprise.

Adelira pressed her back into the cold hard stone in the corridor, clutching her robe closed over her chest and breathing heavily.

A deep rolling crack rattled her bones like the palace itself had split open.

The eery castle corridors had its quiet interrupted by repeated clashes of thunder. So close, she wondered if the storm had somehow managed to climb inside the Keep.

One crack had barely finished before it swelled right back up again, rumbling as it grew and then it struck a sickening smack overhead.

Her body began to tremble.

The scent of fear clung to her; entirely too tempting. The guards shifted. Closing her eyes briefly, wishing the storm away, her attention was divided between the clouds outside and the Vampires sworn to protect her.

She didn't know which threat she was more afraid of.

Benedict tilted his head slightly, he was listening. *For the thunder? No... My pulse,* she realised in horror. The frantic rhythm of prey.

Finn's fingers twitched at his sides. The scent of fear was a rare saccharine sweetness that flirted with instincts to abandon discipline.

They didn't speak, but their tension was tangible. They wanted to soothe her. They just couldn't. They wouldn't move any closer.

She swallowed hard, forcing herself to breathe evenly, though it did little to slow the pulse thrumming beneath her skin.

"I–I..." She wanted to apologise, but she couldn't speak.

Then footsteps, measured and unhurried, came down the corridor.

She knew who it was before she even looked. The *King*.

His figure that stepped into view was dressed in black, the folds of his coat falling against his tall frame. His dark hair, unusually immaculate, without that slightly tousled look, as if he hadn't gone to bed yet. His cloak was draped as if putting on death itself. It didn't settle around him, it smothered all the light.

He walked as though the Keep belonged to him in a way that no one, not even the *daylight*, would ever dare challenge.

His assessing gaze flicked over the scene before him. Her, pale and shaken, barefoot in the corridor in her nightdress. The guards, tense but silent, standing just a little too still.

The King stopped before them.

In a low voice, thick with something, but she couldn't calm her pounding heart enough to make out what it was, he said, "There are no thunderstorms in Ebedene."

She swallowed, still pressing herself into the stone, as if the cold could ground her. Her pulse stuttered in her veins.

If only this had been tomorrow. A third-night cycle.

A time when the third night would have given her a kinder Orahn. Where she might have felt the warmth of his hand instead of the ice in his voice.

She dared to look up at him, her eyelashes heavy with panic.

His eyes almost softened.

The sky cracked apart above them and she jumped, snapping her eyes closed. The rumble rattled the door and she braced, waiting for it to pass.

Her guards braced harder, waiting for her fear to pass. Their muscles locking in place. The sound groaned and pulled back, disappearing before the next one was sure to come.

When she pried her eyes open again, the softness had retreated from the King's eyes.

"No… There are no storms in Ebedene," she said softly, though she knew it wasn't a question he'd asked.

She couldn't decide what terrified her more; the thunder, the silence, or the way none of them moved. She didn't know if she was safer outside in the storm or navigating the strange changes in the King, all while trying to keep out of the teeth of his Vampires.

The King studied her a moment longer.

His stare was sharp beneath the flickering torchlight, like he was cataloguing the shape of her fear. He looked at the guards as if assessing the depth of their bloodlust. He must not have felt it as deeply as she did, already moving away.

She told herself that she didn't need his kindness, but she still flinched when he left. She almost reached for him.

He called over his shoulder, "It's storm season in Tharth. You'd best get used to this."

With that, he continued down the corridor, his stride smooth and he didn't spare her another glance back.

Adelira exhaled a shaky breath and stood trapped between her fears.

Another roll of thunder vibrated through the stone walls, through her and her next breath caught again.

She couldn't move, but neither did her guards.

In that dim corridor, they listened to the storm rage, unsure of which would settle first; her heartbeat or the sky.

35

Chapter Thirty-Five

The next night, Orahn appeared confidently at her side, like he belonged in any place he stood.

She looked up at him.

His eyes only shifted down to her briefly before locking ahead and he said softly, “I have much to do tonight and I cannot stay, but I was hoping I could walk you to dinner. If you’ll let me?”

A small smile escaped as he offered her his arm.

A *third-night* version of Orahn. She released a quiet breath.

They walked in comfortable silence, like neither of them needed to say anything at that moment.

Once they made their way to the dining hall, he tilted his head warmly towards her and brushed his thumb over her hand before slipping away into the clutches of no less than half a dozen advisors who’d followed him there.

∞

Adelira sat at the long wooden table in one of the receiving halls, poring over a map of Tharth she had found.

The hall was quiet, save for the whisper of rain against the high windows. Shadows stretched long across the stone floor, flickering where the candlelight wavered in the wind's draft. The glass rattled as thunder rolled closer. There was another storm that had pulled in that evening and was growing stronger.

Adelira asked questions trying to focus on the map instead.

But her guards only exchanged looks, Benedict keeping Finn in silence.

The thunder crackled in the distance, closer each passing minute. Her hands began a slight tremble.

The few other people in the hall froze at the scent.

Her guards assessed the room, exchanging another weary look between them and then, finally, Benedict exhaled and answered her.

"The mountains surrounding Tharth are called the Fenoria Mountains," Benedict said.

She'd asked them to explain the map. At first, they resisted. But slowly, they seemed to realise that her fear made their job harder.

They began hesitantly still holding back, only speaking quickly and quietly, showing her where they lived, the route they travelled to get to the castle, but then with an expected wave of pride; the place they had their last battle.

"The mountains are broken into three parts," Finn added with reluctance, but since Benedict started, they might as well pass down accurate information.

"The outer ring is called the Veilspine, which can be seen from the North facing windows of the Keep. You would have travelled through the Hallow Peaks," Benedict pointed out the route through the forest covered mountains on the left side of the Keep.

Hallow Peaks, she mused, *somehow the name seemed to fit the innkeeper.*

"This side is called Daggerfell Cliffs and over the height of the mountain is a drop into the coast. The Scarlet Seas," Finn finished.

Finn leaned over the map and pointed along the range. When she tucked under for a closer look, tracing her finger along, his words stalled for a breath too long, just enough for her to glance up and see him holding his breath above her.

She slid back, withdrawing her hand and muttering an apology.

"We have a fortress on the coast, Waters Moot," Finn added, like he was looking for something to say.

"I've never been to the coast, Ebedene is too far inland," she said.

"That's Ivers Pass," Benedict said, pointing to the mountain pass to the sea. "Where Daggerfell Cliffs curve around the city and meet at this point with the Veilspine."

"And here," Finn pointed out, looking up at Benedict with a sly smile.

Benedict traced a path along the map, his voice taking on that unmistakable ring of satisfaction. "We fought our last battle here."

Finn nodded. "Took us three days to push them back."

Adelira loved these moments, when people forgot themselves and simply shared. There was something about the way their eyes burned a little brighter; it made their lives feel tangible, their history something she could reach out and touch.

Rain lashed against the high windows. She curled her shoulders inwards a little. The wind howled through the stone corridors, a low, mournful sound. The candlelight danced.

She tentatively traced the route with a finger. "And you won?"

Finn smirked. "Obviously."

Benedict shot him a stern look, but didn't argue.

Adelira smiled. She liked this. This small slip of camaraderie.

The windows began to rumble. Thunder cracked. She flinched.

The guards straightened, stopped talking, as though her fear had reminded them that they were there to protect her, not reminisce.

She cursed herself.

In Tharth, weakness had a scent everyone could smell instantly. She was a rabbit in a room of wolves. *Little rabbit*, wasn't that what the innkeeper had called her? And here the wolves were trying desperately not to be wolves.

She tapped her trembling fingers along the map, hoping to return to their stories before they retreated from her entirely.

But her guards were motionless now. Their attention had shifted toward the doorway of the hall.

She felt it then, before she saw *him*; the pull of gravity rearranging the room.

The King entered and the tension in the hall caught fire. He whipped his cloak across his back with practiced flare. His steps struck the polished floor with each advance. His eyes scanned the room expectedly. He didn't ask for silence. He *took* it.

The *in-between-nights* King.

Ever so slowly, she turned her head to look at him.

The Vampire King stood just inside the entrance, arms folded neatly, watching her with a look somewhere between amusement and calculation.

Before she could smooth over her fear of the thunder, his voice interrupted, "Is something wrong?"

Her guards had their eyes trained to the wall in front of them. Adelira braced herself for the unpredictability that was the King outside his third night cycle.

"Don't they have storms where you're from?" he asked.

She set her jaw and spoke sharply in Ehvayn, "*You know they don't.*"

"I don't understand you, Princess," he said in Tharic, amused by her irritation. "Predators don't learn the languages of their prey."

Her jaw ticked again and she looked him in the eyes and said in Tharic this time, "You know there is no thunder in Ebedene."

He shrugged, elegant and effortless. "I forget things sometimes."

He forgot how she took her tea. He forgot the weather in her homeland. It didn't make sense. None of these inconsistencies spoke of the calculating, diplomatic warrior she had been told to expect.

A messenger appeared then. His military uniform had the King and guards keenly at attention.

The King was already moving, gathering his weapons from the general as she handed him blades and armour. He left the room with the messenger and general in tow.

Benedict and Finn exchanged a knowing, nostalgic glance.

Adelira frowned. "What's going on?"

No one answered.

The night after tomorrow would be the third night, and with it, she hoped, the return of a King she could speak to; the man who was trying to understand her, the one whose trust felt within reach.

She didn't want to go back to her room and be alone while the storm raged. She stayed in the hall, stayed seated between her stationed guards and studied the map, waiting for the rain to slow.

Hours later, when she was about to retire, when the clouds had broken and the sun was near rising, the castle doors swung open.

The gates opened for the soldiers' bloodied and weary return. At the front, she saw *him*.

Not the King in fine silks who played politics in the ballroom. His armour was smeared with dirt and blood, his black hair untamed, his eyes sharpened red with bloodlust.

He looked *alive*. Too alive. As though war was not just something he endured, but something that fed him.

She stepped back before he could see her. Without a word, she followed her guards to her room.

Adelira didn't need the Vampire King to know her tea preferences or be gentle. She needed him to stand at the Elven gates and crush every enemy that threatened her people. She had come for power. And Orahn was terrifying enough to deliver it.

36

Chapter Thirty-Six

Adelira sat alone in her chambers, thinking. The weeks were passing and she'd made no progress on the Blood Ritual. She would start using these third-night patterns more strategically, and wait for the night after tomorrow.

Enough time was spent *hoping* that the King would trust her, for some unseen bridge between them to form. It was time she learnt to work with stone, if she wanted to belong here. If she wanted to secure the strength she saw last night and deliver it to her people, she needed the Blood Ritual.

Adelira called for her ladies.

A knock came at her door and two ladies appeared seeking permission in the doorway. The first was her usual lady with long dark hair. The second was the newer lady who kept her face lowered, her demeanour trembling like a leaf caught in the wind from the strain of being in Adelira's presence.

The usual lady began changing her bedding and the other one walked over to the fireplace in the wall and built a quick fire. "That's warmer."

Adelira walked towards her, but the woman expertly manoeuvred behind the table near the fire and headed towards the wardrobes.

Adelira's request for help fastening her gown was met with hesitation. When one woman finally stepped forward, her hands were as cold and impersonal as the stone walls.

The second the task was done, the attendant retreated like a shadow fleeing the sun.

Adelira thought of Talion and how he would allow her to rest her head on his shoulder on the nights she stayed up chatting with him while he stood guard by her door. He would grumble a bit, half-heartedly trying to chase her away. But when he had let his head rest on top of hers and breathed a sigh of defeat, she knew he was as grateful for the company as she was.

She wouldn't chase. But she would seek understanding of the world she lived in. If she wanted a place here, she would need to learn the King's patterns.

"Thank you," Adelira said before finding the courage to ask, "Is... is there something wrong with the King?"

They exchanged a quick look she could not gauge before one of them asked, "What do you mean?"

"It's... it's just that he seems so different... all the time... like I can't figure him out. Like he's always changing. His moods swing chaotically. M–maybe he doesn't want a marriage, I'd understand that. He could *say* that," Adelira felt the words spill from her even though she wasn't sure she could or should confide in the Vampire ladies.

Again they exchanged a look she couldn't understand and said, "You're not from here and you're not used to the King, that's all."

"But for everyone else in Tharth..." the woman said.

The other shook her head at her as if reminding her not to say too much. "This is how he's always been."

Adelira bit her lip nervously, trying to decide what to make of that.

The first lady agreed, "Even as a young boy."

"Perhaps more so as a child, more unpredictable," the first lady recounted.

The second lady added, "He's settled as he's gotten older."

Adelira stared in mild horror at the idea that this version of him was more steady than he used to be.

"His mood shifts with the phases of the moons, no different than weather," she said.

"Oh," Adelira said, still unsure if she was relieved to hear she wasn't necessarily the problem or if she felt apprehension knowing even his people found him fickle.

Her mother said her strength came from her ability to love deeply. But was love as powerful a trait as the pure strength of the Vampire King? She didn't know if she could stand before him — stand in his bloodlust and fangs — and open her arms, hoping her heart was enough.

"Could you invite the King? I–I would like to speak with him. I'd like to know everything I should know about Tharth. If I am to stay here, it's time I learn what I can and get to know him better."

"Of course, your Highness."

"Do you have any advice?" she asked tentatively.

They exchanged another look. "Do not be too kind. You give it away too easily."

Adelira took a deep breath and looked them both over. "My kindness isn't... freely made. Or easily given."

"No?" one said.

"No," Adelira affirmed, more firmly than she meant to.

"It seems to be given to everyone," then the other added.

"It's something I work within myself, because I have chosen who I am. T-that doesn't change based on who anyone else is."

"If that serves you best," they conceded, "Let's begin with how to properly dress."

Adelira was sure they thought she was naïve. In truth, she almost believed it herself. Except that she trusted Carys that not all strength had to draw blood. She was trying to step lightly in a place that threatened her light, still she kept walking.

She watched as the lady pulled dresses from the wardrobe and laid them out on the bed in neat order.

"What are your names?" Adelira asked, walking closer.

One lady's eyes flicked up at her, but then returned to the garments in rich fabrics of black, red, and gold. Each dress was heavier than the last, adorned with trims and buckles. The woman explained their meanings; royal colours for public appearances, cloaks for long journeys, ceremonial attire for rituals.

Her hands moved over the thick fabrics. She longed for the silken flow of her Elven gowns; the way they carried the scent of her forest breezes and freedom.

"Everything is so heavy," she murmured.

"For warmth," the attendant replied.

Adelira smiled faintly, but said no more.

When the last dress was packed away, the women curtsied and left.

"Thank you," Adelira said as the door shut.

Turning away from the Vampire attire, she walked to the other end of the closet where her Elven dresses waited. She relaxed as she ran her hands along her familiar fabrics.

She dressed in her delicate Elven dresses. Her silks were too thin for the cold of Tharth, but too comforting to trade for warmth.

37

Chapter Thirty-Seven

A knock echoed through her chamber.

Adelira's pulse quickened as she crossed the room. Her hand trembled slightly as she grasped the door's cold handle.

Orahn waited in the doorway. The moonlight softened his outline.

His long cloak fluttered in the breeze. His dark, peaceful eyes and the stoic mask he wore in public was replaced by the one he wore on the third nights, *only* on the third nights.

Orahn offered her a smile. He extended his arm, the gesture simple as he waited patiently until she placed her hand in the crook of his arm.

"Good evening," she said, the formality of her words were designed to hold at bay the vulnerability that had settled between them.

His eyes lingered on her intensely, but there was kindness too, something she hadn't dared to hope for.

"Lira," his voice silkier than she had ever heard. "Would you like to walk with me?"

She hesitated longer than she'd like, but then smiled with genuine warmth filling her chest.

She stepped out of her room. "I'd like that."

Orahn led her through the castle and out into the gardens.

She didn't know this garden with its twisted vines and flowers in deep shades of red and purple, so different from the indoor garden of her chambers.

As they walked side by side, Adelira noticed the subtle shift in him. His posture was still that of the King, but there was an ease in the way he moved, almost untroubled, like the crown had lifted.

"I'm sorry," Orahn said after a long silence.

She startled, glancing up at him.

"If I've seemed distant," he continued. "There's so much weighing on me lately. I didn't mean to make you feel... forgotten."

"I understand," she replied. "There's no need to apologise. You have your duties, and I... I have mine."

"You are important too, Lira," he added.

He led them to the blossom trees.

She stopped under it, glancing up at the towering branches. The pale blossoms seemed out of place in a region like Tharth. The pink and white flowers were complimented and made brighter by the darkness surrounding it.

Orahn paused before continuing, "I don't want you to feel... *uncertain?*" he thought for a moment and then continued after he settled on the word, "uncertain about your place here. My attention has been divided, I know that. My position... it makes everything harder."

Adelira looked up and said quietly, "I understand why you're distant."

He glanced down at her, his eyes held something in them that could've been regret. "You don't. Not entirely."

Adelira's eyes fell to the ground. He said she was important, but that could mean for their alliance. And even in that he still hadn't actually offered her anything.

"I know I'm not the King you wanted," he said, his gaze averted like he couldn't bear to meet hers. "The Blood King, and that image, still lingers despite my best efforts."

She looked at him as he still avoided her gaze, as though this was heavy for him to say.

He continued, "I've built walls to keep this Kingdom standing. I don't know if I know how to rule any other way. I always end up back here, in this balancing act between chaos and absolute power. But... I will try, for you, because you deserve a place that is less precarious, and because maybe my Vampires deserve that, too. For what this Kingdom could be, I will continue to try."

"Thank you," she said quietly.

Orahn nodded slightly.

They walked on in silence, the only sound the rustle of leaves in the wind.

He wasn't offering her warmth or understanding, but he was offering her something true. She could begin to build on it.

She looked up at him as they stood under the blossoms. The heat of his body radiated from him and she stepped into his warmth. His eyes lowered to her lips for a second too long, then he dragged himself away like the restraint cost him *blood*.

"Could I take you to see something?" Orahn said with almost a breath of hesitation in his usually confident voice. "I haven't shown anyone this. I haven't been here since I was a child."

She nodded.

Orahn led Adelira to an area tucked away in corners untouched by the sun. There was a small courtyard, shrouded in shadow. In the middle was a raised pool that came to her waist. The two moons reflected on the smooth water's surface. A breeze quivered the effect.

"Where are we?" she asked. Her voice had dropped to a whisper without meaning to, like the space was too intimate for anything louder than a breath.

"One of the few places in Tharth where the old magic is still a little overrun. It's older than the castle, older than our Kingdoms."

Adelira stepped closer. "It's beautiful..."

Orahn dipped his fingers into the water, sending ripples across its surface.

As they stilled, the pool seemed to deepen. The reflection no longer showed the moonlight. Instead, it revealed a sky so vibrant it stole Adelira's breath. Constellations danced across the surface. The stars glowed brighter and shifted into patterns unfamiliar to her.

"It's called the Mirror of Ages," Orahn said. "It shows the sky as it once was, before magic began to fade and the world all around grew quiet."

Adelira knelt on the stone bench beside the pool. "I've never seen anything like it."

"Do you like it?" he asked carefully.

"I love it," she said breathlessly.

He smiled and moved next to her, his hands braced along the stone's ledge, his eyes not on the shimmering water sky, but on her.

"The world isn't quiet, though," she said. "I hear it sometimes."

"You're very lucky, few can," Orahn said. "The Elves still sing of the old stars, but even your people haven't seen skies like these in centuries."

She stared into the pool, her reflection mingling with the constellations. She could almost hear the song her people sang in the ripples of the water. He stood as calm as the water, as steady as the surface.

The moment wrapped around her, soft and inviting. "Will you bring me back here again?"

"If it pleases you," he agreed. "It reminds me of what we've lost in the Kingdoms... And what's worth protecting."

For all the mystery he cloaked himself in, for all the danger and power he embodied, there was something raw and vulnerable in the way he looked at the pool. And then he looked at her and she saw the same things in his eyes intended for her. Her cheeks warmed.

"Can... Can we do this again *soon*?" she asked. "Or... s–something? Something like this? Anything else. I just... I... I don't want to stay in my room all the time. I have the guards to see the castle with, but... I'd love to spend time with *you*."

A flicker of uncertainty crossed his eyes before he smiled and said, "Of course. I have a busy schedule, though. Can we arrange it for three nights from now?"

She smiled back. If every three days was all that she got, she'd make the best of it.

"I would like that, thank you."

They slowly made their way back to her chamber. The danger that seemed to follow her every step dimmed, just for a little while, as she lost herself in the old magic of the pool and the quiet company of a Vampire who, against all odds, was starting to feel... *safe*.

It wasn't all rumours and myths. She had seen him command the Kingdom with a single look or in absolute silence, but even so, he was a person beneath that.

He didn't know how to let her in and she didn't know how to make him trust her. But she'd keep showing up, even if she was only given a third of the time to make up the distance between them that grew in the nights apart.

He walked into her room with her. Lingering in the entrance. Like he had the other times before, he filled the room like he belonged there and she reached for his hand.

His eyes surprised, then softened. She saw that the touch was unexpected for him. She was trying to be soft, so he'd lower his walls, return her softness, and he did for a moment.

She wanted to hold him there, so that he might not become someone else after leaving her room. But she was trying to be patient. It was easier to swallow down her knee-jerk reaction and not bolt from the room, now that she felt that she was making real progress with Orahn.

She wanted to find something in Tharth that she could hold onto so she didn't feel so untethered here. She admitted that, *to her*, survival was gentle, almost like love, yet that wasn't what this was. Salvation, but her own personal brand.

He brushed his thumb across the back of her hand, warmth flooded through her veins. Forest frost and pine covered mountains and something stronger like whisky maybe, just the whisper of it seeped in aged-oak. The scent of him overwhelmed her and she wanted his body pressed against hers again.

Orahn leaned closer, so close she could feel the heat of him, the faint brush of his cloak against her gown. The air between them was charged and fragile. His lips hovered near her temple, his breath ghosting her skin, sending a shiver racing down her spine.

Turning her head to close the distance, to let herself be pulled into the gravity of him. But the moment rested on a knife's edge, delicate as a spider's thread. One wrong move and it would snap.

His eyes closed, his restraint drawn tight like a bowstring. His lips brushed her cheek, fleeting, almost imagined. A promise or a warning, she couldn't tell. He was the changing night sky and she was the blossoms in the dark.

And then, he was gone. Disappearing down the corridor.

Adelira stood frozen. Her skin tingled where his breath had lingered. It wasn't love, but it was gentle. In Tharth, she hadn't even dared to hope for that.

38

Chapter Thirty-Eight

The next night she had seen the King only from her balcony in the battleyard below training with his soldiers. He didn't look up, but the way his head shifted in her direction every time she restlessly paced the length of her balcony.

The following night, she'd seen him standing over the desk of a scribe correcting parts of the notes transcribed. The King nodded in approval of something and the scribe beamed with pride as he made adjustments. The King's eyes lifted to hers and left her breathless, before he directed all of that intensity back into his work.

The night after that was the third night.

Orahn appeared at her door, smiling and ready to meet her half-way again. The usual regal posture softened. He still moved with all the power of a King, though more relaxed this evening.

"Ready?" he asked.

"Almost."

Kicking off her shoes, she left them in the room as she stepped into the corridor with him.

He looked down with an amused smirk and led the way to the gardens, past the blossom. Tucked within the inner sanctum of the Keep, hidden behind high, vine-covered walls, was the Midnight Garden. Dark roses and moonbloom vines grew in tangles.

Feet stepping freely over the well manicured grass, she could almost feel grounded in Tharth for once. The earth spoke differently here, in vibrations she couldn't decode, but it was comforting enough.

"Some claim they've heard whispers here, as if the garden itself remembers every conversation it has ever held," Orahn said casually, his dark eyes watching her as she touched the pastel petals of a tall flower.

"I'm sure it does remember," Adelira murmured. "The trees speak. Just not to us, not very often, anyway."

He gave a lazy smile. "I suppose I'll have to start guarding what I discuss out here from now on. Lest the weeds betray my secrets."

The evening was already chilly and she instantly regretted not taking a coat. No sooner had she shivered did the King's cloak wrap around her shoulders, the heat of his body trapped in the fabric.

"Better?" he asked.

"Yes, thank you."

Leaning towards him, he smelled like whisky and pine and frost, like firelight in winter, and her heart fluttered.

Trying to step away, his hand pressed gently over hers, stilling her movements.

"You don't have to pull away," he said softly.

The space between them was shrinking as she sank back into the warmth of him. With the grass beneath her feet and the King next to her, suddenly it didn't seem too foreign here, for a moment.

His breath whispered over the top of her head. She only had to tilt her head up to brush her lips over his, but she held back.

A question lingered in her mind, one she had almost asked aloud before, but never felt it was important enough to voice. He seemed to read her thoughts before she was even able to speak them.

"You don't have to censor yourself with me."

Adelira asked, "How are you always so warm? I thought... I thought Vampires were cold."

Orahn's laughter was unexpected, a sound so genuine that she couldn't help but smile at the amusement in his eyes.

"We dress warmly," he replied in a teasing tone.

She blushed. "Ah, that's wise."

He gave her an affectionate glance. The playful atmosphere wrapped around them, but he also looked at her like he understood how much they had to learn about each other. Like maybe now he was finally ready to begin sharing.

"Why does it seem like you pre-empt my needs before they are fully realised?" she asked, looking down at the coat wrapped around her.

"I pay attention."

"I was half-convinced you could read minds."

"Is that what they say about Vampires in Ebedene?"

"No..." she said pensively. "They say that you can compel us, entrap us under your spells... Is that why I never seem to move when every part of me is screaming to run?"

"We don't have any power over you," he assured her. "Not the kind that could make you stay against your will."

He was telling her she was allowed to leave, if she wanted to... *Did she want to?*

"I think that you don't run away, because the prey that runs," he continued without missing a beat, "is the prey that encourages the chase."

She hadn't considered Elves had instinct as primal as Vampires, and all of hers had been honed for survival.

Nudging her to break the worried expression on her face, he smiled softly. "There's no magic trick, Lira. Magic is for witches, not Vampires."

Adelira broke the silence. "It's quieter than I expected."

Orahn gave a small nod. "The court tires quickly of spectacle, for all their hunger for power, they are creatures of habit. When the excitement fades, they return to their routines. It's the way of Tharth."

Orahn paused, his hand at her back to ask her to stop walking. Her steps slowed near a fountain. His posture was relaxed, but vigilant; a night creature at rest.

"How are you? Away from court, not a princess, just... *you*?" he asked, his voice had softened.

Glancing up at him, his dark eyes held hers and there the question reflected behind them as genuine as they sounded on his lips. He wanted to know how she was.

"I..." She hesitated, gathering her thoughts. "I–I've been trying to find my place here."

He didn't interrupt, and that encouraged her to continue.

"I know what it means to be here. The alliance, the marriage, all of it," she said, glancing down at her hands, "but I feel... distant. Everything is different. *I'm* different." She paused, her voice lowering. "I don't fit."

He wasn't a man who showed his emotions easily, but there was an understanding in his eyes.

"I don't expect you to change," he said, his voice quieter now, more thoughtful. "Tharth is a Kingdom of survival, power and blood. But that doesn't mean there can't be a place for you here. And you don't have to change to earn it. Tharth does not make room easily, but it bends. When I command it. And if it refuses to bend, then I will carve a place in this Kingdom for you."

She sat with his words, and yet there was something gentler still in his tone. It was unexpected.

He continued, "You didn't choose me, your people chose a treaty. It was brave and smart, but more importantly, it was difficult for you. I will ease that as best as I can."

Her lips parted, his kindness settling over her. "I suppose you didn't exactly choose me either."

Orahn's expression softened again, a faint chuckle escaping him. "No. But I don't regret it."

The admission floated between them, humble and offered to her.

Under the watch of two moons, they found something that neither of them expected; an understanding of the lives they had been handed and the possibilities of what lay ahead for them.

He looked down at her then, really looked at her, and there was something new in his dark eyes.

"You've been kind," he said softly, as though the realisation had only just settled on him. "To the court, to the servants, even when you barely know them. Kindness is... rare here. I like that about you, about the difference you bring to Tharth."

A Vampire had never recognised her kindness as a good thing before. Orahn, *the Blood King himself*, recognised it as worthy. She almost hated how much that validation meant to her, hated to admit it had become heavy to hold alone. With him, it was easy to choose kindness again.

She nearly asked why she only ever saw him every third night, but tonight wasn't for questions. Tonight was for the garden and the warmth of his coat and the way his voice softened when he spoke just to her.

Smiling, she relaxed in Orahn's company as he told her the names of the flowers and trees and plants she had never seen before.

She did not think she could remember all the new plants he pointed out, but instead, she focused on the melodic, calm waves of his voice as he spoke.

She liked listening to him and how he was with her when no one was around. Other people seemed to draw out sides of him that he used like a weapon to control the world around him. Only with her, he spoke softly of the flowers in the garden.

His eyes never left her face. She wanted this side of him, always. The man he was between the hush of moonlight and memories.

39

Chapter Thirty-Nine

Adelira waited her three nights again.

One night, she saw the King speaking with his general. Victoria was intimidating, her senses honed and lethal. She moved like a cat, always on the prowl. When the King was with her, his strides matched hers.

Adelira stayed close to her guards and avoided him that night.

The following night he walked past her, he didn't stop. But he took in a breath, so subtle and controlled, she almost missed it. His fingers twitched by his side. Turning to look at him, he continued down the corridor without looking back.

And then, the third night came.

Finding themselves on a now familiar route around the garden.

"Tell me something about your home."

Adelira blinked, surprised by the sudden request.

"My home?" She thought before offering a smile. "I have a brother, Kieran, and a sister, Odette."

Orahn nodded, but pressed on, more insistent, "I know that already. I've heard what my advisors could tell me. About your family, your Kingdom's alliances, your trade routes, the court politics. But I want to know more. The parts they can't tell me."

She glanced up at him curiously. "Like what?"

"Like what you did during the day. Where did you spend your time? Did you have friends?"

His question touched a part of her soul she hadn't allowed herself to speak of since her arrival in Tharth.

"Everyone has friends," she said carefully with the note of caution in her voice. "Ebedene was wonderful that way."

They made their way through the castle and paused in front of magnificent doors of gold and black. She had passed it many times, the other night she thought she heard him talking to himself inside there.

"This is my chamber," Orahn said and motioned to the door, then he pointed down the corridor. "And just down there is yours."

"You're very close," she said in surprise.

"If you ever need me, you'll come straight here, do you understand?"

She blushed. "But what about—"

He shook his head. "Please, don't worry about the formality. Lira, you need not go through anyone else first. If we are to be married, you should feel free to call upon me as you wish," Orahn assured her.

As I wish, Adelira repeated to herself with a flutter.

It wasn't the home he promised. It wasn't even a set date for the Blood Ritual. But it was access to him, above all else. These were the first steps towards the rest of the things she needed from him.

He was offering some small trust in return for all the trust she'd placed in him.

He started to walk her back. He nodded the guards away and Benedict and Finn made a silent exit.

When they reached her door, he stopped, leaning casually against the frame and folded his arms over his chest.

"I know you're homesick," he said lightly. "Maybe I can help. What do you miss most about home?"

Orahn's casual demeanour suggested that he was expecting some small comfort he could replicate.

Instead, her lips *trembled*. Her eyes welled rapidly with tears she hadn't intended to shed.

"I miss Riann," she said, her voice breaking over his name. "The boy who gave me a stone one time, because he liked it. And I miss hearing Mirhan gripe about her husband while she poured honey tea. I miss the farmhands whistling while they cut barley. And Leina's laugh..." Her voice cracked again over rising sobs. "I miss Odette always poking me about my handwriting. And Carys talking to me in the hot springs. I was never alone, not even to bathe."

Orahn froze, his chest tightening as her words hit him. Adelira wasn't listing anything he could fix. She was naming people, memories, pieces of her life that were irrevocably lost.

"But you know what I miss more than anything?" Her voice was raw now, the words spilling out of her. "The clinking of Talion's boots. My personal guard. He followed me everywhere, and I hated it. I hated him for it. I thought his protection was suffocating. I ran from him, avoided him, and made his job miserable."

She looked away, wiping at her cheeks, but the tears kept coming. "He died protecting me. Because I was too stupid to realise how much I needed him. And now... now I just want to stop being afraid all the time. I don't want to be caged in some castle for my own protection.

And I don't want anyone else to die because of me. That's why I'm here now."

He blinked, his voice low and disbelieving, "You were married into a viper pit in a desperate attempt to feel safer?"

Adelira wiped her face dry angrily. "It made sense at the time."

He didn't respond right away. His eyes dropped to the floor, grappling with the depth of what she'd just said. He looked back at her, his expression was twisted in concern, softer than she'd ever seen it.

Adelira took a deep breath, visibly pulling herself together. She firmed up her frame and brushed away the last streaks down her cheeks.

"Alright, I'm done now," she said quietly, folding away her pain neatly after it had run its course.

He didn't know if he should pull her closer... or set her free.

"I don't even know anything about Vampires," she said after a moment, her voice steadier. "Our library has almost no literature on Vampire Culture."

Orahn let out a low and knowing sigh. "That's not an accident."

"What?"

"My father was very careful about what information made its way into other Kingdoms' libraries."

Adelira frowned. "It's exaggerated, then?"

"Some parts, I'm sure," he admitted with a shrug. "Hard to say."

"So, you don't eat children? Or move impossibly fast? Or hunt anything that moves?"

Orahn half-chuckled. "Not really. I mean... sometimes? I *do* hunt."

Her eyes narrowed, but a reluctant smile broke through at his lightness.

He smiled back. "But if you want to know the truth about Vampires, I'll teach you. All of it. Whatever you want to know, Lira."

Grey eyes lifted to him as he offered to bridge her to his world. She nodded, her smile fading into a look of quiet gratitude.

Orahn took a step closer. "I don't mean to hide you away from a world you're used to connecting with. I only want you to be safe until you no longer need me, or anyone, behind you. But I see how I am no different to your guards. I don't mean to suffocate you with my stone walls. I don't wish to stifle you. I said I will carve out a place for you in my Kingdom, one where you are safe, and I will. Please give me time, and while we wait, I'll take you to all the gardens and forests that you want."

She wasn't allowed in the forests of Edebene without a full division of royal guards at the ready. A dozen soldiers would have secured the perimeter, scaring every small woodland creature.

Now she could enter with only one man, not standing behind her, but by her side. She smiled at the irony of having more freedom in Tharth even with the full dangers of Vampires.

"Tell me about Vampires," Adelira asked, not able to go inside and be alone just yet, not after everything she had shared, not after the raw feeling was still catching in her throat.

Orahn glanced at her, his dark eyes glinting with interest. "What exactly do you want to know?"

She hesitated, tucking a loose strand of hair behind her ear. "I... don't know. Is everything they say about the Blood King true?"

"I don't know. What do they say about me in Ebedene?"

She bit her lip, unable to settle on one singular whisper that passed around the Elven realm regarding the Vampire King. There were so many things said, at least half of which were too monstrous to utter now.

He shrugged then. "Probably not. Rumours have their uses. Fear keeps people... respectful."

"You're a myth to us, a legend." Her curiosity deepened. "What's real? What should I know about you?"

Orahn's smile shifted, growing darker, more intentional. "I'm more human than you'd imagine." He leaned towards her, his voice becoming a silken purr.

"I find that hard to believe."

She looked up at him as he towered over her, leaning against the doorframe. He wasn't quite the King right now, but not quite just a man either. His fangs glinted in the light and her heart stuttered.

"There's blood in my veins, Lira. I'm just far more interested in the blood in yours."

Her breath caught.

"Drinking blood isn't always... *intimate*. But I can assure you," his eyes dropped to her throat for a fraction of a second too long, "it tastes better when it is."

A shiver traced its way down her spine.

He looked down at her and she reached out to touch his face, pulled forward by impulse she didn't understand. She lowered her hand at the last second, her fingers trailing down his neck. He flinched.

"Sorry," she whispered, dropping her hand.

He shook his head. "It's only... I'm not used to being touched so softly there."

"I don't bite," she offered with a cheeky smile she smothered.

"No," he laughed, and murmured, "I do."

Orahn straightened, his smirk softening, as though he enjoyed the tension he'd conjured. "Satisfied with your lesson on Vampires or shall I continue?"

Her voice, when it came, was quieter than she'd intended. "That's... enough for now."

"Very well," he said. "What did you do to fill your days? Surely not endless leisure."

A new wave of emotion threatened tears at the thought of her old life, but then Adelira pushed it away lightly. She'd remember some things fondly, she owed her past that without wrapping them in sadness.

"Mostly painting," she began. "I'd read, ride when I could. I love to paint."

"Wonderful," he murmured.

"I also attended formal disputes; farmers arguing over land, resources, or livestock. Those were challenging. No one ever wanted to compromise, and every decision felt like choosing the lesser of two evils. And, of course, my guards ensured I never wandered too far or did anything... improper."

"Ah," Orahn said, his voice dipping into amusement. "The joys of rulership: mediating squabbles, appeasing egos and constant demand for proper behaviour at all times."

She let out a small laugh. "At least no one ever tried to murder anyone else in a council meeting."

His brow raised. "That must be nice."

She passed him a side glance. "Don't tell me you don't enjoy it, Blood King?"

"Blood King..." he said thoughtfully. "Yes... that was regrettable, but necessary. I sacrificed parts of myself I can't ever get back. At the time, Tharth needed a tyrant to bring us out of the Blood Wars. But my intention was never for it to stay that way."

Adelira paused as she considered his words. "You had absolute control and you... gave it away?"

He didn't answer her, but she got her answer in that anyway.

The Blood King's rise to power was a brutal conquest that had bound the fractured provinces of Tharth under one iron rule. But she had never thought of it as an act of sacrifice.

But she saw it then, how desperate he was to step back, to let go. She saw it in simple things like how he let the Council of Shadows have meetings he didn't try to dominate with his voice.

And she also saw how they wouldn't let him. He was the order to this chaos and without him; everyone flung out of orbit.

She said softly, "That takes immeasurable strength."

He softened entirely before her eyes. Like maybe she was the only person who ever saw what it took for him to do what he did.

Adelira's brow furrowed slightly, because beneath all that strength, she saw a soul-deep tiredness. "What now? After all that's happened?"

He hesitated before responding. "I'm not sure what happens now. But I'm not the same man I was."

"Will you let go of fear entirely?"

"I hate using it," he said without breaking eye contact. "But don't worry, I'll spare you from most of the complicated and brutal politics of Tharth."

"I'm just a Princess for show?"

"You're a diplomat, not a disciplinarian. It's my job to spill blood, Lira. Yours is to make sure I don't have to."

"Sounds like you're giving yourself a more exciting role."

"Oh, believe me, *exciting* isn't the word I'd use for council brawls. Brutish, tedious, infuriating; those seem more fitting. But if you ever want a taste of it, I'd be happy to arrange something more... participatory."

She stilled, dropping the banter and looked up at him in seriousness. "Will you really let me have anything to do with the politics of

Tharth? Or will you keep me locked in my room more often than not?"

He looked away then, biting back a sigh. "I don't mean to lock you away, I just..." He took a deep breath. "As for the rulership, I'm not sure yet, I suppose that's something we'll discover along the way."

She nodded. In truth, it was her own people she was looking out for even in Vampire politics and while the Blood Ritual might keep them safe in war, her ability to speak for them in the Kingdom of Tharth might help them continue to thrive in the aftermath.

Orahn peered up at the ceiling, weighing something he wasn't ready to share, then he took a deep breath. She watched him steel himself before he stepped closer.

"Would you like to go to the night market and buy paints tomorrow night?" He offered. "That way you can see the city for yourself."

"But... Tomorrow isn't the third night," she said, her voice quieter now, uncertain of this change in their rhythm.

His face fell like she said something that almost scared him, then he covered it and smiled.

"No, but I won't lock you away in a tower," he said. "I can make time for you each night, if I shuffle my schedule around a little."

"A–are you sure?" She knew these cycles by now, the in-between-nights were difficult for him and if he wasn't ready then she didn't want to push him. But going out more often sounded magnificent.

"You deserve my time as well," he said simply.

Her breath hitched.

"I won't keep you locked up simply because it's easier for everyone else," he said firmly. "If it is difficult for you to remain inside, then I will adjust my schedule, because coming here was difficult enough for you."

"Orahn..." she breathed.

"Paints? Tomorrow night?" he asked even gentler now.

She nodded, more eagerly than she intended to reveal. "I would love that."

Orahn extended his hand, his fingers grazing hers lightly. She laced her fingers with his and leaned her forehead against his chest. His free hand cupped the back of her head for a moment, his fingers lacing between her curls, before he whispered in her ear.

"There's more to Tharth than the court. More to our relationship than this alliance."

Adelira felt it in the quiet gesture, in the unspoken promise in his eyes as she drew back and looked up at him.

"I will send for you tomorrow night," he dropped his hand away from her and gestured towards her chamber doors, stepping just inside her room. "But it's quite late now, the sun will be up soon."

"Yes," she agreed, though she was not tired. Day sleeping was taking some getting used to, even with the teas.

He was just inside her room, but he didn't step in further even when she made space for him to join her. This time he didn't brush his lips against her cheek and she found herself wishing he would.

But he reached out and stroked back the strands of red hair falling forward and he held her face in his hands.

His thumb brushed over the curve of her cheek. Traced lower, hovering to the edge of her mouth. Her lips parted, begging for him to close the last fraction of space. His gaze dropped to her lips and he froze, like a predator pulling back from the kill at the very last moment.

The panic flashed in his eyes, she wouldn't push him. Instead, she nestled her cheek into his hand until his body relaxed and he leaned forward, pressing his forehead softly to hers.

He let go, stepped out of her room and walked into the vanishing night.

40

Chapter Forty

Adelira crossed to her nightstand, brushing her fingers over the pebble.

This would be her first venture beyond the fragile sanctuary of the palace, into the heart of the Kingdom.

She opened her closet and immediately a black gown with gold trims caught her eye. It was a bold choice, as imposing as any nobles might wear. She didn't really want to look like the Blood Families though and her hand drifted towards the simpler design. Dark, less flashy, high collars and structured bodices that gave a militaristic flare. It was more armour than she could bear, though.

Indecision gripped her so she turned towards her own clothing.

The Elven dress was a comfort against the unknown, a reminder of who she was, like her pebble. She knew it only made her stand out more, she still couldn't let it go.

The whole place had fallen into slumber, the Vampires' nocturnal nature had sucked the life out of the day.

As though time stopped every time the sun graced the sky.

She was told Orahn had made sure the market was secure enough for her visit. When she asked what that meant, she was only given silence to work with.

When evenfall finally arrived, the chill in the air deepened. It crept into her bones, making her shiver. Wrapping herself in the Vampire fur-lined coat, she looked again at her reflection. She might not belong here yet, but she wasn't ready to disappear, either, so she kept her Elven dress and left the coat open to reveal it.

She wondered if she looked like a fraud to them, dressed in such a cape. What would they gossip about her? Should she keep her Elven roots or try becoming like them in every way that she could, so that they could try to forget that she's an outsider, a threat, a meal?

Adelira let out a small sigh, turning away from the mirror.

For now, the coat stayed. A small compromise, one that allowed her to feel a bit stronger in a place that threatened to consume her.

She stepped out of her room and glanced at Benedict and Finn stationed outside her door.

Outside, they walked towards the gates. Wind caught her hair. The struggle was in every Vampire they passed. Breaths quickened and their footsteps faltered ever so slightly.

Adelira's chest tightened with guilt and frustration. She hadn't asked for this, hadn't asked to be a source of torment for those around her.

"She doesn't belong here," one muttered sharply. "It's only a matter of time."

"Which of the families do you think will act first?" the other asked.

Brushing her hair from her shoulders, her scent carried through the air. Her guards barely reacted, but the women froze mid-step.

"She's too close," one hissed, their voice suddenly taut and trembling on the edge of control. "Do you smell that? Does she not know? She's playing with our bloodlust and she'll get hurt."

"Touch her and the King will obliterate even the ghost of your memory."

Adelira kept her head down.

"Not even *he* can protect her always. She won't last out the month," the second voice muttered, grim and resigned. "It's not in our nature to maintain this restraint for this long."

They arrived at the entrance. The market was surprisingly peaceful, welcoming even, and her chest rose with hope she barely dared to enjoy. Her escorts peeling off once she was safely deposited into the care of the King.

Her heart fluttered as she saw him standing in front of the gates. The wind tugging at his long dark hair and the ends of his black cape. His eyes gleamed in the light. He was handsome, a night creature forged from constellations, ink and shadows.

"Princess." The Vampire King greeted and turned as the gates opened, flooding them in a warm glow of light.

Iron opened onto the market streets, rolling and curving along the bend of a river. The cobblestone alleys buzzed with midnight life. The pathways were strung with lanterns, their glow an eerie bioluminescent shimmer that cast twisting shadows.

Smiling up at him and glancing around, she willed her feet to slow down. This wasn't a place she could run through. He was silent, but not quiet, his movements were loud like he was trying to be slower than he wanted to be, as well, and straining under the effort.

Children barrelled past them and she side-stepped out of the path for them. She chuckled at their enthusiasm. The King only watched them wearily, stepping back. Sighing in frustration she pushed forward. Then she stopped and ran her hands down the velvet of her cloak and reminded herself to be kind.

This wasn't a third-night and if he could be gentle enough to give her more of his time when it was clearly difficult for him, she could be gentle enough to enjoy it without asking more than he's able to give.

When he was ready, she would be here. He could waver between bravery and retreat. And once he learned that her constancy was real, he would fear her less.

The Night Market was a world apart.

These streets were humming in a way the Obsidian Keep never did. It was an explosion of colour and sounds, mingling scents pulling her in every direction. Silken canopies were stretched over stalls, deep purples, reds, cerulean. Merchants pushed forward their wares as they strolled past tables where everything was sold from enchanted blades to vials of bottled moonlight.

The Vampires moved with seamless elegance, no one ever touched and each step was fluid, like moving through the market was as intricately choreographed as the arrangement of the stall tables.

For all the magic of the marketplace, Orahn's mood did not match it. He walked beside Adelira. Prowling and quiet. His attention was more on the crowd than on her. His jaw was tight.

He was almost constantly in motion, pacing about her. She came to learn that at least one of the in-between-nights, the King had a restless fiery energy and it called to the restlessness in her that made her want to run through the streets with him. She would never do that again. She let him prowl, but she held her own spirit under control.

She basked in the delights of the market. This was a side of Vampire culture she had not experienced.

Her face glowed as they passed stall after stall. The woven fabrics from lands beyond Tharth, the fresh herbs bundled and hanging in fragrant bunches, even the ruby-coloured fruit she had never seen before; which she was sure was special to only her as she saw dozens in baskets across the tables making her believe they were common.

"There, look at that!" she exclaimed, pointing to a vendor selling small, complex wooden carvings. "Have you ever seen something so delicate?"

"Thank you, Your Highness." The lady beamed and she cycled through the carvings on her table, excitedly passing new items into the Princess's open hands and explaining the techniques used to create such detail.

"The wings are astounding." Adelira turned the wooden dragon between her fingers.

"The wings on the fairies were trickier, but I finally got the technique down," the stall holder boasted, holding the delicate craving in the palm of her hand.

Adelira leaned in to admire the craftsmanship. The delicate ornament glinted off the lantern light.

"Oh, yes, the detail is so intricate!" Adelira marvelled.

The stallholder pulled back a little, as though finally the smell of Adelira's blood had overwhelmed her and Adelira smiled in reassurance that it was okay, returned the carving and looked towards the next stall.

The King glanced at the carvings, but said nothing.

His watch returned to the streets warily as though his mind was elsewhere. Adelira wondered if he was burdened with responsibilities that felt too heavy to let go of, even for a night.

Adelira wasn't dissuaded by his silence. Though she had a moment of guilt wondering if it was her fault he was on edge, was he constantly watching for dangers because of her? She didn't feel uneasy like she had in the council with the mad Vampire. Though some stares were a little pointed.

Almost like Talion behind her, the King kept watching the crowd and she wondered if, like Talion, she might win a small smile from him tonight. If she got just one, she'd feel better.

She felt exhilarated and free for the first time since coming to Tharth. She wanted him to know how much this meant to her. She turned to him, her eyes sparkling in the lantern light, and reached out gently, her hand brushing against his upper arm.

"Orahn," she said softly, her face bright, "thank you for bringing me here tonight. It is wonderful."

Her smile was as warm as the lights above them, and for a moment, something softened in his eyes. His eyes rested on her for a moment too long before he nodded, but said nothing.

Still, she continued, his lack of response did nothing to slow her down. She was ready to see and enjoy everything the market had to offer, even if he wasn't ready to let his walls down, yet.

"Oh!" She grabbed his arm in excitement and he stiffened at the unexpected touch. She let go and pointed towards another stall. "Look at those little dolls!"

Small porcelain dolls in lavish dresses , but Orahn did not look. The soft toys allowed her to see something of the Vampires that they did not offer freely within the castle.

"The faces are so realistic," Adelira said, carefully rotating a porcelain doll in her hands.

"It takes two weeks to make one," the stallholder admitted.

"And worth every day," Adelira said, beaming at the artist.

The stallholder was ecstatic at her praise. Open appreciation was often restrained in Vampire culture, but the Princess offered it to them freely.

They looked at her with hungry eyes, but they hungered after her approval most of all. Each one trying to impress her with their wares and she fluttered through the market, seeing each of them.

The King looked down at the dolls before moving further along the street. He peered out at the shadows between the stalls, his mind elsewhere.

In the castle, everything about the Vampires was guarded and mysterious, almost as though they wished her to know nothing of their culture save for the fierce rumours that circled the Kingdoms. But out here, they opened up and let her in and she was as desperate to be seen by them as they were to be seen by her. She loved every item on every stand, and they appreciated her for it.

"This market… I mean, other than the nocturnal hours, but the rest of it, at least, the feeling of it, reminds me of markets I used to explore back home," she said breathlessly, her words tripping over themselves, but her smile wide.

His lips pulled down, it wasn't quite a scowl, but she could tell her words weren't working on him. She looked around the market, thinking.

They stood in front of a stand that had dozens of dark gothic dresses hanging from chains draped between the poles.

"I know you've probably seen everything a thousand times. Like I did back home. But no matter how many times I went, there was always something new to see. Something I hadn't seen before. There's probably things you haven't noticed, either. Oh, like this dress," she gushed as she pulled down a revealing black dress, holding it up against her body and giving a quick twirl.

He stopped and stared for a moment, the scowl erased. She had his attention now and she used it quickly, replacing the dress on the stand and moving towards him.

"The lanterns, the laughter, even the way people drift between the stalls... it is like they are floating." Her hand rested lightly on his arm. "I used to come to markets like these when I felt... restless. They helped me remember that there is more to life than duty."

His expression snapped to her face in surprise before easing. Her words floated through the air, tugging at something buried deep within him. He didn't share it, not yet, but the corners of his mouth curved upward, a short break in the tension he carried.

Her eyes held his and she felt something shift. Her words weren't lost on him. There was a gentleness in their eyes, a quiet understanding.

It wasn't much, but it was enough for him to smile gently.

She smiled back, sensing the small victory. She didn't push him further. Instead, she let her hand fall from his arm and turned her attention back to the market, her excitement undimmed.

"Come on," she said, her voice a touch lighter now, "there's more to see."

He followed behind her, silent and steady as the night. Adelira didn't need Orahn's words to know how tightly he held himself.

She wasn't sure she could break through his walls, but she could try to remind him of the beauty in the small things, this was something she could do for him.

"Vampires always look so gorgeous in their dresses," she said wistfully.

Vampires all dressed in thick and dark clothing, corsets and lace, she stood out like a flower amongst the reeds. Her hair bright red, and her dress thin and illuminated, the cloak she wore did little to hide it.

"What are you looking at?" she asked with a soft blush as his eyes washed over her swaying in her Elven dress.

He scowled. "Nothing. Let's go."

She ran her fingers and thumb over the black velvet material of a vampire dress hanging from a twisted branch and blowing gently in the breeze.

She asked, "Do you think I could pull off this dress?"

"No." He barely glanced at it.

She let the material fall from her fingers, crestfallen.

"You're..." He sighed, running a hand through his dark hair. "You don't need to look like a Vampire, no one expects that of you."

"I know, I just want... to fit in."

"You could wear this dress drenched in blood and I would still never mistake you for a Vampire."

"No," she agreed softly.

He looked down at her. "And that's okay, Princess."

She had a small smile at that, a choice she made to believe it. It was not long before she found her spirit again, determined to enjoy the wonderful evening she was having.

"Where to next?" She asked in anticipation, staring up at him.

"That way." He waved his hand vaguely in front of them.

Refusing to be deterred, she looped her hand through his arm, as had become normal for them. But she felt his muscles tense. He expertly manoeuvred out of her grasp, causing her to stop and look at him. She felt it in her bones then, something she couldn't voice about the King and the strange way he was always changing around her. Always changing...

He shook his head and walked on. "This way, Princess."

She hesitated for only a moment and then followed him, her intention was to fully enjoy the sights and smells hidden in the market. There were so many interesting people and fun things to see still.

"We don't have these back in my Kingdom," She continued a steady stream of commentary.

Then, she stopped by one stall, caught by the glint of something sharp. The engravings in the hilt were flawless.

"Isn't it exquisite?" she asked, stroking her index finger over the blade of a long cutlass.

He was next to her in an instant, pulling back her arm. His bone white fingers locked around her wrist like a vice tightening. She looked up at him with big, frightened eyes and he released his strong grip on her.

"Careful, Princess. If you spill blood here, I'm not sure that even I could hold them all back."

Her wide grey eyes searched the crowded market full of Vampires.

Everyone had stopped.

Stopped talking.

Stopped moving.

Stopped breathing.

All eyes were on her as the market held its breath. Just how strong was their bloodlust? If not all of them, could he protect her from himself? Or would spilling her blood drive him to madness, too?

She pulled her hand back slowly and the collective breath was released. Everyone continued as though nothing had happened.

The Vampire King turned to the blade she was interested in. He picked up the sword with cunning slowness, his hand closing around the hilt. A subtle flick of his wrist; he tested the influence and equilibrium of the weapon.

Polished steel gleamed under the light of the market lanterns, sharp reflections that danced across his features. He adjusted his grip and swung the blade with clean-cut precision. Metal whisked, slicing through the air.

Adelira watched him from a distance, her breath catching slightly as the fluidity of his movements held her attention.

Every shift of his body drew her in. His muscles flexed in his tailored tunic, revealing every chiselled contour. The sword was deadly. Yet when he held it, it became something else entirely, like it fused with his soul; even more dangerous and impossibly graceful.

He swung again, harder this time, and the blade caught the light. He moved with raw hunger, no longer simply testing the weapon, but commanding it. Mesmerised by the confidence in his movements and the way his presence dominated the space around him, Adelira leaned in a little closer.

She was blushing, she knew that much, but whether it was entirely from him or her slow embarrassment for how much he left her wanting, she didn't know.

She bit her lip, trying to hold in a smile. He looked every bit the impressive Vampire King she had watched commanding his army from her balcony and now he was commanding a weapon with the same effect, like it was a private show just for her.

He stopped mid-swing. Rolled his wrist, testing it further, his eyes narrowing in thought. His eyes deliberately flicked to her, catching her watching him, and a slow, knowing smile tugged at the corner of his mouth.

The heat of his attention sent a shiver through her, the intensity of it was thrilling and unnerving.

Setting the blade down, he threw out one final glance in her direction.

"What do you think?" he asked, low and inviting.

Adelira's heartbeat quickened, but she smiled, matching his smooth composure. "Beautiful... And the blade is fine, too."

His eyes widened in shock for only a second, before a grin cocked across his face, and he said, "Oh, my, Princess, are you flirting with me?"

"You wear the blade well," she said with a wink.

"You have a good eye," he praised her. "This is a good sword."

"It is exquisitely crafted," she said.

"I'll take it," he said to the grey-haired Vampire at the weapons stall with the exchange of a vial of blood for the weapon and then he sheathed the blade, attaching it to his belt.

41

Chapter Forty-One

Adelira and the Vampire King walked side by side.

She still looked over everything, he still didn't really look at all, but he had stopped pacing.

They passed a stall with vials of blood. Adelira stopped to examine almost every label. The inscription, *unicorn blood*. The vial gleamed. Another one was written in a language she couldn't read and appeared black and thick.

A potion, or a treat; like a pastry was to her?

She wanted to ask as she twirled another vial between her fingers, but Orahn was no longer at her side. He was walking down the street, distracted.

"You have rare taste. And rare blood of your own, too," the man behind the stall murmured, eyeing the vial in her hand like a wolf who'd scented prey. "Would you consider donating some?"

His eyes were nearly red; she'd seen this look before.

The vial slipped between her fingers.

The stall owner's hand shot out. He neatly caught the vial of unicorn blood and steadied the others.

Panicked, she looked to Orahn who was slipping away into the crowds. She apologised to the man to catch up to the King.

She had allowed herself to forget about the dangers of the outside world because of how wonderful it was, but now the dangers were impressed upon her again.

The King didn't turn to her, but he said, "Here are the paints you wanted."

"Thank you." She slipped past him to examine the stunning colours.

Rich pigments of crushed powders sat in pots with hinged lids snapped shut to protect the pretty dust within. Other glass jars were taller and narrower with thick liquids that rolled around inside, held securely by corks.

There was every colour she'd ever imagined and then a few she couldn't place at all. Perhaps there were more reds than other colours, she thought as she leaned in closer.

The King had a soft, nostalgic smile on his face as he ran his fingers over the jars.

The stall's vendor emerged from behind a curtain at the back with an armful of glass jars. Dressed in a curvy black dress, a corset that was impressive in all the right places, like foxglove; she was gorgeous and fanged. Bottomless brown eyes that Adelira fell into when she stared too deeply.

The paintseller flitted gracefully, setting each jar down with a care. Her hair, long and dark, was pulled loosely over one shoulder, a few strands framing her face.

"Good evening, Your Majesty," the vendor said, nodding at the King. Her voice gave nothing away, there was a note of familiarity hidden in her courtesy.

Her gaze briefly landed on him with a flicker of warmth. Then she looked away, arranging the jars in a neat line. The silence between them thickened, like the King and her were speaking without words.

She flashed a polite business-like smile toward Adelira.

He smiled. "Seyla, your collection has only grown finer since I was last here."

"You've been away for a while," Seyla replied, smooth and casual enough. But her hand, as she picked up a jar to hand it to Orahn, trembled slightly.

His hand moved closer. Seyla's did as well. But they never touched.

Seyla's eyes lingered just a little too long on him when she thought Adelira wasn't looking.

Suddenly self-conscious of her own appearance; hair windswept, dress simpler than the woman's daring robes. Adelira brushed her hair down though it helped little. Seyla was the picture-perfect image of Vampiric ideals, she belonged to the night, to the market, maybe even to Orahn in a way Adelira wasn't sure she could ever belong to Tharth.

Seyla understood him beyond title, in a way Adelira hadn't earned yet. Orahn had had an entire life before Adelira had arrived and now she knew she'd robbed him of it. And she wasn't even a Vampire, she couldn't give that part of his life, of his identity, back to him.

Seyla extended a jar to Adelira.

"Would you like to try?" Seyla asked kindly, her eyes gentle as though she were trying to keep her inner thoughts hidden. "You're an artist, aren't you, Princess?"

Adelira froze. She had only told Orahn that. She wasn't expecting that he would have shared that with anyone else. She could almost believe Seyla would piece it together that they were there for her to get paints since it seemed unlikely that Orahn was an artist as well, but there were pigments here for dyeing fabrics and others for food and hair dyes as well, so guessing what exactly they were looking for felt doubtful.

Adelira turned the jar over and over in her hands, a nervous tick. She forced herself to stop, gripping the jar tight enough to ache a little.

Seyla continued, "The colours here are carefully created. You'll find the richest pigments, ones that last and blend as though made for dreams."

The invitation was generous, her smile kind, though there was something about it that felt... well-practised, guarded, even as it came off as flawlessly friendly. Adelira could sense Seyla's attempt at detachment, politeness that felt a little too perfected, masking something she would rather keep hidden.

"Thank you, I'd love to," Adelira replied, returning the smile.

Adelira dipped her finger into a soft green pigment Seyla handed her and admired the colour. Green was her favourite colour and she appreciated how effortlessly Seyla picked that up, having an instinct for colours. Smearing it between her forefinger and thumb until it dried on her skin.

"It's beautiful, Seyla. Your craftsmanship is incredible."

"Thank you, Your Highness," Seyla replied, her voice warming in response.

She sifted through more colours.

"The way the light catches this azure is magical and I can only imagine the things I could paint with this shade of crimson," Adelira murmured as she pulled jars out from the collection and stacked them in neat towers while she admired the richness of each shade.

Seyla relaxed into a genuine smile at Adelira's unfiltered praise.

"Your hair, your Highness," Seyla suddenly exclaimed, her eyes widening in appraisal. "It's the most *unbelievable* shade! I mean..." she caught herself, blushing slightly, "...I'm sorry, Your Highness. I just... couldn't help myself."

Adelira blinked, caught off guard by the sudden compliment, no one else had complimented her so freely in Tharth before. Adelira smiled, a broad smile that won Seyla over completely.

"Your hair is so striking, it'd make a statement in any one of our dresses," Seyla added. "Red against black, perfection."

"Oh, you think so? Orahn doesn't think I could manage any Vampire clothing."

He didn't say anything, but his lips twitched. She knew she was cutting since he'd framed it nicer than that, but she wasn't feeling entirely nice right now.

Seyla waved a hand dismissively. "Nonsense! I will send a colour palette to your tailors. There's no way those gorgeous curls won't *pop* against the right shades. You'll look divine."

Adelira brightened. "Thank you so much, Seyla."

"But, of course, Your Highness," she said, before letting her eyes drift, landing for a moment on the King again. Seyla seemed to catch herself then, clearing her throat as she gestured toward a new jar of violet paint. "In the meantime, this shade might just complement your gown. Let me know what you think."

"I think you're right, Seyla," Adelira said. "You have a wonderful eye. This colour's perfect."

"It's always been a passion of mine to bring colour into the world." Her eyes drifted to the King for just a fraction of a second before she lowered her gaze.

The kindness in Seyla's voice was tinged with a hint of longing that, to anyone else, would be unnoticeable, but Adelira saw it in the small, careful gestures. Lips pressed together too tightly, even as she smiled.

It struck her that Seyla had once harboured the secret hope that Orahn would set aside his duties for her, would make some grand, romantic choice that would sweep them both away. But, faced with the reality that he would never truly be hers, she seemed to wear her composure like armour.

"Will you be adding any new shades soon?" the King asked lightly, but his gaze was intense.

Adelira could read his genuine interest.

Seyla met his gaze and, for a brief moment, her practised mask faltered. A shadow of hurt passed over her features before she steadied herself and nodded.

"Of course," Seyla said, her tone was gentle. "I'm always adding to what was already there."

Adelira caught her flicker of heartache, quick as it was, hidden beneath her painted eyes. She admired Seyla's grace, her restraint in the face of heartbreak, even though it made Adelira feel small, guilty, as though she were standing in the place Seyla had once hoped to fill.

The silence deepened until he murmured a quiet, "Thank you," and Seyla nodded once, collecting herself with a dignified smile that made Adelira's chest ache for them all.

His fingers brushing over Seyla's as he slipped a vial of blood into her hands as payment. His smile fell away as they left the stall. Adelira looked over her shoulder, Seyla watched them disappear into the crowded streets, eyes lingering on the King.

Adelira clutched the paper bag of paints tightly into her chest like it could hold her together.

The walk home was in silence.

Finally, Adelira worked up the courage to ask, "Who was she?"

He laughed softly at her question. "What's wrong, Princess?"

"I was going to ask you that," she countered, her cheeks flushing red slightly.

He skipped a beat before he responded, "What could possibly be wrong?"

Her marriage wasn't supposed to be about love. Wasn't that what her mother had warned her? But seeing him with Seyla, seeing that sadness in his eyes, made her wonder if she could ever be anything more than a convenient alliance.

The King opened her chamber doors and waved her inside.

She hesitated as though she could wait for some explanation or apology, but when neither happened, she stepped through the threshold and this time he didn't follow her in. Confused by how much trust she'd lost and how she'd make this ground back, she searched his face.

"Don't leave your room alone," he said, clipped, his hand lingered on the doorframe. The sharpness in his voice stung, as though her presence had become a burden.

Perhaps it was meant for her safety, but it sounded like a threat. It was a challenge he dared her not meet.

His eyes flashed with regret, like even he wasn't sure what he'd done tonight. When they connected with hers, his hand brushed over his new sword, his expression almost softening before darkening again and he moved his hand away from the weapon to tug the door shut.

She said goodnight, but he replied with the closing of her door.

Adelira looked down at the jars of paints she crawled in her arms. The colours were perfect, rich, smooth and skillfully crafted. She'd have been excited to use them, if she didn't feel so much sadness for stepping into the middle of a story and changing the ending.

42

Chapter Forty-Two

The next night the scent of nightblooms and burning wicks curled through the air, but it did nothing to settle the restlessness in her chest.

A knock came at her door.

She opened it tentatively and saw the King standing there. Her guards were walking away and she braced herself for the version of him that he still would be during his in-between-nights.

"Adelira," he said, "Would you care to join me for dinner?"

There it was. He didn't call her *Princess*, but he hadn't called her *Lira*, either. It was that strange middle ground she couldn't understand, yet. The him who wielded silence like suffocation.

She glanced him over. He stood in her doorway, his stillness measured. He looked at her with unnerving clarity, like he could see all the way through her.

"No, thank you," she said and started to close the door.

He caught the door, his hand shooting out. It was a clean-cut motion, a scalpel slicing through its target.

She looked up, startled, half-flinching, but she couldn't tell from his expression what he was planning as he held her door open. Her heart raced faster with each passing second. He didn't move away or let go.

He raised an eyebrow, hand still on her door, and asked, "No?"

He asked like it was a challenge he set down before her, entirely clinical and too quiet.

"No," she repeated.

His gaze lingered intensely on her, weighing her response. He dropped his hand and stepped back, giving a curt bow.

Without a word, he turned and left.

She let out a shaky breath of relief. Her legs were trembling slightly. It had been harder to say no than she wanted to admit. The King had towered over her and eclipsed all light. His power in the Keep, in all of Tharth, was absolute.

She'd rather wait for the third night.

He was clearly a man of routine and she was disrupting it by pushing him to spend time with her when he wasn't able to give her what she needed.

What she needed didn't have to come from him.

Adelira wouldn't let a couple of awkward nights take from her. And she wouldn't let Seyla's efforts be wasted. Her paints were intended to be enjoyed and if Adelira had inadvertently taken something from her, she'd give back the only way she knew how, which was to truly and deeply appreciate her craft.

On the floor, skirts bunched around her knees, sleeves pushed up to her elbows, she studied the paints she had gotten from the market. Opening the jar, Adelira selected one of the brushes Carys had gifted her.

Exhaling slowly, she dipped her brush into the green first.

With careful strokes, she traced the shape of trees, their trunks stretching toward a sky she had yet to paint. She'd started this backwards, entirely in the wrong order, but the point was that she *had* started. Her heart had guided her hands and they led her home.

Letting her hand flow, dragging her brush through the paint again, this time shaping the rivers that cut through the woodland. She let the water spill across the canvas in soft blues and white.

Then, she almost painted *him* there. A figure in the distance, standing among the trees, the way he had stood beside her at the magic starry pool.

She stopped.

Instead, she added mist, the way it curled around the trunks in the early morning, veiling everything in quiet mystery.

Sitting back, paint stained her fingers.

Maybe she had not meant to paint him, but somehow, he was *still* there. Hidden between the brushstrokes, in the spaces between the trees, in the water that washed up against the rocks. And behind him stood someone else, someone almost familiar to her. An echo. Like a second him. Close. Almost... But not him.

She swallowed and set the brush down.

When she looked at the painting again, it did not feel like home. Home almost felt like the steadiness of the King, when he was calm, even when he was silent, slowly, she was beginning to understand the different sides to him.

She had painted most of the night. When she looked up, her tea had arrived in her room. She looked at it and knew it would be dawn soon.

Without drinking it, she climbed into the bath to wash away the paint. Scrubbing the colours from her skin and thoughts of the King.

The water was blues and greens running together. The colour hadn't disappeared, she was swimming in it.

Some nights, he was warmth itself, making her feel like they shared a secret. Charming and kind and everything she had never dreamed she could have from the Blood King.

Tonight when he had stood at her door, questioning her. He searched for her certainty, waiting until *she* believed in the 'no' she gave him.

He'd hurt her feelings last night.

Or maybe, she'd hurt her own.

And tonight, she wasn't ready to accept his distance disguised as effort.

Even if it had been the third-night, she wasn't sure she was ready, yet. She'd ached for her past, and for his, for the lives they had lived before the war. Everything they had lost when their worlds collided and everything they had yet to gain from each other. She also ached because a part of her yearned to be near him, but he was impossible to understand.

Even the fierce side of him was thrilling. There was something intoxicating about standing so close to death and knowing it would not touch her.

Softer moments undid her. When she caught him looking at her. When he reached for her hand absentmindedly, as if the action was as natural to him as breathing.

When she was clean, she stepped out and walked past the gown intended for sleeping in. In her closet she found a long Elven dress; lilac sleeves came down to her hands and the cut fell to her ankles. She combed through her wet red hair, pinned it up and walked up to her chamber doors.

Do not leave alone, his words echoed in her mind.

Maybe she did like something about every side of him she saw, but she wasn't about to stay locked away just because he had said so.

She listened through the door, but heard nothing, no danger, but then most of Tharth's dangers moved in silence.

Pulling back her shoulders, she took a deep breath and opened her door.

Adelira peeked her head out first and her door was guarded, even on the verge of daylight.

Benedict and Finn were startled by her sudden appearance, but she didn't slow down. They called her back, but she didn't stop. She listened to them clinking behind her and tried not to think it should be Talion behind her instead.

It was almost sunrise and the thick curtains were already drawn. The palace seemed empty as she made her way through corridors and halls.

She examined high, detailed paintings and touched smooth, marble statues. She opened doors and peered within, there was a room for everything in the Keep and she lost track of all the things she saw.

She found the Observatory in the upper section of the castle where they had done the Vow of Intent. A huge circular room with a glass dome top where the sun beamed in like the entire room had been set ablaze. The room glowed too brightly in contrast with the gloom she'd walked through to get here.

Benedict and Finn wisely stayed safely in the corridor.

She stepped into the sunlight. It felt forbidden to do in Tharth. The warmth on her skin was strange after so many cold, candlelit rooms. She closed her eyes and tipped her face toward the dome, letting it pour over her.

Before she could stop herself, she twirled.

Then she moved again, more slowly. The light caught in her red hair making it shine like fire.

Behind her, Benedict shifted his weight. Finn cleared his throat. She glanced back and saw the way their shadows pooled just outside the sunlit floor. Still guarding her. Still waiting. They could wait, she wanted to touch the sun.

Her skirts flared, catching the light. For a moment, she wasn't in Tharth. She wasn't watched. She wasn't anyone's bride, anyone's captive.

Swaying, light glancing off like spun gold. When she turned, Finn was watching her, expression unreadable, jaw set. But his hand quivered, like he'd reached for her, even in the light, if he needed to.

Her fingers drifted through the air, unsettling the dust motes that shone like stars in the light, and she soaked up as much warmth as she could.

She stayed in the sun until their anxiety began to crackle like static behind her. With reluctant grace, she drifted back; not because they called her back, but because she wanted to ease their hearts.

Even if they pretended to be hardened soldiers, she still felt their anxiety in the restless way they shuffled when she was out of their reach, locked behind a wall of sunlight they dared not breach.

"I'm alright, I'm right here," she said to reassure them as she stepped back into the shadowed corridors, slipping between them.

Benedict's face twitched like he wasn't impressed, but Finn almost smiled. She was almost winning smiles from her guards now. And she smiled back.

43

Chapter Forty-Three

Adelira made her way back through the Keep, her guards close behind her. On the other side of the castle something caught her attention.

The library spanned an entire wing of the castle. It stretched so far that the expanse of shelves turned into shadows in the distance. There were ladders on tracks and winding staircases leading to the uppermost levels.

A feeling of being watched again, those unseen eyes in the back of her head and the King's warning not to leave her room flared in her mind. A mix of guilt and exhilaration washed through her. Whoever it was who always watched at the back of her head, didn't seem to care what the King had said. They never revealed themselves, never reminded her that she shouldn't be out.

Her guards stepped back, allowing her the space to explore. She flashed them a grateful smile. Rayno would have followed right behind her. She appreciated the chance to breathe. She knew it was likely for their own benefit, her blood was testing, but she chose to believe it was an act of kindness. Mercy for them all, maybe.

Fingers trailed lightly along the spines of book, Adelira picked up a particularly hefty tome; the dust jacket faded, but still legible, *Shifters: A New Age*. Gingerly, she pulled the book from the shelf. Its spine settling into her lap as she curled up in one of the lounges near a fire.

"Your Highness."

She glanced up in surprise.

Standing before her was a woman with dark tightly curled hair. Her brown eyes were warm and observant, framed behind gold-rimmed glasses, and most importantly, they were locked onto Adelira without hunger or strain. She wore a sweet, but elegant black dress and a small smile on her lips. Her posture was relaxed, but there was a quiet confidence that put Adelira at ease. This was no Vampire, of that Adelira was immediately sure, but what she was remained a mystery.

"Hello," she replied informally. She didn't want to play by the stiff courtesies of court here.

The woman let her smile broaden as she pointed to the book Adelira held. "That one is very popular."

Adelira blinked in surprise at how daringly this woman broke the 'no-talking to her' rule that seemed to be followed by everyone else in Tharth.

"You're talking to me? Oh, no, I mean, yes... Yes, I'm sure it is read by many," Adelira replied in bursts, her curiosity piqued on the woman before her who willingly engaged with her, "Why don't you want to eat me?"

"I'd rather consume books than princesses." Her voice was reassuring, but there was a playful glint in her eyes and a smile pulling at her lips.

"W–what's your name?"

"I'm Evie Naledi," the woman responded. Her smile was bright. "I am the keeper of the library."

Adelira's brows raised in surprise. She glanced around at the seemingly endless shelves and then back at Evie.

"The whole library?" she asked.

Evie chuckled softly; the sound rolled in the stillness of the library. "Oh, not by myself!" she said with pride. "There's a fleet of us."

This kind of warmth had become foreign, but Evie made it feel familiar again. It was something rare to find someone so bright and hopeful in the cold and formal atmosphere of the palace. It wasn't often she met someone without an unspoken threat of hunger hanging between them.

The simplicity of their exchange wasn't just refreshing, it was everything Adelira needed. Evie saw her. They stood in the library surrounded by the tale of a thousand different lives, but it was Adelira whom Evie chose to give her time and respect.

"It must be wonderful," Adelira said, glancing at the shelves again. "All this knowledge at your fingertips."

Evie nodded. "It is. The stories they tell, the histories they keep alive. Every book here has a life of its own." Her hand motioned toward the shelf behind Adelira. "Some are just waiting for the right reader to come along, and sometimes if I'm lucky, I get to help them find that person."

"You're amazing. Sorry. *That*. That is amazing," the words left Adelira before she was able to stop them. She winced, she sounded too earnest, even to herself.

Her words were equally stunning to Evie, whose lips parted in surprise before she smiled brighter than before.

Evie said slowly, "You're not like anyone else here."

Adelira wanted to say no one else had dared talk to her, but she was afraid if she voiced that out loud that Evie might remember that she wasn't supposed to speak to her either. Instead, Adelira just offered an awkward smile.

"I'll be here looking for silverfish around here, I'll try not to disturb you while you read."

"I would absolutely love the company. Disturb me... please?"

Her whole face lit up. "Hold on!" And she was gone, dashing through the library and darting behind some shelves.

Adelira settled deeper into the soft velvet of the chaise lounge. She'd only just found where she'd left off when a pile of books thudded onto the coffee table besides her.

"These are good, too!" Evie announced eagerly as she set down a pile of books on the table.

Looking at the hefty pile, she said, "Talk me through them?"

Evie said, "Yes, Princess."

"Adelira, please. If one more person refuses to use my name, I might forget I have one," she said lightly, but she was mostly serious.

"Ah, so you've experienced the Vampires' particular flavour of hospitality. They can be a bit uptight. Especially with your tasty blood type." Suddenly her face fell and she apologised, "I–I'm sorry, I shouldn't have said that!"

Adelira laughed heartily. "You acknowledged that out loud! You're truly delightful. What blood type are you?"

Evie said with a grin that suddenly seemed predatory, "I'm a Shifter."

Her grey eyes showed first panic, but she forced it away, holding the book tightly. Orahn would not let dangers in his castle, at least, no more than the usual Vampire ones. Knowing that allowed her to swallow her fear and meet Evie with intrigue. "But not a wolf? You're not from the Rip."

"No, of course not. I was born here."

"So, what are you?"

"Guess." Evie said the word with a smirk that played across her entire face.

Her eyes sparkling with mischief as she leaned against the towering bookshelf nearby and exhaled a heavy breath of thick smoke.

Adelira looked up, a smile began to bloom on her face. She leaned forward, resting her elbows on her knees. "That's what you are, then? A book-hoarding dragon?"

"Exactly." Evie winked.

Adelira laughed again. There was something about Evie's playful energy that put her at ease.

Tilting her head as she teased, "So, is there a hoard of gold somewhere behind all these books, too?"

"Oh, definitely. Gold. But it's well-hidden," Evie replied, her voice lowering to a playful whisper. "No one's found it, yet. The books keep them distracted."

Evie leaned casually against the armrest of a nearby chair, but slipped off and caught herself giggling. Adelira grinned and leaned back into her chair. Evie was charmingly ungraceful. In a castle where she couldn't connect with anyone, Evie was her first real hope that she may survive Tharth.

Adelira often felt self-conscious of her own nervous chatter that flowed too freely, but Evie made her feel safe, like maybe it didn't matter so much that she was entirely different, because Evie was different, too. It was refreshing, being in her presence was like standing in the forest breeze without actually leaving the castle.

"So, tell me, is there anyone else who reads as much as you?" Adelira asked, her hands resting on the open book in her lap. She wasn't sure what to talk about, she just knew she wanted to keep talking, she wanted to hear everything Evie had to say.

Evie sighed theatrically, settling down into a nearby chair with a slight shrug.

"There are some who might, but I'm an unusual breed. My love for books is... unparalleled." Her eyes gleamed. She spoke of her books with the same hunger the Vampires had in their eyes when they looked at Adelira. "There's something about them, though, isn't there? The way a story can carry you to a whole different world. I suppose it's the closest we'll ever get to magic now that all the Witches have left the world."

Adelira found herself sharing as well, "When I was younger, when the world seemed so much bigger than I could understand..."

She tried to put the book on the table, but her hands trembled slightly, and it slipped. Evie caught it and placed it gently on the table, glancing over the title again rather than drawing attention to the mishap. Adelira closed her eyes and tried not to hear Talion's voice reading to her.

Evie studied the book for a moment longer, reading deeper into her words. "Is that why you were drawn to this book?" she asked gently. "Did it help you manage your fears about them?"

She blinked, slightly taken aback. Evie's insight was cherished. Adelira felt exposed, her feelings had been laid bare. But the sincerity in Evie's eyes reassured her. It made her feel seen rather than judged as Evie returned the book to her. She looked down at the book in her lap, tracing the embossed title with her fingers before answering.

"Yes," she admitted. "When I was a child, the thought of Shifters from the Rip kept me up at night. They aren't a part of our world or our equilibrium. That terrifies me. I read everything I could find about them. I suppose I thought that if I understood the wolves, I wouldn't be so afraid. Plus, I couldn't stay under the blanket any longer."

"I'm not entirely sure what staying under a blanket means, but I understand how books help arm me against the world."

Adelira still felt watched, but she let herself believe it was Benedict and Finn, not the unseen eyes that seemed trained to her just as closely.

Tilting her head slightly, she studied Adelira more closely. "It must be strange for you... being here," she said. "The palace, the Vampires... it's not exactly like your home, I imagine."

Sighing, she glanced down at the thin Elven dress she wore. "It's very different," she admitted. "Tharth feels... cold."

"Have they shown you the dresses?"

Adelira rolled her eyes when Evie looked like she was about to burst out in laughter.

"Tease me all you want, but it's not just in the air. Everyone is so closed off. It's hard to know where I fit in, or if I will ever fit in at all. I hope it is better after the Blood Ritual... whenever that might be."

"This place can be overwhelming. But you're not alone in feeling that way. Even some of us who've been here our whole lives still feel out of place at times."

"Y–You feel that way, too?"

Evie gave a small shrug. "King Orahn values knowledge. He built the largest library in the twelve Kingdoms. Which is why I'm here and not with my people. I've spent most of my life here. I don't fit in, but this," she looked around the library with loving eyes, "this place is mine."

Adelira smiled at that, feeling a sense of kinship with the woman. "I envy you, in a way. You've found a place that's truly yours."

Evie's eyes twinkled with quiet pride. "It took time. And patience... And the King. But you'll find yours, too."

"Thank you, Evie," Adelira said, wondering how the King helped her and thinking about how he promised to help her, too. That promise felt more real now. "I needed to hear that."

Evie leaned back in her chair, satisfied. "Well, that's what dragons are for. We're full of wisdom... and fire."

Adelira now knew of a place in the Obsidian Keep that was warm and inviting and, most importantly, welcomed her in.

Throughout the day, the two women continued to talk. Their conversation flowed easily from books to life in the palace, to their hopes and fears.

The library, once vast and endless, now felt smaller and cosier. Evie created a haven shared between two kindred spirits.

44

Chapter Forty-Four

Orahn arrived on the third night, as normal.

But this time, Adelira didn't turn, her gaze still fixed on the horizon and the trees there. Seated by the window, legs tucked beneath her, fingers wrapped around a book from Evie.

Benedict and Finn stood on the other side of the room, even they had the sense to give her space. A sense the King had not discovered, yet.

"Lira?"

The silence stretched and then he crossed the room with deliberate quiet, stopping just short of her.

"Did you think I wouldn't come?"

"I thought you might," she said finally, still not turning to face him. "You usually do."

Orahn was silent for a moment, then pulled a chair to sit across from her. "Something's different."

The scent of frost and whisky drifted between them.

"Is it?" she asked, and this time she did glance at him, just long enough for him to see the coolness in her eyes before flickering back towards the window.

"I was looking forward to tonight," he offered.

"You only miss your third-night-cycle. I'm the one here every night, waiting to see who shows up."

He exhaled, short and sharp through his nose. "You're angry."

"No," she said quietly, and she meant it. "Just not sure who you are when you're not... here. Even when you *are* here."

She turned in time to see the panic flash across his face. Then he looked pained. He turned his face away, realising he couldn't mask himself quickly enough. Once he returned his gaze to her, his expression was solemn, his eyes distant, reminding her that she was still an outsider, not just in Tharth, but to the King, too. Was this the secret he was hiding, his heart wasn't free to want...

"I should let you rest," she said, rising and gathering her things. "Good night, Orahn."

Orahn didn't try to stop her as she crossed the room. He just said her name, softer this time, almost like it might break. He leaned back in the chair, staring up at the same stars she had been watching.

∞

Adelira moved through the library while Evie worked with a scribe.

She pushed open the bottom floor doors and stepped outside. Benedict almost protested, Finn almost stopped her, but the sound of steel rang sharp through the chill night air and gave them all pause.

She looked back at them and then walked quietly through the shadowed garden corridors towards the battleyard. Her guards were close behind her as she followed the sounds to the training arena.

She didn't belong in this space, even less than she belonged in the Obsidian Keep itself. The last time she was here, she'd been invited to hear about the Blood Ritual, without an invite this time the arena felt unsafe. She almost turned and went back inside, but something drew her in.

Adelira paused at the side lines of the battleyard, half-shrouded in darkness. The yard itself was dimly lit by lanterns set high on the walls.

The Vampire King stood alone at the centre, his shirt discarded, his chest heaving, skin gleaming with sweat. His blade moved with relentless precision. This wasn't elegant like in the market, this was brutal, like each strike was meant to punish the world into submission. When the wind picked up, she smelled frost and smoke.

He didn't pause. Didn't look up.

His sword struck the training dummy again and again, driving it back on its post. A splinter cracked and fell. He adjusted his grip. Swung again.

She looked up at her guards. Finn was grinning, a little too hungrily, like he was holding back by sheer willpower not to join the King in training. Benedict was subtler about it, the longing hidden in his eyes, but she imagined even he would rather be training with the King than following her around the gardens.

The fire that burned through his veins, that burned itself out in his training. That same fire was what stopped her, she could no sooner reach for him than she could place her fingertip in flames. She stepped back and watched instead, her heart racing.

Just then the King's sword paused, raised above his head, and his head tilted down and back ever so subtly, like he'd heard them in the shadows.

A gasp froze on her lips.

Then he brought the sword swinging down, again and again, with even more brutality than before. Unrelenting until the training post exploded into nothing but chunks of wood across the yard.

He obliterated the targets in front of him with the force that she now tied to The Vampire King.

Whenever she saw him with a weapon in his hand, her confusion melted away. She trusted this version of him to destroy her enemies.

War hero, not lover.

She didn't need to earn his love. She needed to earn his trust so she could get her Blood Ritual.

Alright Adi, time to try again, she told herself.

She took a deep breath, finding her way back in the dark.

She hadn't realised just how far away he could go in the in-between nights, but at least now she knew there was a pattern that'd bring him back to her.

Maybe third-night Kings were all the affection she could hope to get from him, and, in truth, that was more than most arranged marriages got.

∞

Dinner was served in the dining hall. Though no servers stationed the wall, the table spread was already laid out, minimal, but an amount she finally felt confident she could eat. Her guards remained outside the hall, this evening was intended for a private affair.

Adelira arrived first, choosing a seat that didn't face the door. She didn't want to be caught watching when he entered. She picked up a slice of watermelon and nibbled while she waited for the King.

When the King did arrive, he gave a polite nod, nothing more. Frost and parchment laced over the smells of dinner. He looked... composed. Too composed.

And her fingers were sticky with juices running down her arm and a half-eaten piece of fruit in between her fingers.

They ate, the clink of silver on porcelain filling the room in place of words. She was surprised to see he actually did eat.

"You're quieter than usual," he noted after a time, voice low, but not cold.

Adelira glanced at him, expression neutral. "You're quiet."

He smiled faintly, and for a moment it almost looked like something familiar.

"I suppose we're both adapting," he said, spearing a piece of roasted root vegetable.

"To what?" She asked in Ehvayn, just to test him.

The King looked at her for a moment, but didn't answer. He didn't ask her to repeat it in Tharic either, though. The last time she'd spoken in Ehvayn, he'd been frustrated. The time before that, he'd stopped, like he understood. But how could that be when he'd had such a strong reaction to not understanding? His silence offered her nothing.

She'd finished the bowl of watermelon and started on a glass of wine. The silence between them didn't feel like punishment anymore. Just tired of being so... What was the word Orahn had used? Uncertain? Yes, she was exhausted by uncertainty.

He gave her so little reason to trust him, but tonight his stillness felt like kindness.

"Will you see me tomorrow night?" she reached out to him in Tharic again.

He blinked in surprise, then nodded. "Yes."

Her shoulders dropped, letting go of the tension of the last few nights. "I'd like that."

45

Chapter Forty-Five

Orahn arrived at her chambers.

His smile immediately warmed her chest. He was unguarded and hers, a *third-night-kind-of-hers*.

The skies were clear of clouds and the twin moons shone into the gardens, gliding over her silks. She glowed and Orahn, dressed entirely in black, was a part of the night itself. He slowed pace as she touched the delicate veins of the plants.

"I know I stepped into the middle of your life and changed what it might have looked like without me. Perhaps you could have had someone else, someone from your own Kingdom," she said softly as they walked through the gardens. "I'm sorry for that."

"I meant what I said when I told you that I don't regret this. It was unexpected, yes, and I've had to rearrange pieces of my life, but that is life. You've surprised me, not overwhelmed me."

"Even so, it hasn't been easy for you."

"On the contrary, nothing's been easy for *you*," he said quietly.

She blinked and looked up at him. He had noticed.

"And you still arrive every night," he continued. "I was built for hardship, but you are not difficult for me."

"Only my impact here. My blood."

"Sure, that's had some impact. My Vampires can learn to adjust to you."

"Just your Vampires?"

"I will learn," he whispered.

"Orahn..."

"I don't promise perfection, Lira. Perhaps I cannot even give you nights like this every night, but I can promise they will happen, from time to time, as long as you want them."

He held out her arm to her and she tucked herself into the crook of his arm as they walked, her head resting gently against him.

∞

The next two nights, she spent with Evie. She wasn't avoiding the King, she just wanted her friend, especially during the in-between-nights.

She smiled up at the King as he walked into her chambers.

Orahn entered dressed in travel clothes, his riding boots tapping on the polished floor. Her pulse quickened, her eyes on the boots — his riding boots.

"You're leaving?" she asked, trying to sound casual, though her voice betrayed her panic.

"Yes." He shrugged slightly, almost as though he didn't want to say it aloud.

"Where?" She closed her eyes, cursing herself. "You don't have to tell me."

"It's not a secret."

"Where?" she asked again, softer this time.

"There's steel to be bargained for. I have to negotiate a better price with the miners in the South so we can fashion enough weapons." His eyes studied her face for a moment, like he was trying to read her reaction to that. "I don't even know if you want to know any of those details..."

"I do, I–I want to know."

Orahn gave a slight nod. "There are usually people I send for these discussions, but the South won't engage with anyone but me. They want the King."

She raised an eyebrow, the hint of a smile tugging at her lips. "I think they want a steep price for their steel if they'll only engage with a King."

Orahn's smile deepened, that familiar playful spark in his eyes. "Naturally. But I'll see what they want first." His voice dropped into a private whisper, "Perhaps the pirates have a better price for a King."

"I thought you were at war with the fae pirates?"

"We are." His grin only grew wider. "They'd still take the gold for it. We can continue to fight about the rest afterwards."

The ease at which he stood there like the world bent to his will; she half expected him to return with the steel and the pirates' ships as if it were nothing more than a game.

"You can tell me who had the better deal when you're home."

She heard a horse neighing from outside her open windows and was reminded how little time they had tonight.

"There's still so much I want to know about Tharth and Vampires..." she said.

He leaned back against her door frame, his arms folded casually over his chest. "I have a few minutes if you've thought of more questions to ask me."

The question that she wanted to ask most was what made him so unpredictable on the two in-between-nights, but that question wouldn't come.

Instead, she said, "Do you ever miss the sun?"

His lips pulled into a small frown. "I've never felt the sun."

To her the sun was memory. To him it was a myth.

It seemed such an impossible thing to have never experienced. He probably hadn't even thought about it except as a cruel thing, the exact opposite of what she viewed it as.

Just a few nights ago, she didn't know if she ever wanted to see the King again, now the thought of not seeing him twisted inside her.

Stay, she almost said.

"There's more," Orahn guessed. "I can see it turning over in your mind."

"I thought you said you don't read minds."

"I don't, you're just not very subtle."

Adelira gave a small smile, trying to ignore the heat rising in her cheeks at his implication.

She fidgeted with her sleeve before she blurted out, "Well, since we're skimming over subtlety, I was wondering... do Vampires have ways to avoid pregnancies?"

Orahn blinked, then laughed; genuine and surprised, caught him off guard by her question. He held up his hand, the single gold band glinting on his finger. "This wards off fertility. A necessary precaution when you're not... always in control of your... strength."

She'd never heard him have to search for the right words like this before, this was fun. She raised an eyebrow, half-teasing, half-testing. "You sound like someone expecting to need it."

His expression softened a fraction though the amusement still in his voice, "Not expecting. Just prepared."

Adelira shrugged lightly, trying to be casual about it now. "I was only curious."

His eyes lingered on her face though she wasn't quite ready to meet his gaze yet. "You ask the kind of questions that stay in a man's mind."

"There's probably a hundred questions I want to ask you," she admitted.

"And *that* came to mind first?" He raised an eyebrow.

Her cheeks reddened. "No. It's just one of them. I have many others."

His smile turned gentler. "I'll answer them all, but it might have to wait until my return."

"One more?" she said softly, not looking up.

"Ask," he said, his voice just as low.

Adelira hesitated, her voice quieter now, "Do you... need to take your ring with you?"

Orahn tilted his head, a flicker of amusement and something unreadable in his eyes. Then, without a word, he slid the band off his finger and offered it to her.

Her eyes widened. "I didn't mean—" She broke off, unsure what she had been trying to say.

He gently pressed the ring into her hand. "I won't need it. Will you keep it safe?"

She stared at the warm band in her palm, unsure what the ring meant for her... if it meant anything.

"I'll be back in a week or so." His words were simple, but his eyes lingered on her face.

"I'll be here," she said even though that seemed obvious.

He didn't respond immediately. Orahn stepped closer until the space between them felt dangerously small, only a breath between the warmth of his chest and the stutter in hers.

"Goodbye, Lira," he said as he tucked a loose lock of her hair tenderly behind her ear.

Orahn's eyes softened in concern and then it was gone. He strode from her room with the same authority he always carried.

Her cheek burned where his fingers brushed her. She placed the ring next to her pebble. He hadn't said what it meant.

She walked out onto her balcony and watched as general Victoria waited for the King with their mounts in the courtyard. The general was all tension and control in her muscles as she sat on her steed.

Adelira was surprised to see the King travelled so lightly, but then the general and the King were an army all on their own.

46

Chapter Forty-Six

Stepping out of her room into the castle, Adelira felt unseen eyes on her, tracking her movement and knew she'd find no one if she looked.

Her guards shifted their stance as she passed and they waited the briefest pause before following her through the Obsidian.

But they were always behind her, no different from her old guards in that way, except these two men never spoke to her unless absolutely necessary. Talion pretended not to speak unless necessary, but he was an *expert* at finding reasons to.

Orahn's absence left behind a mournful palace that seemed dimmer and distrustful without him. Adelira felt the chill beneath her fingertips as she pressed a hand to the window, peering out longingly. The city moved under a shroud of mist and moonlight.

Without turning from the window, Adelira asked softly, "Do you ever feel like someone is watching you?"

Neither of the guards answered her, both of them remaining perfectly still as though they hadn't heard her. She caught Finn's eye before he turned away.

Her voice cracked, more fragile than she meant it to be. "Please don't ignore me."

His eyes closed briefly.

She turned to them, blinking fast against the sting in her eyes. "I can't stand it if no one in this Keep speaks to me. I know you're under orders, I know I'm just a responsibility — but *please*. Just talk to me. Even if it's to say you won't."

Shame bloomed across her chest, tight and aching. She felt like she might cry or maybe just retreat to the library.

Then, softly, Finn spoke, "We're watching you."

Her breath hitched in surprise that he spoke and she searched his face.

"No, Finn," she whispered. "You're standing guard. That's not the same. Someone *else* is watching me."

At that, Benedict's face twitched just enough to make her heart thud. He said nothing, but his hand moved over the hilt of his sword in reflex.

Finn scanned the corridor again, more thoroughly this time, his gaze lingering in shadowed corners and the stretch of halls behind them, listening for any movement.

"This must be unsettling for you," he said, then.

"To feel someone's always watching?"

"No, the quiet. The King's absence is felt by us all. Like something is never quite right when he's away."

Benedict passed him a hard look.

Finn lowered his gaze, almost in shame of Benedict's swift correction, but he continued in defiance, "I imagine you feel it harder than the rest of us."

She stared at him. No one, save Orahn on rare nights, acknowledged her feelings, her fear, her *being*. This was an unexpected mercy from her guard. A reaching towards her that she hadn't even dared to hope for. And he voiced something she felt deeply, yet couldn't believe it was how the rest of the Blood Court felt. Orahn's place in Tharth was so foundational, everyone was a little off centre without him.

The urge to reach out gripped her; just for the *contact*, reaching for something she could almost believe was Elven in its honesty. But she stopped herself. She folded the ache inside and offered him a small nod instead. That was the appreciation he could accept from her, that was the Tharathi way.

"I'm going to walk in the garden," she said, the words half-invitation, half-test. "Would you care to join me?"

Finn's lips curved faintly, like he might have laughed if he were allowed to be anyone else tonight. She caught the edges of it, even passed Benedict.

"As if I'd let you go alone," he said, gently. "Lead the way."

She turned toward the arching stairwell that would take her down to the gardens, her steps slower now. Finn followed a pace behind, and Benedict moved into place at his side.

And for the first time since arriving in Tharth, she wasn't entirely sure she was alone. They were risking scrutiny, speaking to her, any warmth her guards showed was a weakness in their armour. She understood what they were risking, tonight she cherished that risk more than ever.

She wove through the gardens first, where dark ivy curled up black-stone walls, their pale blooms glowing in the low lantern light.

"Can I ask a question?"

Benedict sighed and nodded.

"You have no reflection in the mirrors in the halls, but I see you in windows..."

"That's not a question," Benedict said gruffly.

She narrowed her eyes at him, half-rolling them, half-smiling. "The question is why?"

"The old magic that suppresses Vampires used to do a lot more to us than it currently does. The mirror is left over from that, we took back the glass," Finn said.

"You took it back?"

"Took back some power," he shrugged, "Or the fading magic is weaker in places? I'm not sure the difference matters."

"It matters," Benedict said. "We don't know which though."

47

Chapter Forty-Seven

The gates opened not for her, but at the smallest nod from Benedict, revealing the city of Tharth sprawled beneath the ink-stained sky.

The night market was a glitter of movement and conversations. Charred meat wafted through the chilly evening air. Musicians played haunting melodies on string instruments.

Adelira wanted to stop and take it all in. Some stalls sold bottled laughter or a memory from a stranger.

Laughter in a bottle, she thought, *how easily Tharth caged happiness.*

She kept walking, leaving the market behind and moving into the city itself.

She passed Seyla's stall last. Adelira smiled, hand lifted in greeting.

"Good evening, Seyla. Your paints were a blessing to work with, thank you!"

The paint seller waved back with a small, polite smile. Then she saw the direction Adelira was walking, *leaving* the market toward the city and the smile faltered into alarm.

"Your Highness, wait, where are you going?" Seyla called, her voice tight with concern.

"Simply a walk," Adelira called back and gave a final goodbye wave.

Seyla's panicked eyes darted to the guards.

Finn gave her a lazy shrug. Benedict didn't even bother to glance her way, ignoring the panic rolling off the paint seller. He followed; a silent shadow to the princess.

The market noise and bustle gave way to the city which spread out like spilled ink in the night with winding cobbled streets and brick alleys.

Streets were slick with recent rain and glistened under the twin moons. Buildings leaned close together like they were passing secrets back and forth through the night. The hairs on the back of her neck bristled as she made her way through the streets.

A child sat on a low wall carefully folding a piece of paper and dropped it into a gutter of flowing rainwater. The boy said a name and the paper burst into flames, the ashes quickly sinking into the water.

As she walked she heard the fluttering of wings and looked up at the tall curled street light above her. The glass jar was filled with fireflies instead of flames. Her hand twitched at her side as she fought the impulse to set them free.

A woman in rags hugged a cup in her sinewy fingers. She hurried over to Adelira and Finn stepped neatly in her path, but still the old woman peered around him and held out the cup to Adelira.

"Take a sip and let the coffee bones at the bottom reveal your future," the old woman said in a hoarse voice.

Adelira almost reached for the cup.

"No," Benedict said firmly, speaking for the princess.

Adelira shook her head to reaffirm what Benedict said. The woman walked away muttering things in a language Adelira didn't speak.

A man stepped forward. Benedict and Finn stepped closer to her.

The man said, "You can step into my alleyway, it will only cost you a memory. Perhaps one you've long forgotten, you won't even miss it then. What do you say, Your Highness?"

She backed up into Finn's chest. He didn't move, though his hand was on his sword hilt and his body coiled for attack. She felt all of his muscles tense along her spine and she didn't know if she wanted to lean into him or run from all three of them.

"I want my memories. E–even my forgotten ones," she said nervously.

"Ah, I could help you retrieve the forgotten ones," the man said eagerly.

"N–no," she said quickly. "No, thank you."

Benedict stood in front of the man and nodded him back into the alleyway, still standing in front of Adelira, shielding her from view with his body as though the man might try to pluck the memories through proximity. She wanted to step away, though Finn still stood solidly at her back.

The man bowed and slunk back into the shadows.

Still flush with Finn, she tilted her head up and he looked down at her, as soon as his eyes connected with her, he stepped back, putting distance between them.

The soft slosh of river water pulled her towards the bridge.

The River Vein cut through the city, splitting it in half.

The surface caught fragments of starlight and lanterns in its waves. Stone banks overtaken by nightblooms; violet flowers with ink-dark petals that only opened in darkness, a scent between incense and decay with roots that broke through into the mortar between stones.

The city was slowly being devoured by its own beauty.

Adelira stood on one of the narrow bridges that crossed the River Vein. Her fingers brushed over the cold stone walls and looked down at the water. Finn leaned against the bridge's railing with idle alertness, his posture casual, but there was a glint in his eyes like he enjoyed the danger of the city.

Good, Adelira thought, he was enjoying his night. She smiled.

A couple approached. Pale makeup, dark velvet, blackened silver jewellery in baroque layers; clothing like funeral finery from centuries past.

"Excuse me, do you know where this river comes from? It's beautiful."

The man offered a slow smile, his teeth just slightly too sharp. "This is the River Vein, my lady. It flows from the mountain springs in the cliffs above us. The city was built around it. They say it fed the first gardens of Tharth... and the first crypts."

His partner added with a quiet laugh, "And sometimes it brings things down from the peaks..."

"What things?"

"Things better left upstream."

Adelira glanced at the water, suddenly unsure whether it glistened with starlight or something darker. She smiled faintly, offering her thanks, and continued down the bridge.

A child darted past, dropping an armful of logs.

Adelira gathered up the wood quickly.

Finn tried to take it from her but she flashed him a 'thanks, but I've got this' smile and pulled the logs back. Finn dropped his arms and slipped into the shadows behind her.

The boy was surprised, but he showed her where to take them.

At the top of the stairs, the boy turned. "Thank you," he murmured.

Benedict's voice broke the quiet at last, low and dry as old parchment. "We should not linger too long."

"Perhaps," she said softly. "But I wanted to see what was real."

Benedict didn't answer. Finn stifled a surprised cough under his breath. What was *real* in Tharth, they both knew, was rarely what it seemed. And rarely safe.

They made their way back through the city. As soon as they entered the night market, Seyla's eyes locked onto them in obvious relief, her features instantly relaxing. Adelira threw her a small reassuring smile as they passed.

Through the fortified Keep, they moved into the castle, which felt like it was still holding its breath.

Could stone really feel this unsettled by the departure of its King?

Her fingers brushed over the stone. The Obsidian Keep only seemed to sulk harder.

Chapter Forty-Eight

Adelira pushed open the library doors.

Evie was curled up on the green chaise under the circular window, book in her lap, spectacles low on her nose.

"Evie!" Adelira's voice rang out. "You wouldn't believe how beautiful the city is."

"I would believe it," she said, looking up. "I just wouldn't trust it."

"There was someone selling memories. And there was a spell that set a paper boat alight. When the river rushes too quickly under the bridge, it sounds like it's laughing."

Evie tucked a pressed leaf into her book, setting it aside. "Did anyone follow you?"

Evie's gaze landed on the guards for reassurance. Benedict gave away nothing as he moved to the corner of the room to wait for Adelira. Finn offered Evie the barest shake of his head before he retreated as well.

"There was a couple on the bridge. They spoke like they were quoting something. One of them smiled like... he knew a joke I wouldn't want to hear." Adelira dropped onto the chaise beside her. "You think I was foolish."

"No," Evie said. "You're just finding your own way in Tharth, because waiting feels endless."

"You belong here, I still don't even know what here *looks* like."

"It wasn't always that way for me. It takes time."

"I want that belonging... But I don't like parts of it, like how the city made it feel," Adelira admitted quietly, "like I could vanish there and no one would stop it... Or notice."

Evie set her tea down. "Indifferent, that's what Tharth *is*, Adelira. It's beautiful and dangerous that way." Evie exhaled, brushing her dark curls back. "You're the kind of person who chases the parts that might kill you."

Adelira rested her head against Evie's shoulder, knowing her friend spoke of the King. "You make it sound like I'm a reckless romantic."

"You are."

"And you're the cautious scholar who sees ghosts in every footstep."

"Because sometimes they're real," Evie murmured.

Adelira curled in closer and asked, "Do you truly not like it?"

"I'm practical," Evie replied, sipping her tea; steamed almond milk with rosemary. "Too many people out there. It's loud. I don't like guessing how to navigate everyone out there. Here, people come to *me*. The ones who love books, who speak softly, who care enough to linger in silence. The rest filter themselves out."

Adelira laughed in delight. "You never have to go anywhere, curating all of your interactions this carefully."

"I am wise." Evie flashed a bright smile, eyes twinkling through golden glasses. "You're the one coming home trailing stardust and trouble."

"I'm not looking for trouble. I *do* love seeing people and hearing their stories. It reminds me that the world is bigger than the Obsidian Keep. Bigger than me. Older than my time here. It reminds me that I haven't broken anything just by being here. And if it's truly this big, then there must be space for me somewhere here, right, Evie?"

Evie's expression softened, the affection barely held back in her dark brown eyes and she pushed back another bouncy curl with a sigh. "Please promise me you will be careful."

"I will."

Adelira reached for her tea, the cup already brewed to perfection under Evie's careful preparation. It occurred to Adelira then, that Orahn *only* trusted Evie in his absence with the teas to help her sleep and Adelira nestled in closer.

"Tell me about your mountains, Evie."

Evie pulled a shawl around them and leaned into Adelira's warmth. "There's a kind of lichen that only glows after the first frost. You have to watch it before dawn; can't breathe on it, or it fades."

Adelira sighed contentedly, already getting sleepy on the tea. "Of all the magic I saw tonight, you're my favourite, Evie."

49

Chapter Forty-Nine

Benedict said, his words carrying through the door, "You think it's mercy. That it will save her. It won't. It'll just mark you next."

Finn said tightly, "Then let it."

"You forget the Blood King has a temper that is only in hibernation."

"I forget nothing. I know where my place is."

"You best remember your place is *silent*."

Adelira waited a moment and opened the door. Her guards straightened.

"I'm going for a walk."

She returned to the city, but as she passed a merchant, the man froze.

Finn stepped between her and the man until she could no longer see the Vampire. Benedict brushed her arm with his elbow, he never quite touched her but the signal was clear. *Eyes ahead.*

Once they had passed, she looked at them. The tension was still coiled in her younger of the two guards.

"Finn?"

He sighed, like he wasn't going to answer, but then he said, "What are we truly doing here?"

Benedict shot him a hard glare and he straightened up again, remembering his place and scanned the alleys.

"I want to see the world I live in."

They didn't speak after that, silent behind her.

"Ah, the King's pet is out, again," a man leered as he and his friends passed.

Benedict took a step towards them and the man laughed with mock-nervous deflection and raised his hands like he meant no harm.

Adelira lifted her chin and continued, her guards close at either side. Gazes burned too sharp when the wind blew through her hair.

"You could share a truth with me for access to my alleyway," the same memory-man tried his luck again. "Or perhaps you'd prefer to give me one of your lies? I'd take either from you."

The man stepped out of his alleyway. He moved towards the Princess. Finn stepped around as she backed up. Benedict flanked him, making a wall of guards in front of her.

Benedict spoke, "The answer is still no. It will always be no."

Adelira hadn't meant to back away so much, but now there was just a fraction too much distance between her and her guards and not enough between her and the Vampires in the street behind her.

A greedy hand locked around her wrist. "You're a brave little thing," a voice murmured behind her, spinning her around. "Or foolish."

Before she could answer, movement erupted behind her.

The Vampire released her, stumbling away from her.

It wasn't Benedict or Finn who scared him.

The King arrived like night falling too fast. No one could breathe, the streets went silent, their bodies remembered his danger.

He only looked at the Vampire who had dared to touch her and the weight of that gaze was enough to make the man cower.

Adelira turned slowly. The King's gaze sweeping over her, lingering on the bruise forming at her wrist. His lips pressed into a hard thin line.

Her guards froze as the Blood King emerged like a storm rolling into the street.

"Your Majesty, forgive us," Benedict said. "Punish us."

Both guards dropped to their knees. Benedict kept his chin lifted, ever the soldier. Finn's gaze stayed on the ground. The King didn't look at them, but he waved them up and they rose.

"*You're home*," Adelira whispered, barely a sound at all. How did he know she was here? That she needed him at that very moment?

When he finally spoke, like it'd taken too long to compose himself, his voice was quiet and coated with steel, "You're done here."

Adelira swallowed hard. "I—"

"You're done," the King repeated. He sounded calm, but his fists shook at his side.

The finality made her insides twist. But she wasn't finished. She needed to understand this world, him. And she couldn't do that locked within her room.

She shook her head, taking a small step back. "No."

A muscle ticked in his jaw, but he didn't reach for her.

The public was trying to slip away unnoticed but her defiance carried. People turned to stare. The King's attention barely flickered away from her before kicking in fully and he stepped closer. His voice was dangerously low now.

"You don't belong here."

"How can I belong with people I don't understand?" she asked, searching his face in frustration that pulled into a plea for him to understand.

Her plea warred within his dark eyes.

She waved her arms around at the emptying street as Vampires sought refuge from the tempest brewing inside their King. "How can I ever be part of something I don't see?"

"You don't need to do this," he said, his own panic lightly coating his words.

That gave her pause. She had worried him tonight. She hadn't meant for that. It wasn't enough to change what she needed though.

She said softly looking up at him with big grey eyes, "Yes... I do."

His expression was unreadable, his silence stretching long enough that she thought he would refuse her again.

Finally, the King exhaled sharply. "Then, I'm coming with you."

Finn and Benedict fell into step behind them, silent shadows in the King's wake.

Power that stepped into the street could be measured and measured things could be challenged. Somewhere behind them, the night would remember the King was within reach.

Adelira glanced up, the King tense beside her, hands clasped behind his back. His eyes lowered to her and then flickered away, looking over towards a small blood café where patrons were seated and chatting behind the windows.

When a merchant moved with his wares, the King stepped closer before he even realised he had done it, just to see the items for himself.

Adelira saw the flicker of surprise in his expression. His interest was betraying his indifferent act. He had walked these streets before, but never like this. Never with his ears open to hushed grievances, never with his hands brushing the rough grain of a labourer's workbench.

And she saw it, that thing he always hid. He cared, very much. The Obsidian Keep was impenetrable. Those same walls designed to protect, also kept him locked away.

50

Chapter Fifty

The castle felt restless.

Even though the King had returned home early from his negotiations with the South, the castle still seemed to mourn for Orahn, just like it had on the night he had left. But that didn't make any sense.

He had come to her aid last night.

And yet, the halls felt hollow. Like the walls were waiting for someone.

Then she saw the King stop in the corridor in front of her. He was right here, in front of her very eyes. So, why was the castle acting like a piece of its soul was missing?

It wasn't the third-night, she tried to slip past the King. She wanted to ask what changed him every three nights. Or why the kindness came like the tide; rhythmic and fleeting. But it wasn't a night for honesty from him.

Her guards moved away, giving them privacy. She had been grateful they hadn't been punished for what happened in the city.

She kept her head down, her steps quick.

But his voice rolled off the walls towards her, halting her in place. "Who?"

Slowly, she lifted her gaze to his and saw the fire in his eyes.

The King's eyes fell to her sleeve where the bruises darkened her skin. His fingers twitched at his sides, then curled into fists.

"Who?" She asked in confusion, but he knew. "It's nothing," she dismissed, it didn't hurt.

His jaw tightened. His hand hovered near the hilt of his sword, the one he had taken to carrying on his persons since their walks through the night market.

She thought; *he only wore it sometimes... but never on the third-nights, just an in-between-night...*

"Nothing does not leave marks," he said. "Nothing does not make you flinch when a shadow moves too quickly. Who in my Kingdom has touched you like this?"

She swallowed hard. Silence stretched.

"Orahn... I don't understand," she confessed.

His fingers twitched again. And then so gently it nearly stole her breath, he reached out and brushed his thumb over her bruised wrist.

Her breath stilled. He never reached for her during the in-between-nights.

"Please," he said, voice low, strained. "Take *me* with you. Every time."

Her heart stuttered.

She hesitated, feeling the weight of what he was asking. Did he mean it as a command? A plea?

A flicker of shame behind his deep brown eyes. He thought she was hurt and that upset him. She had first imagined he wanted to trap her in his castle, because her value was important to their war effort. But she saw something more in his eyes that betrayed the pain he felt when he looked at her bruises.

He made threats on the people in his Kingdom and demands of her. He took up space in the hall, in her life, because his bold presence hid what his eyes were betraying; he didn't want her to bleed.

Her safety was tied to his sanity. Maybe even his heart.

She searched his face. "Is that what you want?"

He swallowed hard, but he did not answer.

That was an answer in itself.

She made a vow to herself, then; until the Blood Ritual was complete, she would stop going to the city.

"I'll stay inside," she promised. "I won't go out until we do the Blood Ritual."

He looked pained, like her words struck somewhere deep within.

51

Chapter Fifty-One

Finally, the castle took a full breath like it just took longer than the rest of Tharth to believe Orahn's return was real.

Adelira sat in the private dining room. It was much cosier, the space stripped of staff and minimal. Porcelain bowls filled the table.

The small room was lit softly by lanterns strung above their heads. The illusion was broken by the silence between her and the man seated across from her.

She glanced at the King who seemed so much like a stranger to her tonight. Had his travels changed him? Was it the market still? The attack in his streets? She sighed.

He had a pile of books stacked on the table next to him and one open on the table in front of him. He took a bite of food, flipped the page of his book, read for a bit, then repeated.

Adelira tried to catch his attention with a smile.

"The food is wonderful." She had never seen him make much effort to eat.

He barely glanced up. His response was a curt, "Yes."

Did he keep her at bay when they were entirely alone tonight, because there was no one to perform for? Was he thinking of someone else? She did not know what to do with that if it were true.

"What are you reading?" She hoped to draw out some sign of the man she thought she was getting to know.

He paused considering his answer, but then he resumed eating. "It won't interest you," he said, without meeting her eyes. "It's non-fiction."

Adelira's smile faltered. The delicate curve of her lips dropping into something unsure. She could feel him slip further away from her with each passing moment. She searched his face for something familiar or something that made her feel safe, but all she found was a stoic mask.

She thought that she knew him or at least all the sides of him that were strange and dark. But new horrors awaited her. He could be so much colder towards her than she had imagined.

Her gaze drifted and then froze on the gold ring resting on his finger. She knew that ring. *She had it.* It lay beside her bed, a silent, private symbol of something shared. Was this a replacement?

She shook her head, trying to ignore the ring.

"Your Kingdom..." Adelira tried a different approach. "I've never seen so much splendour, what your people can do with stone is unmatched. The sculptures are breath-taking."

His attention remained focused on cutting through the meat on the serving board. "Yes."

"I would love to learn more about Tharth. Perhaps we could—"

"—That's great, tomorrow," he cut her off and offered a distracted smile.

She looked at the bowl of watermelon in the middle of the table. *How odd.* This room was designed to be intimate; made for the two of them. It was obvious that he intended to spend the evening with her... except that he wasn't.

She picked up a piece of fruit.

"Is everything alright?" she asked. "You seem... distant tonight."

He looked up with a fleeting glance. His eyes darted to the wall behind her, as though he saw something there, and then his eyes snapped back on her face. He volunteered a half-smile.

She followed where his gaze had gone, but there was nothing. No sound. No shadow. Only blank stone.

"I'm fine," he muttered. His voice was as distant as his eyes.

She took a breath. "It's just... if something's wrong, you can tell me... I want to help."

His lips pressed into a thin line. It looked like he might say something, but then he returned his focus to his meal. He didn't need to eat, so why was he trying so hard?

Adelira looked down at her own untouched food, fighting the impulse to demand what was happening. But it wasn't in her to confront so directly when she barely knew how to begin unravelling this strange coldness.

"The Summer Ball will be hosted tomorrow night for the Blood Districts. Would you care to join me?" His voice was casual, as though he were offering nothing more than a passing suggestion.

"Yes, of course," Adelira replied, her eagerness for anything he had to offer was only too obvious.

His dark eyes did not meet hers again.

The quiet clink of the dishes and the occasional flip of a page was the only sound he gave her.

She shoved her bowl aside and rebelliously reached for one of his books scattered on the table.

The King didn't bother to acknowledge her defiance. His gaze remained fixed on the book in his lap.

She glanced down at the book in her hands. *Supply Routes in the West.* The title meant little to her, it was the words inside the pages that offered her an escape.

The crisp pages were a welcomed relief. Tharth was so foreign, full of things she didn't understand. But in the descriptions of trade routes, logistical concerns and the flow of commerce; she found something grounded and real.

Hungrily eating up word after word, her mind categorised facts, slotting the world around her into an order that made sense. Each new fact kept her steady, no longer off tilt.

She felt the King, watching her from across the table. He didn't interrupt. He merely observed her with that same unreadable expression. His posture still, as though waiting for her to reach some inevitable conclusion. That the book wouldn't interest her, perhaps? Or that she was proving him wrong? But she didn't care, he wasn't her focus any longer.

The book had become her world. The darkness, the pressure of the distant royal marriage, the tension with Orahn, all of it melted away. She turned the pages with growing urgency. Her eyes scanned the details for the lifeline that it was.

Adelira's fingers skimmed the brittle parchment page as she leaned closer. There were networks of trade routes spanning the Vampire Kingdoms. One line of text caught her attention. A single road in the West that funnelled nearly all the region's fabric trade.

She surveyed the adjoining map. That road, narrow and twisting through treacherous terrain was the only way silk reached the capital. Even the fabric on the chair she sat on had likely travelled along that perilous route, after being harvested in the farthest reaches of Tharth.

She tapped her finger against the margin. A solution might lay in a route travelling along the Ebedene Kingdom where the terrain was more forgiving.

Maybe she wasn't just running from everything; maybe she was beginning to understand how she could reshape it. An idea born of a single road, but there were other secrets to unlock here, more texts to read.

The King's book closed with a sharp snap, startling her.

He stood just as suddenly, his chair didn't make a sound against the floor though, like he could move around anything without disturbing it.

"I have matters to attend to," he offered as the only explanation.

Adelira barely looked up, unwilling to give him any more of her attention tonight. What she needed was something stable. This book was the only thing offering that.

"You can keep the book," he added as he turned to leave.

Adelira didn't respond. His departure was another part of the same world she was beginning to understand in pieces; detached and full of hidden motives.

Once alone, she closed the book gently, the words still fresh in her mind. She stood slowly, clutching the book to her chest like a shield against the shadowed castle.

She walked through the empty corridors and her guards appeared eerily silent behind her until they reached her chamber doors. In her hands, *Supply Routes in the West* was something she could rely on.

Inside her chambers, she sat by the window, the candlelight swayed across the pages; a calm created in ink and parchment.

She held onto the certainty of the written word, which never changed.

Every time she opened the book, it was constant. She read a line. And read it again. And reread it as the same line, *every time.*

52

Chapter Fifty-Two

Adelira flipped through the book.

She read that Nightvine was the basis for several potent Vampire tonics, also an important ingredient in the dyes that gave Tharathi ceremonial robes their deep, shimmering black.

Nightvine was often used to combat poisoning. But the supply line itself was surprisingly narrow, handled almost entirely by a single merchant family who controlled the trade with an iron grip. The plant itself required very specific conditions to grow; cold temperatures, low sunlight, and soil rich in certain minerals.

Her fingers traced the supply routes mapped in the book. She recognised the region, Benedict and Finn had travelled through some of it.

Her mind spun. Could Tharth cultivate nightvine in another region? Perhaps in the under crofts of their cities? Or even in any one of the impressive castle gardens.

A quiet determination settled within her. She would learn more. She would understand the vulnerabilities not just of this Kingdom, but of the man who ruled it.

Her chamber door slammed into the stone wall with a force that ricocheted through the room. Orahn stormed in, his expression berserk.

"Adelira!" he barked, reaching her in a single stride.

His large hands seized her, yanking her from the windowsill with a strength that sent her sprawling onto the floor. The air knocked from her lungs.

"Wh—?" The question died on her lips as a deafening crash erupted above her.

Shattered glass rained down in a lethal, glittering storm. A masked figure burst through the window, a blade gleaming in the moonlight as he drove it into Orahn's back.

Orahn roared and threw the attacker off of him. The intruder landed agilely. Boots crunching broken glass as he straightened.

Adelira's hands covered her mouth as she watched, wide-eyed in horror. The blade would have lodged in her back had Orahn not shouldered it instead.

The assassin lunged in a deadly arc, blade aimed towards Orahn's throat.

Orahn ducked under the swing, his black coat swirling around him. The blade stuck stone behind him, sparks flying. The attacker pivoted for another strike, Orahn shot out and caught the assassin's wrist mid-swing in a bone crushing grip. The blade trembled in the assassin's grasp before Orahn ripped it off him, throwing the weapon aside.

His pale blue eyes and scarred flesh pulled a horrifying realisation from her.

Orahn clamped a bloodied hand around the attacker's throat, lifting him effortlessly, feet dangling above the floor. The assassin struggled, clawing at Orahn's wrist, arms, reaching for his eyes. Orahn simply held him further away. The assassin's strength was no match for the King's fury.

The window gaped behind them and the courtyard was a dizzying drop below. Orahn growled deeply, the sound vibrating through Adelira's chamber as he flung the assassin outward.

Adelira scrambled to her knees just in time to see the figure plummet backwards into the abyss, his scream swallowed by the howling wind.

Orahn's laboured breaths rattled through him as he braced against the frame of the shattered window. Blood dripping steadily from his fingers stained the broken glass at his feet.

Adelira's voice trembled as she squeaked, "Orahn...?"

He turned away from the window to look at her. The sight of him set an entirely different uneasy rhythm to her pulse. His face was pale.

"Are you okay, Lira?"

Orahn trembled at the sight of glass in her hair. He stretched out a hand towards her, stopped either by the pain in his shoulder or the panic plastered all over her face.

She shook the shards free, shaking herself from shock. "M–me?" she squeaked. "Are you okay?"

A thin smile touched his lips, then. He stumbled, his legs betraying him, dropping to his knee.

"Orahn!" The name escaped her lips in a terrified gasp.

She pushed herself off the floor and to his side. Her hands hovered over him, afraid that any wrong move would make it worse.

Dark, spreading crimson soaked through the front of his tunic. He had more wounds than she'd seen. She crawled closer, her palm slipped in a slick pool of blood, and she caught herself, wide eyes returning to his face.

"You're bleeding..." The tremor in her voice twisted with the panic swelling in her chest.

Her hands moved instinctively, pulling aside the fabric to reveal the deep, angry wound in his abdomen. Blood seeped through her fingers as she pressed down, desperate to stop the flow. The tell-tale stained veining around the laceration was unmistakable evidence of poison.

"I need help here!" she screamed.

She started to move towards the door, but the blood flow increased the moment she released pressure and fear rooted her in place. Her hands reapplied to his wounds.

Orahn winced under her weight, a weak attempt at a smile ghosting across his lips. "I was scared..." His voice was rough, each word dragging. He shook like he was still afraid something might happen. "I couldn't... I... not until I knew you were safe."

The wounds on Orahn's body could only have come from the element of surprise and with the wound draining the strength from Orahn's body, he had still come here. To her.

She pressed her hands harder against his wound, trying to stem the warm stickiness that coated her skin. "You should have tended to yourself first!"

His eyes dimmed. It was eroding him from the inside out. His skin a sickly grey tint and his veins stark against his skin.

His eyes found hers, steady, while hers still frantically darted over his pained expression.

"I couldn't risk..." He winced, swallowed it down and continued, "Couldn't risk losing you," his voice breaking on the last half of that sentence.

“You cannot do this,” she whispered. “Please. We need you. *I* need you.”

Her tears fell onto his chest, mingling with the blood. The chill coming in through the broken window was a biting contrast to the warmth of his wounds in her hands. Very quickly he was starting to become cold to the touch.

His hand lifted weakly. His fingers brushing against hers. A touch so faint, she barely felt it, was the only thing keeping the world from falling apart.

His grip slackened, his hand slipping away.

“No,” she choked. His eyes fluttered closed, his breathing growing faint.

Orahn, lying there on her floor, his life slipping away, because he had come to her, because he had cared more about her than himself.

She held her one hand to the wound, brought the other up to stroke the black hair back from his face. He usually looked so intimidating. Here on her bedroom floor, in a state of half-consciousness, he appeared more fragile, more Elven than she ever imagined a Vampire King could look.

“Stay with me,” she pleaded. “You promised to protect me. Please? Stay. You promised—”

53

Chapter Fifty-Three

Everyone arrived at her door and Adelira jumped. Permission hastily given to a group of guards storming in to secure the area, to help their King.

Leading them was the lithe, cat-like general Victoria. Her movements were sharp and commanding as her piercing eyes scanned the scene, taking in the sight of the King collapsed. Before Adelira blinked, Victoria was at Orahn's side and shoving Adelira out of the way with a strength that was startling despite her wiry frame.

"Out of the way!" she barked with command.

Adelira stumbled back, careful to avoid the glass for everyone else's sake. Her throat choked out a breath as healers descended on Orahn to assess his condition.

"Get her out of here," the head healer ordered, looking at the Princess.

"No!" Adelira protested. "I'm not—I can't leave him. H–He needs me."

The general was already moving and in one swift motion, she grabbed Adelira by the arm and lifted her to her feet.

"We can barely hold our bloodlust together around you with the King at full health."

Adelira tried to wrench her arm free. "But he—"

"—He's dying," the general snapped like a slap.

Her black eyes narrowed as she dragged Adelira toward the door. Adelira didn't feel her legs move.

He can't be dying, she wanted to scream that they were wrong, but no words came. She pulled back, trying to stay in the room.

"Then.... Then I should be here."

"Your blood helps no one!"

With a hard tug, Victoria removed her. The door slammed shut behind them. Chaos in the corridors turned to look at her and the general barked orders at the soldiers.

The general hissed. "I need to clear the halls for when they move him to his chambers. No one can see him like this. *No one.*"

Adelira glanced down at her guards unconscious on the floor with healers over them, the sight threatened to hurl her back inside. Victoria's fingers curled tighter as she felt the impulse through Adelira's muscles.

The general's voice softened slightly, grip remaining firm. "Stay away, your Highness."

The thought of Orahn, proud, powerful Orahn, simply being vulnerable as reason enough for his court to turn on him was horrifying. She missed a step, legs giving way under her. Victoria caught her and pushed her up against the wall. Her chest tight, ribs pressing together, and Adelira gulped for air that wouldn't come.

"Look at me!" the general snapped. "*Look at me.*"

Adelira's eyes darted around before landing on the General's face, lips parted, though she was no longer gasping for air.

"Good," Victoria said, slowly easing her hands off. "Now... stand up."

Adelira pushed herself back into the wall and used it to help her upright.

Victoria's black eyes searched hers for a moment longer and then she nodded her approval.

The general released her grip completely, turned and strode ahead, already barking orders at arriving guards to clear out of the area.

Adelira wasn't sure she would survive it. Their blood alliance, and her heart, threatened to break, but her spine held.

Chapter Fifty-Four

Adelira adjusted the folds of her ballgown, her fingers trembling slightly around the fabric and she willed herself steady.

The last time she had seen Orahn, he was barely clinging to life. But the attendants had insisted that he would still maintain his schedule, despite her protests to postpone.

As she prepared for the evening, a new worry gnawed at her. How would he fare in such a public setting? Their combined vulnerabilities, laid bare before a room full of watchful eyes.

Vampires weren't allowed to be weak, certainly not injured. She didn't know how he would manage tonight, perhaps with something strong for the pain.

A knock at the door.

She smoothed her dress one last time before walking to the door to greet her guards, half-prepared for them to tell her the King was too unwell to go after all.

As she opened the door, a gasp caught in her throat. It wasn't guards. It was the King himself.

As his eyes lifted to hers, he smiled.

His face betrayed nothing of the nightmare they had endured last night. His colour restored to a warm glow. He stood steady before her.

Her eyes dropped to the bruises on her arm from where the general had dragged her from the room. *It had been real*, she told herself.

"Orahn," she breathed, blinking away tears that stung her eyes. "I was so worried about you."

He glanced at her, his expression taken aback.

"Thank you," he said, his voice low. "But you never need to worry about me."

"But...are you... y–you're okay, aren't you? They said you were fine, but I couldn't believe it. I thought you were going to... " Her voice trembled as she fought back tears. "But you're *here*... Does it hurt?"

Despite his miraculous recovery, the world was still all wrong somewhere hidden from her. Her trembling fingers hovered just in front of his chest, but she couldn't bring herself to touch him, in case she hurt him, in case he shattered before her eyes.

"*Are* you Okay? Truly?" she asked, unable to mask her concern, she pulled her hand back.

"I'm real, and I'm okay. I promise." He gave a small, reassuring smile.

She bit her lip as she considered this. She still really wanted to hear him say that this wasn't something that happened often or might happen again.

"Let's not let last night take this moment away from us," he said instead. "We deserve to have tonight. Just us, no shadows hanging over it."

She stepped back and took him in again, assessing him for herself for another moment of reassurance. His stance was confident as though he leaned into the evidence of just how well he was for their evening together.

The King was dressed in the traditional Tharathi formal attire, deep navy with silver embroidery. He was dressed to match her, in the colours Seyla had sent to the castle for her. The collar of his coat was high, making his sharp jawline even more pronounced.

His dark hair fell just slightly over one eye and he casually pushed it back.

"You're okay," she said at last, relief coating her words.

"Yes," he agreed softly.

And now, standing before him like this made her acutely aware how close he was and how powerful he looked. Before her eyes, she saw the true strength of the Vampire King. He was a myth. A legend. She had been wrong, there was *nothing* exaggerated about his power.

"Princess, shall we?" His eyes traced her figure, taking in her Vampire gown, a dark blue that clung to her in all the right places.

The midnight-blue gown wrapped and fell in a sweeping cascade of silk around her. Her shoulders and collarbones were a delicate contrast to the structured bodice that held her chest tightly. Her long red hair was gathered into an elaborate half-up style, with curls spilling down her back, adorned with delicate silver pins shaped like falling stars.

The soft flicker at her neck revealed her rapid pulse. His eyes torn between that tender spot and somewhere just a little bit lower.

Flustered, suddenly all too aware of the structure of the dress and the plunging neckline, she felt exposed.

The King was a force to be reckoned with, that much was clear to her now. Here she was worried needlessly about him, nervously talking, fidgeting in a dress that looked Vampire enough, but couldn't make her *feel* Vampire enough.

"Is this dress okay? I still don't fit in, I don't know if I can wear this well enough."

He quickly turned his gaze away when she caught him staring. Took a moment and then slowly, he brought his dark eyes back to connect with hers. "No, you're... beautiful."

Adelira felt her cheeks heat under his gaze. Still, she hesitated. He'd just called her beautiful. That should have been enough. So, why couldn't she move?

Adelira bit her lip and the words rushed out of her in a ramble. "I know they coordinate our outfits so that we would match tonight. But I've never worn anything quite this revealing before. Vampire dresses are so daring and I don't think I'm pulling it off. Even drenched in blood, I could never be a Vampire—"

"—I know," he interrupted. "It's wonderful."

"Wonderful?" She looked at him in surprise.

"Yes," he said and a genuine smile graced his lips. "Even if you tried with everything you had, you could never be just another Vampire. You're *you*. And that's infinitely better. Never apologise for that."

Hearing him say that was the acceptance she'd searched her whole life for and still couldn't quite find it in the royal spaces of Ebedene, and here he was in this rigid place of stone and tradition and he was asking her to be herself.

The King revelled in the delight that was glowing on her face, his smile carrying mischief that softened his usual stoic expression.

"Shall we?" He offered his arm to her.

Adelira slipped her hand into the crook of his arm.

Glittering lights and swirling gowns of silks filled the ballroom. The music flowed until they stood just at the grand entrance. The herald cleared his throat. Their names were announced. This time her name was pronounced correctly. They stepped into the light of the ballroom.

They sat on the thrones overlooking the dancefloor where she expected they would remain for the evening.

After some time drinking and watching the room, a realisation struck her. This was the first time, outside of her room, that she did not have the quiet but certain sensation of being watched by someone unseen behind her. Was her mystery watcher here, as part of the guests, perhaps?

The herald began the formal proceedings, introducing the houses in attendance. "Representing House Crowe, Lord Derek and Lady Lavian with their four daughters and nine sons..."

They bowed before the thrones, one by one. Almost every pair of eyes in the room was sharply fixed on Orahn, and Orahn, leaned forward slightly with a grin, watched them back just as closely.

The King had shrugged off an assassination attempt as though it were a trifling inconvenience. The myth, the legend, grew three times in size that night.

"Everyone's staring at you," Adelira murmured.

He only smiled wider.

"They're surprised you're okay."

"You're surprised I'm okay," he corrected. "They're scared."

"Why should they be scared?"

"Because someone here tried to have me killed. And I didn't die," he said in a low whisper.

Her hand flew over her mouth and her heart started pounding. She never imagined they would be in attendance tonight. She took in the crowd again, trying to see if there was anyone obvious who meant them harm.

"Calm down, Princess," he said softly. "It's them who should be scared, not you. Tonight we get to have fun. And they get to be scared."

She hesitated, nibbling at her lip as she tried to process his words. She trusted him. Trusted him enough to take a steadying breath.

Fun. She could try that, for him. After all, he'd saved her life, and tonight, she wanted to give him whatever he needed: her presence, her joy, her gratitude.

"Enough," the Vampire King declared loudly, ending the announcement mid-speech with a flick of his hand, his ring glinting in the light.

A giggle escaped her.

He turned to raise a questioning eyebrow at her. She pressed long fingers to her lips trying to hide her smile behind them.

"My apologies," she murmured. The faint smile at the corner of her mouth refused to disappear.

"Why are you laughing?" he asked, his voice quiet and smooth, as though they were conspirators in some mischief.

"It just seemed... very unlike you to stop the speeches," she admitted.

He seemed surprised by the observation. Then, he quickly covered it with an assured smile. "We're having fun tonight, remember?"

He stood and raised Adelira up beside him in one smooth motion. Her smile broke through before she could stop it, sudden and bright.

55

Chapter Fifty-Five

Music erupted with an explosion of movement as dozens of dancers took to the floor. She didn't have time to ground herself before the King swept her off her feet.

His hands around her waist, hers hovered at his shoulders.

"You can touch me," he whispered.

"I'm afraid of hurting you," she barely allowed the words to sound above the hush that had fallen over the dancefloor.

"You could never," he said as he moved her hands to his body.

His effortless stride revealed a body untouched by the violence that had so recently threatened it. She felt the armour beneath his suit and felt better for feeling it, though her own dress had some as well, none of it did as much as the press of his body against hers to make her feel safer tonight.

"I've got you," he said and pulled her into his arms.

He began a dance so flighty and reckless that she could not help but laugh. She was spinning near chaotically around the room with him.

The King dipped and dived Adelira as they circled the room. Every time he dipped her suddenly, almost a beat too soon for the music, Adelira laughed and clutched him tighter when he pulled her back in.

The mirrors along the ballroom walls revealed only the Princess, in her long crisp ball gown, swinging across the floor like a puppet more than a dance partner. No reflection of the King, or anyone else and somehow in that glass with no other comparison, she looked like she *belonged* in this world.

The music in the grand ballroom floated around the room, carrying the energy of the evening through the walls of the castle. Suddenly, the quiet castle of stone and blood was alive and growing around them. Candlelight bounced off the chandeliers, casting a warm glow over the sea of dancers, but it was the King and Adelira who commanded the room.

"I won't let you fall." His voice was a velvet rasp tracing a shiver down her spine.

Her breath catching as he pulled her even closer, his thumb brushing lightly along her side as they turned. She could feel the strength in him. Like he had never been injured.

The music rising in a crescendo seemed to melt away. The other dancers. The eyes on them. None of it mattered. Only Orahn. And the way his touch lingered just a moment longer than necessary.

Her hand rested on his shoulder. Her blue incandescent gown caught the light with each subtle twirl. The King spun her out and brought her back into his embrace, her laughter made a soft, delicate sound.

His mouth curved into that dangerous, mischievous smile. With a bold turn, he spun her out again. His grip was light enough to let her choose how far to go. Instead of slipping neatly back into place, she spun again, defying the rhythm.

For a heartbeat, he hesitated, caught off guard. Then she locked eyes with him, the glint of a challenge in her eyes.

"You're out of time," he murmured, low and teasing.

"Am I?"

She twirled again. He was impossibly fast; catching her hand and pulling her back into his orbit.

"You don't know these dances," he teased.

"Is it that obvious?" she replied, her cheeks flushing.

"Painfully," he said with a grin. "But that's good. It means we don't have to follow the rules."

She glanced down at her gown. The intricate folds trapping her in composed confinement. "I don't think this dress is designed for that much... improvisation."

"Then we'll push it to its limits," he said. "Unless you're afraid."

She laughed, a soft, almost nervous sound. "I grew up dancing in the forests. Your court wouldn't know wild if it danced in front of them."

The King's grin widened. "Show me."

Her breath caught. "In this?" she asked, gesturing again to the elaborate gown.

"Yes," he said, his voice was inviting. "Dance anyway. I dare you."

Her lips twitched into a smirk, though there was a small uncertainty in her eyes. "You dare me?"

"I double dare you."

For too long, she had folded away her wildness to fit into a world of Elven poise and grace or the stiff silences of Tharth. He sparked her fire, her thirst for freedom.

"Alright," she whispered, stepping back.

She lifted her arms above her head and twirled. Swaying around the room, eyes closed and feeling for the rhythm that spoke to her soul.

When she heard it, her eyes opened, bright and alive, she began to dance like she did in her forests, like she did when she and her friends escaped in the middle of the night and partied between the trees.

"Do all Elves dance like this?" he called, his voice teasingly rich and stoked with admiration.

"We're usually naked when we do," she wink, spinning past him.

That won a wide smile from the King.

Other couples danced out of her way. She didn't know if they avoided her for the smell of her blood or the hungry way the King watched her like she was his meal, not theirs.

With a sharp rip, her corset gave way, the fabric tearing at the seams as she attempted a daring leap. She froze, clutching the ends of her gown. Cheeks burning, her eyes locked up on him in mild panic.

He didn't move closer. His eyes lowered to her three exposed ribs that shone through the torn dress.

"Dance," he murmured.

It still wasn't an instruction. For the softness of his voice it could almost have been a plea...

Dance... She let go of the fabric and felt the cold night air along her ribs. She let out a laugh.

Someone gasped. People whispered as she passed, but none dared to linger their gaze while the King watched her this keenly, no one would challenge him quite that boldly.

Dancing wasn't enough. With a sharp pivot, she darted toward the string quartet.

"Adelira, what are you..." he began, a laugh caught in his throat.

"Expanding the rules," she replied, plucking a fiddle from a stunned musician.

She lifted the instrument. The bow slid over the strings. A song of galloping horses and roaring winds and touching the sky when she sat above the canopies.

Her feet skated along the smooth marble in time with the music. Her body swaying and spinning, uninhibited. The King was captivated by her. His dark eyes never left her. He had wanted to break the rules, so she was shattering them.

Her hair tumbled free from its pins. Cheeks flushed. Eyes alight with joy. She spun and drew the bow over the final note, letting the melody melt away in one low drawl before she lowered the instrument back into the hands of the band.

The King strode up to her, taking her in his arms, lifting her and spinning her. She laughed and clung to his shoulders until he placed her back on her feet.

He didn't let go of her waist, but leaned back slightly to take her in again, drinking her with his eyes. "Why haven't you done that before?"

Adelira met his gaze. "Because I've spent so long trying to be what everyone else wants me to be."

The look in his eyes was fierce. "Let them see you, Adelira. Don't you ever hide yourself for anyone."

"It's not that easy," she said softly.

"No," he said, stepping closer, his eyes locked intensely with hers. "But it's worth it."

He held out his hand. She took it, and he swept her into another dance.

They spun around the room in a fast rhythm. The musicians tried desperately to match the beat to their King's dance.

Adelira and the Vampire King were locked in a duel of wills. Each step became a challenge they dared each other with.

The other Vampire couples were well and truly unsettled by the night's events, from beginning to end, nothing went as expected. The King and the Princess were both unscathed by the assassination attempt and they were completely unphased by anyone else in the room.

Finally, the upbeat number came to an end. On the final note, a slower song began to play.

Adelira faltered at the change in tempo, but he effortlessly guided her into the slow dance.

She was pressed to him now, the constant closeness of her body against his suddenly felt very intimate. He held her possessively like he didn't want any space between them. His hand was firm yet gentle against the small of her back.

Leading her in sweeping circles across the polished floor, his dark eyes never left hers. He led with the fluid confidence of a King, every step coming naturally to him. In his arms, Adelira felt light as a dream, her body melting into his.

He held her close. Their bodies only a breath apart, the heat of him seeping through her. His touch, a silent promise in his fingertips brushed over the bare skin of her arm, like he would keep her safe and cherished.

Her hips against his and she sank against his chest, surprising herself with the ease in which she fit into his space. She felt the tension in his body, the restrained want. It hit her like a spark: he *wanted* her. His lips lingering at her neck, as though fighting the urge to bite down.

The song faded to an end and the King quickly stepped back.

He cleared his throat, not looking at her. The band took their cue from him and played calmer background music that signalled to the dancers to return to their tables.

Adelira turned, taking a step to follow and swayed slightly. He reached out to steady her, his hands around her waist. She leaned back against his chest.

Tucking his chin over her shoulder, he murmured in her ear, "Are you alright?"

"Just light-headed, that's all," she responded quietly.

"I think we should retire for the night."

"Yes," She agreed.

His eyes connected with the herald who quickly stepped forward and announced that the King and Princess would retire for the night. The party bowed as they made their exit.

56

Chapter Fifty-Six

The Vampire King helped Adelira back through the corridors, his arm around her waist.

"I can walk on my own," she insisted, though even as she said it, she didn't want him to let go. And he didn't.

They arrived at her chambers. He paused outside, uncertain.

"May I come in?" he asked for permission to enter.

"Yes, of course… I've already given you permission… Does that need reaffirming?"

"The first time was because of a curse. This time I wanted you to say it."

She unwrapped herself from him and stepped carefully over jars of paints and brushes that she had left awkwardly in the way. She swayed, a little unsteady without him.

He stepped in and caught her, kicking the door closed behind them.

"I've learned that you cannot drink and dance," he said like he was organising his thoughts about their night.

"I'm fine." She didn't want to admit *he* made her feel light-headed, that he was making her feel all sorts of things tonight.

"Sure thing, Princess," he dismissed.

"What else did you learn tonight?" she asked coyly.

He looked around the room at the canvases littered across the floor, choosing something safer to remark on, "You've been busy."

"Yes."

Adelira glanced around. Most of them were places from Ebedene, the forests, smiles of everyone she knew.

"I've had a lot of free time since I can't go anywhere without… well, you, really."

He frowned, but didn't respond. Instead, he nodded towards the mattress. "Into bed with you. You need to sleep."

He walked to the bed. She followed and leaned against the nearest post of the four-poster bed. Wrapping her arms around the bed poster, she rested her flushed cheeks against the cool wood. The warmth in her face deepened watching him move around her bed.

Her bed was too large for her. When the King stood next to it, it almost seemed like it was made with him in mind.

Something howled in the mountains and he closed the balcony doors with a click and built a fire quickly in the hearth. He turned down the corners of her feathered duvet. Satisfied, he turned to her.

She bit her lip and looked at him daringly. "Help me with my dress."

His eyes widened as he straightened up away from the bed. His gaze dragged down the length of her, over her dress and then back to her face. A moment of panic or guilt crossed his face, but beneath it she caught the look of desire.

"Please?" she asked again with mischievous eyes. "I can't reach the back."

Finally, like his reservation cracked, he stepped towards her. She slowly, slowly turned around. Her back to him and he hesitated again.

Then, his fingers worked through the laces and he pried the sides apart. His hands down her bare shoulders, pausing like he wasn't sure if he should continue, he let the dress fall to the floor.

Beneath the dress, she wore a thin piece of lace that fell midway down her thighs, her back bare.

Without thinking, he ran his hand along her exposed skin, down her spine.

She melted into that touch, craving his touch. The smallest uncontrolled breath escaped her. He pulled his hand away quickly.

"I was thinking..." Her voice was careful as she turned slowly to face him. "You don't have to leave... Not tonight."

He inhaled sharply, his eyes meeting hers with an intensity that made her skip a beat. For a while, he didn't respond.

"To bed with you." He spoke with more force this time and ushered her lightly towards the bed.

She pursed her lips, but climbed onto the soft mattress. Dancing closely all night, his distance bordered on rejection now. She wasn't ready to let this retreat if what she felt was real, if he felt the same way she did.

He pulled the covers up around her and she reached out to touch his face, reaching for him again. He stopped, hovering above her and looked into her pale grey eyes for what must have been for the hundredth time tonight.

"Stay with me?" Adelira watched the surprise of her request cross his face. He had resolved to leave, he just needed an excuse to stay, she could give him that. "Even if you just lay here with me for a while?"

He stepped away from the bed and looked back to the door.

"That's okay, if you're not ready..." She hesitated, the words catching in her throat. "After Seyla, I'd understand if you needed more time."

The name fell between them like a stone dropped into still water. The ripples of its impact were visible in the King's expression.

His eyes widened and for a split second the carefully composed mask slipped just enough for her to see beneath.

"How..." he began, his voice barely audible. "How did you—"

"—I could tell," she interrupted gently. "I know it's over now, but that doesn't mean it's gone and I understand that."

She didn't want to rush him if he needed more time to heal. She didn't feel Vampire enough compared to Seyla, but tonight he'd let her believe it was alright to be Adelira. She held onto that belief, because both were true. They were each allowed to be themselves and loved for that. And he was allowed the space and respect to sort through his emotions. She waited.

He stood completely still.

His breathing was shallow like her words had struck a chord too deep to even acknowledge. He searched her face, saying nothing and she dared not move as he steadied himself.

But then, his shoulders eased and his eyes softened with a look of gratitude. She didn't know if he was grateful she seemed to understand he wasn't without his complications or that she was offering him time.

"It's gone. I'm here, now," he said simply, his voice certain and she felt it in her chest, the tightening around her ribs eased.

The King strode towards her, shedding his jacket. His piercing gaze locked onto hers, his eyes changed from mixed emotion to resolve. Like he'd weighed something he wouldn't voice and decided to remain.

He kicked off his shoes and loosened his collar. Slipping in next to her, fitting perfectly into the bed designed for him, and he pulled her into his arms.

"Does it hurt? Where you were stabbed? Am I too close?" she asked in the quiet, nestling into him, he wrapped around her.

"No," he murmured back.

The steady rhythm of his heartbeat in her ear. His eyes closed and breathing slowed. She almost thought he might have fallen asleep, except for the pressure of his fingers on her arm which gripped her just a fraction too tight for sleep. His attention honed to every movement she made.

Her mind kept taking her back to the final dance, his body flush with hers as they swayed across the room. He felt safe and warm. For the first time in Tharth, she felt safe and warm, and *held*.

Her head lifted. Her hand slid up and over his chest and neck, her fingers curling along his cheek. His eyes flashed open as she lowered her face towards his.

"Adelira," he warned, his voice a low growl that held no bite.

"Is it because—" she didn't get to finish, he stopped her.

"—No," he interrupted. "There is no one else."

She paused. There was no one else, their night was magical, *and* he was still holding back.

"We had fun tonight, didn't we? I am your bride." She pleaded, her face achingly close to his, her eyes falling to his lips. "What is stopping us? I want you. Do you want me?"

His eyes searched hers. She saw it, the excitement, the need, held tightly in check, but there all the same for her to see. Every breath they took tangled together until they were at the edge of control.

"Please," she whispered. "I just need a taste of you." Her words were almost on his lips, she was so close.

His fingers combed through her hair. The touch was both tender and possessive as he locked in place behind her head and pulled her close. The instant his lips found hers, their worlds collided; sparking in the darkness. She surrendered to the kiss and its fire consumed her. Adelira was breathless, her pulse fluttering.

Her chest brushing over his with each heated stroke between them. The warmth of his skin burned through her lace, igniting her every nerve until a delicious shiver crawled up her.

She didn't know if her body moved on its own or if he drew her in without meaning to. Gliding over him, her legs wrapping around his hips. Everywhere he touched blazed her skin, she was losing herself in him, forgetting how to breathe.

"Princ–Adi–," he couldn't quite say anything before his mouth was on hers again. His firm hold keeping her lips on his, as though he couldn't bear the thought of letting go of her.

A moan slipped out of him.

His desire was raw and she could taste his hunger burning through him. His hips lifted against her, hand on the small of her back, holding her to him. His need pressing against hers created a thrilling ache within her centre.

His fangs grazed her lip.

The sting barely registered until copper spilled between them.

He broke away. His hand gripped the back of her head and with a sudden, almost desperate, force, pulling her back from himself.

Adelira gasped as she sat up, trembling.

Her hair tumbled around her shoulders. Chest rising and falling quickly to catch her breath again, impossible to calm her heartbeat. Staring down at him, her widened eyes reflected her arousal, confusion, and a flicker of fear she couldn't quite push away.

His eyes held her gaze, fierce and filled with something so intense that she wasn't sure whether to lean into it or run from it.

He reached out a trembling hand, using his thumb to wipe away the trail of blood falling from her lip. He sucked his thumb and closed his eyes against the moan rising in his throat, his body shuddering beneath her.

She leaned down and brought her lips to his again.

"Adelira..." he warned, his eyes opening to fix her with a look.

"It's just a kiss." She looked down at him, her plea softening her features.

"It's not just a kiss," he corrected, "and you know it."

"I want you," she whispered.

She lowered her lips to his, but at the last moment he turned his face away. *That's okay*, he could say no. Instead, she kissed his cheek, a small gift.

He stilled beneath her, and then melted completely into her kiss. Like he'd never been kissed on the cheeks before. Her gentleness was almost enough to disarm him. Then he built his walls back up, layer by layer, and his resolve hardened.

He grabbed her around the waist so she couldn't try again and slid her off. He set her in the bed next to him.

"Then it can wait until we are married."

"Will you stay?"

"You played dirty, Princess. Staying sounds like it will only end in trouble."

"I'll be good, I promise," she lied.

He grunted unconvinced. "No. Go to sleep."

She pouted playfully after him and he rolled his eyes at her, a smirk threatening across his features. She grinned up at him, his look meant she hadn't actually lost ground.

He rolled out of bed, collected his things and strode towards the door.

The door clicked closed behind him and she let herself fall back on the pillows.

Chapter Fifty-Seven

Adelira found the King standing by the full-length window in the library as the clouds came in fast and heavy. His silhouette stood against the storm-lit glass, tall and regal.

She approached carefully. Her steps were so soft on the stone floor and stood beside him. Though he never turned to her, his attention shifted focus toward her, an unspoken acknowledgment, before returning to the world beyond. She looked up at the black clouds.

A sudden flash of lightning split the sky in half, illuminating the room in brilliant light. His black cloak was the most sheer white for the breath of a second, before the shadows took it back.

A low, rolling rumble vibrated the windows all around them.

Adelira held her breath and looked up at the unfettered beauty of the storm. She had never let herself look at it before. It was breathtakingly beautiful. She couldn't understand now why she'd ever been afraid. The wind howled through the night as it chased rain across the mountains.

With the Blood King beside her, the storm didn't feel menacing. It felt alive and untamed like him. Each clash of thunder sent a thrill down her spine.

Adelira and the King stood in silence, side by side, while the library around them became a forgotten thing. The storm was for them alone and the space between them narrowed with a charge that was unspoken.

Cautiously, Adelira let her fingers drift toward his, seeking to close their small distance. He clasped his hands neatly behind his back before her hand could reach his.

But he hadn't moved away from her, and that, she decided, was something. There was still something between them, quietly growing, not waiting for him to move, but waiting for when he trusted himself with her.

He had pulled away after he pushed her up against the wall. And then they had shared kisses ending in a trace of blood. There was always a whisper of danger between them. The thrill and horror of his fangs grazing her lips.

Finally, the world outdoors returned to stillness as the last droplets of rain streaked the glass and the clouds rolled apart to reveal the star speckled night sky.

When the storm ended, the King turned to her. His dark eyes locked with hers, almost with gratitude.

He bowed before her. It was both formal and deeply intimate, honouring something they had shared.

Then, without a word, he walked away, leaving her alone with the scent of rain and the memory of lightning.

58

Chapter Fifty-Eight

The King

Adelira woke with the taste of the King still on her lips, the memory of lightning flashing behind her eyes. That next in-between-night she spent alone painting, now it was the third-night again.

She got ready for the evening, bathed and dressed for the King's request to join him for a picnic.

Stepping over the empty jars of paint; the remnants of a few stormy days, she moved the finished canvases aside to reclaim some of her chamber from the painting frenzy she used to distract herself from the night of the assassination attempt.

Opening the door, her guards straightened, hands too close to their weapons.

"Hello," she greeted. "I'm ready."

Benedict and Finn led the way to the King. Neither of them spoke much anymore, not since the city, not since the assassination attempt a few nights ago. She knew they were on high alert, but she wished they'd come back to her, at least in some small way.

If Talion had been there, she'd have asked him if she looked okay. He'd have told her to twirl so he could judge, but it didn't matter what she wore, how Carys did her hair, Talion always said she looked too pretty to spend her day in a tree. And up the tree she went, anyway.

"I'm relieved you're both okay," she said.

Benedict's hand clenched around his hilt and he looked wounded just from knowing that she even worried about them at all. Finn was subtler about it, but his pride was still bruised.

"We're grateful the King arrived when he did," Finn said. Then his voice darkened and said, "He's been a better guard to you than we have."

"Even the King struggles with my blood. You've both done well."

Now, neither of them would look at her, but she wished they knew what their silence did to her.

The walk through the castle was slow. All the Blood Houses and their families had returned to their districts after the ball and the Keep was quiet without them. The few guards in alcoves stiffened as they passed, but as always, she moved quickly. They were outside, walking through the courtyards.

By the time Adelira stepped through the archway into the midnight gardens, the two men behind her had caught sight of the King and eased as tension left their bodies.

Her heart stumbled when she saw him in the distance. Three nights since the dance, since he was in her bed. It took everything not to run into his arms.

Orahn turned around when he heard their approach down the winding pathway of the gardens. The moons bathed him in light and he was the most beautiful nocturnal creature she'd seen. Her breath hitched. She waited for which side of him she'd meet tonight.

"Your Majesty," she greeted formally with a curtsy. He bowed, the hint of a wince on his face that almost went unnoticed by her.

"Lira," Orahn said, reaching out to take her hand and he nodded away her guards, who without missing a beat, continued down the pathway and out of sight.

A third-night Orahn. She rested her head against his arm as he tucked her into his body, walking towards the large blossom tree he'd taken her to see the first time he took her to the midnight gardens.

He led her to a blanket where a picnic had been laid out and they sat down next to each other. The blanket was thick, keeping out the chill of the ground.

"This is lovely, Orahn," Adelira said.

The blossom tree branches stretched with delicate pink petals swaying in the breeze, occasionally a shower of blossoms rained down. There was a carpet of petals on the ground. They sat in the silence that was filled with the soft whispers of the wind in the trees and the fall of pink between them.

She watched him with a mixture of longing and uncertainty. No crown, no formal armour, just Orahn in a simple loose tunic, the dark fabric almost casual except that it still held the look of power he so effortlessly carried.

Briefly, she wondered why he wasn't wearing his armoured clothing. Was this another defiant act to his court? Or a gentler tone he set for his evening with her?

His eyes, those hauntingly intense eyes that made her heart race, were focused on the glass of wine in his hand.

He looked up and flashed her a smile and she felt calm wash over her. He was still here with her, still her Orahn.

"I thought... after everything," Orahn began, his voice deep, rich, but softer than usual, "you might need some time away from all of that." He gestured faintly to include the whole Kingdom; the act they had to maintain in front of the Vampires. "I wanted you to have a moment just for yourself."

The gentleness in his words kept clashing against the formidable King she was told to envisage. He was fierce, but he could also be kind.

She reached inside her dress pocket and pulled out his ring. It had warmed in her pocket.

"I thought maybe you had already replaced it," she said with a small smile, too practiced to be unaffected. "But I wanted to give it back, anyway."

His fingers hesitated around the ring. For a fraction of a second, his composure cracked, a flicker of pain, maybe even guilt, and then it was gone.

"Thank you," he said simply, sliding it onto his bare finger like it had never left. Like his hand had been waiting for its return.

Deciding then that it didn't matter, whatever rings he wore or didn't wear, the distance he needed to spin to keep her at arm's reach wasn't working so well anymore. He cared about her and he could no longer pretend he didn't. He'd come to save her, he'd danced with her, watched thunderstorms with her. He was careful, and scared, even if he wouldn't admit it.

An owl flew over them and landed in the tree, head turning all around in search of something to eat.

She smiled up at the bird as it began to preen its feathers. Watching the owl, she thought; she was scared too, but she also knew how to be careful and gentle enough for Orahn and herself both.

Orahn picked up the wine and held out a glass to her. He winced again, moving the glass to the other hand and this time she frowned.

"You're in pain," she murmured, it wasn't an accusation, but the way he instantly deflected hinted he took it that way.

"I'm okay," he assured her with a smile, sitting a little straighter, more confident and assured than before. In an effort to convince her of his statement, he only served to prove hers true.

"You're mortal after all, I almost believed you were invincible," she said coyly, to show she wasn't judging him.

"Almost?" Orahn raised an eyebrow.

"You shouldn't have pushed yourself at the ball, despite your remarkable recovery, it's clear the extra time would have helped you," she said and then she added in a whisper, "It's okay to need more time to heal fully. I am the one person in this castle who will never judge you for a moment of weakness."

That drew a flicker of surprise from him and she leaned into it.

"You know, I don't expect you to be *perfect* all the time. It's okay to be yourself, to be just a person," she said.

His eyes burned into her and she held his gaze.

"I stayed awake the entire time painting to distract myself, but I can't forget how you looked in my room. They said you might... I–I don't know what I would have done. I was so worried about you."

"I know you were," he said. "And I was worried about you. But we're both alright now."

There was still lingering pain from his stab wounds and she felt guilty for any roughness she caused him at the dance, thinking perhaps she pushed him to his limits and he was paying for her recklessness tonight.

"I understand why you left after the ball. I hope I did not embarrass myself too much, or hurt you, at all," she said shyly, by way of apology.

"Hurt me?" he asked as though the idea was absurd.

"Just a little, *maybe*?" she asked tentatively.

"Never. You were wonderful," Orahn assured her.

She shifted slightly closer, just enough to catch the faint scent of him, rich and dark, like the night air after rain.

"It's strange," she said, "I've lived here for a while now, but I don't think I ever truly believed I could belong here, but the last few nights..."

His hand reached out. The tips of his fingers grazing the tips of her own.

"You deserve a place you can call home," he said. His voice low, almost a rumble, like the thunder they'd listened to last night.

His hand was still there with hers, waiting for permission to go further.

"Lira..." Orahn said her name like a secret, one he had grown to cherish. His voice was deeper now, filled with something unspoken and held back like he couldn't quite bring himself to confess, just yet.

She looked up into his warm dark eyes. No longer any pretence or guarded distance, he looked at her as though she were the only thing in the world that mattered and the intensity of it stole her breath.

"I thought I could hide from you," Orahn murmured. "But you have a way of noticing things I try desperately to conceal."

His words nestled into her chest, warm and tender, spoken only for her.

"Orahn..."

"It's more than that," even quieter now, "You see the best in everyone, things that others might overlook. Even... in me, I think."

She trembled, the honesty of his words and the vulnerability it unveiled in both of them, made her soul feel exposed to him. He was opening up in a way he had never softened for her before. His fingers brushed along hers in his strong grasp.

"When you do that," he said, "when you look at people as so much more than what you're presented with... It reminds me why I walked away from the Blood King and it gives me strength to keep walking towards something kinder."

Often her compassion felt a small and fragile thing that wavered like a flame in a breeze. But now in the glow of his words, her fire reignited.

"I didn't think Vampires appreciated such things."

His lips curved up. "We're not used to being seen without a blade in our hands."

A wind rustled the petals across the picnic blanket as she turned her hand over in his, watching the way their fingers fit together. His ring back on his hand, even warmer now than in her pocket.

Some of the trees had begun to get a yellow tint, the first signs of autumn. She'd arrived in the spring and it was hard to imagine so much time had passed. When she read letters from Carys or her family, they spoke of the safety of Ebedene, how there'd been no recent attacks and the Shifters' army settled at the borders had vanished without a trace. This gave her hope that time was on her side.

"I think that besides the dance, this is the nicest time I've had here," she said, offering him a quiet truth.

Orahn's expression shifted, something nearly sad flickering across his face. "I see."

Guilt pressed against her ribs, that wasn't the turn she had intended, she only wanted to match his honesty with her own, but hers was a little too sharp for the moment. She had a way of doing that, letting words tumble from her, when she should consider them a little more first.

"It's okay, really, I understand you are busy and that there's a war and you're not entirely ready to let me in, yet... I shouldn't have said anything."

"I think you should learn to speak your mind more," Orahn encouraged.

She blinked up at him, his offer surprising her and she didn't know if she believed him.

When he saw her hesitation, he leaned in slightly. "You're often so reserved that I don't think you ever get to really say how you feel. And I'd like to know the things you think about."

"Not all the things I think should be said out loud."

"Perhaps," he said, a small smile ghosting his lips. "But if it's on your mind, it must be spoken nonetheless."

"My family would prefer I were silent."

Orahn's gaze darkened slightly, but his hand only tightened around hers.

"I would not." His voice was firm, like she could lean on it for the truth he cut into each word. "I would trade silence for your whispers if every whisper you spoke was true and not something you were taught to say."

She let herself smile, just a little. "But sometimes the truth and the etiquette align, like; I feel content in this very moment right here with you."

His eyes softened. "Indeed, they can align." A chuckle rumbled in his chest. "I've had a wonderful evening with you."

"I know," she said with a soft smirk.

"There, that's you, the real you. And I'd like to see more of her."

His laugh was full, warm, and when he smiled at her, it reached his eyes.

Adelira bit her lip, trying to contain the grin threatening to break free.

"I know we're to be married," Orahn started, "But I want you to only marry me when you are ready and comfortable here with me, with who I am. I am a creature against your every instinct and I won't corner you with this."

"My instincts pull me towards you," she whispered.

The owl hooted and flew silently from the tree, across the gardens until it vanished into the darkness.

He brushed a stray lock of red hair from her eyes. His touch so gentle, so very tender that it made her ache. Cupping her cheek in his hand, holding her gaze steady, she nestled into his warmth. His palm and fingers splayed across her cheek, deep eyes searching hers.

"I've been pretending for too long," he murmured. "I can't anymore. Not with you."

Before she could speak or even think, he leaned in. His lips brushing hers in the softest, most hesitant kiss. It was tentative, as though he were testing the waters.

Adelira's eyes closed as she leaned into him, her hand tightening around his. The kiss deepened, the intensity spilling over until finally they pulled apart and the world felt still.

Orahn rested his forehead against hers. His breath ragged, his voice barely escaping as a whisper.

"I don't know what this is," he confessed. "But I can't stop it."

"Neither can I," her voice trembling with the truth of it, with everything she wanted to say and couldn't find the words for.

"Lira?" He saw the struggle behind her eyes.

"Marry me, Orahn..." she held onto her courage, fought to be brave, "I want to do the Blood Ritual with you."

59

Chapter Fifty-Nine

After their picnic, she had been too energised to return to her room. She went to the library instead.

Adelira curled up in a chaise next to a roaring fire and read into the early hours of the morning. Before dawn broke, the words blurred together in one large ink spot, the book slipping from her fingers.

Adelira stirred, the faint crackling of dying embers pulling her from the depths of sleep.

Then, she felt the weight on her shoulders. A heavy black cloak draped over her, its faint scent of frost and ink.

The King. Her fingers tightened on the soft fabric.

He had been here. She sat up. Books she'd been poring over scattered around her.

She glanced toward the closed library doors. Rising, she crossed the room. She closed her fingers around the cloak, swishing softly behind her. The handle was locked. Her brow furrowed as she slid the latch free and the door swung open easily.

The blur of a figure retreating into the darkness at the far end of the library caught on her peripheral and vanished.

Clutching the cloak tighter around her shoulders, she turned and made her way toward her chambers. Her guards were stationed outside and escorted her back silently. She had to hurry. The night market was calling and Orahn would be waiting for her.

Night settled quickly by the time she readied and stepped out of her chambers freshly bathed and dressed in Elven clothes and a Vampire coat. She left Orahn's one on her bed to return to him later. Did she have two of his now? Three? She was slowly collecting his cloaks, but he always seemed to have more of them. The scent of him stayed in her hair.

Approaching the door, her soft slippers silent against the stone floor. "Shall we go?"

"Your Highness," Finn greeted. His gaze remained fixed on a point just above her.

Benedict nodded, eyes averted, and they set off.

Both of the guards took visible strain every time she stepped closer. The royal guards they passed, usually motionless in their alcoves along the corridors, stepped *back* as she passed.

"I... I can walk the rest of the way alone, I can tell today my blood is having an especially... trying... effect," she offered her own guards softly. "I'll be fine."

Benedict straightened in what might have been concern or pride, or both. "With respect, Your Highness, our orders are to remain at your side until you are with the King."

Moving through the Keep, they headed for the gates leading to the market. In front of the large iron gates the Vampire King stood. He stepped forward as they approached, his towering figure casting them in his shadow.

The guards bowed, their movements stiff. "Your Majesty," Benedict said. "The Princess is in your care." They retreated quickly.

"Princess," the King said with a slight nod of his head.

Finn and Benedict left while she took a moment to release any lingering tension from her shoulders and turned to the King. He was handsome in the dark, but as soon as the gates opened, the entrance flooded him in light, a glimpse of his fangs as he smiled.

She smiled brightly at him as they walked through and let the market welcome them. The night market burst to life. They walked closely together, shoulder to shoulder and there was a near-smirk on his face as he tried to keep his eyes on the world around them. His dark gaze kept finding her, instead.

The wind picked up and the Vampires closest to them tensed in response and moved away quickly.

The King breathed her in deeply and then looked away like he'd betrayed himself.

She nudged her shoulder affectionately against him to show him she didn't mind. He could breathe her in, drink her up, just as long as he stayed close to her.

"Thank you, for keeping watch over me in the library," Adelira said.

He hummed a response, looking around the market, an act that tried to appear more casual than how he'd actually stitched himself to her side.

"You could have woken me up, I'd have made my way back to my room... Or... you could have carried me into my room," she added with a cheeky wink.

His mouth pulled down, but all he said was, "It was no trouble to watch over you."

She glanced up at him, his voice was like frost, but the way he hovered next to her was warm, like he was always one reckless moment away from pulling her into his arms and kissing her.

60

Chapter Sixty

The King walked beside her, eyes alert. She could sense that he was surveying the crowd, though he'd said nothing even as the wind drew eyes their way.

She still fawned over every small carving that caught her eye, but this time, he stayed tentatively by her side, smiling with her at every small find she held triumphantly up at him.

"Are you looking for something specific?" he asked.

A pensive look crossed her features. "Maybe. I suppose I'll know when I find it, though I'm not sure what, yet."

His eyes scanned the market lazily, almost like he felt he should rather than he wanted to. His attention was focused more on her and the items she explored with her excited yet careful hands. The heat of his body close to hers, the scent of frost forest and smoke. She fought the urge to lean into him, finding more delights to hold up for him to see.

"Do you want help?" he asked, his voice almost sounded eager.

"Can you think of something Benedict and Finn might like?" she asked, raising an eyebrow at him.

His eyes widened. "You asked them their names?"

"Of course I asked their names."

"Why?"

"Because names are important."

He looked like she had *cut* him with her words and he turned away, distracting himself with something idle on a table. She frowned, confused by his hurt, but stayed close and he settled into her steady comfort.

After a while, he asked, "Why do you want to get them something?"

"They go with me nearly everywhere. I'd like to thank them for that."

"...It's their job."

"And it's a difficult job. One that I appreciate," she said. "I'd like to show that appreciation."

His eyes didn't soften; they broke, and he looked away. When he looked at her again, it was gone, replaced by a solemn expression.

He pointed out a few items and she showed him a few things in return. Things her guards might like, things she liked, something for Carys. He agreed that he could afford to send a well-guarded messenger with gifts and letters back to Ebedene.

"Have you thought more about what I asked? The Blood Ritual and..." she let her words fall off.

He shifted under her watch. "I think it would be best if we waited a bit longer for the Ritual."

"Why?" She asked quietly. "If... the war is coming soon, the Elder Celestite alone is not enough to bind you to my people. I would feel better, knowing they had your full protection."

"You have my word, I will protect them," he promised.

She shook her head slightly in confusion. She watched as his hand tense at his side and suddenly she wondered if there was some consequence for her, or for him, that she hadn't understood when he explained the Blood Ritual.

"But..." she started, though the words were unsure on her lips, so he spoke up instead.

"I have garrisons across the borderlands bolstered with supplies and reinforcements. Patrols move nightly to keep the pathways secure for trade and travel. In the Eastern Woods, where your people's settlements are most vulnerable, I've scouts who know the terrain as well as the Elves themselves."

"Oh, I—" She backed up.

He stepped closer, his voice steady, but carrying a streak of defiance. "In the capital, I've an entire company of soldiers. Under the command of Elven officers."

"Under my father's charge?"

"That has never been done before. My men have *never* answered to Elves. My soldiers grumble about it, but they follow my orders. With the sheer number of blood donors I'm sending there nightly, they pose no risk to your people, either. You are protected inside and out."

She gasped. "I didn't—"

His intensity never broke, he stepped closer, his body nearly touching hers. "—The Elven warriors wear armour forged by my finest smiths. Their weapons are sharpened by my steel, because I *know* what's at stake."

"That's why you left," she whispered piecing together his journey South.

"They are tasked with not just defending the city, but also Elven dignitaries that need to travel. Even on the roads, you are not undefended. My army protects your Kingdom in its entirety."

She found the wall behind her before realising he'd stepped even closer. His hand came up, flexing by her face like he couldn't decide if he'd cage her between himself and the wall or touch her cheek. He did neither, his hand falling to his side, his fists clenched.

He met her eyes squarely, his words unyielding. "I've made alliances, strengthened borders and ensured that if anyone dares to threaten them, they'll face more than an army. They'll face the Vampire Kingdom prepared to defend its people, all its people, with everything it has."

His jaw tightened. "Don't, for a moment, doubt that I'm doing everything in my power to keep them safe. Because I am."

His declaration moved her to tears, which she tried to blink away.

He might not want to give her the Blood Ritual, but he was still giving her what she desperately wanted from him. Vampire protection for her people.

"Thank you," she said with so much sincerity that it disarmed him and the tension fell from his shoulders.

Tears traced the curve of her cheek and fell from her chin and he stepped back, eyes wide in shock.

He could only look away, nodding and walking further along the streets.

Adelira brushed her tears away and took a breath, shrugging out her shoulders and followed. He didn't watch her cry, averting his gaze, and she appreciated the privacy to compose herself again. He hovered near enough, just a pace ahead of her, but she felt the weight of his attention on her.

The hairs on the back of her neck stood on end.

"Orahn..." she started to call him.

No sooner had her hairs prickled, did they stand down again. A quick sweep of the market led to no more than the usual predators and she shook it from mind.

He slowed his steps and turned to her, then his eyes darted around the market and back to her face. She shook her head, as if to say, *never mind, it was only imagined.*

"Did I scare you?" he asked quietly, still not looking at her completely. "I–I didn't mean to make you cry."

"You misunderstand, I am *relieved.* Grateful beyond words that my people have you."

His fists balled again. "We should keep looking if we hope to find something for Benedict and Finn."

The market swept them along as she kept replaying the things he'd said over in her mind.

61

Chapter Sixty-One

Spiced herbs and nightblossoms filled the air, the phosphorescent lights strung overhead provided enough light to see the tables. Adelira glanced down at the stall they stood near.

"There's new carvings, look!" She gushed as she picked up the small figurines recently added to the collection and turned them to show the King.

He exhaled deeply and turned away. The King had been slipping into that cold, controlled mask he wore so well, the one that had made her doubt if she truly knew him, at all. They had started the night with so much hope and now they had so much distance to cross again.

She gave a smile to the stall holder, complimenting her latest additions, before turning to follow the King. The sword he bought last time was the only thing he ever seemed to connect with, even when he had humoured her by looking at some things she'd found. The distance between them always seemed impossible after she imagined they'd made progress.

She said to him, “Can’t you appreciate anything here besides a weapon?”

He turned to her, his eyes serious. “Appreciating it won’t keep us alive.”

“There’s more to life than that, though. Not everything is about survival, Orahn. Maybe one day you will see that.”

“And maybe you’ll see sometimes, it has to be,” he shot back.

“I live here too, now,” she said. “I know what the world is here. I can still admire delicate and precious things.”

“You really don’t know when to quit when you’re ahead, do you, Princess?”

“Actually, I’ve always known, it’s just that I’m adjusting to the Vampire way, as you suggested. You wanted me to speak my mind.”

“Is that so? Did I say it quite like that?” He raised an eyebrow at her.

“Something like that, anyway,” she said with a shrug.

“Tell me more of these ‘Vampire ways’ that you’ve come to learn so much about, Princess.”

“Well, it’s apparently quite common to be a complete enigma, a whirlwind of unpredictable emotions,” she started slowly with her finger pressed thoughtfully against her chin, as though she was trying to remember what else.

He stifled a sigh. “You were much more pleasant to dance with.”

“What an odd thing to say,” she murmured thoughtfully.

“Why is that?”

“Well, it’s just that we had a pleasant night at our picnic and the dance was a few nights ago already.”

He snapped, “So what, now I’m not allowed to remember you dancing in my arms?”

Adelira was about to respond, when instead silence fell upon her lips.

She felt it first.

A change in the crowd.

A ripple of unease.

She turned. Her eyes flicked across the faces of those passing by, one by one paid her no mind and she dismissed each of them… until she saw him. A Vampire, tall and gaunt, his eyes gleaming deadly in the night. He wasn't like the others. His limbs were jerky, erratic, coiled for pouncing.

The Vampire lunged at her and she was torn away from the King's side.

A sharp gasp fell from her lips. The world tilted. The Vampire, upon her in an instant, was faster than her mind was able to process. Clawed hands grabbed at her, dragging her into the shadows of a narrow alley. Her back slammed up against the stone wall; the wind knocked from her lungs.

The Vampire's fangs gleaming, bared, snapping inches from her. He knocked her against the wall, the brick cutting into the side of her head and spilling blood down her face and dripping off of her chin. Chaos erupted in the streets as her spilled blood drove the crowd berserk. She could barely see the King fight his way out of the thick of it; the wild Vampire snarling inches from her face.

"Smell… better… you bleed…" the feral Vampire said, a mixture of hunger and madness, the words couldn't form a coherent sentence.

Struggling, Adelira couldn't fight to free herself. He was too strong. Too overwhelming. He leaned in for the kill.

In an instant, the Vampire King was there.

But it wasn't the calm, regal Orahn.

His eyes glowed with a dark unholy light, flashed red. His fangs, which she had only glimpsed before, were fully extended, sharp and menacing.

His entire presence seemed to transform, the air growing heavier around the man she was to marry. In an instant, he was unleashed before her eyes. He became the *Blood King*.

The feral Vampire ripped away from Adelira and crashed against the opposite wall with a force that cracked the stone.

The King crossed the alley in a blur and hauled the man up with one hand, an unstoppable force of nature.

The attacking Vampire snarled and recovered quickly, his movements thirsty and desperate. But it was too late. Bloodlust and the promise of death ripened the air. Up against the King of violence himself, the feral attacker was no more than a shadow clawing at the fringes of a tempest. His attempt meant nothing once the Blood King decided to destroy him.

The King advanced with precision beyond any instinct, each strike destruction. The other vampire began panicking; thrashing and scratching. He tried everything to break free. The King's hand wrapped around the Vampire's throat with iron strength, completely unmoved by the feral Vampire's life and death struggle in his hands.

"*She's mine*," the King growled, reverberating ancient and terrifying. The words striking Adelira as harshly as the violence around her.

The Vampire struggled, but the King's grip tightened and cut off the gargled sound. With a single brutal motion, he slammed the man to the ground, pinning him there. The predator was now prey, irrevocably helpless beneath the King's strength.

Adelira couldn't move. She watched Orahn's vicious aura in stunned silence. Every shadow of the alley bent towards him.

A sickening crack then the Vampire's body went limp and lifeless, his neck twisted in an unnatural angle.

The beginnings of a scream bubbled within Adelira. Shock clipped it into a horrified yelp.

The silence that followed was deafening.

The Vampire King stood over the corpse. His chest heaving in rage and he scanned the alley in search of the next victim.

Her breath became shallow gulps. The wrath in his eyes made her heart slam against her ribs.

The scent of her fear pulled his attention sharply to her.

The King's eyes connected with her. Adelira let out a blood curdling scream. She stumbled backwards. He was a monster, completely transformed, and she was next. Who could possibly save her from *him?!*

His stance tightened as he braced for a fight, looking around the alley, finding no other attackers. His eyes widened as he looked her over again. His predatory demeanour gave way as he watched her cower away from him.

Immediately, he took a knee.

Lowered his face to the floor, hidden behind one hand, and held his other hand out to her.

She looked over at the mangled body of the feral Vampire and then back to the King kneeling before her, and in the street outside this alleyway; Vampires fighting each other over the smell of her blood as the guards tried to bring order back to the market. It was too much to take in.

Frantic grey eyes fell back on him.

He was offering *himself* in the only way he could. Kneeling and stripped of the power and menace until nothing of the monster within him was left.

She raked her fear back enough to say, "Y–you were... protecting me."

She swayed, her knees couldn't decide whether to flee or hold. Her eyes flicked from his bloodstained hands to his face, and something collapsed in her. She touched her bloody head... and fainted.

The King scooped her up before her body hit the ground.

Though the arriving guards offered to carry her, he refused to hand the Princess over to anyone.

62

Chapter Sixty-Two

Adelira woke with the crisp night air stroking her cheeks. Bundled in the King's cape, his scent of frost, the cold almost metallic smell of him, and smoke wrapped around her.

Curled on the cold stone of the castle rooftop, above her stars scattered the dark sky. Adelira blinked and rolled over onto her back, staring up at the sky.

She sat up and felt a sharp pain at her temple.

She gingerly touched it and remembered she'd hit it against the wall. The blood there was dry now. Her long red hair whipped around her face, tugged by the wind. She didn't need to be able to speak the language of the trees in Tharth to know they were whispering about her near-death.

She sat straighter, pulling the cape tightly around her shoulders, the smell of him trapped between the folds. Her eyes drifted over the view before her. The city stretched below, lights like embers in the darkness.

The two full moons lit the space around her and she spotted the King perched on the ledge of the rooftop.

Head bowed, staring into his hands in his lap, legs dangling over the side of the ledge. His shoulders were heavy with an ache that gripped her just as deeply when she looked at him.

She could feel the words growing in him like a thorn that tore through his windpipe.

"I'm sorry," he said softly. The edges of his voice were broken and raw. He didn't turn to her; his eyes fixed on the city lights stretching out in front of them.

Adelira stood, clutching his cape closer, drawing in a breath that tasted of night and secrets. His sorrow was visceral. There may as well have been a canyon between them.

"You're sorry for saving my life?"

He glanced over his shoulder at her. His eyes flashing over the blood at her temple like he couldn't believe her version of events. Her injuries told him a different story, one where she'd still gotten hurt and so did others.

His eyes filled with a sadness she hadn't seen before. In them, was the pain of someone who couldn't bring himself to confess his shame.

"I panicked," he said at last. "That's never happened to me before... You must think I'm a monster."

Her heart throbbed against her ribs. She crept closer to him, slowly, not to startle him.

"You're the monster I need," she said.

His eyes snapped to hers, a glint of panic there. Her words struck terror in him.

Before she could close the distance between them, his eyes widened with fear, and he dove backward, disappearing over the ledge into the darkness.

"Orahn!" She cried out, but the wind swallowed his name.

She sprinted to the edge. The ground was far below, but there was no sign of him. He was gone; taken by the wind and melted into the night itself.

She drew in a shaky breath. Swallowing down the ache in her chest, she slipped her hands around the vines that crept along the castle walls. Carefully, she lowered herself over the side. The wind whipped her hair around her face as she descended, but she was a sure climber.

Finally, she reached the balcony to her chambers. She understood he didn't want to be a Blood King anymore. She wanted him to know his guilt, even exposed in the light, was okay. He didn't need to banish himself to darkness...

Instead, she hooked her foot over her balcony and slipped inside. She kept his cape wrapped tightly around her shoulders, like the hug she couldn't give him.

An owl hooted, unseen. Somewhere out there the King was walking alone. But now she knew that Vampires didn't crave solitude. He just didn't trust anyone, not even himself.

63

Chapter Sixty-Three

Adelira woke up alone. Hand flying to her neck, she let out a shaky sigh. The feral Vampire's breath was still hot on her neck. Her skin was smooth. He hadn't bitten her. Hadn't had the chance.

She wanted to find Orahn. Maybe actually thank him this time. After the night she'd had, he was the only thing in Tharth that still felt safe. She just wanted to be close to him. Wrapping his cloak around her shoulders, she willed herself to be brave, opening the door.

"Finn," she whispered, looking up at him.

"Your Highness."

"Um... I..."

He looked down at her sympathetically, eyeing the cape she wore. "Do you want to see the King?"

She gave a small nod.

Finn passed a silent look to Benedict. For once, Benedict didn't look stoic. He just looked tired. Her guards had fought their way through the market after the attack in the alley, but the streets demanded all of their attention just to hold back Vampires drawn in by her blood.

She touched the cut on her head and both guards tracked the movement, bracing against the faint smell of her dried blood along her temple. They looked upset to see the cut.

"Alright," Finn said and they led the way.

She followed closely, walking through the dark and quiet castle made her heart race. She kept glancing over her shoulder. No one followed behind her. They walked to the study and her guards bowed and walked away.

Adelira pushed open the door and found the King reading through a stack of papers at his desk. He was intense, focused solely on the reports in front of him.

Everything was too much. Tears welled in her eyes.

Here he was, just a man writing at his desk. Pen scratched across the parchment. The fire popped lazily in the hearth. The smell of ink and frost filled the room. The smell of him.

Orahn. She ran over, wrapping her arms around him.

His eyes widened. He sat upright, eyes ahead and didn't move.

His cloak fell from her shoulders to the floor, but she held onto him, not moving to retrieve it. Her arms tightened around his broad shoulders, breathing in the smell of him deeply.

"I wanted to say thank you," she mumbled into his clothing, for a second the image of him transforming into the Blood King flashed before her eyes and she flinched, burying her face deeper into his neck. He had shown her she did not need to fear him. Not even at his worst.

She said it a little louder, "Thank you for saving my life... Orahn."

"You're welcome."

She pulled away tentatively. He pushed his chair back and looked up at her expectantly. She wanted to hold him again, she bit her lip and stayed pressed against his desk. She wanted to say so much, he wasn't a monster, she wanted to be with him... So many things, she just didn't know how to say any of it. Her slipper slid on the cold stone and she caught her footing, steading herself against the wooden desk. It was solid beneath her.

"I–I know... Maybe, I think..." her voice failed her.

He pushed back further in his chair. He was constantly slipping away from her. She closed her eyes, watching him move away hurt. Forcing them open, she looked him over again. He was simply watching her, head slightly tilted, waiting.

"I know this is hard on you, too," she said softly. "I've been making things difficult without meaning to."

Her mind raced, piecing together the fragments of the attack. His hands had trembled when he'd held her afterward.

"I promise to stay in my room from now on."

"No. That's not fair."

"It's not fair to put you against your peopl—"

"—They can accept it and so can I. I'm sorry that this is happening to you. You deserve better."

Glancing down, she thrummed her fingers along her leg.

He took a breath, almost unnoticed by her, before he said, "You didn't ask for any of this."

Adelira bit her lip again. "Well, actually I *did*."

"What do you mean?"

"You didn't know? The marriage proposal was my idea."

"I assumed your Kingdom decided your fate..." After a moment, his eyes narrowed on her sceptically. "Why would you do that? Vampire leadership has been carefully cultivating an image of savagery. Why would you *choose* that?"

"Well, for exactly that reason..."

"I don't understand."

"I knew it was the best way to secure safety for Ebedene. And it'd give you the best chance at defeating the Shifters. I want to protect my people. If I am the price, but they are safe... I'll have been a good ruler to them."

He didn't say anything.

"M–My people needed me."

His eyes were searching her face with an intensity that froze her in place.

"I know that you've kept your word so far," she couldn't stop the words from coming, even when he looked at her like that, "Your reinforcements and protection of Ebedene are deeply cherished by me. I don't doubt you. You've proven yourself over and over again. But I hope that you can understand why the Blood Ritual was so important to me."

He stood quickly. His voice abrupt, startling her, "I will grant you your wish."

She blinked. "What... wish?"

"The Blood Ritual." His words were clipped. "Tonight."

"I—" she started, but the words tangled in her mouth. The coldness in his voice left her uncertain; unable to find the right response.

He didn't wait. Without a second glance, he walked out of the door. After a beat, he stepped back into the room, throwing her a long look. "Are you coming?"

"Oh, now??" she asked. "Right, yes."

Legs moving on their own, she followed him outside. Her mind spinning. *Why now? Why like this?* Her heart clenched, this was more for her than him. Still, she was relieved to finally be doing what she'd set out to do when she journeyed to Tharth. *Something's wrong*, she thought for half a second. Yet, she followed, because she needed this so much. Her steps sounded unsure along the tiles.

"We could wait. If you need more time to be ready," she offered.

He said nothing.

So, Adelira asked, "Are you... ready?"

"No. I don't think we'll ever be ready," the King said, finally, and she almost faltered.

"Oh, I, um—"

"—But right now, both of us need this. I need the protection it will give you. And you need our part of the contract to be honoured. In the face of your bravery, I owe you at least that much."

A sound fell from her lips without forming a single coherent word.

"Ready the priests," he barked at the guards stationed outside.

They snapped to attention and hurried off.

Adelira and the King walked in silence through the grand corridors and out into the night. The Obsidian Keep behind them, the forest before them, and into that darkness they walk.

She almost reached for his hand, but the silence of the trees was so unnatural that her outstretched fingertips brushed over the rough bark instead as she followed him deeper into the woods.

64

Chapter Sixty-Four

At the clearing awaited bundles of deep inky fabric. The ceremonial robes were black as the void and unmistakably nightvine. Adelira recognised it immediately from the King's books she had read.

"Put it on," he instructed.

The fabric was strangely heavy like it was trying to root her to the earth itself. She liked that, she felt like a tree.

The King shrugged into his own robe with practiced ease.

The sacred space was illuminated by the two full moons, like the sky had aligned for this. The remnants of Taipan's old magic could almost be felt in the air.

The King's expression turned stern as his look fixed on the priests. There was no hesitation in him now. Adelira straightened her shoulders to match. There was no turning back.

She was surprised to see the priests given the suddenness with which he spurred this spontaneous idea into action, but then most things happened at a speed the Vampire King ordered. Everyone was always poised at the ready for anything he wanted. Tonight was no different.

She trembled, taking the delicate knife handed to her by the priestess. The altar was stone carved with runes so old that even her people's elders could not read them all. In front of the altar was the Sacred Blood Chalice, dark as obsidian and lined with silver.

The King stood opposite her, just as motionless as the forest trees. His eyes were locked on her. There was a shimmer in them, a barely perceivable concern that vanished before it was fully realised.

He was nervous, though his face barely betrayed the emotion. She thought in a moment of panic; *if he was nervous, then I should be, too.*

He trusts me, Adelira told herself, *he might even love me, this is best for everyone... So, what is he not saying?*

His black hair hung over one eye before he swept it back in an effortless motion. His angular face was highlighted by the fading light. There was beauty in him, yes, but also something terrifyingly fierce. She could not shake the image of him being so monstrous, but right now he was utterly restrained, like he was caging his reactions with an icy grip of control that threatened to shatter everything around him. How different he could be from one encounter to the next.

The priestess pulled the words from the earth itself, invoking the blessings of the forest through whispers too low to be understood even by Elven ears. On the ground, the silver sigil beneath Adelira's feet began to glow, shimmering like flickering fish scales in a dark river.

On the other side, Orahn's priest spoke in guttural tones that rumbled a storm and reverberated in their chests with each word spoken. His words were spoken in the old Vampire tongue that called upon the shadows that tied them to the darkness and locked them in eternal night. The ground beneath Orahn's feet quivered like liquid, scattering like fallen beads; the red sand shifted as though it were alive, writhing and twisting, trying to remember what form to take.

The King stepped forward first.

His eyes never left hers as he held his own ceremonial blade. Natural was the act of spilling blood to him, his blade drew across his palm and bled into the chalice.

The deep crimson hit the bottom of the chalice like a clap of thunder reverberating through the clearing and birds were chased from the treetops; spooked off into the night sky.

Adelira took a deep breath as she looked at her blade. Her hand shook as she pressed it to her skin. If she thought the needle prick was an uncomfortable task, this one was worse. Bunching her eyes shut, she dragged the knife into her skin and let her blood fall silently, mixing with his.

The crimson pools of blood swirled together, lighting up the chalice with an ethereal glow that was almost too bright to look at. The bond was visible, a faint shimmer in the air around them, like heat rising off stone.

Deep within her chest, old magic was begging to come alive in her. It had once felt so lost to her before and now just within her reach.

They were asked to recite their Blood Oaths.

The King's voice was deep, weighted by the voices of every Vampire over centuries, "By blood, by shadow, by the eternal night, I bind my life to yours, my people to your people. From this moment, I am yours, and you are mine, in strength and in power."

Adelira's voice was clear as she followed the reading, "By blood, by light, by the stars above, I bind my heart to yours, my people to your people. From this moment, we are one, in grace and in honour."

The blood in the chalice flared with a brilliant light before igniting into flames, extinguishing just as rapidly, leaving the chalice empty and smoking. The sigils beneath their feet merged. Silver-red becoming one; created a new symbol in light and darkness.

Adelira felt an overwhelming rush of energy, multiple heartbeats thrumming in her veins, thousands, millions.

She lifted her eyes to his, as though barely able to raise above the pull of his Kingdom crashing inside her mind. Threatening to buckle her knees under the weight of it, but as she stood in defiance of it, very slowly the noise began to fade and it wasn't so overwhelming, anymore.

"Is this..." she asked as it pulled away from her. "Was that Tharth?"

The sensation narrowed, condensed. Bit by bit, the presence of everyone faded until she was left with just the Vampire King within her blood.

He felt alive, constant, like heartbeats layered together in perfect synchronization in her chest.

Their eyes locked and she could see the flicker of something there. Something more than the charming, distant, complicated King she had come to know.

The intensity of his emotions, too raw and new for her to decipher; as if she had only seen them on his face and not felt them in her chest, as well, so much was lost in interpretation.

The thing she could feel from him, was it relief? ... Or resignation?

The priests returned to the castle, leaving the couple alone in the forest with everything that had just transpired.

Adelira stood there, her hand still in his, feeling the Blood Ritual settle into her bones.

She looked at the King. His face was still, but she thought she saw a tremor in his jaw. He had changed, too. Though he wouldn't show it.

She looked up at the sky, expecting something awful to happen. The world had not broken apart though. The Blood Ritual had not thrown the world into chaos, no fires rained from the skies and the ground did not tear apart and swallow them whole. Yet, he had fought this every step of the way.

65

Chapter Sixty-Five

Under the two moons, the Blood Ritual completed. Adelira stood alone in the forest with the Vampire King. Pine filled the air, but it was his frost and ink that encircled them. A single wing flap disappeared into the dark.

He was under her skin. The blood bond linked them. His frenzied eyes locked with hers.

Legs trembled as a surge of emotions overpowered her.

Pushed to panic, she leaned over. Hands on knees. He held the space steady around them until the calming presence of the King allowed her to draw breath. Breathing him in, leaning on his strength to find hers. He carried as much of the storm as possible, so not everything hit her at once.

She rose and locked eyes with him. He nodded his approval at her, but... he hadn't moved. Did she only *feel* his approval, then? In her chest? In the bond they now shared?

A new and thrilling thought washed over her. In the rare moments Orahn had lowered his walls and allowed her in, she'd grown close to him. And that closeness was now amplified by magic. Now, they weren't separated by anything, at all. The line between them dissolved entirely.

His eyes darkened as she stepped closer to close the space between them. Fingers hovering just above his chest, so close. And yet, somehow, she *couldn't*. The magic ignited an undeniable pull between them. But something in his eyes halted her.

His desire for her heated through her. His passion flooded her veins until it was all she was. He craved her, the depth staggering. It bled through the bond, setting nerves alight. His need filled her from the inside out until she was devoured by him.

And then, it hit her.

Like a dream, she witnessed his imagination.

He *imagined* her pressed against him. Bare skinned and held in his strong arms. His hands tracing every curve with a possessiveness that left her breathless.

Adelira watched as the vision of her tipped her head back for his lips to claim her throat. A growl rumbled deep in his chest.

But there was something unfamiliar in his fantasy. Beneath it was deeply observant. His focus lingered on small details; her shiver when he touched her skin just so. The slight tremor in her fingers as she touched his bare body. His fingers threaded through her long hair. And they were in the *light!* The vision he imagined was in sunlight. Her hair glowed. He smiled. Fangs. Light.

The *her* in his mind clutched him dearly. Pulling him in deeper, she was losing herself in him. His hands grasped her tighter, whispering her name. Offering him her neck, though he only trailed kisses there.

The images in his head were fading as he turned them away.

Adelira blinked. Still, the sensations flooded her standing in the dark forest, just a step from him, as his mind betrayed his deepest desires through the blood bond they shared.

Tension flirted with temptation. His as much as it was hers.

Leaning in, a kiss on her lips. Led by an instinct she barely understood, faces inches from each other. Her lips parted like he was drawing her in. Eyes lowered to his mouth.

Her lips almost touched his.

The distance he kept her at and the withdrawal of his intimacy were at odds with what lay beneath it. She could still feel his suppressed hunger. The raw, undeniable need to claim her.

A lash of his shame.

Dark turbulent eyes locked onto hers. Her own longing reflected back at her. His need for her blazed in his eyes, yet his body was rigid with retreat. He recoiled, pulling back through the unseen threads between them. It cut through his desire, leaving behind unbearable agony.

He fought with his need. And the bond carried it to her; revulsion for the depth of his own craving.

The bond's deep connection was everything she'd ever chased. Having someone so close she could guess their thoughts and feel them always. The height of the Elven experience. She revelled in it... while he recoiled from it.

He hated every minute of sharing his most private experiences with her and she loved every minute of it.

Fingers twitched, drawn to him by her own desire that didn't silence. Even when his desire stopped speaking to her. She hesitated again. Heat of his body radiating against her palm. Stopped only because she knew that he was holding back from the closeness between them.

The King took a sudden step back, breaking the invisible pull between them with a swiftness that left her reeling.

He lifted a hand. Almost in a gesture of apology. As quickly as the images had disappeared, the hunger in his eyes dimmed, too. His jaw tightened.

"Orahn..." Her voice was a whisper, desperate and questioning, but his response was just as uncertain.

His eyes flashed a fleeting vulnerability that made her heart lurch and ache for him all at once.

It's okay, I won't hurt you, she wanted to say as he tried to hide.

She sat with her pain carefully balanced away from him, so he wouldn't have to hold that, too. She sat along the rim of his mind, willing him to trust her, asking him if he was okay.

He wouldn't answer her.

He spoke her name like a plea, "Adelira..."

Her lips parted, but no sound came.

"I can't," he said.

The forest was silent. Not even the wind blew. She felt cold.

His shoulders stiffened with the effort it took to hold himself together. The space between them turned hollow with his retreat sounding through the bond. He took yet another step back. Visible resolve solidified in his eyes.

They might have spoken more. The details eluded her now. Lost in the haze of their emotions. All she could hold onto was the sting of his rejection.

Adelira's heart sank. Confusion spread across her face. Followed by a new horror of realisation.

The world might not have broken open and rained chaos down on them. But he was *still* scared.

That meant that the consequences of their Blood Ritual were still to be realised. What was so terrible about the Ritual that he could not even bring himself to speak out loud?

"No one will touch you now," he said out loud, looking out into the forest and avoiding her. "You're not prey to my people any longer."

"Prey..." she murmured, the word curdled in her chest until she was small inside. She had forgotten the reason why they did this tonight.

"You're safe," he said. Voice hardening even further, "And the crystal will obey me, now."

He needed the Elder Celestite. He had promised her nothing more than safety. So why did this feel like such a betrayal? Did she only imagine the love he felt for her?

Looking into the bond at the tangle of their emotions for the answer, she couldn't find her way through the storm of feelings crashing over her all at once. Whatever his true feelings were, they were lost to her in all the noise.

"That's all this was for you? A way into the Rip?" She asked, stepping back from him. Her voice dripped with anger, the only emotion she could easily hold onto.

Then softer, her voice revealing too much of the hurt she felt, she asked, "Was it *ever* anything more?"

His eyes flicked away.

"Or only a strategic move?" The words were barely a whisper on her lips.

He took a further step back, distancing himself so much now that there was no mistaking his intention to leave.

His words were dismissive, as though the Blood Ritual hadn't happened and they hadn't just been on the verge of something more. "I have to return to the castle."

Before she fully understood it was his, a storm not her own battered at the corners of her mind. Guilt cut through her like steel, followed by humiliation that dripped like poison into her veins. A heat seeped through her core and left her shaking. Her thoughts tangled up in his. A man fighting against himself, desperate to master the tempest of his own desires.

He was disgusted. With himself, with the wanting, with the possibility of giving in. That disgust was a blade turned inward, carving him up inside with every breath he took.

Adelira pressed her hands to her head, trying to separate her feelings from his. But it was impossible. His torment had become hers. Leaving her unmoored, lost in emotions that weren't her own.

Shaking her head, she refused to lose him. Refusing to let him leave without knowing that she'd stand by him, no matter what the consequence of the Blood Ritual was. Even if he wanted her crystal, beneath that he wanted her, too. She needed him to know that was okay, too. He was allowed to have both... the crystal and *her*. Both were his.

She stepped into the bond; walking into his storm.

She strode forward, undeterred by the chaos. Pressing through the fury, until she found him, hidden in it all. And as she stood in the eye, everything died down.

Adelira waited there at the fringes of his fractured mind. Cracks spiderwebbing through his thoughts. He stayed hidden. His walls were paper to her; little more than a comfort blanket, hastily built and trembling. She could tear them down with a whisper. But she wouldn't do that.

If he needed to hide, like a wounded fox cornered in the garden, then she would grant him that mercy.

Patient, hand outstretched to offer herself in an unspoken promise. She waited. He had shown her how when he had waited for her; when she was lost and afraid on her first night in Tharth.

And yet, no matter how long she stood there, hand steady, he never took it.

He only turned away.

And in that moment, a slow, creeping certainty settled over her.

This was *not* Orahn.

She didn't know who he was. But he wasn't Orahn.

66

Chapter Sixty-Six

A soft voice called through the quiet forest, "Your Highness?"

Adelira startled, turning toward the sound.

A Vampire woman stood a few paces away, her lady with the amber eyes.

Adelira braced herself for her lady's warmth to be a fleeting illusion.

"I'm Amber," the woman said. "Would you like me to walk you to your chambers?"

Adelira blinked. No one had ever introduced themselves before. The gesture, small as it was, caught her off guard.

She hesitated, lingering in place. "Amber..." Her voice trembled as though testing the sound of the name. "I–I feel unsteady. Will you help me?"

"Of course," Amber replied without hesitation, wrapping an arm around Adelira for support.

She glanced at Amber, but there was no bloodlust fought against. Amber was calm as though Adelira were simply another person, not a dangerous temptation.

Amber said encouragingly, "Lean on me."

Adelira let out a sigh of relief. Finally, there was a Vampire who didn't flinch at close proximity.

"You'll feel stronger soon," Amber said as they walked through the castle. "That must have been quite draining! You're very pale. Let's make sure you rest up."

Adelira nodded.

"I noticed the flowers in your room, Your Highness," Amber said when they stepped into her chambers. "They are from Ebedene, correct?"

"Yes, the King sent them last week," Adelira murmured, too distracted to notice the guards were no longer stationed outside her door.

"It was hard to notice anything before, your scent was so overwhelming, I couldn't even smell the flowers," Amber said with a blush.

Adelira made her way to the bed as Amber busied herself around the room, straightening out her dresses. One caught her eye and she held it up.

"You should wear this to your next dinner with the King," she said, holding out a Thathian dress in a dark green.

Adelira didn't look at it.

"The colours will make your red hair glow," Amber offered to try to win her over.

Adelira knew what Amber was doing, she did it herself often after all. Steady chatter often softened the evening. But Adelira couldn't take anymore softening, anything more tonight might just unravel her entirely.

"These next few days might be a bit draining for you, given the strength of the Blood Ritual. If you need anything," Amber said, pausing at the doorway, "call for me."

Adelira's lips parted, unsure of how to express the gratitude rising in her chest. "That you can even look at me without... flinching... I've felt like a living curse these past few months, like something people fear to touch or even see."

Amber's brows furrowed. "Your blood... You feel like standing in sunlight. Dazzling, but much too much for Vampires. Under the King's power, it's softer like the glow of the stars instead of the intensity of the sun."

Adelira looked up and their eyes met. "You'll never know what it means to me that you simply held eye contact."

"Goodnight, Your Highness," Amber said with a small, sad smile before stepping out.

Adelira took in the emptiness of her room, the hollow that had greeted her every night since her arrival.

The Blood Ritual had done what was promised. She was no longer a disruption in the fabric of this aged and dangerous world. But it hadn't mended the ache in her heart and the confusion she felt when she thought of her time in the forest.

Adelira couldn't shut out the storm of emotions bleeding from him, no matter how much she tried, caught in the push and pull of emotions that weren't hers.

His guilt shot through her with a bitter undercurrent of shame.

Unfiltered emotions hit her, he was fighting something within himself. He wouldn't give in to her; she knew that much, even though the wanting was there, clawing at him and tearing him apart.

She felt her own anger and betrayal burn within her.

Climbing out of her bed, her thoughts tumbling through her.

Retracing the steps that had led her to this impossible situation. That man in the forest... He had not been Orahn. She felt it in her bones as an undeniable truth, but logic refused to yield an answer.

The Blood Ritual had changed him.

She had known the Ritual carried a cost. Though no one spoke of what that might be. Perhaps this was it? Once complete, it transformed him. Stole some integral part of him and reforged him into something else.

Was that why he never wanted the Blood Ritual in the first place?

But... no, that didn't fit.

Because the moment she let herself feel, she knew. The man in the forest wasn't Orahn...not because he had changed, but because he had never been Orahn to begin with. She shuddered.

A curse?

A man who was one way by day and by night another. Maybe cursed to shift between two selves: one cold, the other warm.

One night, he felt like a storm. The next, he was the eye of it.

Adelira then sat cross-legged on the floor of her chamber, surrounded by scattered parchment and smudged charcoal. She started to draw the King.

His fear of the blood bond was not a magical consequence of the curse, but a logical one.

And that consequence was she would discover his *secret.*

The answer had been there all along, in every inconsistency, in every small hesitation, in every detail that hadn't quite fit.

There had never been just *one* King.

That was why he never wanted the Blood Ritual. Not because he feared what it would do to him... But because he knew what it would reveal to her.

And now, she *knew.*

The first sketches had been quick, instinctive strokes of ink and shadow, impressions of him as she had seen him in different moments. She had started with two, because she was sure of at least two.

One was quiet, still as stone. His presence coiled and heavy, a force that could hold the room in its grip without a single word. He measured his silences carefully, moving with a calculated slowness, watching, assessing.

The other was restless, a creature made of movement with sharp dancing words. His charm had an edge. His smile never quite reached his eyes. He paced when he spoke like something caged. This one had called her *Princess*, teasing and testing, pushing her to react.

Which of them called her *Lira*?

Adelira exhaled, setting aside her charcoal. She looked at the sketches.

There are two, she told herself. *And yet...*

She reached for a clean sheet of parchment and hesitated. She didn't know why she was so certain of it. But she felt it. There was something missing... Someone was missing.

She had been trying to piece it together through sheer logic. Nothing felt logical. Separating them by observation, by sketches, by notes, by her shaky memories, ignoring the Blood Ritual until now.

The blood bond was too loud. Whenever she turned her focus inward, she was overwhelmed by emotions that did not belong to her. Restlessness, tension, hunger, grief.

She tried her hardest not to feel anything at all, to bottle her emotions for the first time in her life; so she wouldn't have to drown in the emotions of men who let theirs rage and flood the bond with hurt and desire and things she could barely begin to label.

Emotions are the problem... she thought slowly.

If she could not separate the Kings by feelings, then she would separate them by something else. Something more tangible inside the bond.

Heartbeats.

She had felt it before in the forest. That strange, eerie synchronization, like multiple rhythms being forced to beat as one. Almost too perfect. She took a deep breath, closed her eyes and let herself listen.

It was impossible to tell them apart, at first. The bond was still full of too much noise, emotions bleeding into each other.

She ignored all of the noise. Listened only for the heartbeats, steady, identical, perfectly synchronized.

One. Two.

And then, a breath of a pause; a hesitation that was so faint she nearly missed it.

Three.

Her eyes flew open.

There were *three.*

Three Kings. Three night cycles.

She looked back down at the two near identical figures she had drawn. Slowly, she reached for another sheet. With a certain hand, she began to sketch the same face, but a different person.

She had been lied to for months.

This wasn't just deception. It was a careful orchestration so seamlessly no one had ever questioned it. No one except her.

67

Chapter Sixty-Seven

She had ignored the signs. Now, those inconsistencies stood over her, screaming the truth.

There was another, a third presence wearing his face, stepping into his role as though it were a mask to be donned and discarded at will.

It was unbearable, the idea that she'd been tricked all this time.

But deeper than that, what disturbed her more, was the knowledge that she had actually always noticed. Some part of her had always known.

She scrunched up all of her sketches and threw them in the heath, watching them turn to ash.

Her own anger blended with theirs; Orahn and the not-Orahns.

Maybe this was the true consequence of the Blood Ritual, that they all knew about each other, and were forced to constantly and repeatedly crash into each other with their uncontrolled emotions.

The door opened quietly behind Adelira. She didn't need to turn to know it was the King, he was undeniable.

"Lira," his voice was hesitant, something she wasn't used to hearing from him.

She didn't look at him and kept her attention fixed on the fire.

He walked over and reached for her.

"—Just stop!" Slamming her palms against his chest, though it did nothing to move him.

His eyes widened in shock, but he didn't retreat. When she looked at him, she found an opening, a crack in his armour that had always seemed impenetrable until now.

"Lira..." he barely uttered her name.

"Are you insane?" Her fists falling. "I can't keep up with you! You barely care that I exist and then other times you act like you can't live without me!"

"I *do* care! I—" his words were swallowed by his anguish of not knowing what more to say than that.

Her heart paused, his words sincere enough to stop her for a moment before all the hurt came rushing back.

"If you care then why do you do this?" Her voice was rising. "Why this constant back and forth between kindness and — and *hate*!?"

"I don't ha... Please, I can explain, Lira..."

"How can you explain any of this?"

He stepped closer, trying to close the distance between them, but she folded her arms across her chest, a physical action to protect her heart against him.

"It's not just *you*, Lira... it's everything," he said, taking a step out of her space, shaking his head.

"If I'm a bride you accepted in war times, then I can live with this being only about the treaty," she said, her voice sharp. "But don't pretend it's more."

His face pulled in anguish. For a moment, she saw something that made her regret the harsh words. He reached for her face, but she knocked his hand away, eyes flashing with anger.

"I'm *not* pretending," he growled, his voice low with desperation. "I'm not!"

"I can't go on wondering which side of you I'll meet."

"You don't know how right you are," he said, the words full of exasperation.

He had to be the one to say it first, because if she did it, then she'd always wonder if he would have ever told her the truth. She couldn't live with another giant question bearing down on her soul.

If she had stayed, if she hadn't run that day, would Talion be alive today? This was the question that weighed her down and there was no space left in her heart for another big haunting uncertainty, like would Orahn have confessed if she hadn't said the words for him.

"What?"

"If it feels like you're seeing different sides to me, it's because you are!"

Her breath caught. She stared at him. Everything was about to change.

"I'm not who you think I am."

She stumbled back slightly. She *knew* this, but wholly unprepared for the words that left his mouth anyway.

"What... What does that mean?" She asked slowly.

"I am Orahn. But you're not always with *me* when you're with the King."

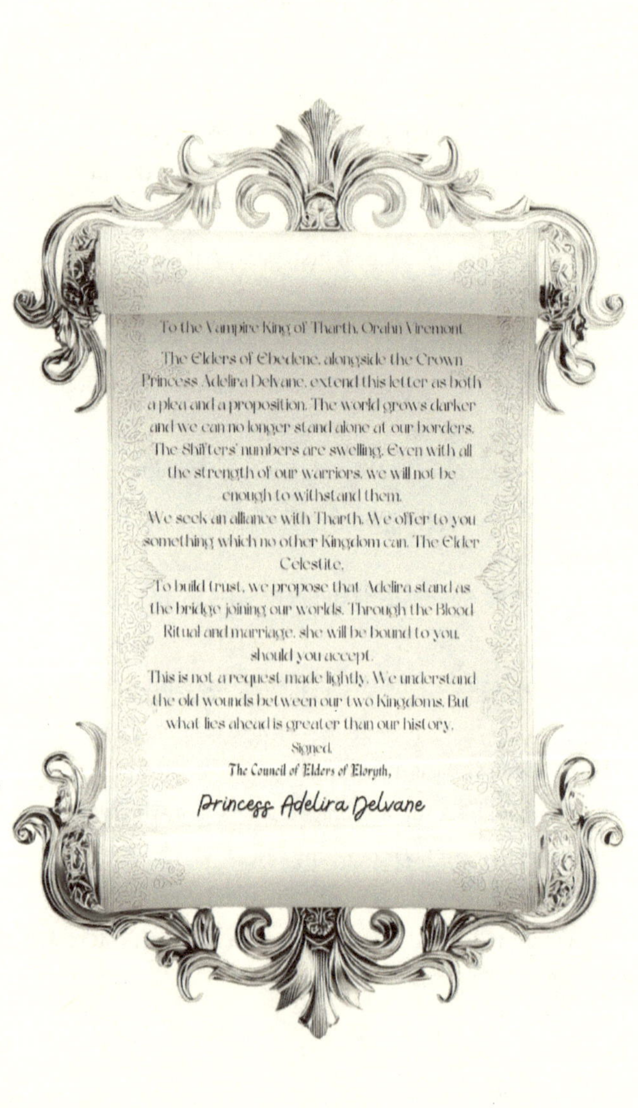

To the Vampire King of Tharth, Orahn Viremont

The Elders of Ebedene, alongside the Crown Princess Adelira Delvane, extend this letter as both a plea and a proposition. The world grows darker and we can no longer stand alone at our borders. The Shifters' numbers are swelling. Even with all the strength of our warriors, we will not be enough to withstand them.

We seek an alliance with Tharth. We offer to you something which no other Kingdom can. The Elder Celestite.

To build trust, we propose that Adelira stand as the bridge joining our worlds. Through the Blood Ritual and marriage, she will be bound to you, should you accept.

This is not a request made lightly. We understand the old wounds between our two Kingdoms. But what lies ahead is greater than our history.

Signed,

The Council of Elders of Eloryth,

Princess Adelira Delvane

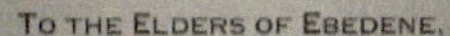

To the Elders of Ebedene,

I have read your letter. I have considered your plea. And I have decided.

Your offer is but trinkets of Elven power. That alone is not enough to earn my allegiance. A key into the Rip is hardly tempting enough.

Your people do not trust mine. Mine do not trust yours.

You ask me to take a wife not of my kind. To bind my fate to yours. To fight your war. You mistake me if you think I bend to the will of prey.

However, I have no interest in waiting for war to find me.

The Shifters will not stop with your lands. They will come for us all.

I accept your offer, because I will not watch as enemies gather strength.

Send your princess. Let her step into the darkness and prove she is more than an offering.

Understand, I do not need Ebedene. I will wage war on any foe at my doorsteps. I enjoy the opportunity to walk through their door first.

Now, bring me my bride.

King Orahn Viremont

68

Chapter Sixty-Eight

THE KING

Cormac slapped a copy of the letter down on the table. "You call *that* a diplomatic response?"

Lorcan didn't even look up. "I call it honest."

"That's why *diplomats* write these, or better yet; *me* — which I *did*, by the way. You only had to send it."

Lorcan shrugged. "I wanted them to know where they stand."

Cormac's jaw tightened. "You wanted to pick a fight."

"If they scare that easy, what use are they to us?"

Orahn finally spoke, voice even, "We need allies, not corpses."

Lorcan flashed a grin. "Then, I did us a favour. They were desperate. It bled through every line of their proposal, I won't match them in that. I know you think we need the crystal, but I don't want a Princess."

Cormac shot him a glare. "No one wants the Princess. Not even the Blood Families, who've gathered tonight, ahead of her arrival to tell us that as much. Let's hope this Princess thinks your response was worth the travel."

"You're late on this. What have you been doing? It was sent officially weeks ago."

"What have I been doing?" Cormac asked incredulously. "Keeping the Kingdom running while you keep trying to burn it down. I had no reason to suspect my proposal wasn't sent."

"Your letter was boring. Besides, she accepted the terms. She came anyway, off of my invitation. That tells us exactly how desperate she is," Lorcan said. "I also got her here in one piece. You're welcome. *Twice.*"

"Enough, it's done now. We don't have time. The Blood Families requested an audience."

"Fantastic." His fingers tightened around his bloodwine.

Orahn rolled his eyes at Lorcan's sarcasm, but he remained mindful of Lorcan's tiring weeks of playing hidden bodyguard.

Orahn shrugged into his traditional robes and placed the crown on his head. His brothers; Lorcan and Cormac, still bickered, a constant background noise in his life. His eyes flashed to each of his brothers, and they both reflected his exact appearance back at him.

They were identical triplets.

Their parents declared a *single* heir at birth. The brothers were raised and trained to rule as one person; three minds behind one throne.

The public image of the fictional King was impossibly perfect. An undeniable and unfair advantage that made the Vampire Kingdom flourish under its deceitful Kingship.

When they were young, attacks on the crown of Tharth were common. The constant threat made their parents grateful they ensured the safety of their lineage by allowing two heirs to grow up auxiliary to secure their place.

Each night, a different brother stepped into the spotlight, and to the Kingdom the King was a formidable creature of legend who never required rest.

At the end of each night, the brothers would meet to share details of their evening that may be important for each other to know. The court itself was none the wiser to the deception on their throne.

"Cormac?"

"I'm already on it. The war strategy is coming along well, I just need to confirm the funds' final figure." Cormac pulled out wooden devices to run calculations from his desk and opened his accounting books.

"Lorcan." Orahn fixed him with a serious look.

"What?" he asked defensively.

"Help our brother."

"Maybe if he was doing something fun like, I don't know, the actual war plans?" Lorcan said, rolling his brown eyes. "Stabbing someone? Maths doesn't win wars."

"*You* know it does," Cormac muttered.

Orahn tracked the weariness hidden beneath their well-oiled façade of invincibility. Lorcan had driven off a dozen Shifter packs that came too close to the Elves during their journey.

Yet, Lorcan wasn't just expected to survive out there. He was expected to thrive. They were always an indestructible force, untouchable in every way. Anything less was unacceptable.

But then the tiredness in his brother's eyes betrayed the truth to them all.

"Lorcan, you've just come off a two week escort mission, keeping the Shifters from the Elven travelling party. You need rest, because you'll be back at your duties soon enough." Orahn's loyalty to his brothers outweighed his own exacting standards. "This time, you get a pass."

Lorcan lit up like a child released from chores. "Sleep!"

Cormac, already seated at a desk piled high with ledgers, didn't bother to glance up. "It's not like you're any help with the numbers unless there's actual battle strategy involved."

Lorcan smirked, unabashed. "Don't let me stop you."

"Lorcan," Orahn said with his best impression of oldest brother's sternness.

Cormac began running through calculations and scribbling sums across reams of paper, and muttered, "Sometimes I think he's more exhausting than the military drills."

"See!" Lorcan waved his hand at Cormac. "Look how happy he is! He doesn't even need me."

Orahn's sharp gaze cut to his brother, his voice full of warning, "If you're not going to bed, Lorcan, then you're helping with the numbers. Those are your choices."

Lorcan groaned dramatically, slumping against the doorway. "I want to sleep, I do. But the Elves are coming tonight and I never actually got close enough to see this princess of yours. Too busy fighting off Shifters." He smirked. "Still... maths." He shuddered like it was a horrifying option.

Cormac huffed, flipping a page in one of the ledgers. "Then sleep and leave me to it. I'll do it faster without your distractions, anyway."

Orahn started to turn away, confident his brother would shuffle off to bed.

"I'll help you," Lorcan muttered, shoving his hands into his pockets.

Cormac looked up, blinking in mild surprise. "What?"

"I'll help," he repeated. "I hate maths and I *hate* missing sleep, but... You're my brother." He dropped down in the chair opposite Cormac, his eyes were already moving over the documents.

Cormac's features softened, though he tried to hide it by immediately thrusting a sheet of numbers under Lorcan's nose. "Fine. Here. Just match these columns. Try not to set the desk on fire."

"Yeah, yeah, I got it," Lorcan grumbled, snatching the page. "Why do these numbers need to be matched? What are we proving?"

"That you can still count, apparently," Cormac quipped.

Orahn paused at the doorway, watching the two of them. A small, rare smile tugged at the corner of his mouth before he strode away. Whatever happened, no matter how they bickered, one thing was certain, they would always have each other's backs.

"Fine. But I'm doing the royal tour of the army." Lorcan begrudgingly pushed back his chair and started rampaging through papers.

Cormac snatched the papers back and reorganised them. "Stop messing things up. Here, take these and tell me how much is left from your battle with the Jin District."

Lorcan sighed exaggeratedly and started running through the figures.

"Thank you," Orahn called over his shoulder without agreeing to Lorcan's demands. They all knew he did not need to, Lorcan was always going to do the war tours and training. That was how he served the crown best.

In Tharth, it wasn't an aspiration to have a King as a legend; it was their reality. This was the only Kingdom that could afford such daring risks in all areas of rule, because they weren't bound to a single King.

To outsiders, the King of Tharth appeared a tireless, unassailable, singular ruler who could be everywhere at once. A King who fought in the blood-soaked chaos of battle, yet still governed with an iron grip behind palace walls that very same night.

Orahn stepped out of the chambers he shared with his brothers. His long cloak trailed silently behind him.

A restless energy brimmed unnaturally through him. He often saw it in Lorcan. Once, a long time ago, when they were more connected, he'd felt it in Lorcan as well, but he'd long since tried to bury the memories of their childhood.

Did his brother always feel this uncomfortable and trapped in his own skin? Orahn hoped not. This was just nerves for Orahn. *Nerves*? Was that something he *could* feel? He thought that had died in childhood. Maybe not.

Passing the grand hall, its doors ajar. He glanced inside to see a flurry of preparation. Servants moving briskly, draping crimson cloths over banquet tables and fluffing cushions in a rare effort toward comfort. The room, like the castle itself, strained under the pretence of softness.

Orahn shut the doors softly, his fingers brushing the iron handle, and moved on. Tall arched windows let in long streaks of fading light. Mountains surrounding the castle rose like pointed teeth with peaks that bit into the clouds.

His thoughts were always foremost with his brothers. They sacrificed so much, it was his duty to put them first every chance he could. Second came the Kingdom. But now... now there was an Elf and he had to protect her while he protected everyone else's interests at the same time.

Adelira was an enigma to him. What would it mean for her to leave behind her sunlit-filled world for the shadows of his world?

Adelira's arrival brought with it a vulnerability he hadn't anticipated. If he thought about the Elves and the light by which they lived their life, was that a thing he could have? Was he allowed to enjoy her light?

They were a singular force, their brotherly-bond forged in blood and united by the crown they shared. His life stood on that foundation.

The idea of romance, of anything personal and selfish, had always felt like a luxury Orahn couldn't afford. He had convinced himself that he was content to let go of such indulgences. He was certain that no brief connection could ever compare to the sacred duty he carried with his brothers who would always have his loyalty first.

But there was a strange ache growing in his chest, difficult to ignore now when he thought of his future.

He reached the great doors of his meeting hall. Beyond the door, his advisors would be gathered.

But his mind remained on her, this Elven Princess who would soon walk through these halls ruled by shadows and blood.

Would she be able to bear it?

Would *he*?

Orahn straightened his shoulders. Pushing open the doors, the night fell fully upon him as he stepped into the hall.

69

Chapter Sixty-Nine

The Making of a King

Long ago when the Blood Princes were young:

Behind warded doors no other Vampire had permission to enter; the royal family rehearsed a *lie.*

From the first moment, they were taught to speak and walk the lie. Then they were taught to guard it like a knife held inward.

The boys knew they had to live as one always. But now they were old enough to start to ask if they'd die as one, as well. It seemed to matter less lately; they were dying, piece by piece.

A polished black table reflected the faces of three identical boys. Young Orahn sat rigid, hands folded, like he could disappear into his chair. Young Lorcan lounged, lips curled into a smirk. Young Cormac hunched between them, trying to make his silence match their dissonant noise.

"Again," the old-King commanded.

Orahn began, voice clipped and steady. Lorcan echoed him, every word an insult disguised as precision. Cormac stammered to find the rhythm between them.

Mother's fan cracked the table. "You are not three. You are one."

They straightened instantly. Obedience wasn't just expected, it was survival.

"You, Orahn," she snapped. "Your voice is clear. But where is your heart? Words without weight are whispers. Do you intend to whisper at your Blood Court?"

He didn't answer. He couldn't find the words. His heart was buried beneath iron layers of duty, too dangerous to acknowledge.

Her gaze shifted. "Lorcan. You reek of disdain."

Lorcan's spine stiffened under her scrutiny. The urge to please flickered, died, and left only the ash of defiance. He'd been so eager to impress them once, but that eagerness only set him apart from Orahn and Cormac, inciting their wrath.

Lorcan said, "Would you rather I lie with a smile?"

Her hand snapped out, her fan struck his cheek.

The red line across his cheek stung, but not as much as the silence that followed. Could he train on the battlefield harder than anyone else and be a person; forged in pain?

"And you, Cormac. Stop hiding in your brothers' shadows. A king does not follow."

Cormac shrank back, the contradiction was impossible. He was supposed to be one with them, but also *more* than them. Somehow, he had to be just as strong yet distinct... And erased. He didn't know how to be everything they wanted, both less and more at the same time.

"Again," the King commanded.

They spoke together with perfect timing. And when they were told to walk, they moved in pace with each other, every step mirrored, over and over, and over again. Unity tightened its hold, like fingers choked around their throats.

"The Blood Ritual is dying. You must maintain the illusion without it to help you."

The Blood Ritual, forced on them when they were much younger still, was designed to keep them in sync, constantly aware of each other's emotions so they could present as one. Without any privacy between them, they were driving each other mad.

But as it began to fade, they were slowly unravelling the bonds which kept them standing upright before their parents and the entire Kingdom. Ripping slowly from their bones and sinew. Without the blood bond, they felt the terror of being separate for the first time in their lives, and the terror of knowing even after the magic faded, they'd never be allowed to be alone.

Each boy was handed a sword to practise with. Lorcan's blade glinted in the light and he swept it through the air, metal whistled. His brothers didn't follow. He glared at them, but they didn't meet his gaze.

"Lorcan, your fire will destroy you if not leashed."

"So, leash it," Lorcan muttered.

The Queen's hand grazed his cheek, he almost flinched, though it was gentle this time, almost like a mother might touch her child. He wanted to lean into it; believing in the softness. But that lie would wound more than her fan ever had.

"Discomfort isn't a signal to stop. We push to failure. And we *do not* fail," their mother said as they moved through the forms and grapplings.

Grunts punctuated the room, ripe with sweat.

Later they weren't granted rest; instead, they instead had to write dissertations on the Kingdom's trade channels and current laws.

"Cormac," the King said, examining his quiet notes on their reports. "You see cracks. Good. But kings must act, not just observe."

"Yes, Father."

Cormac closed his eyes, he knew his brothers could still feel his anxiety in the fading bond, the sickness that rose up in him whenever they failed to impress their parents. He had acted more when he was younger, but the consequences of that still fluctuated through him. Now, he wasn't sure he could move at all without someone suffering for it.

The lessons blurred; decree, movement, weaponry, posture, fighting. Endless training was drilled into them until they were shaped as one and stripped of identity. Even the way they chewed their food was exact. They didn't even need to eat, but their parents ensured that if they ever did, the very act would be identical across all three of them.

"A king does not blink unless all three blink. You will not breathe alone."

They remained hidden from court, watching from the tunnels and from within the darkness their parents watched *them*. When Lorcan laughed at a noble's feathered hat, Cormac followed with a quiet chuckle. Orahn, against all control, smiled.

The King's voice slashed the moment: "Drop the illusion again, and you risk everything."

Lorcan's smile died. Cormac stared at the wall. Orahn folded his hands. All of them more hollow tonight than they were the night before, less hollow than they would be tomorrow.

"What if we can't keep this up?" Lorcan asked.

The silence after was immediate and dangerous.

"You must," the Queen hissed. "There is no *you*. There is only the King."

"If you falter, the Kingdom dies," the King said.

Their room was the only place the walls didn't watch. But even there, their breath stayed synchronized. They almost always moved together now, spoke in the same tone, trained to the same rhythm.

There was nothing Orahn kept for himself, because there was nothing left of himself. There was no item in the room that distinguished him from Lorcan and Cormac. It hurt too much to lose more of himself that he would inevitably have to give up for this lie their parents insisted on and it ached to force his brothers into the shape of who he was. Whoever he was. So, he chose to be no one, for all their sakes.

Lorcan clung to his daggers, desperately, like an identity he was almost allowed to hold for how useful it appeared to their parents, but he heard Orahn's voice inside his head like it was his own and he couldn't turn it off, anymore. He sometimes caught himself counting breaths, like Cormac. Orahn did too, and they hated that obsession about their youngest brother.

Cormac turned to his books, just to fill his mind with something that wasn't *them,* if there was so much else in his head; then maybe his brothers couldn't take over the one place meant for him. But Cormac found his brothers between the lines of ink, anyway.

Lorcan spun a dagger between his fingers. "Do you ever think... what it'd be like to just be *us*? Not a crown. Or a mask. Just brothers?"

Orahn's voice was flat. "It doesn't matter."

"But what if it did?" Cormac whispered.

No one answered.

The fire crackled and three identical shadows stretched across the floor.

70

Chapter Seventy

Back then, Orahn had convinced himself it didn't matter. But tonight, with Adelira on her way, he wasn't so sure.

He shook his head and let the memory fall away.

"Thank you for your patience," Orahn said, striding across the hall where men and women rose from their seats at a long table.

He took his place at the head of it. He could almost hear his mother's fan cracking the table, a ghost of correction at his back and he straightened his spine. The act slid into place. King always. Held in place like the blade his parents had once pressed to his throat to ensure he breathed in time with his brothers.

They'd bleed so much that night, but by the end, the habit had solidified and even now Orahn sometimes found himself gasping if Lorcan held his breath. Fortunately, that was something Lorcan hadn't done in defiance since they were children, though sometimes if the prey was just a little too tempting he held it until the bloodlust passed.

Now, even when alone, Orahn carried all three of them within him and none of them left space for the man he might have been. Cormac and Lorcan were too loud. Yes, *even* Cormac was too loud. They'd traded three lives for a single crown. At some point, the crown had to feel less heavy. *Right?*

The great hall was filled with the familiar faces of noblemen and the aristocrats of Blood Houses from across Tharth. His spy, Sterling, suspected some of the more loyal Houses hoped he'd view this as a warning for what the others might plan. Orahn needed no warning, he and his brothers were constantly watching everything.

The stone walls of the grand hall held in displeased voices, an illusion of privacy that was true for once. Often Cormac would be listening from the tunnels within the walls, but tonight he had other plans. The Vampire nobility argued. Orahn sat unmoved as the nobles aired their grievances.

Lady Le Rouge sat forward at the table, her eyes blazing with disdain, trying to sway him one last time before the Vampire's future was set on this path.

"Your Majesty," she said, "I don't speak alone when I say the Houses do not stand with this decision."

"Speak for yourself," General Victoria said. "House Cazimer stands by the King and his choices."

Orahn nodded subtly towards her.

Lady Le Rouge huffed. "I didn't expect Cazimer to favour weakness so quickly."

"Our House isn't afraid of what an Elf might do, though I understand why Le Rouge might panic a little," Victoria said, admiring her nails, shaped like lethal claws.

Lady Le Rouge glowered, ignoring the insult, and turned her attention to the King instead.

"Surely you see how marrying an Elf is...unacceptable. You're the King of Vampires. You must wed, but we implore you; wed one of your own. A noble of pure blood."

"Pure?" Orahn asked.

"Perhaps one of my daughters? We need strength in the line, not. ..fragility."

"Viremont, from your own family. We can find you a strong match there," his cousin said.

Orahn knew the houses had spent decades bickering over which of their daughters were best suited for him, which house had more strength and riches, and who got the most power from such an alliance.

Three lives secured the crown. He didn't need their approval nor an heir weighing on his shoulders tonight. He had never allowed himself to consider children. It was too indulgent an idea to entertain.

He spun the gold fertility ring around on his finger.

However, things had changed with this war. A bride had come unexpectedly into the brothers' equations. A bride didn't get to have their future though. She got to help them win a war and by Vampire standards, that was a much more prodigious outcome.

Lady Viremont, his aunt, said, "The Elves are weak. Our power lies in our bloodlines, the strength of your bloodline, Orahn."

She used his name too personally. It grated underneath his skin, but he let it slide, they were family, after all.

"The Celestite is what matters most," a Crowe Lord pointed out. "Take it if we must, but don't bind us to Elves for it."

Orahn's calculating look swept over his council, but he held his silence.

As Blood King, he could do almost anything he wanted. Still, the houses would only take so much before an assassination attempt on the crown might yield better results than arguing with the stone wall they knew he could be when his mind was set. His mind was most certainly set. He and his brothers were always prepared for moments when the Blood Houses might try to steal power, but now they had to be prepared that they might go after the Elf, as well.

Lord Le Rouge snapped, "Why risk everything for a union that will only make you weaker?"

The King raised an insulted eyebrow.

"You'd make a fine match with a Vampire of our own blood," the man continued, "A daughter from my House Le Rouge, or even Delarosa, their House has dozens of daughters to pick from."

"Let us find you a suitable bride. The finest matches in all of Tharth are right here for your choosing, Your Majesty."

"Your people would be far more loyal to such a union."

Orahn spoke calm as ice as he said, "The Elves are our allies. Taking their Elder Celestite will do nothing but turn them against us."

Lady Delarosa's eyes flashed and Orahn's own irritation flared in response.

"Allies?" she sneered. "They have had that crystal all these years and now they want to marry into our strength. You could take the crystal."

The room shrank as Orahn rose. "And risk another war? Plunge us into another bloody century, with enemies surrounding us on all fronts?"

He remembered what endless war did. How the screams didn't stop when the swords dropped. It cracked a Kingdom from the inside, long before any enemy breached the gates.

He remembered what he and his brothers looked like when they didn't recognise themselves anymore. When the Blood King was the only madness they understood.

"The Elves are our only remaining allies who would stand with us against the Rip. Stealing the Elder Celestite would create enemies, Lady Delarosa. This marriage is about stability, not some grand bloodline you've concocted."

Obsession with power and addiction to violence blinded Vampires to the worth of anything that isn't a weapon they could understand. The weapon was her crystal. She was obsolete. It was a mindset deeply rooted and difficult to overturn, especially when every effort to do so risked making Orahn appear weak. A fatal flaw in a world where his hold on peace demanded the appearance of unyielding strength.

The entire foundation was forged by the secret and paid for with their lives.

He was never allowed to ease his death-grip. Vampire society was a demon he had to keep back or all of Taipan, the entire world, might fall under his rule. Tharth was a ravenous beast that snapped at anything within reach. To loosen his hold would mean destruction of everything he and his brothers had carved new of themselves to shed. The Blood King had fought not to be this.

A chilling silence fell over the hall. The nobles exchanged wary glances, palms beginning to sweat.

Finally, Lord Le Rouge spoke, "You risk your bloodline for the Elves. Marry her and you isolate yourself from your people. The Houses could rally and challenge—"

"—Challenge me?" Orahn growled.

No one spoke for a minute. Heads bowed.

"For securing peace? Over heirs?" he continued, "Don't forget, I sit on this throne not only because I know how to keep it, but because I could throw us into war just as effortlessly."

The Vampire Houses balked at the idea of this marriage with an outrage that simmered beneath their elegant facades. To them, the

Vampire King taking an Elven bride was an act so disruptive to their society that it was nearly a declaration of diplomatic war in and of itself.

Lord Le Rouge spoke, "With this marriage you'll not only lose the support of Blood Houses... you may find yourself with more than whispers against you. There are those who would rather see you dead than wed an Elf."

Orahn's eyes darkened. His words rolled like thunder.

"Have you no faith in me?" Orahn let his piercing gaze sweep the room, daring any of them to challenge him. "There has been no other King in our history to have accomplished the feats I have. Under my rule, this nation has reached heights of prosperity unimaginable to our ancestors."

He leaned forward slightly. "I defeated the Giants of Killmanagh! What other King could have lasted three weeks in the trenches of the Antilliones, where even the earth sought to devour us whole? Or brought down the Alvain fortress, the last stronghold between us and the East?"

Orahn's frustration grew that they still needed convincing. He was impossibly strong to them and it still wasn't enough. His Kingdom was broken by the legend of the Blood King, something he and his brothers had forged in desperation. Now, they could barely contain it and the people still demanded more.

"Your Majesty," someone started but he shut it down.

"Do you think I am so weak, so fragile, that my bloodline would falter because of *this*?" Orahn asked in disgust.

Then, he paused. If the Blood King was what they wanted, they would get him. He would be every bit as ferocious as they insisted he be. If his deception was a weapon, he'd use their fear to secure peace. The room darkened around him, candles extinguished without wind.

Orahn's voice dropped sardonically.

"I could marry a songbird and my children would conquer the skies."

A hush fell. Some nobles froze mid-gesture, eyes wide, jaws tightening. A hand tapped nervously against the table; another ran through a lock of hair. Gossip swelled like a current: He's survived the impossible, this too could be true.

No one dared to breathe.

"Your feats are undeniable," someone finally spoke. "You are but one man, Your Majesty."

His eyes flashed red.

"If you falter, the power doesn't die with you," Crowe continued. "It spills into the hands of other families, other ambitions. Elven hands. That is what we fear. Not your reign, but what follows."

Orahn's jaw clenched.

"Then let me make this clear," he said, pushing his chair back as he stood. "I do not falter. And if any of you are foolish enough to think otherwise, then step forward. Let's see what your ambition is worth against me."

He waited.

They all waited. But no one came forward.

Orahn said with finality, "I will marry the Elf and we will keep our alliances intact. Those of you who oppose this are free to leave this court and relinquish your titles along with your grievances."

The nobles stared, seething, but none of them moved to exit.

One by one, they lowered their eyes, some in reluctant submission, others in open resentment. Orahn walked out of the hall without another word to the outlying blood districts.

He stopped by the guards stationed outside the doors. "Ensure that they leave before the Elves arrive."

They bowed to the Blood King. Not Orahn. He could never just be Orahn. That name had been bled out of him long ago, made sharp enough to rule and large enough to share with his brothers.

71

Chapter Seventy-One

Orahn returned to his brothers in their private chambers.

Lorcan groaned, running a hand through his long, dark hair. "I thought you'd never come back."

Orahn ignored him and walked over to the table. He picked up the papers next to Cormac. "Is this the final figure?"

"No, but it's close," Cormac explained.

"Looks like you're getting those upgraded steel weapons you wanted, after all, Lorcan."

"Delicious," Lorcan said with a dark grin.

"Let's neaten you up," Cormac said and stood in front of Orahn to make him presentable. Orahn let Cormac fuss. "How was the meeting?"

"Awful. Remind me never to entertain a meeting from them again; especially when they were given so many chances to raise concerns before tonight."

"I told you to deny their request," Lorcan said with a scowl.

Orahn scoffed at him. "Next time I'll let you handle the formalities."

"Great!" Lorcan flashed him a deadly grin. "I'll murder them all and we won't have any more of these ridiculous meetings."

"They see the Elf as weakness," Cormac stated.

"It's more than that."

"They always hoped one of their families would secure the line of the crown and now that that reality is slipping away, they feel their power slip," Cormac went on.

"I sent them home, leaving only the minor representatives of each house to witness the Elves' arrival."

"That was wise for tonight, but it will wound their pride," Cormac said.

"Let the wound land," Lorcan dismissed.

Orahn chuckled, at least his brother would have fun with that. He grew pensive and asked, "Should we tell the Princess?"

Lorcan asked, "Tell her *what* exactly?"

"About the three of us? If she is to be our bride, then maybe she should know."

"We've discussed this before," Cormac said. "She is to be *your* pretend-bride. On our rotations in, we will spend time with her, get to know her enough to keep up the illusion, but ultimately focus on the usual duties that we perform to the crown. You handle diplomatic and public matters, and a bride is a part of that role."

"We can't share our secret with a stranger," Lorcan added.

"Having an Elf here is risky," Cormac cautioned. "We must ensure her safety from the Blood Houses."

"Let them try," Lorcan muttered. "They've got enough to worry about with this war without risking an assault on her now. They will have to learn to relinquish their control until after the war is won and then they can fight about who sits on the throne."

"Those who can't control themselves, will be controlled by us," Cormac affirmed.

Lorcan started, testing the waters to gauge his brother's response, "But if she were to conveniently..." he waved his hand nonchalantly, looking for a polite way to say it, "... *die*... then we are free of all of this."

Orahn's eyes narrowed in on him immediately. "If she's killed by a Vampire in our charge, we make instant enemies of the Elves."

Cormac felt his finger tremble with the energy he got whenever he was making a plan on the fly. He hadn't intended for her to die in Tharth, but Lorcan's proposal was not without his consideration.

"But if she is killed in a Shifter attack, I can turn her into a martyr. We could grieve our way into a stronger alliance with the Elves. A shared desire for vengeance would give us both freedom and allies."

"No one is dying in our charge!" Orahn was reminded of the brutality of his brothers.

Lorcan's face twitched, but he said nothing.

Orahn watched Cormac, he was still calculating the risks and rewards. His youngest brother was always a few steps ahead, half of the reason Tharth still stood and always the reason why ethics were under threat. Considering how explosive Lorcan was, Orahn almost saw it as a feat that Cormac managed to be just a little scarier.

"Regardless of the potential benefits,", Orahn said, "we are better than the scheming snipes that constantly nip at our ankles. We are strong enough to protect her, so... We. Do. That. She's not to be left unguarded. We control ourselves and our Vampires. Understood?"

Softer, Orahn said, "We're all thinking it, aren't we? That giving her the Blood Ritual would keep her safe from our people. They'd have to recognise her as one of us."

Cormac's expression was colder than usual. "The Blood Bond isn't just about protection. It ties us to her as much as it ties her to us."

"The bond would strip away the last barriers between us," Lorcan said, his timbre shaking from the thought alone.

"Once she's bound, she'll feel everything we feel. She'd be part of the three of us." Cormac said quietly, his voice low. He paused, his jaw tightening. "Do we really want that?"

Orahn shook his head with slow reluctance. "We're supposed to be her guardians. Not bound to her in a way that leaves us with nothing left to ourselves."

Lorcan said in disgust. "We'd have no private lives from each other."

"I love you both," Orahn admitted quietly. "But I don't know how much closer I can stand to be to you two."

"She'll be another chain around our necks," Lorcan's voice wavered. His fists clenched and unclenched, wrestling with the words. "Another reminder of what we gave up for this throne."

"It doesn't matter what we want," Cormac continued. "It never has. This is a choice we've made to protect our Kingdom, and to protect our secret. We don't know her and we don't trust her, so we tell her nothing. She is secondary to everything else."

Orahn shook his head, shaking the thought free so he could continue, "Is she though? Because her life is valuable."

Lorcan let out a frustrated breath. "We keep her in her room, no Vampire could get in."

"That only protects her from a Vampire attacker, what if they hire someone else to remove her as a threat?" Cormac asked. "I agree, she must remain in her room as much as possible, because our people can be unpredictable. But we have to admit she is still vulnerable, we'd need to take it in turns to watch over her."

"Great," Lorcan rolled his eyes. "More watching the world pass me by from the inside of a hidden passage."

"That is a lot, on top of all our duties," Orahn said reluctantly. "We will need to make it seem like we're still honouring our terms with the Elves. We gain enough of her trust that she doesn't feel us stalling at every turn."

"We can do that," Cormac said, though his voice betrayed the faintest hint of doubt, "We keep her in the dark, we will fight for both Kingdoms, win the war, and then..." His voice trailed off.

Protecting Adelira might cost them the last pieces of themselves they still held as their own.

"Then we let her go home after the war is won," Orahn finished, steely but with an undertone that hinted at a reluctance none of them wanted to voice.

"Won't that insult the Elves?" Lorcan asked, trying to assess if the Elves might become another enemy he had to (or was *allowed* to?) defeat.

"Insult? A war won *and* the return of their Princess?" Cormac scoffed. "I can spin it like a gift."

"We keep her for as long as it takes us to open the Rip," Orahn agreed.

"Why keep her, after we have the crystal, what's the point?" Lorcan grunted.

"I don't think the Elder Celestite is all that easy to work. They'll have considered that possibility. We likely need her to get it to work," Cormac said, his jaw clenching, hating that control outside of his hands.

Lorcan asked, "What happens when she realises we're holding something back? She will want what she was promised."

"She'll be smarter than the Elven Council lets on," Cormac said, already piecing together an image of the Princess from his advisors and Crowe spies. "It won't take long for her to see the cracks in our story."

Orahn turned to the window. The lights of the city burned like embers in the darkness beyond the Keep and wrapped in a blanket of mountains. Somewhere out there he could almost feel Adelira's presence in the cold night, drawing closer.

"All we can do is keep her safe, through sheer physical strength and well executed strategy, so she doesn't feel the need for the Blood Ritual. And hope we work the Elder Celestite quickly enough," Orahn said, his voice steady, though the words dragged at him.

Cormac's voice hardened. "The three of us have surely achieved more difficult things? It won't be easy, but neither was Condorf."

The three of them shiver in unison.

There was a silence as each brother weighed what it meant for her safety and for their own sanity.

The Blood King was a scar none of them could heal.

Lorcan already looked restless.

"The week won't be that long," Orahn tried to offer him.

"Says the brother who gets to spend the week on stage."

"Don't be such a child, Lorcan," Cormac said with no heat. "You need a week to recover from the Shifters you fought to keep off our Elven guests."

"You make it sound hard."

"You only pretend that it isn't."

"Then it's settled," Orahn said at last, pulling them back to focus. "We don't do the Ritual with the Princess. We keep her at arm's length, protect her without binding her, and... hope that it's enough." He took a steadying breath.

"Ready?" Cormac asked with a great deal of calculation.

His brothers could see the look on his face as he grew pensive while he worked out the course of the evening for them.

"Of course." Lorcan smiled at him, carefree and less concerned about the minor details of the evening's plan.

Orahn stifled a sigh. It felt shameful to hide his brothers from the world and it felt lonely in the spotlight without them. He robbed them of a full life by only letting them out a third of the time. But then he only lived a third of a life, as well.

"It's not 'fighting for your life' fun, but who knows, brother," Lorcan said in jest and patted his back, "it might be fun in that 'Elven blood' sort of way."

"We're not drinking the Princess," Orahn said and swatted his hand away and Lorcan grinned, swinging for his brother.

Neither of them would ever hit Cormac, he was different, although he could fight just as well; he preferred not to and his brothers respected that.

Cormac almost smiled as his brothers wrestled. "Lorcan, you still do that thing where you close one eye before swinging. Thought you'd have grown out of it by now."

Lorcan mocked disbelief, "Close one eye? It's called *aiming*. Might improve your 'combat,' if flailing counts at all."

"It's purely strategic," Cormac dismissed. "Now, you underestimate me."

"Is that a challenge?" Orahn asked, playfully throwing an arm over his brother's shoulder.

They laughed, a low deep sound that rang out at exactly the same pitch and length as each other.

They didn't do that often, but it still surprised them when they did. It was unintentional and that's why those small acts of unity meant something to them.

Lorcan and Cormac stepped through a hidden passageway in the wall. Orahn walked with them on the other side of the wall. He made his way through the palace.

Orahn sometimes envied his brothers' roles as part of the machine or part of the violence. His role as diplomat required endless grace and balancing in real time.

He'd let Lorcan do the March of Arms for the Elves, not just because Lorcan fought most closely with the soldiers, but because locking Lorcan away for too long had consequences the Kinship could not afford. And Orahn would let Cormac do the Council of War, because that's where Cormac came alive, a focus that kept them three steps ahead.

Orahn glanced briefly to the wall next to him and knew that his brothers shadowed him on just the other side.

72

Chapter Seventy-Two

Lorcan walked through the secret tunnels in the walls of the Obsidian Keep with Cormac next to him. Their steps sounded in sync down the tunnels. It didn't matter how old they got or how much Lorcan rebelled, the way they'd been warped into one person never quite faded.

The tunnels made his skin crawl with memories he'd rather bury. His thoughts turned to their childhood, as it often did in the dark...

Lorcan remembered as he and his brothers stood by one of their bedroom windows that had a sharp drop down the side of the cliff. There was one partially flat piece of rock that jutted out meters below and just below that was a window back into one of the lower sections of the castle.

The boys looked down. The drop wasn't fatal though it was high enough to make most people avoid it. Or at least think twice.

Lorcan never thought twice.

Pulling himself up into the window frame. He balanced on the ledge and dangled one leg over the ledge, swinging it freely.

Grinning, he declared, "Let's jump."

Cormac stood behind him, eyeing the drop, arms crossed over his chest. "This is idiotic."

Lorcan laughed. "You say that like you're not tempted."

Cormac's mouth twitched at the corner, but he held back his own smile.

"Are you afraid of heights?" Lorcan asked, but then he felt the rejection of that idea almost like a spoken 'no' coming from Cormac through their shared blood bond.

The rejection was a silent certainty that settled behind Lorcan's ribs. A shared and unspoken feeling, like it had always been between them just waiting to come to light. That was how the blood bond worked, the brothers could feel how each other felt instantly, incessantly.

"Are you afraid to die?" Lorcan asked. The 'no' came again and Lorcan tilted his head. "Seriously? No? Heh, I respect that." He grinned in approval. "So... it's just Mother you're scared of, then?"

Cormac rolled his eyes.

But there was something awakening in them all, a thirst for adventure that matched Lorcan's.

In one fluid motion, Cormac brushed past, and perched on the ledge beside Lorcan, both his legs dangling over.

In unison, their heads snapped back into the room and they looked expectantly at Orahn.

Orahn stood watching them, his arms folded, a scowl still on his face. He was supposed to be steadfast, the voice of reason in their little trio. Still, he ended up getting dragged into their madness.

Cormac wanted to explore and understand the world around them. It was quieter than Lorcan's restlessness that pulled him to adventure. As they grew older, he learnt to leash it and turn to books for that outlet.

Lorcan didn't care how old he got. He'd always throw his body or his sword against something just to see which broke first.

Cormac and Lorcan were pressing back against their parents' control, probing for weakness.

Tonight, that weakness was an open window.

"You're both insane," Orahn said.

"You mean, all three of us are insane," Lorcan teased.

Orahn moved to the window, because Lorcan wasn't teasing; he was right. Orahn might not fight his parent's control, but he'd always meet his brothers where they were. It was the only time he got to live and feel something.

"Hell," he muttered, climbing up between his brothers into the open window. "I want to see if we can make that jump, too."

Lorcan looked around the dark corridor as he walked with Cormac. It was the same suffocating space it had always been. Though now there was something new on the other side of the wall, the scent of *Elven blood*.

Lorcan felt like they were all about to jump again now. This time he was old enough to know they'd broken bones in that fall. Here, he wasn't sure what the cost would be.

73

Chapter Seventy-Three

Orahn halted outside the doors. His guards and Marshall averted their gaze. He refused to take a deep breath. Nothing that might make it seem like he had to prepare himself. The decision was made. He simply had to follow it through.

A guard moved to get the door. Orahn, already moving, pushed it open himself. He crossed the grand hall. He stepped up the low-rise platform to his throne.

Behind him, the walls were draped in banners with his family's sigil. A single upright sword at the center, with two others crossed behind. Was he the middle sword? Or just one of the crossings? Intercepted at every stage of his life by his brothers.

The evening chill was trapped inside the Keep now like the Elves' arrival had let it in when they opened the main gates. The fires along the wall did little to help. Orahn wondered if Tharth had begun to nip at the Elves' bones. The cold never bothered him. The sunlight creature who would join him soon, how would she fare here in the winter months?

The Marshall announced, "Presenting Elven King Hara and Queen Juli. They have travelled across the Veilspine Mountains for their daughter's hand in marriage."

The royal Elven couple entered.

Orahn rose, his tall figure casting an arresting silhouette. His crown, blackened metal. Armour beneath his ceremonial attire moved with him. He was dressed up tonight. Beneath it, the truth of who and what he was still rubbed against his skin.

King Hara and Queen Juli moved quietly as a breeze. Through the hall and came to a stop before him. Hunger stirred through Orahn's congregation as the Elves entered and soon quietened.

"King Orahn, thank you for agreeing to our terms," King Hara said formally, "And inviting us here tonight to begin our alliance."

Queen Juli stepped forward. Cradling a small wooden box, she opened it to reveal the Elder Celestite resting on a bed of satin.

He closed his hand around the crystal. The vibration shook his skeleton. It was heavier than it looked. This was *it*. All he needed now was to master it.

He said, "With this, we will secure victory."

His focus was entirely on the prize he'd gained. The Elven King and Queen exchanged a look. He caught enough to understand their concern.

His attention cut to them. "I will take care of her, too."

Queen Juli's head snapped up at his words. Surprise crossed her features. The Blood King spoke like a protector. The tension fell from her, exactly as he knew it would.

"She will be safe here," he added, the words spoken purely for diplomacy.

"Thank you, King Orahn," the Queen said.

They were escorted to seats along the side of the court. Orahn didn't notice. The crystal in hand. Its power in his palms now. After years of fending off Shifter attacks and fortifying their blood supply, he had the only thing that mattered. He allowed a satisfied smile. Placing the crystal on a stand beside him, he took his seat. Waved for the night to proceed.

"Presenting Princess Adelira Delvane of Ebedene," The grand Marshall announced next.

The doors opened, again.

Adelira stepped through.

They slammed shut behind her like a death sentence, and yet, for a heartbeat, the flames brightened in her wake.

His grip on the throne eased without him meaning to.

Orahn straightened, instantly tracking her every move. A sharp unexpected catch in his chest stilled his breath.

There was something heartbreaking in her slow approach, each step too careful, and it pulled the curve of his mouth down.

Iridescent as sunshine, her red hair caught the flames and was tucked into loose curls beneath an Elven tiara. The crown he bore was heavy and threatening, that design was intentional. A weapon he could wield if needed. Hers was barely a trinket by comparison. Adelira's clothes had no built in armour, if someone attacked now, she'd die in an instant. He marvelled at how unprepared Elves were and how it seemed as though they wanted to die.

On top of her head was a garland of slightly wilted flowers. An odd addition, he didn't quite know what to make of it. As though the flowers lifted her up by some invisible force he couldn't understand, her head held high. Even in *this* hall. The dress she wore was a soft shade of pink; flowing material that did not belong in his world of stone and darkness.

It was the look in her grey eyes that drew him in; too large and wary.

She knew everyone wanted to drink from her. She likely didn't understand why. He could see her tremble. He could taste her fear in the air. The unexpected urge to soothe her fought against his fangs.

The court had been on the verge with the Elves' arrival, but Adelira was pushing them over the threshold. Every ravenous eye was on her, watching her exquisite approach against the backdrop of candlelight

Eyes flashed red. *Gods*. He almost dropped his face into his hand, but he pushed his nature away with willpower alone until his eyes were dark and steady again.

Shaking as she walked down the long aisle toward him, footsteps tapping against the marble tiles.

Orahn had never heard an Elf make a sound while walking. Their steps were silent as a breeze.

It occurred to him then that perhaps she had done this on purpose, breaking the unnerving quiet with the rhythm of her heels. A small act of rebellion? Surrounded by the sunless, unblinking eyes of his people, each one a predator in their own right.

Even refusing to look at anyone, he noted her attention was keenly on every Vampire she passed, almost like she was making sure no one moved an inch.

Her blood sang sweetly. So close now, it was a scream.

Suddenly, he understood she wasn't just in danger from his politically hungry Blood Houses. She was in danger from his very literal-hungry Vampires. Their bloodlust was always beneath the surface, but he hadn't imagined that *her* scent would be this difficult to manage. His Vampires could snap, turned mad by her.

He felt half-mad just breathing her in.

She called upon every ounce of courage just to walk alone through a room of hunters. And he found she had not even noticed him, yet. He grinned in amusement.

She reached the platform, coming to a surprised stop before him.

Orahn looked down at her. His expression caught somewhere between curiosity and a look that was a little... *hungrier*... if he were honest.

A selfish desire for her trust began to stir within him.

She dipped into a small curtsy; the motion fluid and graceful. Her long lashes cast soft shadows as she lowered her grey eyes. It was perfect. Yet there was a tremor in the air, a hint of vulnerability that was impossible to miss this close. Orahn caught the hesitation in the rhythm of her breath. Subtle, like a whisper only he could hear. He wanted to lean in, just to hear it again.

When she rose, their eyes met.

He offered her a gentle smile. A gesture of reassurance, though it felt like a lie in the face of the future that awaited them both.

Usually, his instincts would align with his Vampires. Fear would trigger his killer impulses, too. But with her, the urge in him was entirely different and almost unbearable.

Orahn clenched his jaw, suppressing a shiver as famine warred with an ache that went deeper.

He wanted to show her his hands free of weapons, as though that might deny what his bare hands could do. Lowering his voice until he discovered the pitch that would stop the tremble in her shoulders, secure her belief that she was safe in Tharth. More than that, he wanted her to feel safe with *him*. Longing for her trust in him, even when he knew she shouldn't.

A darker thought sprung to mind.

Saccharine, everlasting-sunshine to match the melody within her veins. Her kind had a lightness that bled into every part of them. He imagined, for just a moment, the feeling of her skin breaking beneath his teeth, that gentle *pop*, her gasp, her warmth filling him, flooding every corner of his being with light.

Orahn's hands gripped the arms of his throne. She was breakable in a way that made him want to defend her from every danger, including himself.

Could she survive in a place like this?

He didn't know if she would survive *him*.

Eyes lingered on her a moment longer before forcing himself to look away. He was just starting to grasp how much they were all about to struggle. His brothers. He closed his eyes briefly. Nor would this be easy for his Blood Court... And certainly not for her.

He extended his hand toward her. The gesture was as careful as offering crumbs to a wild bird. Breath held as if the slightest exhale might startle her. His fingers stayed steady in silent offering. Conflict in her eyes was at war with the invitation of his outstretched hand.

He waited, unassuming, hand open.

She had to choose him. To step toward him on her own terms. He would never force her. He could never chase her, that'd only make her feel in her heart what her shaking bones already knew about him. This had to be her decision or it would mean nothing at all.

An Elf could never truly trust a Vampire. But the thought of it, his irrational craving for it, consumed him.

Orahn made a silent promise as he stared into her scared eyes and found that her vulnerability reflected back at him, haunted and hoping. He'd battle the very instincts that dictated his existence.

Even if it meant losing himself to her.

And then she placed her hand in his,

and he was undone.

74

Chapter Seventy-Four

Lorcan pushed into the tunnel. The darkness ate him up.

What Lorcan really needed was something to fight. Not drills, numbers or nobles playing power games behind silk screens.

He choked it down, like he did everything else in his life and prayed for a concealed dagger in the crowd or a battle in the mountains.

"The Elves hopefully won't be staying long." A whisper on the other side of the wall.

"They are distracting, though none more so than her," another voice said.

The whole court was saying the same thing. Adelira didn't belong here and he understood that better than anyone.

Lorcan followed the familiar paths until he found Cormac.

Cormac didn't look up. He stood in the narrow passage peering through the small crevices cut so discreetly into the rock that no one would spot them behind the textured stone and artworks hung in the hall.

Lorcan strode up, pressing his cheek against the rough wall by the nearest crevice. Dark eyes landing on the Princess and a smirk tugged at the corner of his lips. She moved to her seat beside Orahn, graceful and slow, her dress catching in the chandelier light, making her too bright to fix his gaze on.

"Oh, yum, I can smell her from here," Lorcan said in a playful drawl.

"She's overwhelming," Cormac replied, far less amused by that fact than his brother was.

Unmoving, Cormac's eyes fixed on the events unfolding on the other side of the wall. He wasn't about to be pulled into his brother's mischief.

Lorcan swept the room with his own glance. No Vampire actually ate. The glasses of bloodwine were drunk quickly.

His smirk fell as his gaze landed on a disturbance so subtle it barely deserved more than a half-glance from the people seated nearest to them. On the other side of the long table the head House Marquis, Lord Tavadin, seemed locked in heated exchange with the sons and mother of House Le Rouge.

Lorcan side-glanced at Cormac and they both made a mental note to monitor them all a little closer from now on.

Lorcan didn't like that people plotted at the same table where his brother was seated. Though it'd take a lot more than that before he ever worried about Orahn. The man sat like a God, laughing, charming, winning over everyone within earshot.

Boredom tinged his words, "The Princess? Overwhelming? No. She's pretty enough... I guess."

For the first time, Cormac pulled back just long enough to throw Lorcan a frustrated look. "I mean her blood is going to be difficult for our Vampires to be around."

Lorcan considered that, then shrugged as though it only made things marginally more interesting to him.

Rolling away, he slumped against the wall, his back pressed into the cold rock. It was damp with the scent of stone and candle smoke.

Every minute spent trapped felt like an entirety to him. Even if they did get to return her after the war and life continued as it had, when he looked at her, he didn't feel like anything would be normal ever again.

"Her effects look lasting," he growled, trying to look at the glow of the Elven Princess again. *She's too much.* Instead, he shifted focus to his other brother seated beside her. "It's been *years* since Orahn needed us to play warden."

"It's our job to watch for the things Orahn can't while his attention is elsewhere," Cormac said simply.

"That makes him sound weak," Lorcan said, the faintest smirk tugging at the corner of his mouth.

"We're *all* weak around Elves until we adjust to their presence and her blood is more powerful than most."

Lorcan scoffed. "*That* Elf isn't enough to make me weak."

Cormac's eyes flicked to him, cold and knowing. "Then you're lying to yourself or you're lying to me."

"You're just bitter that my willpower is stronger than yours."

"Bitter? Of that famous self-restraint of yours? Orahn and I have never had to clean up your messes," Cormac shot back with heavy sarcasm that didn't bother his brother in the slightest.

Lorcan had done this a thousand times; sat watching from the back of a room. This was the first time there had ever been a woman involved in their life with so much power at her fingertips. She didn't even understand what her cost in their Kingdom was. Her ignorance grated his nerves. With each step she took further into his domain, Lorcan felt his freedoms melting away.

Sweeping her hair over her shoulder, a whiff of Adelira's blood assaulted their senses through the walls. Cormac stiffened beside him, his interest dragged from her to his brother.

"What's this Cormac?" Lorcan poked fun. "Does her blood sing to you that loudly? But you don't drink from the living. So, why are you drawn to her?"

"I never said that," Cormac said through gritted teeth.

"You didn't have to," Lorcan teased. He'd never seen his youngest brother react to anyone before and he grinned wider, maybe this would be more fun than he first imagined. Torturing Cormac had a certain appeal, especially when he made himself so untouchable.

Ignoring him, Cormac's keen attention fixed on the scene beyond the wall. The banquet was beginning, platters of food now being passed down the table, though few Vampires paid attention. The wine goblets were filled, but it was the darker liquid served in smaller, more discreet glasses that caught the interest of the Vampires at the table.

Lorcan stretched lazily, his arms folding behind his head, his boots scraping against the uneven floor, exhaling a dismissive breath.

"I don't see what's captivating," Lorcan murmured, a drawl that barely carried through the gloom. "Just a bunch of Vampires posturing and pretending to care about some arranged marriage."

"They care," Cormac said. "Because they're deciding if this marriage is worth keeping Orahn as King."

"*This* marriage," Lorcan scoffed, shifting to glance at Cormac with a sardonic smirk. "That timid little Elf? And she's the one we're all supposed to orbit around now? She walks in and suddenly the court, the King, turns to her and we're nothing, but shadows. The nobles see her for what she is, a liability."

"We were always shadows. The nobles will see her as leverage, if not for anything other than the Elder Celestite," Cormac corrected.

"It's our job to make sure that leverage doesn't come with a dagger to Orahn's back."

Lorcan rolled his eyes. Cormac's logic pressed against his boredom and he looped back to the obvious jab.

"And if they try? Do we leap down and announce we've been spying like thieves in the rafters?"

Cormac didn't respond.

"Look at us. The *three* of us, tied to one Elf's life. Even without the Blood Ritual, she's holding us hostage." His voice dipped with bitterness. "It's pathetic."

Cormac finally turned his attention to Lorcan, the barest hint of warning in his steady glare. "Our focus is on the war. Not the Elf. We're not here to interfere unless we have to."

Lorcan's lips curled into a thin smile completely devoid of any humour. "Oh, I know." He leaned forward slightly, his voice too harsh. "We're watching, Cormac. That's all we're ever doing."

Cormac's expression gave away nothing. "For now, yes," he said. "But if the Vampires lose their control around her from the smell of her blood? And if Orahn can't hold the court, then what?"

Lorcan didn't answer immediately. His smirk faded as he stared at Adelira, the allure of her blood drawing the attention of everyone at the table. Every predator locked in on her as their target and she had nowhere to hide. She was completely exposed; surrounded by predators and put on display.

For a second, something softened in him as he thought what that must feel like for her. *Scared. Prey. Alone. Brave. Gods, was she brave?* Lorcan scowled again.

"We should let the court tear each other apart trying to get to her, before we drag her out," he muttered, cold as ever. "Let half the problems kill themselves."

Orahn's hand occasionally brushed hers. Orahn's smiles were all well-timed and carefully charming. His posture was open and confident. He played his role to perfection and no one doubted his place at the head of the table.

Cormac turned his eyes over to Adelira. Her composure remained flawless, though there was a flicker of uncertainty in her eyes. The give away was so slight that Cormac was sure he and Orahn were only people who knew how nervous she was. The only one that actually concerned him was Orahn; his control softened minisculely around her.

The tunnel was dark and intimate and comforting to Cormac. A place that was his while he ordered the outside world.

To Lorcan it was a coffin. Shadows imprisoned him and his whispers felt like a betrayal to the silence.

Here, Cormac was free to shed the burden of being a man. Lorcan was denied the chance to even be one.

"A nightmare, that's what—" Lorcan didn't finish the thought.

A movement flashed.

Instantly, he stood at attention, senses honing in on a noble making his way towards Orahn and Adelira.

Awareness flared towards Lorcan, before Cormac tracked the same noble across the room.

A Vampire's eyes turned red with bloodlust, pulled towards Adelira by his own hunger he could no longer control. The chair made an ugly scraping sound as he rose.

Lorcan's hand moved to the hilt of his sword as his breathing stilled and they watched the noble's movement become jittery and sharp, the flash of his fangs catching in the candle light.

"Hold," Cormac murmured. He didn't need to say anything.

It was instinct to touch his sword when teeth flashed, that was all.

Just then, Orahn's gaze lifted from Adelira's face and his eyes connected with the noble. The man sat, immediately, head bowed, the red dulled to the original shade of blue that his irises were. Orahn's gaze lingered until satisfied the man wouldn't rise again before he turned back to Adelira, like he hadn't skipped a beat.

Lorcan's hand fell away from his sword, disappointed.

Adelira was talking to Orahn, completely unaware of the threat that tried to cross the room to get her. Orahn barely blinked and the threat vanished. Lorcan ground his teeth. She laughed, too unaware, and he felt the weight of what keeping her alive would cost them all. Lorcan rolled his eyes at how oblivious she was and he moved away. She was still unnervingly bright and he bristled at her laugh.

Muscles tensed, Lorcan bit back a growl, his thinning patience.

Orahn had taken on lovers in the past. Lorcan had several on hand, any time he wanted. Orahn kept his tucked away somewhere in the court where if Lorcan or Cormac were King neither would need to interact with them.

Now, Lorcan would face the Elf in the corridors and between duties and have to seem like Orahn specifically for the kindness he'd shown her tonight.

Lorcan couldn't conjure up that kindness. The thought made him feel physically ill. When he stepped out of these tunnels, she'd be expecting an Orahn who was laughing and leaning into her space and charming her endlessly.

Fists clenched at the thought. There'd be nothing left of him by the time she left Tharth.

He wouldn't do that. Couldn't do that. He'd bite her before he ever spoke to her the way Orahn did. If one more word left his lips that belonged to Orahn, he'd never speak again.

"I'm going to fall asleep back here if nothing happens soon," he muttered, though he knew Cormac wouldn't care what he did right now. He tapped his fingers idly against his knee, the small sliver of light spilling through the peephole onto him.

Cormac remained steady, his focus inexorable. "I want to be sure I don't miss anything. I have a meeting with the Elven King and Queen at the end of the week, and when I step in there, they must not suspect a thing."

"You know Orahn will give us a run-down tonight, right?"

"He isn't always as thorough as I would like."

"We've done this all our lives."

"It's that relaxed attitude that will get us caught one day."

"Honestly, I think we deserve to let our guard down, be more ourselves. Who'd know? Who would *dare* question the Blood King himself?"

"You'd burn the world down just to prove you could," Cormac dismissed.

"No," Lorcan said thoughtfully. "I'd watch it burn, the heat makes it feel like I'm alive."

Cormac froze. If that was possible. If he could move any *less* than he did already. He was stone now and neither of them dared confront what Lorcan had just said. It wouldn't be the first time he'd tried and Cormac knew it wouldn't be the last either, but the reason struck something that *even* Cormac felt a stirring for, reluctant as he was to admit it, alive in a way the brothers had never been allowed.

Shaking off the confession, Lorcan returned to his usual jabs for both their sakes.

"You just like looking at her, don't you?" Lorcan teased, stealing another glance himself.

"Despite what her blood would suggest, she's not my type."

"Do you even have a type?" Lorcan asked. "Come to think of it, I've never heard you talk about any women."

"Is there a point in indulging in romantic affection knowing that it can never be real?" Cormac replied, giving his brother the faintest glimpse of a reaction.

"Doesn't have to be real to be fun."

"I like my fun in the dark."

"I bet she tastes great." Lorcan flicked his tongue over his fang.

"Thinking about how she tastes isn't going to help anyone."

"Everyone's thinking about how she tastes," Lorcan said. "I bet even *she* is thinking about how she tastes for the first time in her life."

Lorcan realised, "Every fibre of her being must be screaming at her to run, and yet, she walked right into the viper's nest..."

He almost admired the bravery of such an ac. He couldn't quite feel the admiration, not when he felt enraged by her presence, instead.

"Yes, but confidence won't make her belong here," Cormac said.

Lorcan shrugged. "She doesn't belong here. Yet, we're all expected to reshape the world to fit her into it. I'm not interested in something that costs me everything just to keep it alive."

"As good-natured as Orahn is compared to the rest of us, she will be out of place here which is going to make it more difficult for her to accept waiting for a Ritual that will never come."

"What does it matter, really? An Elf could never belong with Vampires anyway, everyone knew that. That's why the families are against this marriage."

"It doesn't matter," Cormac said curtly. "It's only important that other Vampires don't lose their self-control around her. Now that we know the pull of her blood, we have to accept that the court is even more dangerous."

"Every Vampire knows not to risk their King's wrath," Lorcan countered, surveying the people in attendance to reaffirm his statement. "No one out there is stupid enough to even think about it."

Cormac paused, his glare steady. "I agree," he said. "There probably isn't anyone out *there* who is stupid enough."

"Exactly," Lorcan said, and then stopped and glared up at his brother. "Wait, just what exactly are you implying?"

"Nothing at all, brother," Cormac said with a faint trace of a smirk.

Orahn and Princess Adelira, seated together at the grand table in the centre of the hall, their heads bowed slightly as they spoke in low tones.

"What are they talking about?" Cormac asked, his voice barely more than a whisper, the sound almost swallowed by the dense silence of the hidden passage.

The brothers had gotten good at lip reading over the years, but this angle was awkward. They'd selected one that gave them the best advantage overview of the room, to watch the players in the crowd. Their attention kept falling back to Orahn, though they couldn't easily read the exchange. In full study mode, Cormac was cataloguing every shift, every laughter.

Lorcan watched the exchange with disinterest. Orahn's dark, brooding figure slightly angled toward Adelira. She was still too glittering in the room, like she eclipsed everything, further reminding him of how she had come to take over his world. How could there ever be any common ground between them? For once he was glad it was Orahn out there instead of him, because Orahn could find the common ground, even if that ground was something he built in real time out of sheer diplomacy and lies.

"I dunno," Lorcan muttered, with a huff and sinking to the floor. "Probably something boring. It's Orahn and an Elf, can't get plainer than that."

Cormac didn't respond. There was tension in Orahn's posture, though it was subtle, the kind of tension only a brother would notice. And the Princess... She looked calm enough, though there was a nervous flicker in her movements and just enough curiosity.

Cormac's eyes never shifted from the scene before him as he noted the subtle gestures between them. Adelira responded softly to Orahn, answering his questions carefully. Orahn's hand near hers. Adelira's eyes darted up to meet his, her eyes uncertain. *Grey eyes*, Cormac noted — *No, storm-grey.*

Orahn's dark hair slipped forward as his face closer to her, a quiet intensity in his movements, and Cormac instinctively brushed back his own hair. A moment later, Lorcan brushed back his own. They still had to fight not to stay in sync with each other.

Sighing, he finally pushed himself up from the floor.

"Well, you keep watching if you want, but I'm done with this." He gave the wall a soft thud with his fist before turning down the passage, his footsteps barely audible as he disappeared into the shadows. "Call me if anything interesting happens," he muttered lazily. "But I'm betting it won't."

Something stopped him as he walked down the tunnel. He froze. With more hesitation than he'd felt in years, he pressed against the wall and looked through the spyhole. His eyes fell neatly on Adelira.

And as though she felt him there, she turned. And looked directly at him.

Lorcan jumped back with a start as her grey eyes connected with his.

But she couldn't see him, hadn't seen him, he convinced himself. It was impossible from that angle. He couldn't shake the feeling that somehow, against all odds, she knew he was there, watching her.

She felt *him*.

His jaw locked and he stalked out of the tunnels without looking back.

The End

The Kingship Serries

Book 1 – The Deceitful Kingship

Book 2 – The Fallen Kingship

Book 3 – The Blood Kingship

Book 4 – The Ripped Kingship

Book 5 – The Secret Kingship

Book 6 – The Eternal Kingship

www.ingramcontent.com/pod-product-compliance
Lightning Source LLC
La Vergne TN
LVHW050911080826
845145LV00001B/57

* 9 7 8 1 9 1 9 1 7 7 6 0 1 *